Where the Hurt Is

Chris Kelsey

Black Rose Writing | Texas

ISBN: 978-1-68433-071-3
PUBLISHED BY BLACK ROSE WRITING
www.blackrosewriting.com

Printed in the United States of America
Suggested Retail Price (SRP) $20.95

Where the Hurt Is is printed in Palatino Linotype

To Judy Kelsey

ACKNOWLEDGEMENTS

Thank you to my early reader Gisele Bryce, whose eagle eye caught things I'd never have noticed in a million years; my earlier reader, my mom, who couldn't find a single thing wrong with it; and my earliest reader (and cover designer) Lisa Kelsey, who always tells it like it is.

Where the Hurt Is

CHAPTER ONE

It all started the night Mingo from the Daniel Boone show tried to teach Johnny Carson how to throw a tomahawk.

At ten-thirty the temperature sign over the First National Bank read 91 degrees, down from an afternoon high of 95. It was what I believe the TV weatherman call "unseasonably warm." Like my daddy used to say: "It was so hot, I saw two fire hydrants fighting over a dog." I don't think he actually ever did, but you get the idea.

It was a Friday in late April, even if it felt like midsummer. The coming weekend beckoned with the phony come-hitherness of a forty-year-old stripper with athlete's foot. Still, a day off is a day off. I'll take one when I can get it.

I'd finished work an hour before, after which I'd pounded a few beers over to Edna's Eats, the only bar in downtown Burr, Oklahoma, population 1,280 (the persistent rumor that 279 are coyotes, skunks, and/or armadillos is of questionable veracity).

Before we go any further, I'd best introduce myself. My name is Emmett Hardy, and I have the dubious honor of being Burr's chief of police. If I think of anything else of a personal nature that's relevant, I'll toss it in as we go along.

Anyway, I was about to explain about Edna's, which I've been known to patronize on the not-too-rare occasions when I feel like drinking in the company of our local rednecks and lowlifes.

Edna's Eats has been a beverages-only establishment since The

Great Grease Fire of '56. Changing the name would require either altering or replacing the neon sign in the front window. The former would've been an offense to the eye, the latter a frivolous misallocation of funds. Edna is as sensitive to appearances as she is the balance in her bank account. The cost of cleaning-up after the fire was steep enough. It's been nine years since the fire. The name's stayed the same.

I partook of a few glasses of the cheap skunk piss Edna's calls beer and headed home, intending to prepare myself a gourmet meal and relax with some late-night TV. When I say "gourmet," I am in fact being what Mrs. Adkins, my high school English teacher, would call "facetious." In fact, my dinner would be something I call Okie Beef Stroganoff: Piggly Wiggly store-brand macaroni & cheese mixed with fried ground beef. A simple dish that stretches my cooking skills to the limit.

Piggly Wiggly's macaroni and cheese is almost as good as Kraft, and at six boxes for a dollar, the price is right. I also eat Piggly Wiggly fried-chicken-and-apple-cobbler TV dinners and wash my clothes with Piggly Wiggly laundry soap. I'd probably treat my hemorrhoids with Preparation Piggly if there was such a thing. Maybe there is, but I don't have hemorrhoids, so I never had cause to investigate. Their stuff costs less than the famous brands, but I can't tell much difference, except the packaging isn't as fancy and I don't care about that. About the only non-Piggly Wiggly product I use is Brown Derby beer, and that's Safeway's store brand, so it's cheap as water, too (and has about as much kick).

It pays to be thrifty. A poorly-compensated small-town cop can't afford not to be.

I stripped down to my t-shirt and BVDs and plunked down on the threadbare brownish-green La-Z-Boy I'd bought slightly used for 20 bucks when Larsen's furniture store over in Alva went out of business ten years ago. I turned on the TV in time to catch the last few minutes of the late news. Reception around here normally isn't too reliable, but I splurged on a huge aerial a while back and mounted it way higher than is technically legal, so the Oklahoma City stations come in loud and clear.

I propped my feet up and sat with the bowl of hot orange goop in my lap. My yellow Labrador retriever Dizzy lay on the floor next to me, snoring and chasing jackrabbits in her sleep. An evening of low-quality food and high-quality entertainment beckoned, courtesy of Piggly Wiggly and the Tonight Show and the cow who died so I could have fried meat in my macaroni and cheese.

Ed McMahon had just finished his "He-e-e-re's Johnny!" routine when there came a knock on my door. Dizzy woke with a start and howled like we were being overrun by an army of Jehovah's Witnesses. The effects of the aforementioned beer—not to mention a Flintstones Jelly glass twice filled to the brim with Old Grand-Dad bourbon, consumed while preparing my meal—made getting out of the La-Z-Boy an arduous task. I did not rise in undue haste.

"Go away," I shouted. I can be uncivil when I'm tired and inebriated.

A voice strained to be heard over Dizzy's caterwauling. "Chief Hardy, it's Bernard, could you please open up?"

That would be Deputy Chief of Police Bernard Cousins, Burr High School Class of 1958. Bernard wears braces on his teeth and thick round eyeglasses that make him look like Don Knotts in *The Incredible Mr. Limpet*. A few years back, he graduated with honors from a mail-order police academy he discovered in the back pages of *True Detective* magazine. I hired him anyway. Never had cause to regret it. He helps me immensely and I like him a lot.

But I'd had enough of him at work.

At the moment, I preferred the company of Johnny Carson.

"What do you want?" I yelled, hoping but not expecting he'd go away. Bernard is not the type to be easily deterred.

"Could I come in, Chief?" he hollered back. "I'm on official business and I'd rather not be shouting through the door."

"Alright, hold on, I'm coming."

I managed to haul myself upright after a couple of tries. I examined my jockey shorts to make sure everything was properly contained and took a serpentine route to the door. Dizzy jumped all over Cousins the second I opened up, sniffing and licking him like he was her best friend. Not to slight Bernard, but Diz isn't picky about who she takes a shine to. I've had her jumping all over prisoners in my jail with just as much enthusiasm.

Bernard stood in the doorway as the combined aromas of alfalfa and cow manure that make each new day in Burr a little sweeter than the last, wafted in, uninvited.

"I'd offer you a drink," I said, "but that'd mean less for me."

"Oh, no sir, that's fine, I'm on duty." Bernard doesn't have much of a sense of humor. Nor is he much of a drinker.

I let him in and Dizzy out. I did not offer him a seat.

"I hope you didn't just drop in to say hello, buddy."

"Oh, no sir," he said, shocked that I would suggest such a thing. "You know I wouldn't bother you if it wasn't important."

His eyes wandered to the television. A few seconds passed without him saying anything else, so I snapped my fingers in front of his face. "Why are you here, Bernard?"

"Sorry, Chief," he muttered. "Edgar Bixby called. Daffodil's missing."

He might as well have said Moe from the Three Stooges had kidnapped the Queen of England. Daffodil Bixby is Burr royalty, after all.

Daffodil is also a pig: Edgar Bixby's 1800-lb. Oklahoma State Fair prize-winning sow. Folks around here crow about her being the biggest pig in the world. God knows, we don't have the biggest or best of anything else, although hope springs eternal every high school football season. Some smart-ass reporter from The Daily Oklahoman who came to do a story on Daffodil said the Red Chinese government claims they got one that's bigger. Of course, no one in these parts believe much of anything a communist says, especially when it comes to livestock.

That said, while Daffodil's a celebrity around here, a pig's a pig, and not even so uppity a swine as Daffodil has a say in how the police department is run. I'd already put in long hours and sure as hell didn't want to get dressed and drive out to Edgar Bixby's.

"Doesn't Edgar have a hired hand that takes care of that pig?" I asked.

"Edgar says he gave him time off to take care of his sick mother."

Sick mother? Edgar must be getting soft.

"Maybe she got out and wandered off," I said. "Anyway, I can't do much if anything about it right now. Why don't you go out and talk to him? Let me finish my dinner and drink my bourbon and watch Johnny Carson. I'll worry about Daffodil tomorrow, which, as a pretty lady once said, is another goddam day." As if to emphasize my point, I plopped back down into my chair.

Bernard remained unswayed.

"Sir, I've been inside that fancy indoor pen where they keep that pig and I can tell you there's no way she up-and-left on her own."

"So, you're saying she didn't run off to join the circus."

"No sir, I think it's likely she was stolen," he said, ignoring or not getting my joke. "I really think we should go. Edgar's about to have a cow."

The seriousness of the situation began to penetrate the fog of drink.

Edgar hates me. His little brother Deke, who sits on the town council, hates me. The two of them basically run the town. Both would love an excuse to take my badge.

The writing was on the wall. Or maybe the insides of my eyelids. In any case, the course was clear.

Oh well, I thought, maybe I can make things interesting. Tie Daffodil's disappearance to Castro or the Kennedy assassination or something.

Sometimes I talk shit to myself when I've been drinking. Once again, I summoned sufficient effort to stand. Wobbly, but erect.

"Alright," I said out loud with all the heartfelt enthusiasm of a 40-year-old Sinatra fan on his way to his first Beatles concert, "let me drink a cup of coffee, and we'll head on out there."

CHAPTER TWO

I drank my Piggly Wiggly instant coffee and watched Carson tell jokes while I put on my uniform. My fingers were discombobulated from the bourbon, so it took longer than usual.

The actor Ed Ames was Johnny's first guest. Ames plays Mingo, the Indian sidekick on the Daniel Boone show, which dramatizes the adventures of a "real-life" frontiersman who lived in Kentucky around the time of the American Revolution.

I say "real-life" because while there actually was a Daniel Boone, and he really did live in Kentucky, his adventures as depicted on that show bear no relationship to reality or even common sense.

Take the casting of Mingo. I got nothing against Ed Ames. He seems to be a nice fella. For all I know, he draws straws with Boy Scouts for the right to help little old ladies cross the street. He is, however, about as much of an Indian as Groucho Marx. In fact, I read somewhere that Mr. Ames is of the Hebrew faith, which means he's also about as Jewish as Groucho Marx.

Ed Ames was preparing to school Johnny in the intricacies of throwing a tomahawk. His target was a full-sized cartoon silhouette of a cowboy painted on a big wood panel, because—ha-ha—that's what Indians do, don't they? They fight cowboys. They also smoke-um peace pipes and drink-um too much firewater. It's bad enough we stole their land and killed most of them off. Now they're the butt of our jokes for eternity. Goddam, sometimes I wonder about this country.

But I digress.

"Sir, with all due respect, we should go," Cousins said. "Edgar was very upset."

"Alright, hold your horses. I'm not going out to see him in my shorts," I said, although by that time I was more-or-less fully clothed. I gulped down more of my coffee and strapped on my service weapon, a Smith & Wesson Model 28 .357 Magnum, which I only carry in special emergencies like pig abductions.

I turned off the lamp. The TV's blue glow was the only light. Ames threw what was supposed to be a tomahawk. Damn thing looked more like a hatchet you'd buy at the hardware store. It spun through the air and struck the cartoon cowboy right in the crotch—embedding itself in the wood with the handle sticking up at a 45-degree angle, making it look a lot like a man's stimulated private parts.

The audience thought it was hilarious. Even Cousins laughed, and he's not a big laugher. It was undeniably an unusual thing to have happened. "I didn't even know you were Jewish," Carson said.

"What's he mean by that?" Bernard asked.

I've learned to be patient with my young deputy.

"That's one of those New York jokes."

"Oh," he said, as if that explained everything.

I took one last slug of coffee. "Well, that was almost worth the wait. Time to see a man about a pig." I put on the wide-brimmed fedora I wear instead of a cowboy hat, and made for the door.

I left the TV on so people would think someone was home. I left Dizzy out. She basically has the run of the town.

We walked across a weed patch disguised as my front lawn, to my driveway made of dried mud and some chat a local company digs out of a pit outside town. "Summer's getting an early start this year," Bernard said.

I didn't respond, not being in the mood for small talk.

Lit-up all pretty by a full moon was the pride of the Burr Police Department, a black and white 1961 Plymouth Fury police cruiser. The Fury's our one and only official vehicle. It looks like something out of a science fiction movie, with side-by-side dual headlights topped by a pair of angry, eyebrow-like fins on either side of a grill that looks like something a Martian might use in place of a mouth. That Fury is one scary-looking automobile. Cousins loves it like it was his own flesh-and-blood. I reckon you could tell how many times he's waxed that car by slicing through a section and counting layers like the rings of a tree. God help any civilian who dents it in a parking lot. I'm sure Bernard would push the prosecutor for the maximum sentence. The State of Oklahoma has an electric chair and she's not shy about using it.

The Bixby farm sits on about a thousand acres southwest of town, on a dirt road a mile-and-a-half north off US Highway 14, which also serves as Burr's main street. US 14 runs along the South side of train tracks that cut across the county on a diagonal. The tracks are built on a rise, a few feet higher than the highway, for drainage purposes. A trickle of water like Dead Arapaho Creek, which crosses underneath the highway and tracks just outside town, can be as treacherous as the Amazon when the nearby South Canadian River floods, which happens on occasion.

The tracks accommodate freight and passenger traffic. A Santa Fe Streamliner stops in Burr four times a day, twice going west-southwest, twice going east-northeast. Ride to the end, you'll find yourself in San Francisco or Chicago. It runs alongside Route 66 much of the way west. I've only ridden as far as Amarillo in that direction. In the olden days, the train did a bustling business, but automobiles have pretty much done-in the passenger service, in Burr, at least. Hardly anyone ever gets on or off.

I let Cousins drive, in consideration of my impaired condition. I'm not a cheap drunk by any stretch. I can hold my liquor. Even if I get stopped, I've gotten pretty good at talking myself out of tickets, owing to the professional courtesy one cop extends to another. But folks are getting more agitated these days about the dangers of driving with a load on. Anyway, I had no reason to tempt fate. I had a perfectly willing and able chauffeur.

At its busiest, US 14 never has much traffic. This time of night it was completely deserted. Local high school kids would rather cruise Temple City or Watie Junction—a couple of slightly-less piss-ant towns than Burr—on Friday nights. We passed Edna's and drove through Burr's lone traffic light at Main Street and State Highway 43. It blinked yellow like always. Red and green lights are for big towns. Like Temple City and Watie Junction. We drove southwest toward the Bixby place.

I looked out the passenger side window. My eyes passed over everything without seeing much of anything. The scrublands and pastures glowed like an ocean of fireflies in the light of the full moon. I reckon you might say it was a beautiful sight, but I barely noticed. I've been living here so long, sometimes I'm blind to the things that make it special.

I couldn't remember what crops Edgar Bixby pretended to raise or how many and what kind of animals he kept other than Daffodil. Whether one fella plants soybeans and another one wheat doesn't have a whole lot to do with how I do my job, though for political reasons it's a good thing to know. Edgar is what they call a gentleman farmer, although if he's a gentleman, I'm the Prince of Wales. Mostly, Edgar collects money from mineral rights on land he inherited from his daddy.

"What exactly does Edgar grow out here, again?" I asked Cousins.

"Hay," Cousins replied.

Hay.

"You ever wonder the point of raising crops to feed animals, just so you can eat the goddam animals?" Bernard didn't answer. He knows better than to talk back when I get like this. "Raise crops to feed people and leave the goddam animals in peace, that's what I always say."

That's not what I always say. In fact, I like a good cut of meat as much or better than the next man. I've never been too fond of vegetables.

Bernard gently pointed out the inconsistency of my position.

"Sir, with all due respect, you and I just had a steak dinner at the Piazza last night," he said. The Piazza is Burr's only sit-down restaurant.

"That was *chicken-fried* steak." I glared, trying to keep a straight face. "*Chicken-fried*. More chicken than steak."

Not sure if I was being serious or not, he gave me nervous sideways glance and dropped the subject.

I wouldn't tease Bernard so much if I didn't like and respect him. He isn't the brightest penny in the jar, if you want to know the truth. But he makes up for his general awkwardness with grit and a strong sense of right-and-wrong. I never met a man of any age who tried harder to do the right thing. He's a good hand in a scrap, too. You wouldn't believe it to look at him, but he'll fight until he drops. I once saw him take down two drunkards twice his size in a bar fight. A copious amount of blood was shed, none of it his. Both miscreants ended up in my holding cell, much the worse for wear and wishing they'd known better than to attack the skinny local cop with the coke-bottle glasses and braces on his teeth.

By normal standards, this had already been a helluva day. That afternoon, some woman's Buick broke down on Main Street, and her husband tried to tow it home with a rope behind an old Kaiser pickup. He built a fair head of steam and was going along at a pretty good clip when a Chevy Bel Air backed out of a parking space in front of him, causing him to stop short. The wife, who was steering the Buick, panicked and hit the clutch instead of the brake. The husband looked in his mirror and saw the Buick about to rear-end him, so *he* panicked and accelerated, causing him to crash into the Bel Air. Naturally, the Buick squared the circle and rammed the pickup. I considered issuing three separate tickets but ended-up writing just one to the idiot towing the Buick. Coupled with Daffodil's disappearance, we were in the midst of a full-fledged crime wave. A stolen celebrity pig was another break from routine. I might've welcomed it, if not for the lateness of the hour.

Bernard and I passed the billboard where we set up our speed trap ("Temple City Motor Hotel 19 Luxurious Rooms! AAA Approved!") and Wesley Harmon's Sinclair station. In the daytime, the Sinclair is the last place to fill your tank before you get to Watie

Junction, which is on the western edge of Tilghman County along the Texas border. The Sinclair was dark when we drove by. Wes closes at six.

A half-mile past Wesley's is the turn-off to the Bixby place. I was thinking about how to handle Edgar—I determined that Bernard would do most of the talking since my tongue was still feeling too big for my mouth—when I glimpsed something out-of-place lying on the train tracks. My first thought was that it was a dead calf.

"I saw something back there," I said.

"What was it?" Bernard asked. He looked in his side mirror.

"I don't know," I said. "Maybe a dead calf. We should check."

Cousins turned around and drove back slowly. The Fury's spotlight was broke, so we had to use a flashlight. Bernard braked. "Uh-oh," he said. "That ain't a calf."

"No, it is not," I said.

Edgar Bixby's pig-napping would have to wait.

CHAPTER THREE

I've lived in Burr most of my life. Most of the time it's been as peaceful a place as you could imagine.

That's not to say it's some kind of heaven on earth, because it's not. We had us a little rough patch after World War II, right before I graduated from high school. A big natural gas processing plant opened north of town in a place called Butcherville. You can't expect roustabouts to be choirboys and these weren't, by any means. They caused some trouble at first, but eventually the majority learned to behave. Even at their worst, few engaged in anything strictly criminal, unless you count patronizing some of the brothels that briefly sprung-up in the vicinity of the plant right after it was built. These days, they come into Burr on weekends, drink at Edna's, flirt with local gals and mostly mind their p's and q's.

On the other hand, boys will be boys. We've had ourselves some hellacious brawls, although usually everyone comes out in one piece.

Usually, but not always.

I'd been on the job for a couple of years. I'd handled a few fights, but nothing I couldn't deal with myself. At the time, I naively attributed a lack of serious casualties to my imposing presence as the presiding officer of the law. In truth, it was just dumb luck, and it ran out one night in the winter of '57.

I was about to hit the sack when I got a call about an incident at Edna's. In those days, I was the sole member of the force. When someone needed a cop after hours, they called me at home. This night it was sleeting and the roads were slicker than snot, so I drove slow. It took five minutes to get there, instead of the usual two. I didn't think it mattered. All I expected to find was a couple of drunks duking it out. Later I wished I'd gotten there quicker.

I asked the bartender what was going on. He made a disgusted face and said something I couldn't understand because the juke box was too loud. He gave up trying to explain and hooked his thumb towards the rear of the bar.

I exited out the back door and found a pair of gentlemen sprawled on the pavement—one sitting against the wall, one laying on his back. Both wore oil-stained t-shirts with jeans and work boots. The one against the wall held a can of Schlitz in one hand and a pipe wrench in the other. The one on the ground could've been sleeping one off, although the pool of blood around his head and the imprint of a pipe wrench on his skull suggested a more malign state of affairs. Both men were coated in a thin crust of ice so they sparkled in the moonlight. The most notable difference was one was a lot deader than the other.

The guy who wasn't dead saved me the trouble of putting two-and-two together and confessed on the spot, blubbering and remorseful and ready to take his medicine.

He needn't have worried about paying for what he did. He killed a colored man.

The day-and-a-half that fella spent in my holding cell turned out to be the full extent of his incarceration. I handed him over to the county and they let him out on bail before I could process the paperwork. The case went to trial quick. The jury took a whole morning to deliberate, long enough for them to get a free lunch courtesy of the State of Oklahoma. They came back with full bellies and hearts overflowing with forgiveness. They declared the defendant not guilty. Self-defense, they said. I didn't get credit for solving the crime, but it got my name in the Oklahoma City papers, which was nice.

Such was the extent of my experience investigating murders,

which was fine with me. Better to leave those kinds of things to the state or county boys. Well, maybe not the county.

The Town of Burr didn't hire me as their police chief on account of my sterling qualifications. They hired me mainly because I'd been a local football hero. I'm still remembered as the captain and starting tailback of the Burr High School team that won back-to-back state Class D championships in '48 and '49. My police training consisted of serving as an MP in the Marines; most of that time was spent in the field. I studied local, Oklahoma, and federal law on my own after I got the job. I worked hard and became a good small-town cop. But I'll tell anyone who'll listen: Sam Spade I ain't.

.   .   .   .   .

The railroad tracks were no more than twenty feet or so from the highway. The moon was full and bright and lit the scene tolerably well. I used the flashlight anyway and shined it on what had caught our attention: a young woman, nude and apparently deceased, lying on her stomach against the embankment leading up to the tracks.

I mumbled a quiet profanity or two. A wave of sick washed over me. I felt a lot soberer than I had a minute earlier.

"My lord," said Cousins. That's about as close to cussing as Bernard gets. Nothing he learned in that mail-order police course could have prepared him for this.

A blind man with a bag over his head could've seen the girl was dead, but I've always been one to make sure. "You wait here," I told Cousins. "I'm going to go over and check."

I tried to step on rocks where I could, so as not to disturb footprints or other evidence that might've been left. My balky knees popped as I knelt. Under the circumstances, the sound seemed amplified and disrespectful.

The victim was a light-skinned negro, I'd guess between the age of 16 to 20. I looked for a pulse and did not find one. I touched the skin of her face. She wasn't warm, but she wasn't real cold either. I'm no expert, but I didn't think she'd been dead for too long. I stood and my knees creaked some more.

I quit smoking a while ago, but in stressful situations like this, I still get the craving. I tried to push it aside.

I examined the scene as carefully as I could. The full moon helped, but even with the flashlight, I couldn't see much I wasn't standing right on top of. Most of what I could see, I already knew was there: the coarse rocks that made up the track bed; brush and hard red soil in the gully and next to the highway; scrubby pasture on the other side of a wire fence. I vaguely remembered the land belonged to Edgar Bixby. I peered across the fields and saw his house in the distance. The porch light was on. I reckoned he was waiting for us. I'd forgotten about his pig.

I had more pressing matters to attend to.

The girl had not been laid gently to rest. On the contrary, she reminded me of a broken doll thrown by an angry child. Her left arm stuck out to the side at an unnatural angle, like it had been yanked out of joint. Her right arm was trapped and twisted beneath her body. Her legs were awkwardly crossed and contused, no doubt by the crushed stones lining the embankment—chunks of which were embedded where her skin had come into contact with the ground. I saw a few pieces of what appeared to be freshly mowed grass stuck to her back, which struck me as out of place. There was no other grass in sight.

She was small, no more than an inch or two over five-feet. Her body was that of a teenage girl who had yet to cross all the way into womanhood. Her hips and waist were narrow, her legs slender. My guess was she weighed 100 pounds, give or take.

Her head was turned to the right, her left cheek rested on the rocks, her eyes stared unfocused into the distance. Even in that condition, her face was remarkably pretty and peaceful-looking, which made her harder to look at, somehow. I felt like a party to her violation. Lying naked and broken in the middle of nowhere and being gaped at by a couple of strangers is about as undignified as it gets.

We wouldn't need Sherlock Holmes to help us discover the cause of death. The girl's throat had been slashed from ear to ear. The cut was deeper than was necessary to achieve the desired effect, which made me think strong emotion was somehow involved. I couldn't know, of course, but that's the feeling I got. Some blood was evident on her neck, but not nearly as much as you'd expect. Hardly any was on the ground. It seemed plain she'd been carted here after being killed someplace else. Some place with fresh grass.

I bent over to get a closer look. Her face powder was a shade lighter than her skin. I thought she used a lot more than a girl her age would normally wear. Her eyelids were painted sky-blue, her lashes black with a thick application of mascara. Her eyes were large and oval-shaped and as green as a 7-Up bottle, their natural beauty contrasting sharply with the garish cosmetics. She looked like a little girl who'd been playing with her mother's makeup.

Her eyebrows were thicker than is fashionable, but not too thick. Her nose was small and slender and had a slight bump in the middle. Her mouth was wide, lips full and slightly parted, painted a dark red. She had a small space between her front teeth. Her black hair was styled in that short, natural way some negro girls wear it these days.

If not for the gash in her throat—if I just focused on her face—I could've been fooled into thinking she was still alive. Those green eyes looked past me, like she'd decided I'd proven myself useless and hopefully any minute someone more competent would come along.

Those eyes held me.

Cousins broke the long silence. "You think she got thrown off a train?" he said. "It don't seem like she was exactly laid down careful."

I shook myself out of my trance. "Could've been, after her throat was cut."

Cousins made a comment to the effect that she'd probably been raped. I agreed that was likely. "We'll get the forensics people out here and see what they find," I said. By now I was so tired, I could hardly get the words out. "Call the sheriff, have them call the highway patrol and the OSBI," the latter being the Oklahoma State Bureau of Investigation. Bernard nodded and retraced his steps back to the Fury.

Considering my condition when the evening began, I was more alert than I had any right to be. Which is not to say I didn't feel like shit, because I did, but the booze wasn't totally to blame. The death of the girl was the biggest reason, of course, but there was something else:

The understanding that ten tons of trouble had landed on my plate, and I might not have the appetite or ability to deal with it. That particular dark cloud seemed likely to follow me for the duration.

CHAPTER FOUR

I had Cousins get on the horn to our dispatcher, Karen Dean. I needed her to call Edgar Bixby and tell him we wouldn't be coming out until tomorrow. "Say we're working on something important." It was true, but I knew it would piss-off Edgar. It doesn't take much to piss-off Edgar.

"He won't like it," Bernard said.

"I don't give a good goddam if he likes it or not. Maybe I'm crazy, but where I live, a murdered girl takes precedence over a missing pig. Personally, I'd be more worried about getting Karen out of bed this late."

Bernard nodded ruefully. "You got a point."

It took a couple of minutes to apprise Karen of the situation, after which we took another look around. With just the lights from the Fury and the moon disappeared behind a cloud, we didn't accomplish a whole lot.

The first highway patrolman arrived within a half-hour, which I counted as good time, considering the closest barracks is 50 miles northwest, in Guymon. I'm at least somewhat acquainted with most of the troopers out this way, but this fella was new to me.

His nameplate said, "Dickshot," which might explain his attitude. I once heard of a ballplayer by that name. I considered asking this fella if he was any relation, but this wasn't a good time and this fella didn't seem like the type who'd appreciate being asked. He strutted around like a tom turkey the day after Thanksgiving—chest puffed up, chin stuck out, hands on his hips. His Smokey the Bear hat was pulled so low over his eyes, I reflexively pushed my fedora further back on my head just to compensate. His ears stuck out like a pair of handles on a loving cup and he frowned like a spoiled kid who'd finished his all-day sucker in five minutes. From his comportment, I figured it was likely that Trooper Dickshot joined the patrol so he could abuse beatniks, only to be bitterly disappointed when he found there weren't any in Oklahoma.

He immediately commenced pacing back and forth, ordering Bernard and me around. Another time I might have given him the what-for, but for now I managed to keep my smart-ass comments to a minimum and let him think he was in charge. I reckoned the best thing to do was fake as much corn-fed charm as I could and wait for the higher-ups to arrive.

Trooper Dickshot placed blue sawhorse barriers around the scene and Bernard and I tramped back to the Fury. "Did you notice his fly was open?" Bernard said.

"I did. I thought I'd let him discover it for himself."

We sat on the trunk of the car and watched Trooper Dickshot secure the crime scene. I remembered I had a stick of Juicy Fruit gum in my shirt pocket. I started to work on that, hoping it might curb my urge to smoke. It didn't.

"You recognize her?" I asked Cousins.

"No sir, I never seen her before. You think she's from Jackson Corner?"

Jackson Corner is an unpaved street on the eastern edge of Burr—literally on the wrong side of the train tracks. Our poorest of the poor live there in a few dilapidated shacks. What few colored folks we've had always lived on Jackson Corner. But that was a long time ago.

"Unless I missed someone new moving in," I said, "there haven't been any colored folks here since Clarence Younger and his people moved away. I doubt you even remember them. They left when you were little."

Bernard shook his head. "I've heard the name. Didn't their house burn down?"

"Something like that," I said. That was a story best told another day.

We didn't say much else. The flashing lights on the Fury lit up the night in that scary way peculiar to police cars, ambulances, and fire trucks. I was so tired I could barely keep my eyes open. I wanted to focus on where this girl might've come from and who did this, but I couldn't set my mind to anything and do it justice. My bourbon high was long gone, replaced by the general gloom brought on by extreme fatigue.

I don't know how long we'd been sitting there when Sheriff Murray drove up in his blue and white Dodge pickup. Tilghman County is the least-populous county in Oklahoma, a place where a whole lot of nothing happens. If Burton Murray had to be sheriff somewhere, this is as good a place as any. He's of that common species of elected lawman who loves being a big deal but hates doing any actual work. He knows how to get elected, I'll give him that, but if there's a crime that needs solving, you might consider doing it yourself, because he's generally of little help.

Burt can regularly be found at his favorite diner in Temple City, the county seat, drinking coffee all day and swapping tall tales with a group that includes some of the richest cattlemen in the Southwest, all of whom trade campaign contributions for various and sundry favors. He's a distant relative of Alfalfa Bill Murray, one of Oklahoma's founding fathers and one of its more eccentric governors. Like Burt, Alfalfa Bill was all hat and no cattle and a total nut, but the folks who liked him *really* liked him. I got to admit, I kind of like Burt myself, even if he is as crooked as a bucket of chicken wings.

A caravan of vehicles arrived, led by another highway patrol cruiser and a dark blue State Bureau of Investigation car. Behind that was a white van carrying the forensics crew, followed by a red Ford Fairlane station wagon with the letters WKY painted on the side. I wondered how in hell an Oklahoma City TV station had gotten wind of this so quick, then realized the sheriff probably did it himself. Burton Murray never misses a chance to get his picture taken.

They all parked on the shoulder behind the Fury and Trooper Dickshot's unit. The crime scene folks and the TV crew unloaded their gear. A pair of troopers started positioning the camera and lights, aided and abetted by Trooper Dickshot, who was visibly happy to have civilians to order around.

The two men who got out of the OSBI car could've been a pair of mismatched characters out of a Warner Brothers cartoon. The first was a tall, balding fella of about 50 or so. His face looked like it had been inflated with compressed air then popped like a balloon. A beer belly the approximate size and shape of a beach ball stretched his dingy white dress shirt to its limit. His wrinkled gray suit coat hung open; it wouldn't have buttoned closed even he had a mind to try. His crimson necktie looked like it had been tied once many years ago and slipped on-and-off over his head ever since. On his feet were oil-stained brown corduroy slippers, worn without socks. A lit cigarette hung out of one side of his mouth; a pack of Marlboros was visible in his shirt pocket. He carried a tall plastic mug with a Phillips 66 logo.

The second fella was about 20 years younger and looked as slippery as an eel coated in Vaseline. He stood no more than five-foot-four on his tip-toes. He wore a light gray Stetson with a medium-wide brim, and a tight-fitting, double-breasted dark suit. His white western-style shirt had mother-of-pearl snaps and narrow blue pinstripes. A braided leather bolo was held together by an ornately tooled silver slide with an oval chunk of veined turquoise in the center. On his feet were a pair of snakeskin Tony Lamas. He looked like the type to admire himself in the mirror for a half-hour before leaving the house every morning. Put a fiddle in his hand and he was the spitting image of a young Spade Cooley.

I watched from a distance as Sheriff Murray greeted the OSBI men. Burt gestured in my direction as he spoke, which I took as my cue to traipse over and get introduced.

"Emmett," said Murray with the solemnity befitting the occasion, "this here's Agent Ovell Jones and Agent John Joe Heckscher. Boys, Emmett Hardy, Burr Chief of Police."

The first thing I noticed about them is their smell. I imagine the clear night air made it seem worse than it was. The big one—Jones—had a kind of beer-and-cigarettes-and-bowling-alley-men's-room aroma. Heckscher's was harder to pin down: a mix of cigarette smoke, wintergreen snuff, and half-a-bottle of Aqua Velva would be my best guess. Of course, I'm one to talk. I hadn't bathed in two days and probably didn't smell too good to them, either.

We shook hands and I got them up-to-date. "If it's ok with you, Emmett, these boys will handle this," Burt said.

I said that was fine.

"If you need me, you know where to find me," he added.

Yup. Wherever there was a camera or a microphone.

I escorted the agents over to the body. The crime scene technicians had illuminated the area. They'd already found some footprints I didn't see before.

We stood in silence for what seemed like a long time. Jones bent down for a closer look. "Well, shit," he said at last. "You know her?"

"Never saw her before," I said. "We don't have any colored folks in Burr. I doubt whether there's a dozen in the whole county."

Jones took a last drag on his cigarette and dropped it in his Phillips 66 cup. "Burr ever been a sundown town?" he asked.

They don't exactly advertise that term like they used to. A sundown town is a place where a negro is liable to get beaten or worse if he has the gumption or bad luck to find himself there after dark. They used to be all over the place. When I was a teenager, I saw a postcard in a cafe in Edmond, a suburb of Oklahoma City, that boasted "No Negroes" among the town's finer qualities. My daddy swears there used to be signs on the roads into Norman—home of our state university—saying, "Nigger, don't let the sun go down on you in this berg."

"I wouldn't say we were a sundown town, exactly," I said, "but we did have some troubles about twenty, twenty-five years ago. What few colored families we had moved away around that time. We haven't had a race problem since then. Probably because we haven't had any negroes." I remembered those days, although I'd prefer to forget. "I reckon we still have a few unreformed Klan members, but if we do, they're not as loud about it."

The one who resembled Spade Cooley interrupted my train of thought. "I'll bet you anything she was some hobo's girlfriend," he said. "Got tired of her and cut her throat in a freight car. Pushed her out the door."

I began to think my impression of this fella being slippery was on the money. I'd say I wouldn't trust him far as I could throw him, except I suspect I could throw him a fair distance, as scrawny as he was.

"I don't know about that," I said, feeling a little heated. "See those pieces of fresh grass on her back? I don't know how she would've got those in a box car."

"There's about a million things it could be," said Jones, like he wanted to interrupt Heckscher and me before we got into a fistfight. "It looks like we can rule out is her being killed here. There ain't nearly enough blood. We'll have the forensic team scour the area, look for tire tracks and whatnot. Might be blood somewhere nearby." He turned and handed his coffee mug to a flunky, who tried to decide what to do with it. Holding it seemed to be the best option.

Cousins came over and I introduced him to Jones and Heckscher. "Chief, I just got done talking to the Santa Fe dispatcher," he said. "Next train comes through around three-fifty. That don't give us all that much time."

"Officer Cousins," said Jones, "if you would get back to that person and tell him to hold that train until we give him the go-ahead to let her through, I would greatly appreciate it. I don't want my crime scene examiners to have to worry about getting flattened by a locomotive."

"Can I tell them how long it's going to be?"

Jones lit another cigarette. "I got no idea. Tell 'em it'll take as long as it takes." He coughed and waved away the cloud of smoke hovering in front of his face.

Trooper Dickshot and his colleagues were having a hard time

keeping the TV folks at bay. A group of television folks surrounded a fella with a microphone interviewing Sheriff Burton. Detective Ovell Jones saw the scrum and didn't like it. He pulled Burt aside and said a few words. Burt stomped off, leaving the TV crew to scratch their asses and shuffle their feet. Jones came back to where Bernard and I stood.

"Can I assume that, by calling us in, you are formally requesting for the Bureau to take over?" he asked.

"That's what Burt wants and it's fine with me," I said. "This more in your line. Of course, I'm happy to help where I can."

"I might take you up on that. The bureau is stretched real thin. We can use all hands on deck."

"Suits me," I replied.

Jones asked me to give a preliminary statement to Agent Heckscher, and if possible come to the city the next day to give a formal statement. He handed me his card. "Call me in the morning to make sure we're there, and we'll set up a time. This looks like an all-nighter, so we might get a late start."

I told Agent Heckscher what I knew. In the meantime, more highway patrol cars had shown up. Our anonymous little stretch of highway was lit like the midway at the state fair. All that commotion in the presence of that poor dead girl seemed like a desecration, but it couldn't be helped.

I waited around a while just in case. Agent Heckscher make a brief statement to the TV reporter, as Sheriff Murray watched with a jealous eye. Heckscher talked a lot without saying anything, but the reporter seemed satisfied. The crime scene examiners went over the scene with what I hoped was a microscope attached to a fine-toothed comb. One approached Jones and started talking to him in a way that made it seem like they'd found something important. I went over and asked.

"A set of tire imprints running off the pavement up to within a few feet of the body," Jones said. "We'll take pictures and try to get casts, so at least we'll have some confirmation if we ever find the car. They also found a leather work glove with the Santa Fe Railroad symbol stamped on it. It's hard to say if either the tire marks or the glove are related to the crime. The glove could've fallen off a train."

"That's something," I said.

"Yeh, or maybe nothing. We're still looking." A man of few words is Ovell Jones.

CHAPTER FIVE

By three o'clock it was clear my presence on the scene was no longer required. I asked Jones if he needed me for anything else. He looked surprised, like he'd forgotten I was there. He said it would be fine if I left, but asked if he could borrow Officer Cousins until they were finished. That was ok with me. Bernard said he was happy to do it.

I drove home and crawled into bed without getting undressed.

Once when I was about eight years-old, a girl named Elnora Goodpasture told me that if I died in a dream, I'd never wake up. That Elnora Goodpasture was a mean little girl.

I slept poorly. I dreamt that I was called upon to break-up a fight between a giant pig and a restroom attendant at the Piazza, which was strange, since I doubt there's a restaurant in the state outside of Tulsa or Oklahoma City that has a restroom attendant. The Piazza sure as heck doesn't. I woke up in a cold sweat and knocked back a couple of king-sized belts of Old Grand-Dad, which helped me fall asleep but brought on more nightmares. In the last one, I was driving down a lonely highway in a pouring rain. I couldn't remember who I was or where I was going. The road began to shrink in front of me and I panicked. The more I panicked, the more the road shrank. Everything converged on a diminishing point on the horizon. It felt like I was being sucked through a giant soda straw, and the more I struggled against it, the stronger the pull. I jolted myself awake before I got totally consumed. I pinched myself to confirm I was still among the living.

I was.

Take that, Elnora Goodpasture.

I lay there until dawn, eyes open, until it became clear trying to sleep was a waste of time. I got up and let Dizzy out to do her business, then boiled some water in an old sauce pan and made instant coffee. One of these days I'll buy a real coffee pot.

I put a record on the stereo. First song was by the saxophone player Charlie Parker: "Billie's Bounce," an up-tempo tune that puts to lie the myth that the blues is all about being sad. I'm partial to jazz, especially saxophone players, and Charlie Parker was about the best who ever lived.

Around here I'm as much of a misfit about music as I am most other things. Oklahoma is country & western territory. The closest thing to jazz you'll hear is Bob Wills and the Texas Playboys. That's good music on its own merits, but I don't much care for it. I inherited my love for jazz from my mama, Marceline Hardy, who came by it honestly, having grown up in New Orleans. Her folks were poor but cultured and they paid for their daughter's piano lessons. Her teacher schooled her on Beethoven sonatas, but at home she practiced "Maple Leaf Rag." My daddy used to say with some pride that when he met her, she was one of the finest whorehouse pianists in the Crescent City. He was kidding, but mama's piano playing was no joke. Of course, once they got married and moved back to Oklahoma, music took a back seat to being a wife and mother.

Marceline never lost her love of jazz, though, and she handed it down to her son. Somehow in the midst of the Dust Bowl and the Great Depression she managed to squirrel-away enough money to buy me a secondhand alto saxophone. It remains the best gift I ever received. I learned by trial-and-error and by playing along with her records. Marceline even taught me a few licks she says she stole directly from the eminent Mr. Jelly Roll Morton, himself—things he used to play on a piano hoisted onto the back of a flatbed truck at Mardi Gras. She might've been pulling my leg, but it was fun to think about.

My daddy loved music too, although he didn't play an instrument. His tastes ran more to country singers like Jimmie Rodgers and the Carter Family, though he always got a kick out of listening to mama and me play "Swing Low, Sweet Chariot" together at the First Methodist Church after Sunday services, with mama on the wheezing old pipe organ, and me on my Conn Wonder alto saxophone.

So many memories of my mother are tied-up with music. I remember one night when I was real young, maybe seven or eight, she got daddy to go bowling with some men from town. Everett Hardy was a homebody. He didn't know how to have fun except with his family and didn't care to learn, but Marceline needed him to try. Being his only friend was a heavy burden, which I didn't understand at the time.

As soon as his truck leave pulled out of the driveway, Marceline snuck out to the tool shed and liberated a jug of bootleg whiskey daddy thought he'd hidden from her. He didn't like her to drink, maybe because she could hold her liquor better than he could. We had a party, just her and me. She drank sour mash, I drank Coca Cola. We listened to Bix Beiderbecke and Louis Armstrong and Jelly Roll Morton records for hours, dancing and acting like escapees from the loony bin. She even confided to me one of her closest secrets: I'd been named after a trumpeter she'd had a crush on as a girl, even though she'd told my daddy she just liked the name Emmett. It was after midnight that we heard my father's car drive up. We rushed to bed and pretended to be asleep. The next day she made me promise not to tell him about our little shindig. I never did. I'm the only living soul who knows it happened. It's one of my fondest memories. I still have that saxophone my mother scrimped and saved for. I think of her when I play it, and when I listen to jazz. She's been gone awhile and I miss her a lot.

With a trip to Oklahoma City on the docket, I endeavored to make myself presentable. I showered and shaved and ate a healthful breakfast of coffee and powdered doughnuts. I put on a fresh uniform shirt. Instead of my usual blue jeans, I wore my official brown pants with the tan stripe down the legs. I seldom get hangovers and didn't have one this time. Except for still being tired, I felt about as good as I ever feel. Charlie Parker's saxophone helped put the bad thoughts out of my mind.

The sun nearly blinded me on my way out the door. The wind had yet to kick up, but I expected it would, eventually.

The drive from my house to the police station takes two or three minutes if I go the short way, which I seldom do. Most mornings I prefer to drive from one end of Main Street to the other, which adds a couple of minutes. Burr's business district consists of a row of one-story buildings on each side of Main Street, which is what we call US Highway 14 for the three-quarters-of-a-mile it runs through town.

Burr is home to the usual stores and amenities you find in any town its size. Our drugstore is called Miller's and it's been around forever. For some reason—no one's ever been able to figure out why— the air in Miller's smells vaguely like farts, but it sells us our medicine at a good price, and the soda fountain serves great root beer floats. Oklahoma Tire & Supply is a chain store that stocks hardware and such staples of small town life as blue jeans, flannel shirts, and guns. Lots of guns. The Burr Gazette is our newspaper, run by Frank Ickes, who used to have my job before he got smart and went into the publishing business.

We've got a couple eateries that serve different clienteles: the aforementioned Piazza, which features table service and home-cooked meals; and Burger Mart, which sells burgers and fries to folks who prefer to eat in their cars. We also have our own five-and-dime, and what must be the world's smallest Piggly Wiggly supermarket. There's Town Hall, the public library, Edna's, and a few other concerns that serve as a first stop for locals who'd rather not drive to Alva or Temple City to stock up on life's necessities. Recently, we've seen an increase in vacant storefronts. Once upon a time, if a place went out of business, another took its place, sooner than later. These days it's usually later.

The police station is a small detached cinderblock building painted red, white, and blue. It sits in a lot between the Chamber of

Commerce and a building that used to be a feed store but has been shuttered for a few years. Our front office is a space about the size of two Porta-Pottys pushed together. It contains a desk for the receptionist/dispatcher, a pink formica counter, a couple of folding chairs, and a bench pushed up against one wall. The back area comprises my desk and a holding cell just large enough to accommodate one normal-sized town drunk or two boozed-up leprechauns if they don't mind sleeping head-to-toe.

I got to work at eight on the dot. As usual, Karen was there already. My two part-time officers—Kenny Harjo and Jeff Starns—were present, as well. Kenny is always punctual. As for Jeff, well, there's a first time for everything.

On paper, the Burr Police Department consists of four officers, which isn't bad for a town this size. That's not counting Karen, who's technically a civilian but puts in more hours for lower pay than any of us. Bernard Cousins is my only full-timer. As for the other two, Kenny does a fine job.

Jeff, on the other hand, is as useful as tits on a bull. I hired him five years ago as a favor to Ray Midkiff, the high school principal. Ray had his eye on Jeff to teach math and be an assistant football coach, but didn't have enough money in his budget to hire him full-time. He knew I needed help and suggested we combine resources, figuring between the two of us we could pay Jeff a full salary. The boy wasn't very impressive in his interview, but I wanted to do right by Ray, so I agreed to train him. I regretted it almost immediately. Among other of his shortcomings, I found out too late he's a terrible bigot. That doesn't cause too much trouble, to be honest. Most folks around here are prejudiced to some extent. However, I'd prefer not to work with someone like that, if I can help it. A worse problem is that he's as lazy as a preacher on Mondays—the kind of fella who watches the clock until quitting time so he can go home and watch television or get drunk with his buddies.

For reasons I cannot fathom, they love Jeff down at the high school, so I can't fire him. I asked Ray not too long ago about him being able to pay his full salary so I could get someone else. Ray said it could happen soon, but it hasn't yet. To make matters worse, Jeff's wife just had twins, so he's been putting in fewer hours. Once he's gone, I think I'll find a negro officer to replace him. Call it an act of repentance. I know this: having a colored police officer would sure shake things up around here.

It was scandalous enough when I hired an Indian.

Kenny Harjo is the great grandson of Crazy Snake, the Creek leader who led the last great Indian uprising in Oklahoma—except Kenny calls him Chitto Harjo, which is his proper name. Kenny's a born lawman. He came to us out of Bacone College in Muskogee, where he took business classes and worked on the campus police force. At some point, he decided college wasn't for him and decided on law enforcement as a career. When a friend told him about a part-time opening on a small police department in the western part of the state, Kenny hitchhiked the 250 miles from Muskogee to Burr. He walked into the station one day and told Karen he'd heard we were looking for help. She sent him back to my office. I interviewed him and hired him on the spot.

I got some flack from local rednecks, but honestly his being an Indian stopped being an issue quicker than you'd think. Kenny commands respect so naturally, even Jeff gets along with him. We can't afford to pay him much, but I was also able to get him appointed Animal Control Officer, which helps him make ends meet. When he's not working for us or rounding up stray dogs, he stacks boxes and runs the cash register at Oklahoma Tire & Supply. I've been after the town government to let me hire another full-time officer so Kenny can quit one of his jobs.

Karen sat at her desk outside the door to my office, drinking her morning coffee and reading yesterday's copy of The Daily Oklahoman; we get it the day after its published, and the Gazette comes out once a week, on Mondays. On a table next to her is a small gray two-way radio and walkie-talkie handset. Next to the door as you come in, there's a TV tray that holds our jumbo-sized electric percolator, a jar of Coffee-Mate, one of those restaurant-style sugar dispensers, and a stack of paper cups. On the back wall is a framed photo of JFK—we never got around to replacing it with a portrait of LBJ—and a cork bulletin board with a map of Oklahoma tacked onto it. The opposite wall is decorated with FBI Most Wanted posters, including an old yellowed one of John Dillinger that hung in the Burr post office when I was a boy. That one is framed.

The jade green Bakelite radio on Karen's desk was playing "King of the Road," by Roger Miller. Kenny sat in the bench against the wall, eating a glazed donut and using the window sill to rest his coffee cup. Jeff stood leaning against the counter, drinking coffee. My usual routine is to walk in singing along with whatever hillbilly song's currently playing, so Karen can tell me my voice makes her ears bleed. Today I didn't feel much like it.

She noticed. "No singing, huh?"

"Not today. Find me some jazz. Maybe I'll sing along with that."

"That radio just plays white people music," Jeff said.

I didn't think it was very funny, especially after what I'd seen the night before. I started to tear into him but Kenny beat me to it.

"Jeff, how 'bout you keep that nonsense to yourself," he said.

Karen joined in. There are about ten non-prejudiced people in this town and three of them work for me. "I know you think you're funny, Jeffrey," she said, "but you sound like one of those drunk peckerwoods down at Edna's when you talk like that." Like most kids who grew up here, Karen was raised to worship Jesus Christ and discriminate against negroes. At some point, she concluded the two things were mutually incompatible. Karen came down on the side of the Lord.

Jeff just chuckled. "Hell, I *am* one of them drunk peckerwoods," he said. "They's my people. At least they were before the twins was born."

Fatherhood cut into the time Jeff spent carousing with friends from his high school days, who treat him like King Shit of Turd Mountain thanks to a college football career that consisted mainly of picking splinters out of his ass.

Around here, Jeff was already skating on thin ice and about to fall through. I hoped he could swim. At the moment, however, I was disinclined to give him a lesson in brotherhood. We had more pressing issues to address.

"I assume everybody's heard about the body Bernard and I found out by the railroad tracks last night," I said. I looked at Karen. "I know *you* know, because we got you out of bed to help. Sorry we had to do that."

"Don't apologize. It's an awful thing. Did y'all find out who she was?"

"No, we didn't. She had no identification. No clothes, no purse. No nothing." I told them what I knew, which wasn't much, despite the fact that I'd found the body myself and spent half the night at the scene. "It's the OSBI's case. I told them we'd be glad to assist in any way we can, but it's not our crime to solve."

"We're just going to let it go?" said Kenny. "Let them do all the work?"

"Officially, we can investigate it *un*officially, if that makes any sense," I said. "The good news is, the pressure is on them, not us, so we can spend as much or as little time on it as we want. God forbid it takes us away from important work, like finding Edgar Bixby's pig."

I told them the tale of the missing Daffodil. Given what had happened, it seemed too ridiculous to concern ourselves with. But it was our job.

"Jeff, you go on out there," I said, figuring a pig-napping was best-suited to his talents. Also, Edgar's ex-Klan, so he and Jeff speak the same language. "Talk football with him and calm him down," I said. "Take his statement. He'll want us to treat this as the crime of the century."

Jeff nodded and started for the door. I remembered that I'd seen Edgar's porch light the night before. "While you're at it, ask if they saw anything suspicious last night. I could see his house from where we found the body. That means he could see us. You never know, maybe he noticed something while he was out looking for his pig."

"Yup, I'll ask," Jeff said. He passed Bernard going out.

"You're late," I said. "How long did they keep you last night?"

"I got home a little before five and slept for a couple of hours," he said. He rubbed his face and slapped his cheeks like he was trying to wake himself up.

"You ok to work?" I asked.

"I'm fine," he said, stifling a yawn.

"Ok, I'm going to hold you to that." I said to him and Kenny, "How about you two ask around and see if anyone saw a young colored girl in town over the last few days? Maybe you can find a passerby, someone who drove by where we found her." They scooted out like they were afraid I was going to change my mind and make them count paper clips.

I called Agent Jones to set up a time to come in. He asked if I could be there by eleven o'clock. I said I could if I got on my horse. He said that'd be fine and hung up.

"Not much of a talker, I gather," Karen said.

"Not this morning he's not. I don't much blame him. I sure wouldn't want his job."

She frowned and leaned back in her chair. "I predict your own's fixing to get hard enough."

CHAPTER SIX

I had to pass the crime scene on my way to the city, so I reckoned I might as well stop and take a look in the light of day. The murder might not be mine to solve, but I still felt responsible. I couldn't just sit by and do nothing.

In the Marines, I witnessed things so gruesome, I wouldn't describe them in any detail to a civilian. Yet somehow that poor girl, lying there naked and alone, was as sad as anything I'd seen in Korea. Sadder, maybe.

Maybe it was those green eyes.

The skies were deep blue with not a cloud in sight and the sun sat low enough in the sky that it still felt more like spring than summer. Three or four police barriers and a lone highway patrolman were all that was left. I was relieved the patrolman was not Trooper Dickshot.

This fella's name was Johnson. I recalled seeing him the night before. He sat in his car with the door open and one foot resting on the blacktop. Judging by the dinner-plate-sized sweat stains under his arms and the dark circles under his eyes, I'm sure he was more than ready to call it a day.

"Last man standing," I said even though he was sitting. "Been here all night?"

"Yup." Trooper Johnson took a deep breath and puffed-out his cheeks. "Waiting for permission to vamoose. Need sleep."

The poor bastard was too exhausted to waste words.

In the weeds along the side of the road, grasshoppers and other assorted insects had commenced their symphony of clicks and buzzes. The hotter it gets, the louder they get.

"Going to be another scorcher," I said.

Trooper Johnson leaned his head back and sighed. "I expect it will," he said. "Kept the car running for the air conditioner. Had to turn it off. Almost out of gas." He wiped his face with a dirty handkerchief. "That'd be a helluva thing. Running out of gas."

"Yeh, it would," I said.

Neither of us was feeling especially talky, so I got down to business. "Mind if I look around?" I asked. I didn't need his permission, but there is such a thing as good manners.

"Go ahead," said Trooper Johnson. He smacked the steering wheel with his palm. "Dammit, I'm going to run the air conditioning for a few minutes. If I run out, I run out. You take all the time you need, Chief." He slammed the door and started the car.

I walked around the barriers to where we'd found the body. White chalk outlined where it had been. Just like in the movies. I didn't expect to find anything, but figured there was no harm in looking. I saw what I expected to see. The coarse jagged rocks they build the tracks on—I'm told it's called ballast. Scrub. Red ants. Not much else.

The tire marks were a lot easier to see in the light of day. It looked like they'd been made by a medium-sized passenger car of some sort. The ground was mostly red sandstone, but in places there was enough dirt for tires to make an impression. I wondered if the forensic boys were able to take a plaster cast. I reckoned they took plenty of pictures. A cast and photos might help confirm the identity of the vehicle, if it was ever found.

I widened my search a few yards in every direction but nothing special caught my eye. I needed to hit the road, anyway, if I was going to be on time for my meeting with those OSBI boys. I honked at Trooper Johnson on my way out. He nodded back. Either that or he was nodding off. Hard to tell. His cruiser was still running, for the time being, at least.

I drove south until I hit US 66 in Elk City, then headed east toward

Oklahoma City. Route 66 is about to be replaced by one of those four-lane interstates, but for now, it's still the best way into the city from the West. I'll miss it when it's gone. I can't imagine anyone will ever make a TV show or write a catchy song about Interstate 40.

I've been driving to Oklahoma City since I was a teenager, so I know the streets pretty well, although things have changed since the old days. I'd just visited OSBI headquarters one other time and I couldn't remember precisely where it was. When it comes to directions, though, I've got good instincts. I found it without making too many wrong turns.

·   ·   ·   ·   ·

You could say I have a love/hate relationship with the OSBI.

On second thought, love has nothing to do with it. It's more of a pity/hate deal.

The Oklahoma State Bureau of Investigation was founded to combat the epic outlawry running wild in Oklahoma during the years of the Great Depression. Back then, bank robbers could evade capture simply by crossing from one county to the next. Counties could cooperate, but it wasn't a sure thing.

The sole agency with statewide jurisdiction were the US Marshals, and they were spread pretty thin. Up through the early days of statehood, they did an acceptable job of keeping the peace. By the 1920s, however, things had gotten significantly out of hand. The governor at the time decided it was high time to establish a statewide police force. In time, that force became the OSBI.

Despite its well-intentioned beginnings, the OSBI has had more than its fair share of troubles. Whichever tinpot politician who happens to be in power screws with it in one way or another. Frankly, I'm not sure anyone's ever known for sure what to do with it. The OSBI has always been a political football, which I reckon can be as interesting to watch as the other kind, but not much fun to play. As a whole, the bureau is underfunded and abused. From what I've heard, morale is lower than a prairie dog's nuts.

Most of the agents I meet are decent and hard-working. It's not their fault their job has them trying to haul an elephant up a mountain on a tricycle.

•   •   •   •   •

The OSBI building looks more like a modern big city elementary school or a post office than a police station. The blast of refrigerated air I expected upon entering did not transpire, however. A red-faced, pudgy uniformed trooper sat at the front desk, his face buried in an overmatched fan. "Air-conditioning's out," he said. I flashed my credentials, but I might as well have pulled out a Mickey Mouse Club membership card for all he seemed to care. I told him who I was there to see. He directed me to an office in the back.

Agent Jones intercepted me before I could get there. He wore the same clothes as the night before, except for the too-small jacket, which I suspect he had dispensed with in deference to the heat. He'd also replaced his grimy slippers with plain black cowboy boots that hadn't seen a shine for a spell. His hound-dog face gleamed with sweat.

"Thanks for coming in, Chief Hardy," he said, friendlier than he'd been on the phone. "Let's do this in Heckscher's office," he said. "Mine's being painted." He leaned close and winked. "That's what I tell people instead of letting them come in and discover what a goddam mess it is."

Heckscher's cramped, windowless office had all the down-home charm of a gas station men's room, except instead of a filthy urinal and a condom machine on the wall, there was a battered Underwood typewriter sitting atop a cluttered, rubber-topped desk. The white walls were stained yellow by the smoke of who knows how many thousands of cigarettes. The latest had rolled off its ashtray and was currently burning a hole in the top of the desk. A small rotating fan moved the smoke around but didn't make things any less uncomfortable. In one corner stood a rusty water cooler with a paper cup dispenser.

"Good to see you, Chief." Agent Heckscher stood and shook my hand, then sat back down and corralled the errant cigarette. He tweezed it between two fingers and took a puff. It must have tasted bad, because he made a face and ground it out.

Unlike Jones, Agent Heckscher appeared bone dry and cool as a cucumber. "Have a seat," he said with a smarmy grin and lit another cigarette. "This shouldn't take long."

Jones and I sat in a pair of folding chairs. Heckscher picked up the phone and said a few words. Within a few seconds, a tall, slender woman carrying a yellow legal pad entered the room. Her sleeveless dress was made of a coarse fabric dyed an ugly shade of greenish brown. In fact, nearly everything about her was brown: cat-eye glasses, stockings, shoes, hair. She even had a suntan. Jones introduced her as Miss White.

The agents asked me a few questions but mainly listened as I filled out the basic story I'd told the night before. They stopped me once or twice to clarify a point. For the most part, however, they let me have my say. I finished in about 15 minutes.

"That should do, Chief. Much obliged to you for coming down," said Jones.

"You're welcome, detectives. Glad to do it." They stood and offered their hands, which is the universal signal a meeting is over. But I wasn't ready.

"Before I go, I wonder if you boys could fill me in on what was found after I left."

Jones and Heckscher looked at me like I'd just shown them a naked picture of Lyndon Johnson. They excused Miss White and sat back down. With scarcely hidden annoyance, they described what they knew, which didn't take long since I'd told them most of it in the first place. Without an ID, they had no way of knowing who she was or where she came from. All they knew for sure was her throat had been cut by a knife with a non-serrated edge. Also, a near-total lack of blood at the site meant she'd been killed elsewhere.

I asked if they had a theory.

"Right now, we believe she was killed on a train and thrown off," said Jones. "A Kansas City-bound freight passed that spot not long before the body was found." He took a deep drag of his cigarette and fell into a coughing spasm that lasted half a minute. A slappy, high-pitched echo bounced off the walls. "These things'll kill ya," he choked, then took another puff.

He helped himself to a cup of water and cooled his face in the fan. "Based on the position and condition of the body," he said, "it's probable she was killed in a boxcar and thrown off the train, which would explain the lack of clothes or personal effects. Also, the absence of blood at the scene."

"What about that fresh grass on her back?" I asked. "There was no grass on the scene."

He waved his hand dismissively. "You find all sorts of things in freight cars. Wet grass will stick to anything."

"It could also mean she was laying in grass when she was killed."

"It could," Heckscher agreed. "We're not ruling anything out at this point."

Jones extinguished his cigarette, then soaked a stained blue handkerchief in the water cooler and wiped his face. "We sent word to the freight yards in Wichita and Kansas City ahead of that train. Asked them to detain any vagrants," he said. "Frankly, I'm not optimistic about apprehending anyone."

Heckscher shook his head. "Me neither. They uncouple cars on sidings all along the line. Railroad security tries to keep the hobos off. It's not as bad as the old days, but it's still a losing battle. Bums get on and off all the time. It's unlikely our guy stayed on to the end. He could've gotten off almost anywhere."

None of this was news to me. As a boy, I learned more about hobos than I cared to. I saw too many of them up close during the Depression.

"I gather you don't think there's much chance of finding our killer," I said.

"Oh, we've got a chance," said Jones. "It ain't a big one. We could get lucky, but it's a needle in a haystack."

"What makes you so sure she was killed on the train?"

"I'm not saying we're 100% sure," he emphasized, "but going by the marks on the body, it looks like she fell hard from a distance, like off a moving vehicle. Hopefully, we'll know more after the autopsy."

"When will that be?"

"Tomorrow morning," said Heckscher.

"Unless there's a line ahead of her," said Jones, "but we don't think there is."

"What about the glove and the tire marks?" I asked.

"Chief, I reckon if we walked along those tracks between here and Kansas City, we'd find a hundred gloves exactly like it," said Heckscher. "It might have something to do with our case, but I doubt it."

Jones lit another cigarette, this time managing not to cough. "As far as those tire tracks, they might be related, but they don't help much all by themselves. I wouldn't be at all surprised if there were a hundred cars with that same tread in your county alone. If we can tie a car to the crime by other means, the tire tracks might help confirm, but—" He shrugged.

"Y'all aren't giving up before you even get started, are you?" I asked.

"No, no, no. Of course not," Jones said, shaking his jowls in the negative and trying to look insulted. "We'll work on it as hard as we can. We'll be going back to Burr and poking around and asking questions. We're checking missing persons reports across the state, especially from here and Tulsa, where there's a high concentration of coloreds."

No one said anything for a few seconds. Like nature, stupidity abhors a vacuum, so Agent Heckscher felt an obligation to butt in.

"We gotta be realistic," he said with a self-satisfied expression on his face and taking a drag from the last quarter-inch of a filterless cigarette pinched between his forefinger and thumb. "The way most of those folks live, we can't expect much from them in the way of help." He blew a plume through his nose and ground out the cigarette. "Nobody's going to miss one stray nigger more or less."

Jones's bulldog face looked ready to bite. "John Joe, that's enough of that. You don't know a goddam thing about how them folks live."

He motioned to me. "C'mon, Chief, I'll see you out," he said.

Heckscher leaned back with a smirk plastered across his oily face. Jones gave him a disgusted look. We left the office.

"I apologize for that," he said in the hallway. "I have to deal with that smug son of a bitch on a daily basis. It ain't fun, let me tell you." We walked toward the front door. "I'll work this every bit as hard as if it was a white girl, I promise you that."

Maybe Ovell Jones sincerely believed that. I didn't.

"All I'm saying is, we don't expect to find much."

That, I believed.

We walked through a warren of offices on our way to the entrance. Jones went on about how they had their hands full with cattle thefts and some pig that got nabbed from our neck of the woods. *Those ranchers raise a ruckus,* and *the squeaky wheel gets the grease, so far no one's called about this girl,* and so on and so forth. I tuned him out, because the message was clear. A dead colored girl don't matter.

It didn't surprise me. It turned my stomach, but it didn't surprise me.

Still, I held my tongue. I had little hope for a just conclusion, but I didn't want to give Jones any kind of excuse not to work it as hard as he could.

Miss White caught up with us and pushed a typed copy of my statement in my face. I signed it and she whisked it away.

I asked Jones if he planned to do a sketch portrait of the victim. He said they already had. You could've have knocked me over with a wadded-up piece of paper. "Our artist lady drew one this morning, as soon as we brought the body in," he said. "We're having copies printed, but we won't get them back until Monday. I can give you a Xerox of it, though."

The sweaty highway patrolman at the front desk still had his face stuck in the fan. Jones reached around him and opened a drawer. He took out a Xeroxed pencil drawing of a pretty young girl with her eyes closed and handed it to me. She looked like she was sleeping. You couldn't tell her race. The details were blurry, but it was a good likeness.

"Can I keep this?" I asked.

"Sure. We got the original. These Xeroxes aren't worth a shit. I'll be over your way tomorrow or the next day and bring along some printed copies." He mopped his face again and grinned dolefully. "Hopefully, y'all got air-conditioning."

I said the Town of Burr provides us with a window unit that does a pretty fair job and that we looked forward to seeing him. For his part, Agent Ovell Jones once more cautioned me not to get my hopes up.

I didn't bother telling him there was no danger of that.

CHAPTER SEVEN

I stopped at a Burger Chef on my way home and wolfed down a cheeseburger and some french fries. I used their pay phone to call Karen and asked her to set up a meeting with everybody for when I got back. My conversation with Agents Jones and Heckscher had nettled my mind. I needed to talk over things with my own people.

By the time I arrived, three-quarters of my staff were present and accounted for. Kenny sat stretched out in an old wooden chair we'd liberated from the high school last fall when they got new desks. Bernard had the same guilty look Dizzy gets when I catch her drinking out of the toilet, which led me to suspect he'd been trying-out my desk. Sometimes he does that when I'm out of the office. He thinks I don't know.

Karen was taking a break from dispatching. She had no one to dispatch, anyway; the full complement of Burr police was in the room. All except one.

A noise sounding suspiciously like a snore emanated from my office. I looked and saw Jeff fast asleep on the cot in the holding cell.

"He's discovered the secret to getting his beauty sleep," Karen said. "Leave Cindy alone with the twins and take advantage of our accommodations."

"Not sure how much I like that idea."

"Oh, he's not hurting anyone," she said.

I reckoned it was just as well.

All the seats were taken, so I leaned with my back against the wall and tried to shut out the honks and grunts.

"How'd it go with them two agents, sir?" Bernard asked. "What're their names? Smith and Jones?"

"Jones and Heckscher," I said. "Let's say it did not go as well as I hoped. They think the girl was killed in a boxcar and thrown off the train."

"Based on what?" Kenny asked.

"I don't know. Based on what they want to believe, mainly."

"You don't think it could've happened that way?" Bernard asked.

"It could've happened that way, but it could've happened some other way. Their theory has the virtue of being next-to-impossible to prove, since whoever did it could've gotten off that train anywhere between here and Kansas City."

Karen pulled a skeptical face. "What do you mean, their theory has the 'virtue of being impossible to prove?'"

"I said *next* to impossible. I meant that, if I were the cynical sort—"

"We all know that's not the case," she said. That got chuckles all around.

"Alright, very funny," I said. "I should say, *if I didn't know better*, I might think they were looking for an excuse not to work this too hard. Pinning it on an anonymous suspect who disappears into thin air would fill that bill."

Kenny shifted in his chair and the legs screeched against the floor. "You're saying they figure it was a nameless colored girl no one will miss, so there's no use spending time on it," he said. "Write it off as one vagrant killing another. Move on to the next case."

"That's about the size of it." I decided not to mention the next case might well be the disappearance of Burr's favorite pig.

"That's a gloomy attitude," Karen said. "Those boys are professionals. I expect they'll do their job the best they know how."

Karen likes to think the best of people. I am by nature less charitable. "They are professionals, but they're also overworked and underpaid," I said. "There's pressure on them from other cases. They said it themselves: the squeaky wheel gets the grease. Unless someone starts making noise over this girl's death, I expect she'll get lost in the shuffle."

"We know she's not from around here," Bernard said, "which means she'll be hard to identify unless someone comes forward. Without an ID, we got nothing to go on, really."

"They found a glove at the scene, and there were tire marks in the dirt next to the body," I said. "I think it's possible there's more to find. When I went by there this morning, everyone was long gone except for one trooper about to fall asleep in his cruiser. That area should be gone over again in the light of day."

"They have plans to do that?" asked Bernard.

"I don't believe so," I said. "I'm thinking we should do it, ourselves."

"Couldn't hurt," said Kenny. He's always hankering to do anything that at least approximates real police work.

Karen raised a curious eyebrow. "I was under the impression you didn't want any part of this."

"I don't really, but like Kenny said, it can't hurt. It's not like we got anything else to do that's so important."

"We got the Daffodil case," said Bernard.

I pushed my hat back. "I think we can walk and chew gum at the same time," I said.

"We're going to need more than the five of us if we want do it right," Karen said.

I started to ask if she might find it in her heart to ask for volunteers in church the next morning, then quickly retracted my request. "Never mind, I'll do it myself." Under my breath I added, "Rules are made to be broken."

"What rule is that?" Kenny asked.

"His rule against going to church," said Bernard.

"Don't you know your boss is a heathen?" Karen asked. She said it like was joking, but I knew better. Karen takes her relationship with the almighty very seriously.

Kenny grinned. "That explains a lot."

"I guess it does," she said and turned back to me. "You'll have to clear it with Reverend Hankins."

I summoned the counterfeit charm for which I have been roundly derided by single women from Seoul to Temple City. "Would you mind asking the good Reverend for me?" I asked. "He's more likely to say yes to you. Judging by the look he gave you when we were in line at the Piggly Wiggly the other day, I'd say he has designs."

.   .   .   .   .

She sighed. Elaborately and sarcastically. "Number one, Emmett Hardy, you got a dirty mind. Number two, your dime-store Cary Grant impersonation won't help your cause." That got a giggle out of Kenny.

"I'll do it, but I can't guarantee he'll say yes."

The quicker I could steer the conversation away from religion and my lack of it, the better, so I thanked her and outlined my plan.

"We'll ask folks to drive out there after the service and do this thing right. Go over the area rock-by-rock, weed-by-weed. We should send someone out there right now to make sure the scene doesn't get messed with. The highway patrolman was gone when I passed by there a few minutes ago. I should've had one of y'all out there earlier, but I didn't think of it."

"I'll go," said Kenny, rising up out of his chair.

"I'm going to need to you to stay there overnight."

"That's fine. I'll pack some sandwiches and a thermos of coffee."

Jeff was still dead to the world in the holding cell. "Bernard, coordinate a time for Sleeping Beauty over there to relieve Kenny. He tells me he gets woke up in the middle of the night by crying babies, anyway. Might as well put his sleeplessness to good use."

Just for spite, I considered locking Jeff in the cell while he was asleep, but that'd be too mean, even for me. Suddenly I remembered something. "Did Jeff ever go out to talk to Edgar?"

Everyone laughed. "He was fixin' to yesterday, when we got a call," Karen said. "Guess who—or what—turned up in Principal Midkiff's garage?"

"Does it oink?"

"Bingo," Karen said with a grin.

"Principal Midkiff and his wife were in Oklahoma City for a couple days," Kenny said. "When they got back, there was Daffodil in their car port, pretty as you please, a brand-new pink ribbon tied around her tail."

"It looks like it was a senior prank, sir," Bernard said. "They're common this time of year, just before graduation."

It didn't seem especially funny to me, but then again, I'm getting old. "Did the neighbors see anything?" I asked.

"They don't really have neighbors, sir," said Bernard. "Their house is off by itself."

"Where's Daffodil now?"

"Last I heard, Jeff informed Edgar and advised him to go pick her up," said Bernard.

"Jeff didn't go out there?"

"Nope," Kenny said.

I tried to remember if I was drunk when I assigned Jeff that task and decided I must've been. "Bernard, you go. Edgar will want to know what we're doing to find whoever stole his pig. Tell him we're working on it and ask him if he or his family saw anything suspicious the night of the murder. I assume when Edgar noticed Daffodil was missing he went looking for her. Maybe he saw something."

"10-4, chief," said Bernard.

"And I don't care if it's a prank by some kids or the ghost of John Wilkes Booth. We need to find who stole Daffodil before Edgar does. He's liable to shoot the little bastards if he finds them first." I was only half-kidding.

CHAPTER EIGHT

Oklahoma has always had a complicated relationship with law and order, dating back to when it was barely even a territory, never mind a state. There were times—the better part of its early history, in fact—when it was a paradise for the criminal element.

In the 1890s, gangs like the Dalton Brothers or the Wild Bunch would commit depredations in Texas or Kansas or Missouri, then take refuge in "the Nations"—territory the United States government ceded The Five Civilized Tribes as compensation for other, more valuable land they stole from them in the Deep South. The Nations comprised what is now eastern Oklahoma, which, it goes without saying, is no longer primarily in Indian hands. Back then, however, it was sovereign tribal territory. White man's law counted for nothing. Outlaws hid there almost without fear of getting caught.

In those days, drinking and fighting and balling and gambling were as much a way of life here as they were in such notorious Old West outposts as Dodge City or Deadwood. Hard men were required to keep the peace—men like the trio of US Deputy Marshals known collectively as The Three Guardsmen: Deputy US Marshals Bill Tilghman, Chris Madsen, and Heck Thomas. When I was little, I used to listen to the old-timers down at the barber shop tell stories about them. Those stories made me want to be a cop.

Those marshals and others not as famous were charged with making Oklahoma Territory a fit place for white people to live. The

Guardsmen's most famous exploit was the pursuit and eventual apprehension of the villainous bank robber Bill Doolin, leader of The Wild Bunch. Tilghman captured Doolin single-handedly as the malodorous scoundrel was taking a bath. Doolin later escaped and Heck Thomas shot him deader than a day-old plate of grits.

I've heard Matt Dillon of *Gunsmoke* fame is based on Tilghman. For some reason, they didn't use Bill's real name. We named our county after him. Could just be those Hollywood fellas can't spell.

Oklahoma's other major bout with rampant lawlessness came during the '30s, when it was a crossroads for bad guys (and a few gals) from all over the Southwest. Some of the worst were home-grown. Pretty Boy Floyd grew up in Akins, a little place near Sallisaw in eastern Oklahoma. It was there he first learned the tricks of his trade. Local newspapers of that era made him out to be some kind of handsome Robin Hood character who took from rich bankers and gave to the poor. Folks suffering the twin body blows of the Dust Bowl and Great Depression wanted to believe it. Sad to say, Charles Floyd didn't much care if you ran a bank or plowed a field. If you had something he wanted, he took it. Mouth-off to him and you might get a bullet in the head for your trouble. FBI Agent Melvin Purvis shot and killed Pretty Boy in 1934. Forty-thousand misled admirers attended his funeral, making it the biggest in state history.

I never thought Floyd was pretty. He just looked mean and stupid to me.

Other Depression-era gangsters had Oklahoma connections. Bonnie and Clyde regularly crisscrossed the state during their short, bloody career. Ma Barker and her gang of idiot sons got their start in the Tulsa area. A pea-brained bootlegger named Machine Gun Kelly kidnapped a rich Oklahoma City businessman in 1933, bungling every aspect of the operation before the FBI eventually caught up with him. Legend says he cowered and begged "Don't shoot, G-men!" which is where Jimmy Cagney picked up the term.

Things have changed a great deal since the days when robbing banks was a growth industry. Which is not to say we don't have crime. We do. But not because we're a wild, anything-goes society.

On the contrary. These days, the state is run by a crowd of blue-nosed hypocrites with an imaginary hotline to Jesus. Prohibition ended in 1933 for most of the country. Oklahoma didn't get around to repealing it until '59, and even then, they only did it part way. There's still a law—scorned and widely ignored—against buying a drink in a bar.

The way I see it, folks are going to sin. There's just not any two ways about it. As much as certain people try to stamp it out or sweep it under the rug, pleasures of the flesh will be indulged. To pretend otherwise is ridiculous. Look no further than all the bars and night clubs willing to circumvent the law against serving liquor by the drink. Or the multitude of establishments featuring young ladies who gyrate in their birthday suits for men who can't keep their tongues from hanging out of their mouths. The difference between now and the days of Bill Tilghman—who owned a saloon or two himself, or so legend has it—is that today the folks who want to close the bars and clothe the naked ladies have the upper hand.

I do not identify with the killjoys. There's nothing wrong with having a drink now and then. Or even more than one, more than now and then. And while dancing in the altogether might not be the best way for a woman to exploit her spiritual and intellectual gifts, I reckon it must pay better than being a secretary or waitress or schoolteacher, or else those girls wouldn't do it. As far as affecting their chances of getting into heaven, I can't believe the angel tending the pearly gates would be so small-minded.

Instead of fussing over made-up crimes, people ought to spend their energy fighting things that do actual harm. Plenty of that going around. Like the laws keeping negroes down, for example. Too many white folks thump bibles and preach brotherhood on Sundays, then spend the rest of the week trying to prevent negroes from having the same rights as them.

We still have violent crime, of course, even if it's not as flashy as it was in the olden days. Every so often I'm called to referee a pair of feuding love birds who try to rip each other's faces off. Such incidents can be tricky to handle, especially if there's a gun in the house—and in

Oklahoma, there's always a gun in the house. We got our share of bar fights, too, which can be hazardous to a person trying to break one up.

Mostly, however, the stuff I do is of a piddling nature. I'll haul-in the occasional drunk and let him sleep it off in my cell. The city government is always pressing me to give out more speeding tickets as a way of sweetening the town coffers, so I do that. I don't like it, but I do it.

Every fall, I place a plastic crown on the head of Burr High's homecoming queen. I fire a pistol that kicks-off the annual rattlesnake hunt. We got one spry old fella who, for reasons we've never been able to figure out, climbs a tree on his property once or twice a year and needs our help getting down.

In a little town like Burr—where everyone knows everybody else and the doors don't have locks—a police chief's biggest job is simply making sure everyone knows it's in their best interest to get along.

I try not to make a big deal about it. People don't generally need—nor do they appreciate—the law breathing down their necks all the time. I sure as hell don't like *doing* it. My policy is, be seen and not heard until it's time to speak softly and carry a big stick. Something like that. Preventing little things from becoming big is the major part of my job. I'm good at it.

Truth is, I'm mostly an insurance policy the town hopes it will never have to cash in. Something like the abduction of a prize-winning pig is about as interesting as my job gets.

•   •   •   •   •

The afternoon passed without event. I'd dispatched Bernard to calm-down Edgar and Kenny to babysit the crime scene. I called Agent Jones and informed him of my plan for an expanded search. He agreed it was a good idea.

I stopped by the train station just in time to witness nobody getting on or off the late-afternoon Santa Fe. From there, I went to Burger Mart and had a chocolate milkshake.

I occasionally substitute milkshakes for bourbon when I'm on-duty, if it's especially hot outside. Both inflict roughly the same amount of damage to my waistline.

By the time I'd sucked down the dregs of my shake, it was quitting time.

So, I quit. For the day, at least.

·　　·　　·　　·　　·

I sat in a rickety lawn chair in my back yard, a steadily diminishing six-pack of Brown Derby at my feet. Watching the sun dip below the horizon is a cheap and dependable form of entertainment. It doesn't cost a nickel to watch, and you know you're going to get a good show. Sometimes it's a lot better than good.

Looking for things to like about where you live is essential, if you want to keep from losing your mind. Sometimes it's not easy. Indeed, there was a time I thought it couldn't be done—when hopes of getting away from Burr were all that kept me from French-kissing the business end of a .30-30.

I had big plans. I wanted to make my mark.

Instead, I enlisted in the Marines and got shipped to Korea to fight in Harry Truman's "police action." It sure as hell looked like a war to me, but what did I know? I was a dumb kid. I learned soon enough that all the horseshit I'd read about the glory of combat had been written by men who never came within pissing distance of a battlefield.

My mama dying while I was in Korea broke my spirit. After my discharge, I stayed as far away from Oklahoma as possible. I took halfhearted stabs at being a musician and getting married. I failed at both. I was an inch away from hitting rock bottom when I got a call from home. Burr needed a police chief and my name came up. Apparently, my experience as an MP seemed more impressive than it really was. My dad knew how low I'd sunk and convinced me to take the job. Thank God, he did. Remembering how much I'd once wanted to be a cop very likely saved my life.

I'm not a believer in God or heaven or destiny or any of that. But I do believe I'm doing what I'm best cut-out to do. Being a small-town cop isn't a huge deal, but it's important in its way. We can't all invent the airplane or cure polio or run a mile in four minutes, but we can all do small things that make the world a little better. I didn't always think of life in those terms, but I do now. It gets me through the day.

I watched a beautiful emerald and gold sunset stretch across the sky. The lone windmill silhouetted in the distance might not be as spectacular a detail as the buttes and mesas you see in a John Ford movie, but it was pretty enough for me at that moment. I understand they call Montana "Big Sky Country." I've never been, but I can tell you, the name describes western Oklahoma every bit as well.

CHAPTER NINE

In Burr, if you need to put the word out about something, the best way is to whisper it in the ear of the person standing next to you. By the next day, pretty much everyone in town will know.

If that isn't quick enough, you might want to tell it from the pulpit of the First Baptist Church. Or announce it from the press box at halftime of a high school football game. Both events are of a religious nature and draw standing-room-only crowds. Just one of them convenes year-round, however. It being April, I'd say my decision had been made for me.

The First Baptist Church's weekly congregation numbers at least 400 people, maybe more. It's twice the size of the First Methodist, where my folks took me as a boy. That total doesn't count all the sinners who go once or twice a month because they can't always drag themselves out of bed for all the drinking and screwing they done on Saturday night.

With rare exceptions, Reverend Melvin Hankins reserves his pulpit for saving men's souls. One of those exceptions was the 1960 presidential election, when the specter of a Catholic in the White House moved the Reverend to preach against JFK so hard, he had a minor stroke and was hospitalized for 13 days.

Such things happen once in a blue moon, however. Indeed, it's a measure of Karen's persuasive powers that she was able to convince the good Pastor that helping to find a murderer was, in some small way, as important as foiling a worldwide papist conspiracy.

. . . . .

I ascended to the pulpit and commenced my plea. "I'm sure y'all heard by now that we found the body of a colored girl on the tracks outside town night before last," I began.

The congregants' facial expressions ran the gamut. Most seemed indifferent. Some looked concerned, a few just plain hostile. I tried to talk past the latter group. Expecting a crowd of white folks to feel compassion for a dead negro is a lot to ask around these parts. Still, I hoped at least some would help, out of personal affection for Karen and me or a general sense of civic duty.

Who knows? Maybe they'd help because of the badge.

I described the events of Friday night in some detail. Despite the surroundings, I did not prettify my description. I reckoned the grislier I made it sound, the more people would be shocked and want to help.

I told about how her throat was cut, how the rocks had gouged her skin, how she was dumped on the train tracks like a sack of dirty laundry. The gruesomeness elicited a number of gasps and my-goodnesses. After picking at every scab of guilt I could think of, I outlined my plan to search the scene, then handed back the proceedings to the pastor.

Reverend Hankins—a short, stout man whose face is naturally flush and turns fire-engine red after a morning of strenuously extolling the virtues of a life lived for the glory of Jesus—dismissed his flock. I snuck out the side door and rushed around to the front steps in time to shake hands with people on their way out. Some smiled and exchanged pleasantries. Others pretended not to see me, or found an excuse to avoid eye-contact. Karen Dean threw me a smart-alecky look as she passed and said something to the effect that there might be hope for me yet. I watched as she made her careful way down the church steps, and wondered for about the millionth time how women manage to walk in high heels. I'm grateful they're willing to try.

If I were to guess, I'd say the church's parking lot had never cleared faster than it did that morning. Horns honked and tires squealed as 395 of the 400 lambs of God in attendance rushed to put as much distance as they could between themselves and the crazy son of a bitch who expected them to give a damn about a dead colored girl.

Three civilians stayed to help: Martha Pierce, who works as a cashier at the TG&Y and is sweet as molasses but dumb as a stump, bless her heart; Donna Maxwell, a middle-aged kindergarten teacher and president of the Ladies' Auxiliary for the Loyal Order of Moose of Tilghman County; and Carla Midkiff, Principal Midkiff's wife and pound for pound one of the toughest people, male or female, I've ever met. "Ray would've come," Carla said, "but he was so exhausted after our trip to Oklahoma City and dealing with that pig and all, I didn't have the heart get him out of bed this morning." I told her that of course I understood.

That made five of us, including Karen and me. We'd add Kenny and Bernard and maybe Jeff at the scene, for a total of seven or eight. Not the gigantic search party I was hoping for. I thought maybe we could make up in enthusiasm what we lacked in numbers.

The five of us managed to squeeze into the Fury without any trouble. We took things slow on the way out of town. I hit the lights but not the siren. It occurred to me that this might be the closest thing to a funeral procession that girl would get.

I parked behind Kenny's white Dodge Coronet with the magnetic revolving bubble light on the roof. Jeff was nowhere to be seen, which didn't surprise me.

"You been here all night?" I asked Kenny.

"Jeff got here about four o'clock, but the poor son of a gun was so beat, I sent him home."

"You're a better man than I, Gunga Din."

A lot of ground remained to be covered and only a few of us to do it, so I spread everyone as wide as I dared and we got to work. The first thing I wanted searched was the train tracks. No sooner had I given the direction than I spied Carla climbing the embankment. That would've been fine, except she wears braces on her legs as a result of having polio as a child, and I didn't want her to hurt herself. I scolded her, but she was having none of my fussing and scurried right up. Martha and Donna followed along.

Karen and I handled the scrubland on the opposite side of a wire fence running alongside the tracks, careful to avoid hidden deposits of fresh cow shit and keeping our eyes peeled for snakes. The area beside the tracks where Kenny and Bernard searched was no picnic, either, with all the red dirt and rocks and sagebrush and goat-head stickers and whatnot. No one said a single word of complaint.

After nearly an hour, all we had to show for our labors was a sun-bleached rattlesnake skull—that is, unless you count Bernard's cigarette lighter, which he dropped and Donna found. The crew's spirits were willing, but their energy was melting like a Popsicle left out in the sun. By half-past noon, even Bernard was dragging, and I wasn't feeling so frisky myself. I was on the verge of suspending our search when I heard an excited whoop.

"I found something! Praise Jesus, I found something!"

Martha Pierce stood proudly on the tracks, one hand raised to the sky, the other pointing at the ground.

Martha pushes six-feet tall and weighs maybe 100 pounds. She wore a loose-fitting green dress and her short white hair was a sweaty mess of spikes pointing every which way. With her arm stuck up in the air like that, I swear to Christ she looked like the Statue of Liberty.

I clambered up to where she was, scraping my hands on the ballast and cussing my own clumsiness. Martha was beet-red and shaking like a dried leaf in the wind. "Alright, calm down now, Martha, calm down," I said. "We don't want you to fall down off this and hurt yourself." She threw her arms around my neck and about hugged the life out of me. I peeled her off with some effort and handed her over to Karen, who'd followed me up to the tracks. I bent over to get a good look at what Martha had found.

It was a gold medallion or coin of some sort. It lay almost completely hidden under one of the rails, which explained why it had eluded detection. I was amazed that Martha had found it, considering her limited powers of concentration. The last time I tried to check-out at her register at the TG&Y, she got so distracted by a little boy wearing a cowboy costume, it took me forever to buy a pair of socks.

I had Kenny get out his Instamatic and take almost a whole roll of photographs to show where we found what we'd found. I then put on a rubber surgeon's glove and picked it up.

It was about as big as a Kennedy half-dollar. One side had a stylized engraving of an atom. The Indian shield and pipe from the Oklahoma flag was the nucleus, surrounded by lopsided crescent lines that were supposed to be electrons revolving around it. Inside each of the crescents was a different scene representing our state: cattle, an oil rig, a hydroelectric plant, a disembodied propeller of some sort. Around the edge of the coin was written, "Oklahoma at the World's Fair 1964-1965." On the flip side was more engraving and fancy words I almost fell asleep trying to decipher. Soldered on top was a small brass loop meant to accommodate a chain so it could be worn around someone's neck. There was no chain to be found.

I had Kenny snap a few close-ups of it in my hand, then put it in an evidence bag and stuffed it in my shirt pocket.

Everyone was excited by Martha's discovery and were ready to call it a day, but I reckoned we should look around a while longer. We continued for another half-hour but didn't find anything else. I bought everyone lunch at Burger Mart, since it was all that was open on a Sunday. I hoped I might get the city to reimburse me but wasn't counting on it.

CHAPTER TEN

I was sorely tempted to play hooky the next day, or at least go in late like I sometimes do on those rare mornings after I've managed to fall asleep the night before. Unfortunately, I didn't have that luxury. I woke up feeling there was something I needed to do, but for the life of me I couldn't remember what it was. The more I thought on it, the more I drew a blank. I figured the way to find out for sure was to go in to work and hope Karen or someone else would remind me. It must've been important or I wouldn't have remembered that I'd forgotten. If that makes any sense.

I tried to think how much I'd had to drink the night before. I couldn't remember that, either. I don't normally get hangovers, but sometimes my memory fails.

Kenny works nine-to-five at the hardware store on Mondays, Jeff has school, and Cousins had the day off, so I was on my own. Except for Karen, of course. My hours are her hours.

She was already at her desk when I waltzed into the station at eight o'clock sharp.

"You just missed the handsome and charming agents Jones and Heckscher," she said in a tone that implied they were neither handsome nor charming. "They wanted us to know they'd be asking questions of folks and generally nosing around."

That's it, I thought. Jones and Heckscher. I needed to show them something. What was it? I thought. "Nice of them to drop by," I said.

"I told 'em about the coin," she said. "I would've shown it to them but I couldn't find it. I reckoned you had it."

The coin. I patted my shirt pocket. It was still there.

I'd hand over the coin, I thought, then wash my hands of the whole thing.

Bernard called in to relate the details of his conversation with Edgar Bixby. Edgar had been too pissed-off to give Bernard the time of day regarding anything but his lost-and-found pig. "He said if you have questions, you best get out there and ask them yourself," Cousins said. I reckoned I'd have to do that, eventually.

Jones and Heckscher had dropped off a printed version of the artist's sketch. It was markedly clearer than the blurred Xerox from before. They also left a copy of the medical examiner's report. For some inexplicable reason, the coroner had gone to work on Sunday.

I sat down at my desk and read the report. It didn't tell me much I couldn't have worked out on my own. The victim was a light-skinned negro female, approximately 16-21 years of age, five-feet, 3 inches tall, 110 pounds. Green eyes. Good teeth. A few minor scars were mentioned. None appeared relevant. Some faded bruising to her arm and upper torso might've indicated past abuse, though the doctor couldn't say for certain. Overall, she had all the characteristics of a normal, healthy young woman.

I scanned the jargon until I got to the cause of death: "a cutting wound to the right side of the neck by a sharp instrument inserted in a vertical direction. moving upward in a left to right direction," resulting in the "severing of the jugular and carotid arteries." The bleeding caused was "rapid and massive," causing unconsciousness within 30 to 60 seconds and death within two minutes. She'd engaged in intercourse in the last hours before her death, but there was no vaginal bruising or scraping to indicate rape.

The phone rang. Karen answered and handed it to me. It was Agent Jones calling from one of the three pay phones in town. None of them are so far from the station that he couldn't as easily come in and talked to me, but never mind.

He asked me if Karen had relayed his message. I said she had. I also thanked him for getting the autopsy results to me so quick.

"Yeh, we were lucky," he said. "The ME decided to come in on a Sunday. He had to be out of town for a couple of days and wanted to finish this one before he left."

He rushed through our conversation like a man who had someplace he needed to be. It was early, he said, but they were still looking at it like a vagrant assault and murder. They'd be around most of the day and would check in with me on their way out. He hung up before I could say goodbye. I mumbled something I'd rather not repeat.

"What'd he say?" Karen asked.

"What a man who's too busy to be bothered would say. I could've told him Godzilla ate Tulsa and he would've have said, 'too bad, gotta go.'"

She grinned. "Don't give up on 'em yet, hon. It's just been a couple of days."

"A couple of days is a couple of days. The more time passes, the less chance they'll make an arrest."

That's assuming they cared even a tiny bit, which wasn't by any means for certain.

"First thing to do, I would think, is to find out who she was," said Karen.

"I agree. So far they aren't showing signs of doing that."

"Maybe we should, then. We're not exactly riding a gigantic crime wave here. We can investigate on our own."

"I'd hardly know where to start," I said. "She's not from here, that's for sure. It's been a long time since we've had any colored folks."

"That don't mean they can't visit or pass through town."

"True." I chewed on that for second. "But this is the OSBI's case. Those boys tend to be touchy about local cops infringing on their turf."

She sighed dramatically. "Now you're just making excuses. They asked you to help, didn't they?"

I sat on the corner of her desk and studied a crack in the wall.

"Yeh, they did."

She peered at me over her reading glasses, lips pursed. "You're not helpless," she scolded. "You know that the right thing to do is, so do it. Show those state fellas how a real lawman goes about his business."

Her shaming was getting in the way of my heartfelt desire to put this case in the rearview mirror. I wasn't just being timid or lazy on this. The bottom line was, I wasn't sure I was up to the job.

"I appreciate your confidence in me," I said, "but those OSBI fellas have a helluva lot more experience with this kind of thing, even if they're not as highly motivated as I'd like them to be." I pulled at my collar. The top button was unbuttoned, but it still felt tight. "I'll lay low for a while and see how it plays. If it looks like they're not going to work at it as hard as they should, I'll see what I can do."

"I'm going to hold you to that," she said. "Personally, I think you're that girl's best chance." She winked. "I like how bucking the system brings out the Gary Cooper in you."

If she could flirt, so could I. "Does that mean you're not taking the next stagecoach out of town, missy?"

"If I remember correctly, in *High Noon*, when push came to shove, Grace Kelly stood with Gary," she said. "No sir, marshal. I'm not going anywhere."

CHAPTER ELEVEN

Our Tilghman County shouldn't be confused with the Tillman County in the southwestern part of the state. To my knowledge, nobody's ever been able to fully explain why we have two counties pronounced the same but spelled different. Then again, there's lots about Oklahoma that can't be fully explained.

Tilghman is in the Northwest, situated snug against the Texas panhandle. Burr is its third-largest town, within spitting distance of the state line. We're named after Aaron Burr, the third Vice President of the United States, although he's more famous for having gunned down Alexander Hamilton in a duel. In 1804, Hamilton bad-mouthed Burr when the latter was a candidate for Governor of New York. When Aaron lost, he found in the more handsome and successful Alex a worthy scapegoat. Burr challenged Hamilton to a duel, since that's what aggrieved gentlemen did in those days. In a brass-balls face-off outside Weehauken, NJ, the ex-VP got off a lucky shot and killed Hamilton, thereby earning a reputation as one of history's all-time sore losers.

Several decades later, during the Run of 1893, a band of laggardly settlers came upon some sad-looking land along the Southern Kansas Railway tracks in western Oklahoma Territory. Nearby was a trickle of water that looked like a creek if you squinted hard and thought about something wet. Since pretty much everything else was taken, they put down stakes and formed a town.

The leader of these intrepid slow-pokes was an ex-grocer from Ithaca, New York, named Elijah Erasmus Darwin. For reasons lost to history, Darwin idolized Aaron Burr and proposed to that the new community be named after the legendary spoilsport. Darwin was a smooth talker and was able to convince the men of the town without much trouble. I imagine they were fairly ignorant of their American history or he might've had a harder time.

My great-grandfather on my father's side got to the area several hours ahead of the Darwin-led bunch on the day of the Run. He laid claim to 160 acres of prime farmland outside what would eventually become Burr. He farmed that land and bought more from his adjoining neighbors, until he had quite a spread. When he died, it was passed it on to my daddy's daddy, Grandpa Hardy, who subsequently willed it to my father, Everett George Hardy. My father worked the land for a few years, until one day a fella representing a petroleum company came to our house and offered him a lot of money if he'd let them drill on our property. Dad retired from farming the day he received his first royalty check. He sold most of the land (holding on to the mineral rights, of course; you don't sell those), leased the rest for grazing, and purchased the house in town where he still lives. The money from grazing fees and the oil and gas money is more than enough for him to live on.

Before he retired, Everett Hardy had been one of those stubborn farmers who stuck it out through the Dust Bowl and hated John Steinbeck for making Okies look bad in *The Grapes of Wrath*. He did tolerably well raising cattle and planting wheat, better than his own father. He made sure I kept clear of the family business. "You're not cut out for this life," he always said. "You're too soft." He was wrong about the last part, which I must confess I've spent most of my life trying to prove. But he was plenty right about me not being cut out for farming.

My mama died of a stroke as I was fighting frostbite and a company of Red Chinese soldiers at the Battle of Chosin Reservoir in the winter of 1950. Losing her came closer to killing me than the Chinese and North Koreans ever did. Her death had a stranger effect on Everett Hardy. Dad had always been a drinking man, so you'd expect the shock of his wife's death would cause him to drown his sorrows. It did just the opposite. He stopped drinking entirely. In fact, he didn't just give up booze; he gave up just about anything that gave him pleasure. It was almost like he commenced the act of dying through force of will. That's not to say he became a snake-handler, or a tightrope walker or did anything else to speed up the process. It's more like he decided his life was over. Everything from that point was like the credits rolling at the end of a movie.

15 years have passed.

Sometimes those credits can run really long.

.   .   .   .   .

I spent the rest of the morning writing up the events of the last few days. I'd rather have my fingers chewed off by a wolverine than write an official report, but sometimes I have no choice. I didn't want to get caught with my pants around my ankles if Sheriff Murray and the OSBI boys came looking for documentation.

After getting that out of the way, I took the Fury out to make my rounds. Monday means a trip to Dad's—first, to make sure he was ok; second, to stock up on my quota of abuse for the coming week.

Dad is in his late 70s. Like a lot of ex-farmers, he's got a uniform he wears. His comprises a dark yellow Carhartt jumpsuit, beat-up black cowboy boots, and a sweat-stained gray felt Stetson that belonged to Grandpa Hardy. All have seen better days.

Dad was digging with a shovel in the front yard when I drove up. He keeps house neat, inside and out: the lawn immaculately mowed, the hedges trimmed, the driveway and sidewalk swept clean. I was surprised to see him making such a mess.

"What're you digging?" I asked.

"A goddam hole, what's it look like?" he answered, head down, a bulge in his lower lip made by the snuff permanently lodged there. Most fellows around here dip Skoal because of the wintergreen taste. Dad dips Copenhagen. Skoal is for pansies, he says. I don't get why, but that's what he says.

"Well, I can see that," I said, referring to the hole. "Why? Looking for a shortcut to China?"

"No, I'm not trying to get to China," he said, disregarding my little joke. "I'm lookin' for something I buried here awhile back."

"What?" I asked. "Maybe I can help."

"I don't need your help, goddammit, I can find it myself." He excavated a few more spadefuls without another word. Sometimes getting information out of him is like extracting a rotten tooth with a pair of tweezers. I let it drop.

The purpose of my visit was to find out how he was doing. The way he is, I can't ask directly. He'll say, "I'm fine," and that'll be the end. Instead, we have a conversation about the weather or one of his neighbors, and I judge how he is by the way he answers my questions. If he cusses a lot, I figure he's ok.

So far, so good.

"Dad, you mind taking a break and having a cup of coffee with me?" I asked. "I wanted to talk about a case I'm working on. Thought maybe you could help."

He kept his head down and shoveled some more. He slowed a bit, though, which I interpreted as a spark of interest. I expected it to die of neglect, so I was a little surprised when he shoved the spade into a pile of dirt and led me inside.

Besides his bedroom, the sparsely appointed kitchen is the one room in his house that gets much use. A toaster sits on a shelf by the sink. Next to it is a coral-red Westinghouse radio that he turns on once an hour to listen to the news. It's always tuned to whatever station carries the Oklahoma State Cowboys football games, which is the other thing he listens to. He gave up music after mama died. Four chrome and green-vinyl chairs surround a pearl-colored Formica table.

Dad spit his tobacco into the trash bin beneath the counter and rinsed his mouth with water from the tap. He crossed the kitchen and filled a couple of cups of Folger's from the percolator. He poured milk into a small pitcher, placed it on the table, and sat down across from me. I splashed some milk and emptied a packet of sugar into my coffee. Dad brings home those packets by the pocketful from a diner in Temple City.

I told him about the girl's murder. He allowed that he'd heard something about it on the radio.

"Know who she was?" he asked.

"No idea," I said. "No colored folks living in town. Unless they been hiding."

"No place to hide."

"Ain't that the truth."

He asked what she looked like. I described her, mentioning she looked well-fed and clean, not like someone who'd been sleeping in boxcars.

"Light-skinned?" he asked.

"Yeh, and she had kind of high cheek bones. Could be part Indian."

He peered down into his cup like he was looking at his reflection. "Could be creole," he said.

"We're a long way from New Orleans."

"They don't got a goddam fence around that city," he said. "They let 'em come and go as they please."

Anytime something reminds him of mama, you're treading on dangerous ground. "I guess you'd know."

"Never mind," he mumbled into his coffee. We sat quietly for a time.

He broke the silence abruptly. "I'd look around for the nearest whorehouse, if I was you. Them places aren't likely to advertise when one of their girls goes missing."

I hadn't thought of that.

"That makes sense," I said, "but the OSBI boys are pretty convinced she was some hobo's girlfriend who got molested and killed and thrown off a freight."

He snorted. "That's horseshit. I saw plenty of men and women riding freight trains during the depression. They sure as hell weren't well-fed and clean. They were dirty as a Frenchman and looked like they hadn't eaten in a month. Most of the time they hadn't."

"Maybe she hadn't been on the train long," I said. "The coroner said she'd had sexual relations not long before she died. She could've been taken on it against her will, then killed." I took a sip of coffee. Needs more sugar, I thought. "But I'm with you. It doesn't ring true to me. That's what the OSBI seems to think, though, and they're the ones in charge."

"Whoever did it wanted you to think she was thrown off the train," he said. "Someone from around here killed her and dumped her on the tracks. Someone you know."

"I hope to hell it's not someone I know," I said. "Christ."

"People are no goddam good." Dad's opinion of humanity grows less generous by the year.

I told him about the World's Fair medallion we'd found.

"Nobody from around here would be carrying something like that," he said. He was right. New York's not a popular destination amongst Burr-ites. Most citizens of Tilghman County are lucky to travel as far as Amarillo or Wichita once in their lives.

"Maybe it was hers," he said. "Maybe someone gave it to her as a gift."

"Might be it belonged to whoever killed her and they dropped it."

"Might be."

I was surprised how animated he was getting. Most of our conversations consist of me talking, him grunting and cursing. This thing had gotten him wound up. Normally, only the crimes of Republican politicians and the ever-declining fortunes of Oklahoma State football did that.

"You wouldn't know the closest whorehouse, would you, Dad?" I asked.

He jerked up from the table and started clearing the cups. "I heard tell of one. Never been to it." The tenor of his voice coarsened and I thought he might be blushing a little bit,

"Of course, I know you'd never go to one," I said.

He turned where I couldn't see his face and rinsed the cups. "Over the line in Texas," he grumbled, "by Watie Junction."

I knew what he was talking about. Watie Junction is about a twenty-minute drive southwest on US 14, just this side of the state line. The brothel lies just across the border in Texas, which complicates efforts to have it shut down. That my dad even knows it exists is all the evidence you need of its local notoriety.

He set the clean cups in the strainer by the sink, then walked outside with me on his heels. Without another word, he went back to digging. He drove his shovel into the ground with more violence than before and cussed under his breath. I stood there trying to decide whether or not to leave. He turned over a final shovel-full of dirt and turned abruptly to me. "You're going to have to do this yourself, Emmett," he said. His left eyelid twitched like it does when he gets wound-up. "Those OSBI bastards don't care. You're going to have to do it." His face dripped with sweat; he pulled a greasy red rag out of his back pocket and wiped it away. "She needs your help," he said, then started digging again without another word.

Maybe it was my imagination, but it seemed like his eyes shone more than usual.

CHAPTER TWELVE

I stopped by the office of the Burr Gazette and gave them the copy of the artist's sketch to mock-up into a poster, which they were more than happy to do. I thought I'd prime the pump by offering a $1000 reward. I didn't have authorization from anyone and I didn't know what I'd do if it was claimed. I reckoned I'd cross that bridge when I came to it.

Afterwards, I walked up and down Main Street, stopping here and there when someone wanted to bend my ear. Most asked about the killing. A few had already talked to Agents Jones and Heckscher.

Karen spent the majority of the morning on the phone. She basically knows everyone and has the knack of talking like a mother or sister or girlfriend or best buddy, depending on the person. She gathered vital intelligence on the postal clerk's affair with the local postmaster and eyewitness testimony that Michelle Stadler—Ezra Grayson's secretary down at Grayson and Sons real estate office—was not a natural blonde. As for our murder, however, no one knew a thing.

I told myself not to worry. Solving it was the OSBI's problem.

I picked up my flyers around five o'clock. They were as slick as if they'd been made by a big city printer. Frank Ickes always does a nice job. I crossed the street to the station just as Agents Jones and Heckscher pulled in.

"How are y'all?" I said. "We've been crossing paths all day. 'Bout time we hooked up."

"Chief," nodded Agent Jones, his several chins wobbling uncertainly as he squeezed out the car door. "Good to see you. Nice town you got here."

"Salt of the earth," I said, because that's what you say when an outsider compliments the people of your community. The sun was still beating down so I suggested we go inside. Karen offered us all a cup of coffee. We declined with varying degrees of politeness. Even with our little window unit air conditioner running full blast, it was too blamed hot.

Karen sat at her desk in the front office; I teetered on the edge in my usual spot. Jones and Heckscher took a couple of the folding chairs. They were suitably impressed by the flyers. I asked them what they'd learned.

"Not much," said Jones. "In fact, not a darn thing. No one saw anything out of the ordinary last Friday night. No strange cars or folks they didn't recognize. We stopped by your train station and talked to that fella they got working selling tickets. He couldn't help. I been up and down every street in this town and didn't see a single negro, so I'm fairly sure someone would've noticed your girl if she'd been here."

"There was a man who got his pig stolen," said Heckscher, "but apparently it was some high school prank. It didn't have anything to do with our murder, that seems sure." I needed to talk to Edgar. Just making things harder for myself, the longer I put it off.

"I better show you this before I forget," I said, and pulled the bag with the World's Fair coin out of my pocket. I told them how and where it was found. Jones impatiently grabbed the envelope out of my hand and shook the little gold-plated disk out onto Karen's desk. I handed him a pair of rubber gloves. With some effort, he stretched them over fleshy, nicotine-stained fingers. He studied the coin like was trying to discover the secret to unlocking its magic. He didn't say so, but judging by the scowl on his face, I surmised it bothered him his own people had overlooked it.

"I met some boys from New York when I was in the service," he mused. "I've never been and don't know many folks who have." I'd spent time in New York, but I didn't know any other Burr-ites who had.

I proposed that it could've come from someone in state government involved with the fair. Both men responded with a shrug. I presented an evidence receipt for them to sign and turned the medallion over to them. On their way out, Heckscher suggested I post the flyers around town, which I'd already thought of, believe it or not. Jones asked me to explore the World's Fair angle, see if anyone in the vicinity had been. I said I would and asked what else I could do.

"Be on the lookout for someone wearing one Sante Fe railroad glove who's been to the World's Fair and carries around a bloody knife," he said. "Might get lucky."

They seemed to think it was funnier than I did.

No sooner were they out the door when Karen said, "If that was my daughter got killed, I'm not sure I'd want them two being in charge of finding who did it."

"You're the one who said we should give them a chance."

"That was before I met them." She frowned and thumped the eraser of her pencil on her desk a few times. "They don't seem to be in any hurry to solve this."

"Well, let's see how it goes and what they do," I said. In the back of my mind I thought my plan to wash my hands of this might not work out.

CHAPTER THIRTEEN

It would be of some benefit if I spoke at some length about the Bixby family of Burr, Oklahoma, starting with the head of the clan, Edgar Bixby.

Edgar Bixby is not my favorite person, as I have already implied. In fact, although my mama did not raise me to be a hater, I might be inclined to make an exception for Edgar.

If I didn't know for a fact Edgar'd never seen *It's a Wonderful Life* (if a movie doesn't star John Wayne, Edgar ain't interested), I'd think his role model is Mr. Potter, the skinflint banker who tries to ruin George Bailey. Before he grew into a greedy and cruel adult, Edgar was a cruel and greedy child—the kind of kid who'd lend you a nickel for ice cream at 100% interest, and only if you pledged your bicycle as collateral.

Edgar was a couple of years ahead of me in school, which made me the perfect age to qualify as a target for his abuse. That lasted until my sophomore year, when I got big and ornery enough to put a whipping on him if I had to.

Edgar's granddaddy was a cattle baron dating back to when this was still Indian Territory. Edgar's daddy wanted to make his own mark, so he took to raising crops, as well. All that went by the boards once they discovered oil and gas on their land. They sold the livestock and went into the energy business. While the petroleum beneath my dad's small spread provided him with a modest if comfortable living in retirement—and might do the same for me someday—Bixby property sat atop one of the biggest natural gas plays in the state of Oklahoma. Even with the mineral rights split in two upon Mr. Bixby's death, it was still sufficiently lucrative to make Edgar and his brother Deke the two richest men in the county.

Edgar is a prideful man. He doesn't have anything to do, really, but spend his money. However, for appearance's sake, he farms a little bit and keeps some livestock. That's why Daffodil and her blue ribbons are so important to him. He wants people to think he works for a living.

If I had to tell one story that describes what Edgar's like, it'd be about the time he stole my brand new Rawlings Pepper Martin Model baseball glove.

Pepper Martin was a native Oklahoman who went on to play third base for the St. Louis Cardinals's famous "Gashouse Gang" teams in the '30s. Pepper became my father's favorite player after he saw him with the Guthrie team in the Oklahoma State League before he made the major leagues. My folks gave me that glove for my tenth birthday. I loved that dang glove so much, I used it for a pillow for as long as I had it. Which was about a week.

One day, some friends and I were playing ball on the field behind the junior high. Along came Edgar and his abject apostle, Nate Gunter. A smirking Edgar asked if they could play, which was a joke, because they were going to, whether we liked it or not.

Poor Nate Gunter was a piece of work—one of those kids you feel sorry for, even as you find excuses to stay as far away from them as you can. Nate always stunk. He never washed himself and wore the same filthy shirt and pair of dirty jeans every day. He got terrible grades in school and was as throughly and permanently beaten-down as the guy at the circus who follows the elephants with a shovel and pail.

For a long time Nate played with us younger kids because most of the kids his own age wouldn't have anything to do with him. That is, until Edgar took an interest in him. After that, Nate didn't play with us anymore.

Edgar made Nate his puppet when he needed him to do something, and his punching bag when he felt like being mean. He did things like offer Nate a dollar to wash his car then tell him he'd done a shitty job and refuse to pay. One time he stuffed Nate's jeans down the toilet during PE class just so Nate would have to wear his gym shorts the rest of the day. Nate was so starved for friendship he'd do anything Edgar said, even if it got him in trouble or made him look like a fool.

Anyhow, whenever Edgar showed up to one of our ball games, it was as good as over. He always did the same thing: hit the ball into the weeds and watch us turn tail and chase after it. We wouldn't be able to find it, and that was all she wrote. Edgar thought it was hilarious.

Nate knew what was coming, too. He gave me a shit-eating smile and shrugged, like he was apologizing in advance.

In his first time at bat, Edgar performed as expected and slugged the ball a mile. I threw my glove down in frustration and chased after it with the other kids. Edgar laughed like a maniac. We looked under every foot-tall blade of grass, but it was lost. By the time we gave up, our ankles had been bloodied by hundreds of goathead stickers and our faith in the essential goodness of man had suffered yet another blow. Of course, Edgar and Nate were long gone. As was my glove.

Either Edgar or Nate had to have taken it. Nate wouldn't have done it unless Edgar forced him, so no matter how you cut it, it was Edgar's fault. The next day my daddy went out to the Bixby's and talked to Edgar's father. Edgar lied, Mr. Bixby believed him, and that was that. My daddy cussed Mr. Bixby to his face, but I didn't get my Pepper Martin glove back. Thing is, I'm sure Edgar didn't even want it. I'll bet he had ten as good or better. He just didn't want me to have it. That's the kind of person he was. The kind of person he is.

By the time I was 15 and he was 17, Edgar began staying clear of me. I'd grown too strong to push around. Years later, when I was under consideration for police chief, he and Deke—who by that time was on the town council—remembered how much they hated me and fought my hiring like they were afraid I was going to take away their gas wells. Despite everything, I got the job, one of the few times in memory they didn't get their way.

We've had our run-ins in the years since. Typically they involve Edgar trying to steamroll somebody and me coming down on the side of the somebody getting steamrolled. Even when I push back, he usually gets what he wants.

Part of the reason I became a cop was I couldn't stand bullies. Edgar is that in spades. He's always wanted more than his share of everything. Ever since high school, I've been one of the few to call him out when he takes advantage of those who can't defend themselves. He figures I do it because I'm jealous and think I'm better than him. I will admit to thinking most people are better than him and see no reason not to include myself among that number. But I'm sure as hell not jealous. Edgar's never had anything I wanted.

Except for a certain woman.

·   ·   ·   ·   ·

I fell in love with Denise Kinney in first grade and remained in said condition well into adulthood. Maybe to this day, if you want to know the truth.

Denise and I were best friends. There were times growing up that we did everything together. I gave her the nickname "Denny." She liked it and made everyone call her that. For a long time I was conceited enough to think I could turn our friendship into something more. I reasoned because she played hooky and went fishing with me, it made sense she'd want to marry me. I miscalculated.

Denny always ran against the grain. Most girls seemed satisfied to go along with whatever stupid things boys made them do. Not Denny. She wasn't about to be anybody's fool. Not mine, not anyone's.

Denny'd do things like wear boy's pants to school even though she knew the principal would make her go home and put on a dress. When all the other girls made cookies for the football team, Denny laughed and refused. Needless to say, she hated Sadie Hawkins Day. "Every day should be Sadie Hawkins Day," was her take on the subject. At parties, she took immoderate pleasure in declining boys' invitations to dance. Instead, she'd dance with her friends who never got asked.

Which is not to say she was a total rebel. She was practical. She'd do something she didn't want to do if she thought it would help her get what she wanted.

The prettiest girls in any school are always cheerleaders, and of course Denny was one. But she didn't do it because it was expected. If anything, she did it despite that fact. She didn't do it because she liked sports, either. When Denny and I were alone, she was hilariously disdainful of cheerleading. But she did it, hoping it'd pay off down the road.

If it did pay off, you couldn't prove it by me. As far as I was concerned, she was already the most desirable girl in twelve counties. But what I thought didn't matter. I wasn't the kind of man she was after.

For a while I thought it was because I played football. Denny famously did not like athletes. Many times I volunteered to quit. No dice. "You'd end up hating me for making you stop," she said. That wasn't true. I didn't even like football that much. I'd have happily given it up for Denny. Didn't matter. Telling me that was her way of letting me down easy. She was always good at that.

The only time I kissed Denny was one of the most crushing experiences of my life. We were in eighth grade, riding a bus on the way back from an away football game. The cheerleaders rode with the team, and Denny sat with me in back. I'd scored the winning touchdown and the world was my oyster. It was dark. My juices were flowing. I summoned my every ounce of courage, leaned over and planted one on her. At first, Denny tensed in surprise, then relaxed. She didn't push me away, but she didn't encourage me, either. She just sat there, slack and disinterested. I might as well have been kissing a mannequin.

I figured maybe she just needed to get used to the idea, so I dove in a second time. After getting the same non-response, I realized I wasn't exactly throwing kerosene on an open flame. Frustrated, I asked her what was wrong and why she let me do it in the first place since she obviously didn't want to. She said she knew *I* did, and she didn't mind, if it made me happy. I felt like an idiot, like I'd forced myself on her. I apologized. She smiled a little Mona Lisa smile and changed the subject, like my sorry-ass Casanova impression had never happened. It was a long time before I thought about trying it again.

I wanted her to be my girl. She wanted me to be her friend. That's the way it stayed.

Ultimately, it became clear Denny wanted someone with lots of money. She wasn't going to make the same mistake so many of her friends made: marry some local boy who peaks at 17, then spends the rest of his life working a dead-end job and reminiscing about how great high school was. I was determined not to be that type of man, but I didn't plan on being rich, either. I didn't care about money and never would. Not even the prospect of marrying Denise Kinney would change that. You can't make a seagull want to be a peacock.

In Denny's mind, success equaled money. She came into this world poor as a stray cat, so she had to find it some other way. To a woman in her circumstances, that generally means having to marry a rich man. I don't for a second believe she cared much about the things money can buy; I think she saw wealth as a necessary security blanket in a world that doesn't do women any favors. She couldn't afford to take it for granted. Whether or not *I* could was and is an open question. The fact remains, I did, which I'm sure in her eyes disqualified me as a potential husband. Unlike me, Denny had no intention of gambling with her future.

I was a sucker's bet. Edgar Bixby was a sure thing.

·   ·   ·   ·   ·

I had a real hard time coming to terms with Denny's romance with Edgar.

He was the worst person I knew. She was the love of my life. It stands to reason I wouldn't be doing cartwheels.

To be fair to Edgar—which is more than he's ever been to me—he was a different man around her. In general, Edgar treated folks decent only as long as it took to get what he wanted. Not so with Denny. Edgar knew he was lucky to have her and treated her that way. I used to think all his fawning over Denny was just an act. Later on I wasn't so sure. If Edgar loves anybody besides himself, it's Denny. If it *is* an act, he's succeeded in fooling her. And hers is the only opinion that matters.

The two of them started dating during Edgar's senior year. The timing coincided with my adoption of Old Grand-Dad bourbon as my beverage of choice. Whether or not that was a coincidence, I'll leave for others to infer. I will say I was too young to drink as much as I did.

Denny and I remained friends, as painful as that was to endure. While they hadn't made it official, it was as plain as the dimple on Kirk Douglas's chin that she and Edgar were going to marry. Even so, I still nursed a forlorn hope I could change her mind. I spent the next two years trying, during which time Denny and I kept frequent, if chaste, company.

The night she gave me the bad news, we were parked out at Burr Lake, just the two of us. It was Little Red Riding Hood weather—not too hot, not too cold. Crickets chirped, lightning bugs lightning-ed. The brick-red water lapped at the shore. I remember the lake smelled less of sewage than it normally did.

We had graduated a week before. Both of us had gotten jobs— Denny as a secretary for a local insurance agent, me hauling hay for the summer. We sat in the front seat of my car, passing a bottle back and forth, talking about the meaning of life and other things of little consequence. I was feeling better about my chances and thought I might take another shot at kissing her for the first time since that disastrous bus ride four years earlier. She might've sensed where I was going, because before I could make a move she blurted out, "Edgar asked me to marry him and I said yes."

It shouldn't have been a surprise, but hearing her say it hit me like a truckload of fertilizer. I tried one more time to talk her out of it. For every one of Edgar's negative qualities I could name, she'd whisper

"Oh, he's not that bad." I talked and drank until the two activities became incompatible, after which I just drank. Eventually I passed out. When I woke up around daybreak, I felt like a Gila monster had crawled down my throat and laid eggs. Meanwhile, there was Denny sitting on the hood of my car—arms wrapped around her legs, knees pulled up under her chin. Her long blond hair waved gently in the breeze. She looked out over Burr Lake like it was the Atlantic Ocean instead of the dirty Army Corps of Engineers-built mud puddle it was. "Drive me home?" she asked, sober as a judge and prettier than a hundred Marilyn Monroes.

They scheduled the wedding for June, when Edgar came home from college. By that time I was long gone. That night at the lake was my come-to-Jesus moment. I reckoned the best course to preserve my mental health was to get the hell out of Dodge, so instead of spending the summer hauling hay, I joined the Marines.

I was in San Diego for basic training the day they said their I do's. Not that I would've gone, anyway. I'm no stranger to the benefits of being kicked in the nuts with a steel-toed boot, but even I can only take so much. I stayed away long enough to fight in a war, get married and divorced, live and almost die in a big city, among other things. But not long enough to get over Denise Kinney.

To this day it bothers me Denny didn't have enough imagination to create a different life for herself. I recognize I'm probably being unfair. I shouldn't look down on her for playing the hand she was dealt as best she could. But I blame her.

Sometimes I'm not the person I'd like to be.

·　·　·　·　·

Denny and Edgar had one child, a son: Edgar, Jr., better known as EJ.

EJ Bixby inherited his mother's good looks and his father's rotten temperament. Judging by the way he's let the boy run wild, I suspect that combination tickled Edgar pink.

How it affected his mother is another matter. I can't imagine Denny jumps for joy when her son gets caught shoplifting beer from the Piggly Wiggly or pissing in a teacher's gas tank. It must bother her, but given Edgar's influence over EJ, she can't do a damn thing about it. The kid flunked the eighth grade twice. Not because he was stupid—though he's not especially smart—but because it didn't matter to him. His daddy was rich. EJ was going to be rich. End of story.

·　　·　　·　　·　　·

If the tale of my stolen baseball glove best illustrates what Edgar was about, the sad story of Erma Pulver's cat tells us all we need to know about his son. In EJ's case, the acorn don't fall too goddam far from the tree.

Erma Pulver was a sweet elderly widow lady who lived in the house her husband had built her on a side street here in town. One day, she called and told me she was looking out her kitchen window and saw Edgar Bixby's boy stuff her cat in a burlap bag. He rode off on his bike before she could stop him.

By the time I tracked EJ down a half-hour later, Erma's cat was a bloody, headless stump. EJ had tied it up by the hind legs with clothesline and dragged the poor thing to death behind his bicycle. Later, I found pieces of cat strung along a path a half-mile long. A trip to reform school seemed to be in order, but the county prosecutor was Edgar's man and declined to prosecute. I was left to apologize to Erma and contrive a less gruesome explanation as to why I couldn't get her cat back. She died a short time later. Maybe it was a coincidence.

As a child, EJ pulled charming little tricks like that all the time.

Then, in high school, it seemed like a switch had flipped inside EJ's head. He began treating adults with exaggerated respect. Folks would talk about how that Bixby boy had changed, what a nice young man he had become. Behind their backs, though, he was up to his usual tricks—stuffing a potato in the tailpipe of his shop teacher's truck or stealing seventh-graders' lunch money. Same kid. Just sneakier.

EJ's folks gave him a new Corvette when he got his driver's license, after which I spent half my waking hours pulling him over for one reason or another. EJ would smile his plastic smile and promise not to speed—or drive reckless, or flip someone the bird, or run a stop sign—ever again. A day later I'd catch him driving past the elementary school at 60 miles-per-hour while first-graders were trying to cross the street. He likely would've torn-up the tickets I wrote if it wasn't easier to pay. I imagine it was worth it to him and Edgar just to get my goat.

I'm sure Denny loves her son, but it seems obvious she's given up on him. EJ worships Edgar and walks all over her. I wonder if perhaps Denny sees EJ's behavior as the balance coming due from the original deal she struck with the boy's father. A debt like that ain't near as easy to pay as a traffic ticket.

Anyway, that's enough about that.

CHAPTER FOURTEEN

It was nearly sundown by the time Agents Jones and Heckscher left us alone and headed back to where they came from. Going home myself would've been an unimaginable luxury, but I'd put off going out to see Edgar Bixby as long as I could. I closed the door to my office to hide myself from Karen's prying eyes and took a swallow or two from my desk-drawer bottle of Old Grand-Dad. Some things I cannot bring myself to do completely sober. Facing Edgar—or Denny, for that matter—falls under that heading.

I turned off 14 and crossed the railroad tracks heading west onto the newly covered gravel road that leads to the Bixby home place. Clouds of white dust from the chat wafted in the open car windows and it made me wonder why Edgar had never paved the road. I hoped it wasn't coating the insides of my lungs like it did my upholstery.

After his father retired and he took over most of the family business, Edgar built his own house next to the one he'd grown up in. The old Bixby house had been the nicest in the county, but Edgar reckoned he deserved better. He hired an architect to design a copy of the fanciest house in the state, a huge limestone brick monstrosity built in the '20s by the oil tycoon E.W. Marland in Ponca City. The Marland Mansion was itself a copy of some Italian palazzo E.W. had seen in his travels. Edgar built his version—smaller than Marland's but just as gaudy and out of place—within spitting distance of his folks' home, where Mr. and Mrs. Bixby continued to live. Within a week of his father's death, Edgar moved his grieving mother into a spare bedroom in the mansion and razed the old house. He eventually constructed a luxurious indoor pig pen on the spot.

When I drove up, Edgar's tomato-red Ford pickup and EJ's Corvette were nowhere to be found, although Edgar's bronze Lincoln Continental and what I took to be Denny's latest new car—a red-and-white Thunderbird just off the showroom floor—were both present and accounted for. Automobiles are one of the things Edgar uses to bribe Denny into putting up with him. I don't see her too often, but it seems like every time I do, she's driving a new car.

Denny was waiting on the porch, leaning against the fancy wrought-iron-and-glass double doors, a cigarette in one hand and a martini glass in the other. She was dressed—barely—in a slinky floor-length powder-blue silk robe, one very attractive leg artfully exposed. I couldn't tell what she was wearing underneath. I preferred to think not much. Her shoulder-length hair was mussed but not messy. She wore just enough make-up to obscure any middle-age imperfections. Twilight lent the scene the quality of a black-and-white crime film from the '30s or '40s—something like *The Postman Always Rings Twice*, with Denny as the Lana Turner character and me as John Garfield, the designated patsy whose brain resides below his belt. We both knew it was corny but that was kind of the point. Denny and I used to go to those old movies together when we were kids. Back then, she could have persuaded me to do pretty much anything. I reckon she could still lead me a fair distance down the road to perdition, if she had a mind to.

I climbed the steps. "Well, well. Look what the cat drug in," she said.

I didn't have to pretend to feel like a bumpkin. "You dress up just for me?" I asked. We'd played this game before. Not for a long time, but it's not something you forget.

"I suppose I might've, if I'd thought about it," she said, taking a puff and acting all world-weary. Smoking had made her voice huskier over the years. I liked it. "If I was to do it for anybody, it might as well be you."

I smiled. "You're a one-man woman. I know that."

She took another drag, lifted her chin and blew a stream of smoke. "I'm a *no*-man woman," she said, and took a sip of her drink.

"That's a loss to the male race."

"Oh, I reckon they'll survive," she said vaguely. She ground out the cigarette under the heel of her high-heeled pink slipper and looked at me for the first time. "To what do I owe the pleasure?"

"How are you, Denny?"

"Fair," she said with a wan smile. "You?"

I figured there was nothing to be gained by being honest.

"Not terrible, all things considered," I said. "I mainly wanted to check with Edgar about Daffodil. Wanted to make sure the old man's feathers aren't too ruffled."

She stifled a yawn and pretended to admire her manicure. "Oh, you know Edgar," she said. "He was born with his feathers ruffled. He'll get over it." She looked at me through hooded eyes and gave me a mocking smile. "Of course, he blames you."

"I'm sure he does," I chuckled. "He's never forgiven me for making him steal my baseball glove."

She laughed. "He's always looking over his shoulder at you, Emmett."

"No need," I said, wishing there was. "Anyway, as far as this Daffodil thing, I don't want him going off and trying to take justice into his own hands, like he sometimes does. This isn't the Lindbergh baby, it's a stupid prank by some kids at Burr High. We'll find out who did it, give 'em a good spanking. Send 'em to their room. That'll be the end of it."

"Don't worry, he's got other things on his mind." She downed what was left of her drink and sat the glass on a small wooden table beside the door.

"Such as?"

"I don't know and I don't much care, to be honest. I can tell he's got something else on his mind, is all."

"Is he home?" I made a show of looking around. By this time it was too dark to see much past the glow of the porch light.

"No, he's not. He brought the pig home and went out again. He's been gone all day. I don't know where he is." She hugged herself like she was cold, which was doubtful, since the temperature was in the mid 80s. "Out getting some of what he's not getting at home, I'm sure," she said, sounding amused and sad at the same time.

That didn't seem to require a response. For a moment we both peered into the darkness and listened to the crickets. Tried to feel less uncomfortable with each other.

She perked up suddenly. "So Emmett Hardy's gonna solve Burr's crime of the century," she said. Her lips curled in a teasing smile. "It looked like the state fair across the way last night, with all the lights and noise and everything." She poked me playfully in the ribs. "That was you, huh?"

"I was there," I said, "but I'm not the one who's going to solve it. It's the OSBI's case. I might do some digging as a courtesy to them."

"Well, you always were the courteous type," she said. "I passed by y'all on my way home. Sat on the porch and watched for a while. Better than television."

"So that was you," I said. "I saw your light was on."

"That was me. I hear it was a colored girl who got killed."

"A young negro woman, coroner says she was 16 to 21. Bernard Cousins and I found her on the tracks as we were on our way out here to investigate your missing pig."

She made a face like I'd offered her raw chitlins marinated in gasoline. "Not *my* missing pig," she said.

"You know what I mean."

She shrugged. "I don't know anything about it."

"We're asking folks out this way if they seen anything strange after dark that evening," I said. "Over by where we found the girl, especially."

She scrutinized me sideways. "Who else out this way you asked, Emmett?"

I shuffled my feet and tried to sound matter-of-fact. "You're the first one," I said.

"Uh-huh," she said. Her eyes narrowed and she lit another cigarette. "The only strange thing I saw was y'all, with your lights and sirens."

"Where were you coming home from?"

She picked up her martini glass without looking, then put it back down when she remembered it was empty. "If you must know, I had dinner with my husband at the Polly Anna Cafe over in Woodward. Afterwards I went out by myself. Why do you ask?"

"I'm just trying to get as complete picture as I can. If you'd been there the whole time, you might've seen something important, that's all."

"O-kay," she said, stretching out the two syllables to the snapping point. "What else?"

"You remember what time you ate?"

"We barely missed the Early-Bird Special, which ends at four-thirty. But Edgar talked them into letting us have it, so I imagine it was about five."

"Do you remember how long you were there?"

"I don't remember exactly. A couple of hours, I guess." She brought the cigarette to her lips with one hand and waved away a cloud of smoke with the other.

"You say you passed by the scene on your way home," I said, "so that must've been after eleven."

"I'd say eleven-thirty, as a matter of fact," she replied.

"You and Edgar went out after dinner?"

"No. *I* went out. We took separate cars. He said he had errands to run, so I went to a movie. I have no idea where he went."

"You didn't ask?"

"Now, if I'd asked, I'd have an idea where he went, don't you think?"

"I guess you would," I said. "You came straight home after the movie?" I'd turned this into an interrogation without meaning to.

Denny felt it. "You don't sound like you're just doing a some digging as a courtesy," she said, and lit a new cigarette off the old one. Her hands shook the tiniest bit—from the booze or nerves, I couldn't tell. "No, I didn't come straight home," she answered. "I stopped at Junior's for a drink. If you want witnesses, about fifty men hit on me while I was there."

I could believe that.

"Could you give me names of some of those fellas if I needed to know?"

The corners of her mouth drew back and for a split second I thought she was going to spit in my face. "Ask me when you need to know," she said. I reckoned it was best to leave it there for the time being.

"Was Edgar here when you got home?" I asked.

"No, he wasn't. He didn't get in until late. I don't know when. I was asleep."

"So, you don't know where he was?"

"I said I didn't," she snapped. She ran her non-smoking hand through her hair. "Although I suppose I do have a general idea," she added.

"What's that?"

"Oh, he's been carrying on with some woman."

I pondered if I should pretend to feel bad for her then decided I couldn't make myself. "Any idea who?"

She smiled wickedly and sucked on her cigarette some more. "No, but I can smell it on him when he comes to bed." A part of me died when she said that. I'd spent years trying to avoid the mental picture of her and Edgar in bed together.

"What about EJ?" I asked. "Was he home?"

"He was here when I got home. He was in his bedroom. I didn't see him, but I heard him moving around. His radio was playing."

"Has either he or Edgar said anything relating to the girl we found?"

"No. All they talked about was that damned pig."

Some unseen trucker in the distance blew his horn a couple of times. The crickets stopped chirping at the noise, then re-started after a few seconds. I asked Denny when she expected Edgar and EJ. "I don't expect them any particular time," she replied. I asked her to have Edgar give me a call or drop by the station. She said she would.

"Good to see you again, Denny."

"I'm sure it is," she said blandly and turned to leave. Whatever good feelings we'd shared were gone.

Her exit was interrupted by the indignant snarl of Edgar's pickup tearing up the road. It skidded to a stop inches from the Fury's rear bumper. Edgar's face was as red as a baboon's ass and half as handsome. Denny turned and looked, her face blank, then disappeared into the house.

Edgar cut his engine, opened the door and stumbled out of the truck, banging his head on the driver's side mirror. Something cracked—the mirror or his head. I didn't care which.

I don't think he did, either. He was feeling no pain. "Emmett Hardy, you sorry sonuvabitch," he yelled. "What d'yoo thin' yer doin' wit' my wife?" Even from where I stood, he smelled like he'd bathed in Budweiser.

I snuck a look at the doors to see if Denny was watching. I thought I saw her shadow behind a half-drawn curtain.

"Take it easy, Edgar," I said, resisting the urge to put my fist through his bloated one-eyebrowed clown face. Sometimes I'm amazed at how calm I can be. "I'm here to check on you and Daffodil. Wanted to make sure everyone's ok after the traumatic events of recent days."

"My wife don't know nothin' about it," he said. "You want to ask anyone, you ask me."

He staggered up the first couple of steps. That long piece of gray hair he keeps plastered over his scalp to hide the fact he was bald stood straight up on one side of his head like a radio antenna. His fancy blue pinstripe cowboy shirt with mother-of-pearl snaps was still tucked in, but his fly was open and a sliver of shirttail wagged through the opening.

To his credit, he had yet to piss himself.

"Maybe now's not the best time to be asking you questions," I said. "I reckon you're too drunk to make much sense."

"You can go straight to hell, you wife-stealin' piece o' shit. Come on down here so's I can kick your ass."

He was more likely to fly to Mars by flapping his arms. "Edgar," I said, "I'm going to need you to blow into a balloon for me."

"Yeh, I bet you'd like to me to blow me—" His vocabulary—never extensive—had deserted him more-or-less entirely. "—blow you, for me to blow you, you pansy queer-faced bastard, I'll get you, you just wait—" at which point he threw up all over the front of his fancy blue pinstripe cowboy shirt with mother-of-pearl snaps.

He dropped to his knees and teetered forward, managing to catch himself before he fell on his face. He kneeled on all fours and hacked up what was left in his stomach. I stood over him and thought how easy it would be to accidentally on-purpose raise a boot to his face. I resisted the urge.

I was resisting a lot of urges today, I thought.

"So, can I assume you're refusing to take a drunk test?" I said.

He pushed himself up as best he could. "You can't arres' a man for drunk drivin' in his own driveway," he slurred, wiping a piece of what might have been a french fry from the corner of his mouth. Vomit had landed on the length of shirt tail sticking out his fly. He tried to stand, but his legs wouldn't obey his brain and he flopped back down on his stomach. Somehow he managed to avoid the puddle of puke. He lay in the dirt and mumbled incomprehensibly.

"You're wrong there, Edgar old pal," I said. "I can and I believe I will." I handcuffed him as he lay on the ground, motionless. After a few minutes of tugging and lifting and threatening, I managed to get him more-or-less upright and threw him face-first into the backseat. I looked back at the house, but Denny was no longer looking out from behind the curtains. I honked the horn but got no response. I knocked. Denny opened the door a crack.

"Denny, I'm taking him in. He was driving drunk, and besides, in his condition he might hurt himself or someone else. I'll take him to the county jail. He'll make bail or pay the fine. I imagine you'll be able to pick him up in the morning."

"Do what you have to do, Emmett. I'll call his lawyer first thing," she said in a flat voice, then shut the door and turned out the porch light.

I got back in the car. Edgar's head nodded on and off his chest. I started the car and maneuvered around his truck.

"I'll get you, Emmett Hardy," he said Edgar as we turned onto the highway.

I had to laugh. It reminded me of a line from another movie.

"Oh yeh? How 'bout my little dog?"

"What about your dog?"

I saw in my mirror he'd managed to sit up. In the dashboard light he looked like a Halloween pumpkin left out until Thanksgiving. He smelled of vomit and stale beer and I suspected I might've been wrong about him not having pissed himself.

"You going to get my dog, too?" I asked.

"What in hell you talkin' about?" he asked.

"Don't tell me you never seen *The Wizard of Oz*?"

"No, I ain't seen the goddam *Wizard of Oz*."

"Oh, that's right, there aren't any cowboys in it," I said. "That explains a lot about you, Edgar."

"Screw you and your dog," he said.

Then he passed out.

CHAPTER FIFTEEN

The next day dawned hot and dry. Like the day before and the day before that. And tomorrow, I was willing to bet.

Karen was typing something or the other when I got to the office. It's a mystery how she always gets there ahead of me. Some days I'll sneak in before sunrise, thinking I'll get the drop on her, and there'll she'll be. She's not just a typist and a dispatcher, either. Her talents extend to actual police work, even though she's technically a civilian employee. Bernard Cousins is my second-in-command and Kenny Harjo's an up-and-comer. But when push comes to shove, Karen's my right hand.

"What's this I hear about you arresting Edgar Bixby last night?" she asked before I was halfway through the door.

"News travels fast."

"It's a small town, hon."

I related the story in enough sordid detail to satisfy Miss Dean. I then called the sheriff's office to see how things had developed on their end. They told me Edgar's lawyer had gotten Burt Murray out of bed and demanded his client be sprung. Burt acceded, no doubt with the idea of securing a sizable monetary contribution to his next campaign—which, rumor has it, will involve a run for State Senate.

I wasn't surprised, but Edgar getting off scot-free—like he always does—exasperated me, nonetheless. I replaced the phone on its hook with more force than was polite. "Mr. Bixby is on the loose," I said.

"Of course he is," Karen said. "And the sun rises in the East."

She typed a couple more strokes and ripped the paper out of the machine.

"That's not a job application, is it?" I asked.

She rolled her eyes. "No, I'm applying to Harvard." Karen has a sarcastic streak.

"You wouldn't like Boston."

"That's fine, because I'm not planning to go. And last time I checked, Harvard was in Cambridge." She stuck the paper into an envelope, licked the flap and sealed it shut. "You do realize Edgar and Deke will try to string you up for this?"

"What're they gonna do, fire me?"

"You go ahead and laugh," she said. "No telling what story Edgar will come up with to tell the mayor and town council."

Everyone in Burr likes Karen, and Karen likes everyone. Except Edgar and Deke Bixby, which tells you a lot about what kind of men they are.

"Let 'em," I said. "I'll move to Hawaii and lay on the beach and forget I ever heard of the Bixbys."

"What about that girl on the train tracks?" she snapped. "You going to forget her, too?"

"Red, you sure know how to hurt a guy." No one else in town is allowed to call her "Red."

Cousins stuck his head in the door on his way to making his rounds, which mainly consist of him keeping tabs on teenage drivers and being visible along Main Street. I silently welcomed the interruption. The three of us talked about this and that for a few minutes, until Bernard went on his way.

I used his exit as cover to retreat to my office. I needed to think. I also sought to avoid further scolding. At any rate, I like my privacy. I also like a good belt of bourbon, which goes down smoother behind closed doors, although it was a little early for that, even for me.

Kenny checked in before I had a chance to do any actual brain storming. I gave him some of the new flyers I'd had printed, and asked him to post them around town. I also suggested that, while he was at it, he should post some in Watie Junction and Temple City.

With him out the door, I slouched behind my desk and took a half-assed shot at mentally deciphering the nature of evil. I made very little progress and gave up. I decided to take a walk. By lunchtime I'd been up and down Main Street and interviewed nearly everyone in town. I learned nothing of relevance. Most folks just used the opportunity to complain. My tolerance for petty bitching and moaning is limited. On this day, I accepted it in service of a nobler cause. By the time I made it back to the office, my already shaky regard for humanity had diminished another half notch. The afternoon was redeemed by a visit from Dizzy, who jumped for joy all over me. Unlike my faith in people, my faith in dogs remains utter and complete.

I told Karen to hold my calls—it's a joke, she never does—while I retired once again to my office. I spent a few minutes indulging the privileges of command and played tug-of-war with Diz. Unfortunately, a phone call from Agent Ovell Jones of the OSBI interrupted our hijinks.

Jones gave me what I now recognized as his usual line of nonsense, except this time he allowed I could work the case as much as I wanted. I didn't want to work it at all, really. But no one else seemed inclined to, and that irritated me to no end, so I said I would. Jones suggested I call Sheriff Murray and tell him I'd be taking a bigger role.

Burton did a good impression of someone who wasn't relieved to be taken off the hook. Looking at it from his point of view, I could understand why. Tilghman County's whiter than a glass of milk. I'd reckon the three citizens from church who aided us in our search on Sunday were a fair representation of the percentage of townsfolk truly disturbed by that girl's death. I hate to say it, but if Burt caught the killer and the killer was some local good ol' boy, he could just about forget about that run for State Senate. I doubt many of his constituents would think killing a colored girl is a good reason to throw a white man in jail. They may well see fit to express their displeasure in the voting booth. Better to let us local yokels handle it. Burt could always horn-in on the credit down the road if it somehow helped him politically.

I'd just said good bye to the sheriff when the phone rang again. Karen picked it up before I could. The door was shut so I couldn't understand what she was saying, but she didn't sound happy. After a minute or two, I heard her slam it down. She burst into my office.

"Well, I predicted it," she said, her face flushing a shade darker than her hair. "That was Frank Potter." Frank sits on the Town Council. "They're calling an emergency Council meeting tonight and your presence is required. Edgar filed a formal complaint. Says you arrested him because he caught you making a pass at his wife."

"I didn't make a pass at his wife."

"Well, that's good to know, but I don't think it matters."

"I guess not. What time is this hoe-down supposed to start?"

"Eight o'clock at the elementary school."

"I'll be there by seven fifty-five."

She gave me a look that would've shamed a rodeo clown. "You take this seriously, Emmett," she said with her jaw fixed and teeth nearly clenched. "The Bixbys have been looking for a reason to take your badge for as long as I can remember. It looks like this time you were dumb enough to serve it to 'em on a silver platter."

For some reason, I thought it a good time to suggest a course of action that had previously been dismissed as impracticable. "Maybe I'll retire on my gas royalties and move to Hawaii after all."

Karen had still not warmed to the idea.

"Oh, that would be wonderful," she said. "Then Jeff would end up as chief. You want the rest of the people in town to hate you, and not just Deke and Edgar? You go right ahead and quit."

I suddenly felt ashamed for making light of the situation. So many times, Karen's steered me clear of disaster—watched out for me when I couldn't or wouldn't be bothered to watch out for myself. I can count on a couple of fingers how often I'd expressed my gratitude. Fact is, I got it in me to drink myself stupid and go in there and tell the Town Council to kiss my rosy red hindquarters. I probably wouldn't, but I might. Karen was there to make sure I didn't.

I didn't thank her this time, either. Graciousness isn't one of my strong points.

Instead, I asked: "You think they'd hire Jeff before they would Bernard or Kenny?"

"I think they'd hire someone they could push around, is what I think."

That more than rang true. It would hardly matter to them that Jeff believes a cabal of Jewish bankers run the world from a secret vault on Mount Rushmore inside Honest Abe's left nostril. Or that he hates negroes almost as much as he does an honest day's work. Jeff Starns could paint his face purple and wear a diaper on the outside of his uniform; it still wouldn't bother the Bixbys so long as they had him under their thumb. In fact, a good percentage of the town would doubtless forgive him anything, given his exalted status as an ex-OU football player. Even Sooner benchwarmers are celebrities for life in this state.

"Ok, I get the message," I said, humbled and beginning to feel a little nervous. "You gonna come to give me moral support?"

"Can't, darlin'. Meeting's in Room 222."

Regular council meetings are held in the school auditorium. Room 222 is where they hold the closed-door kind.

The kind where they fire police chiefs.

CHAPTER SIXTEEN

I don't know how it is other places, but the Burr Town Council has always seemed to me unusually small, comprising as it does just two councilmen and the mayor. I guess you could say the members are prominent citizens, although to the naked eye there's not much to choose between them and anyone else with a job and a roof over their head.

I'd say the biggest difference is that as a group they are notably less law-abiding than the folks they represent. I've had cause to arrest all of them, usually involving a propensity for raising hell to the point where it's just not funny more. Alcohol is inevitably involved. In all such cases, the judgment of the court has been invariably and suspiciously merciful. Not one has ever spent more than a night in jail.

For over a decade, a rotating cast of the same three men—Frank Potter, Jim Bob Hall, and Jerry Chrisco—have occupied the mayor's office and one of the two council seats. They take turns. One serves as the mayor, another sits on the council, and the third cools his heels until the next election.

It's a joke the town plays on itself—a biannual spectacle in a place starved for entertainment. Folks just sit back and watch. No respectable citizen would dare shoehorn himself into the process. One time a few years back, whichever of the boys was mayor—I think it was Jerry—came up with the idea that they should expand the council so all of them could serve at the same time. The community was so outraged, the proposal never even came up for a vote. Folks find amusement and some comfort in our biannual tradition of political musical chairs.

You could say the members of our town government are more or less typical of the kind of fellas you meet around town any given day. They drink copious amounts of 3.2 beer, of course. They talk about football like it's some arcane science handed down on marble tablets. They hang around the barbershop Saturday mornings and lie about the nookie they didn't get the night before.

The council's second seat never changes ownership. It belongs to Deke Bixby, lock, stock, and barrel. Unlike the others, Deke isn't a good ol' boy and doesn't pretend to be. As president of the First State Bank of Burr, he holds mortgages on nearly every farm, business, and home in the area, giving him power over most everyone who casts a vote.

Deke made it clear early on he would not countenance electoral opposition. One year, Jim Bob decided he didn't want to wait. He ran out of turn. Deke beat him, but just barely. The day after the election, Deke called-in the note on Jim Bob's bait shop. Scared Jim Bob to death. They eventually renegotiated terms, much to Deke's advantage. Jim Bob kept his business, but he learned (the whole town learned, if they didn't already know) not to mess with Deke. No one's run against him since.

Except for Deke, the boys on the council like me well-enough. I've got a history in this town, dating back to the '40s and my time as a local high school football hero, then later, from my experience as a Marine MP. It doesn't hurt that my father is widely respected, as well.

Deke hates me as much as his brother does. I don't mean to brag, but people like me, and they don't like the Bixbys, although some pretend to. The fact I served in the military fuels their dislike almost as much as my general popularity. Old man Bixby got his sons draft exemptions so they could stay home and provide the essential work of running the bank and counting their oil and gas money. People look down on them for this, even if they don't dare say so. When I came home from Korea and got the celebrity treatment, it burned like someone had lined their jockey shorts with Ben-Gay.

From my first day on the job, Deke and Edgar have caused me grief whenever they've gotten the chance. The fact that the rest of the council usually sides with me allows me to keep my job, even if the town government is in most instances under Deke's—and by extension, Edgar's—control. The Bixbys are small and petty men. It follows that their quarrels with me are small and petty. My best defense is to remain indisputably in the right. I've managed to do that so far.

·   ·   ·   ·   ·

I said goodnight to Karen around six-thirty with a promise to call later and let her know how things turned out. I drove Dizzy home and downed a couple shots of Old Grand-Dad for courage, then headed out.

Since the Burr city offices don't have room for much more than a couple of desks and a water cooler, public meetings are held at the elementary school, the biggest and most modern building in town. Community events are held in the auditorium, but when the council has something they want to keep secret, they convene behind closed doors in a sixth-grade classroom on the second floor. The room is right above the cafeteria, which is why room 222 always smells like Salisbury steak and tater tots.

It was hot out but not too uncomfortable, so I walked the couple of blocks from my house to the school. I chewed half a roll of breath mints on the way, to mask the booze on my breath. I realized I hadn't thought about our murder victim since Karen told me about the meeting. Being forced to deal with something as trivial as hurt feelings at a time like this boiled my blood.

Room 222 is like the classrooms I remember from when I was a kid. A blackboard runs across the length of the front wall. A couple dozen one-piece wood-and-metal desks are lined up in rows. Pictures of American heroes like George Washington and Robert E. Lee adorn the walls. An OU Sooners football schedule is taped to the front of the teacher's desk. No public space in Oklahoma is complete without one.

I walked in to find Frank, Jerry, and Deke sitting at the teacher's desk: Jerry on one end, Frank on the other, and Deke in the middle. Deke sat a Dixie cup full of tobacco spit in front of him. The odd-man-out always attends these meetings, too, so Jim Bob was present, squeezed into a half-sized kid's chair in the front row, beer belly encased in a blue-and-orange bowling shirt and spreading over the desk like lava oozing over the base of a volcano.

I nodded to all present.

"Emmett," said Jerry and Frank. Jim Bob smiled sheepishly, aware of how ridiculous he looked, I reckon. Deke just glowered.

"This going to take long?" I asked. "You might've heard how we got something pretty serious on our plate. I'd like to get back to it."

Deke pushed his chair away from the desk so fast and hard, the wooden legs screeched against the tiled floor. "I'd say the false arrest of one this town's leading citizens is pretty serious," he said. "I'd say that attempted adultery with a married woman is pretty serious, too, or don't you think the laws of God apply to you, Mr. War Hero?" Elephants and Bixbys never forget.

Jerry and Frank each gently grasped one of Deke's elbows and tried to pull him down to sit. He did not relent and remained standing.

"Deke, I'm pretty sure God has more important things to worry about," I said. "If he decides he wants to give me some advice on the way I go about my business, I'll listen to what he has to say. Until that happens, I answer to the people of this town. Last night, on their behalf, I jailed someone who presented an imminent danger, both to the public and to himself."

As he often does, Frank figured to play the role of the peacemaker. "Emmett," he said, his voice more sugar-y than a stick of Juicy Fruit, "Deke's already given us Edgar's version of what happened. Why don't you tell us yours? In your own words." Deke sat, grudgingly. He spit into the cup, folded his hands on the desk, and looked at me, shooting flaming arrows with his eyes.

I said I'd be happy to explain, and told the long, sordid story in detail, including the reason I went out to Edgar's in the first place. Frank, Jerry, and Jim Bob seemed satisfied.

Deke wouldn't budge an inch.

"It ain't a crime for a man to move his car from one end of his own driveway to the other," he raged. A dip of snuff bulged from his lower lip. He tried to spit into the cup again, but some of the tobacco juice missed the target and ran down his chin. He wiped it with back of his hand. "I don't care how much he had to drink. And it sure as hell ain't no crime for him to defend his wife's honor from some bastard who tries to molest her under cover of a badge."

"Deke, if I tried anything with Denny, she wouldn't need Edgar's help setting me straight. That I was still in possession of my balls when Edgar came home last night is proof I didn't try anything."

Frank, Jerry, and Jim Bob laughed. Deke got redder and sweatier.

"As for just moving his car, that's just horseshit," I said. "Edgar had been driving on a state highway. He almost slammed into my car. He refused to take a roadside breathalyzer. I had plenty cause to take him in."

"Why didn't the sheriff charge him, then?"

Everyone in the room knew Burt Murray wouldn't charge Edgar for any crime short of murder, and maybe not even that, not as long as Edgar was writing checks to his political campaigns. "You know the answer to that as well as I do," I said. "I'm still within my rights to press charges."

I had no intention of going down that road, but Deke didn't know that. His eyes closed to slits as he considered whether to call my bluff.

He didn't have to. Frank saved face for him by trying to conciliate. "Deke, I can't imagine Emmett went out there to force himself on Edgar's wife. We all know Edgar gets ornery when he drinks. So far, nobody's charged anybody with anything. Can't we just shake hands and let it go?"

"I ain't letting nothing go!" said Deke, spraying wintergreen-scented spit. "I'm charging this man with an abuse of power, and I'm calling for a vote to dismiss him effective right here and now!"

Jerry had been sitting with his arms folded on his chest and his head down, listening but not saying anything. Of the group, he's generally the least likely to leap before he looks. "Deke, you're going to lose that vote," he said. "Right now, it's Emmett's word against yours, and you weren't even there. Why ain't Edgar or Denise here to make their case? If Emmett forced himself on Mrs. Bixby, I'd think she'd be willing to come here and tell us all about it."

Deke spoke faster and louder. Maybe he thought speed and volume would compensate for the paper-thinness of his case. "Edgar's home comforting his wife, who's too upset to do anything but cry her eyes out over this man's inhuman treatment of her. He told me, 'Deke, you're my brother and an honest man, and those fellows down at the city council will listen to you when you tell them about the indignities Emmett Hardy subjected me and her to. You tell 'em about it and they'll do the right thing.' So, I'm telling you, and I expect you to do the right thing."

Or I'll kill you with my bare hands, the spittle on his lips and twitch in his cheek said. Frank looked at Jerry and Jerry looked at me and Jim Bob shifted his oversized butt in the little chair, trying to get more comfortable. Frank gave mediation one last shot. "Deke, you know we think the world of you." His doughy, liver-spotted face crinkled into something like a smile. "But we think a lot of Emmett here, too, dang it. I just wish for the good of the town y'all could set aside your bad feelings, shake hands and make up. I'm sure Emmett's sorry for what he done."

I wasn't and he knew it. He kept moving his mouth in case I decided to say so. "Mistakes were made on all sides." He looked at me, hoping I'd at least throw him a bone. I didn't. "The best thing to do would be to move on like this never happened, don't you think?" He sounded like a five-year-old asking his mama for ice cream an hour before dinner.

Deke wasn't about to back down. "I ... ain't ... forgettin' ... nothin'," he said. "I *am* calling for a vote to dismiss Emmett Hardy from his position as police chief of Burr, effective right here and right now."

For a few seconds, you could've heard a gnat belch into a ball of cotton. Jerry said, "I guess that's that, then. You got anything else to say before we vote, Emmett?"

"I reckon the picture's clear enough. Y'all go ahead and take your vote."

Deke called for a show of hands in support of my ouster. His was the only one raised. Frank and Jerry voted against. Jim Bob forgot he wasn't presently on the council and tried to add one for me, but Jerry set him straight and Jim Bob apologized.

Deke's face turned the color of grape Kool Aid. "This ain't over," he said, and screeched his chair away from the table one more time. He was followed out the door by a long piece of toilet paper stuck to his shoe. We gave him time to get down the hall before erupting in laughter.

"Goddam, Emmett, you got pair of onions on you, I'll give you that much," said Jerry, wiping tears from his eyes.

"Woulda been a damn shame if Denny Bixby'd cut 'em off," added Frank. That got them to laughing even harder.

We relaxed and chatted a bit. "You never did get to ask Edgar if he saw something the night that girl got killed, did you?" Frank asked me.

Jim Bob, always eager to help, interrupted before I could answer. "Edgar, Jr.'s been seeing a nigger girl. I wonder if she knows who that dead girl was you found?"

Jerry and Frank winced and exchanged squirrelly looks.

"Wait a minute, wait a minute," I said. "You're telling me EJ has a colored girlfriend?" No one said anything. Apparently, a cat had been let out of a bag.

Jim Bob knew he'd run his mouth when he shouldn't have. "Well, I don't know if she's he's his official girlfriend," he mumbled. With all the dignity he could muster—and it wasn't much—he slowly unsqueezed his belly out from behind the kid's desk. He rested his elbows on his knees and looked balefully at the floor. "I don't think EJ. wants the word to get out," he said sheepishly, "but I seen him out at the lake with her a bunch of times. They sit in that fancy car of his and kiss or hump or whatever. He don't think I can see him from the store, but I can."

Hell no, EJ wouldn't want the word to get out. Male Bixbys pass their Klan hoods down from father to son. "That can't be," I said. "His daddy would kill him if he found out."

"I didn't say he was fixin' to *marry* her," Jim Bob said defensively. "Probably she's just a piece of ass. But they been parking out at the lake every Saturday night for quite a while now."

Jim Bob admitted he had invited Frank and Jerry out to see for themselves. "Couldn't see much 'cuz the windows was fogged," Jerry offered.

"But it was EJ and some colored girl," Frank said. "We all saw that much. Deke didn't go, but he knows about it."

"Don't tell no one," Jim Bob said. "We don't want no trouble from Deke." No one does, I thought. But that don't mean it's not going to come.

"Does Edgar know?"

"Shit, Emmett, who's going to tell him?" said Frank. "Deke's the only one who could, but I don't think he did."

Edgar the kind to shoot the messenger first and ask questions later. EJ's not very smart, but he's not so dumb he'd tell his father about this.

Jim Bob tried to close the barn door. "You know, Emmett," he said, "now that I think about it, I'm sure it's not the same person."

"Based on what?" I asked. "The fact that the boy's daddy and uncle run the goddam town?"

They all sat there and squirmed like they'd gotten caught watching their parents fornicate.

I felt like hitting somebody or something but I managed not to. The pressure in my head felt like it might pop my eyes out of their sockets. "Anything else you're not telling me? Her name? Where she lives?"

They shook their heads in perfect unison. I felt like I'd been dropped into the middle of a Ritz Brothers movie.

I took a deep breath and counted to ten. No one said anything. Frank horked up a big wad of phlegm and spit it into the cup Deke had left behind. "In that case," I said, "I'll just thank y'all for saving my job and get back to work."

CHAPTER SEVENTEEN

I walked back to the station to pick up the Fury, hoping Karen would still be around so I could talk over what had happened. She wasn't, but Kenny was sitting at her desk with his feet propped up, reading *To Kill a Mockingbird*, of all things. I sent him on patrol so I could get some solitude. I dialed Edgar's number, mostly expecting I'd be talking to Denny. I reckoned Edgar'd be drinking at Edna's and his delinquent son out somewhere torturing puppies.

As predicted, Denny answered. I told her I needed to see EJ in my office first thing in the morning. She asked why, and I told her I needed to ask him some of the same questions I'd asked her. Neither of us mentioned what had transpired the previous night. She said she'd make sure EJ was in my office by nine, and we said our goodbyes. It was all very stiff and formal and polite.

My encounter with the village idiots had taken more out of me than I'd realized. I couldn't summon the energy to rise up and go home, so I unlocked my desk drawer and pulled out my secret bottle of Old Grand-Dad. Karen has the other key to my desk and is kind enough to ensure I always have an adequate supply. I poured my blue enamel cup half-full and drank deep. I find that sometimes a good belt sharpens my thinking.

On the other hand, sometimes it just helps make me feel sorry for myself. This was one of those times. Independent of my will, my brain decided it was a good time to accentuate the negative.

I remembered all the times I'd stopped EJ Bixby for raising hell in that fancy car of his, and how he'd pretend to apologize in a tone that really said: Go to hell, old man. I thought about how apathetic and/or pessimistic those OSBI boys were, and how the men paying their salaries didn't consider the murder of an anonymous colored girl worth solving.

I thought how my experience strong-arming drunk Marines had not provided me with the skills needed to investigate a murder. Not even in a pimple-on-a-mosquito's-ass town like Burr.

Dizzy came scratching at the door. I let her in. She carried a weather-beaten brown work boot in that big soft mouth of hers. God knows whose it was or where she got it. She set it down at my feet and looked up at me, all proud, like it was a big fat prairie chicken she'd caught for our supper. I rubbed behind her ears and told her what a good girl she was. She laid down with her chin on her paws and slept.

I refilled the enamel cup over and over until the bottle was close to empty, feeling more pathetic and depressed with each swallow. By the time I got up to leave, my eyes had forgotten how to focus and my legs how to walk. Through the haze, I thought how this kind of thing was happening more often than was healthy.

I knew I shouldn't drive, but there weren't any other cars on the streets that time of night, and my house isn't too far from the station. Dizzy got in the Fury without being asked. Somehow, I managed to aim the car in the direction of the house. My last thought was how I'd forgotten to call Karen. Everything after that was a blank, but I made it home, because I woke up the next morning fully clothed in my own bed, with Dizzy snoring beside me.

· · · · ·

I learned how to sin at the movies.

When I was kid, a lot of towns the size of Burr didn't have their own theater. But we did. We had the Broncho.

The Broncho Theater—don't ask me where that "h" in "Broncho" came from—booked mostly westerns. Its marquee featured a full-color painting of a cowboy on a rearing horse, outlined in red, white, and blue neon lights. The auditorium walls were decorated with historically inaccurate murals of Indians and cavalrymen shooting at one another from behind oil derricks, and shaking hands with football players.

The biggest movie to hit the Broncho was *Cimarron*, a film about a historical episode near and dear to the hearts of local citizens—the Oklahoma Land Run of 1889. In one way or another, most of the people in the standing-room crowd that first night owed their presence to one or another of the several runs that opened the territory to white settlement. Some of the older folks had even participated. My granddaddy was just a young man when he made the run of '93 in a covered wagon. He was an honored guest at *Cimarron*'s opening night. Afterward, some of those in attendance were angry about what the film got wrong. Grandpa just laughed from beginning to end.

I liked cowboy pictures all right, but my favorites were the crime movies—films like *The Public Enemy*, *The Maltese Falcon*, and *Scarface*. The Broncho showed a few. I didn't miss a one.

For better or for worse—the jury's still out, seeing how I am still able to function with body and soul more-or-less intact—I trace my fondness for hard drink to those films. In many of them, alcohol was practically its own featured character.

I decided that if boozing was the way of the world, I'd better learn how to do it. I started with moonshine when I was 13. Shortly thereafter, I developed a liking for the bourbon my daddy hid in the tool shed. Eventually he discovered my pilferage and found a new hiding place, after which I was forced to rely on my wits in order to quench my thirst. Fortunately, nearby Butcherville was home to a number of freelance bootleggers. My whistle remained wet.

I drank for fun until I joined the Marines and got sent to Korea. There, I learned to appreciate booze's anesthetizing qualities, for which I continue to be grateful, however much I've come to over-rely on them. A gunnery sergeant taught me how to short-circuit hangovers by chug-a-lugging a glass of Alka Seltzer before I went to bed. It worked so well, I lost my fear of waking up sick. That allowed me to drink past what had been my cutoff point. I eventually built up a resistance and didn't need Alka Seltzer anymore. I'm sure there's a scientific explanation for that, but I'm not smart enough to know what it is. It might be all that booze—combined with those licks to the head I got from playing football with a leather helmet—killed the brain cells responsible for giving me those allergic-to-sunlight, morning-after headaches. My memory ain't what it used to be, but hell, remembering is overrated. I still remember more than I care to.

So it was that I woke up the next morning in the same condition as always after a bender: breath like a septic tank, foggy on the details of how I'd gotten home, but tolerably well-equipped to dodge the daily shovels of shit sent in my direction.

Karen was at her desk when I arrived, angry because I'd forgotten to call her after the meeting. She said she tried to call me but I guess I slept through the phone ringing. I gave her a detailed rundown, downplaying the fact that, but for the grace of God and my winning personality, I might've lost my job. She was about to lay into me on that account, when I told her the part about EJ having a negro girlfriend. That about knocked her for a loop.

Before we could talk more about it, EJ arrived with his father's lawyer, Jimmy Jack Preston, in tow. I escorted them back to my office. Karen asked if I needed her to take notes. I could tell she was silently begging me to say yes, so she could come in and hear what was going on. But I was feeling contrary, so I said I figured I could handle it myself.

You'd expect a man named Jimmy Jack to have been born on a horse with a dip of snuff jammed between his cheek and gum. Not our Jimmy Jack, who's a redneck by affectation, not birth. His grandfather—the original James Johnson Preston—hailed from Connecticut and worked for one of those New York robber barons, I forget which one. Impressed by James Johnson Preston's ability to sell ice to Eskimos or popcorn to Indians or whatever flimflam he was put in charge of, he sent him to Oklahoma to run one of his railroads.

Grandfather Preston subsequently got filthy rich in his own right, as railroad magnates tended to do back then.

James Johnson Preston's grandson attended an elite private school in Oklahoma City. When it came time for college, his folks shipped him back East, to Yale, where he studied law. He graduated but failed the bar in New York, so he came home and opened a lawyering business in Tilghman County. Before long, he was calling himself Jimmy Jack, talking like a hick, and looking after the interests of rich assholes like Edgar Bixby. Jimmy Jack is a mediocre lawyer, but it doesn't matter. He doesn't need to be especially good. The laws in this state are expressly written to favor his clients.

Jimmy Jack compensates for not being an honest-to-God good ol' boy by driving a pickup and wearing the flashiest western gear money can buy. Today he went all-out. He wore a powder-blue western suit with white leather-lined pockets and shoulder patches; a plain white cowboy shirt; a string tie with an elaborate clasp made of red jasper turquoise set in silver; and a pair of fancy-stitched white Tony Lamas that I'm sure cost more than I make in a month.

His overstuffed posterior hovered a few inches above the chair, like he was unsure he wanted to commit to sitting down and risk having it collapse under his considerable weight. He opened his suit coat to relieve the pressure placed on it by his oversized belly—no doubt, the result of a steady diet of prime rib and baked potato with butter and sour cream.

Next to him, EJ sat with no fuss.

We shook hands. "I'm surprised to see you, Jimmy Jack. This isn't anything EJ needs a lawyer about."

He pushed his gray businessman's Stetson back on his head. "I guess EJ's daddy figured I was still on the clock for gettin' him cut loose down to the county courthouse yesterday mornin'," he said, a big phony grin plastered across his face. "Just what exactly is it you want to talk to EJ about?"

For a second I thought he was kidding, then I realized he honestly didn't know. Maybe calling him mediocre gives him too much credit.

"As I'm sure you've heard, Jimmy Jack," I explained, "we're

looking into the killing of a young negro girl whose body we found outside of town on the train tracks."

"Ok," he said, "but what's that got to do with young Edgar, Jr?"

"I've been told young Edgar's been keeping company with a colored girl. I'm looking to see if it's the same girl."

Jimmy Jack looked like he'd been hit in the crotch with a sledge hammer and was trying to pretend it didn't hurt. "You didn't tell me this was about that," he said, turning to EJ.

"You didn't ask," EJ sneered.

"Chief, if you don't mind, I'd like to confer with EJ in private."

"Y'all go right ahead."

I left them in my office and sat on the edge of Karen's desk. She was typing and smoking a cigarette. I thought about asking to bum one, but I've been quit of them for so long, it'd be a shame to start again.

"They run you out already?" she asked without looking up.

"Apparently EJ kept his lawyer in the dark."

"About the colored girlfriend?"

"Yup."

"You're going to tell me all about it when you're done in there."

"Yup."

"I wasn't asking, I was telling," she said.

"Ok."

We didn't talk much after that. I could tell she was still mad I didn't call the night before. She typed while I cleaned my fingernails with one of the toothpicks I keep around the place.

"I checked your desk this morning," she said after a few minutes, without looking up from her work. "Looks like your bottle needs replenishing."

"I hadn't noticed."

Jimmy Jack stuck his head out the door.

"You can come on in, Chief."

I went back in.

"EJ here says he don't know any colored girls," Jimmy Jack said. "Never spent time with one, never even met one that he can remember. Says whoever told you that is wrong."

EJ sat there sulking and avoiding eye-contact.

"That's interesting, EJ," I said, "because I got witnesses who say they seen you out by the lake on a number of occasions parked in that Corvette of yours with a negro girl."

The boy looked me in the eye for the first time. I held his gaze and he looked away again. "Whoever said that is lyin'," he muttered, his face as sour as a carton of spoilt milk.

Truth-telling don't come natural to male members of the Bixby clan.

"Almost the entire town government is saying it, son," I said. "Jim Bob Hall saw you parked out there with a colored girl several times. Frank Potter and Jerry Chrisco saw you at least one time themselves. You calling them liars?"

I could see the hamster wheel in his head going around and around, trying to contrive an explanation that didn't sound like total bullshit. "Maybe it was someone with the same kind of car," was the best he could come up with.

"That don't wash, son," I said. "I'm willing to bet there ain't another car exactly like yours in the whole county, never mind Burr."

His eyes appeared to have settled on a piece of old bubblegum that had probably been ground into the linoleum some time during the Coolidge administration. He seemed to have trouble comprehending how the world could suddenly turn on him the way it had.

I didn't feel sorry for him, but I reckoned it might help my cause if I pretended I did. I told him I understood how he might be embarrassed for folks to know he'd been dating a colored girl. "I know you must be worried how your daddy would handle it," I said. "But you don't have anything to be ashamed of, son. It ain't a crime."

Of course, this time it was me who was lying. Sexual congress of any kind between black and white folks—inside or outside the bounds of holy matrimony—is against the law in Oklahoma. Even Jimmy Jack must've known that, but I suspect on this count he thought it best to keep his mouth shut.

EJ was sweating around the eyes like he'd drunk a whole bottle of tabasco sauce, causing him to wipe his face with the collar of his t-shirt. He leaned back in his chair and looked at the ceiling, his long legs splayed out, hands locked together behind his head. Playing for time. He's a handsome kid, I thought. I'll give him that. Takes after his mother.

After a time, he sat upright. Suddenly, like he'd come to a decision.

"Ok, I've been seeing a girl." I could tell right away he wasn't about to give up the whole truth without a battle. "But I ain't seen her in a long time. Not for a month, at least."

That got Jimmy Jack's attention. "EJ, don't say nothing else. We need to talk about this with your daddy. He should—"

"You leave my daddy out of this," EJ barked like a hungry dog who thinks you're trying to steal his dinner. "It don't matter, anyway. I ain't got nothing to hide because I ain't done nothing wrong. Her name was Sheryl. I picked her up at that whorehouse outside Watie Junction."

The brothel my dad had mentioned.

I gave EJ all the time he needed to spin his yarn, which he did at some length. He insisted this Sheryl wasn't his girlfriend, but rather just a form of hired help. He said for a while he was going out there once a week, paying her five dollars every time. "Sometimes we'd drive out to the lake," he said. "but it's not like we were going out on a date, like you would with a regular girl. It was just more private that way."

I told him I thought that price sounded low. He said maybe she gave him a discount because she liked him. That sounded unlikely but I didn't say so. He asked if I was going to arrest him and I told him if I arrested every man in the county who paid for nookie there'd be no room in the county jail. He smiled and appeared relieved.

"What I need to know," I said, "is if the girl you were seeing is the one who got killed."

He went quiet again.

"I reckon you've seen the posters we've put up," I said.

He nodded. Jimmy Jack looked at his gold watch and cleared his throat. The boy's chin quivered a little bit. I could hear cars driving by out front and dogs barking in the distance. No one spoke.

Finally, EJ said, almost inaudibly, "Yeh, that's her. I mean, I didn't want it to be her, but it's her."

"If you knew, why didn't you come forward?"

"I don't know," he said, his chin resting on his chest. "I guess I was afraid."

"Where were you and what were you doing Friday night?"

Jimmy Jack started to interrupt but EJ wouldn't allow it. He had something to say and was going to say it. "I was in Anadarko with the baseball team. I played first base. Got three hits and scored a couple of runs." He sounded suspiciously like he'd been practicing that story.

"What time was this?"

"The team bus left at noon and the game ended around five. I don't know exactly when we got back. We stopped at a Dairy Queen, so it might've took a little longer to get home."

"Was this Dairy Queen in Anadarko?"

"Maybe. I forget."

His chin stuck out in that odd, arrogant way he shares with Edgar, but his eyes looked everywhere except at me. The boy was hiding something, I was sure of that. Then again, he always acts like he's hiding something.

"Alright, I'll check with your coach. We'll leave it there for now."

He relaxed.

"I assume you knew her name," I said.

"Just her first name, and I'm not even sure if it was real. Sheryl."

"Alright, son, I'm going to need your help on this. We need to identify who she was and where she's from and notify her kinfolks, if she has any. The more we know, the more folks we talk to who knew her, the better the chance we have of finding out who did this."

"Whatever you want me to do, I'll do." All of a sudden, his tone was eager-to-please. "Those other girls who work out there know her better than I do. You should go out there and ask them."

"Tell you what, why don't you come out there with me?" I said.

He hesitated, then shrugged. "I don't see how that'd help," he said. "but if you want me to, I will."

"If nothing else, you can show me how to get there. I never been."

He looked at me like I was trying to put one over on him, which, of course, I was.

"Mm ... ok."

We made plans to meet me that evening at seven-thirty and drive over to Watie Junction. He pleaded with me not to tell his father or uncle about any of this. I said I wouldn't, feeling no obligation to honor such a promise, if push came to shove. He seemed to think he'd dodged a bullet, not understanding that he remained square in my sights.

I told Jimmy Jack he didn't need to come, not thinking he'd actually agree, but he did. Perhaps the young ladies there might be familiar with his face, which could prove an embarrassment. Apparently, it didn't occur to him that it would be in his client's best interest to tag along. Possibly he didn't care. Like I said, he's no Perry Mason.

We said our goodbyes. The room got 50% smarter by them walking out the door. I tried to read what few notes I'd taken, but they were almost indecipherable. Should've let Karen do it. Oh well, I thought. I'll remember the important parts. I threw the scraps of paper in the trash.

CHAPTER EIGHTEEN

The hours running up to my visit to the house of ill repute were chock-full of the usual earth-shattering crises I am called upon to quell in the course of a typical day.

Benny Courtland, the Chamber of Commerce president, called to nag me about posting an officer on the crosswalk in front of his candy store. He says it's for the safety of kids walking home from school, but I think it's a way of funneling them into his establishment. I don't like it. The way the town's configured, hardly any kids need to cross the street at that point. I said I'd consider it just to stay on good terms with Benny, but I have no intention of doing it.

Ethel Blankenship's a nice old lady who calls in regularly to report a certain stray dog that keeps getting in her garbage. Burr doesn't have regular pickup, so folks burn their trash in barrels in their back yards. Ethel's is an inviting target for scavenging dogs, since she's a great cook and only burns her garbage once a week. The offending pooch is frequently my own, so I feel obligated to go out there and clean up the mess whenever she calls. Today on my way over, I collected a guilty-looking Dizzy and drove her home before I went to Ethel's. Mrs. Blankenship seems to be the one person in town who doesn't know Dizzy belongs to me. I'd like to keep it that way.

Cathy Stallcup, one the hairdressers at Jesus Is Lord Hair Salon (so-called because the building used to be a Pentecostal church), came in to complain her boss wouldn't give her a raise. I told her I was sorry to hear it, but I couldn't do anything about it. She said that was ok, that she just wanted to get it off her chest. "She's got a crush on you, Emmett," Karen said after Cathy left. Karen thinks every woman in town has a crush on me. I believe she's right in this case, but I'm too much of a gentleman to say so.

Kenny relieved me at six o'clock. I decided to forgo a visit to Edna's and went home instead. I pounded a couple cans of Brown Derby, which is no better than what Edna's serves but has the good manners to be cheaper. I also don't have to listen to drunks jabber when I drink at home, which is an added benefit.

Refreshed, I put on my civilian clothes so as not to alarm the working girls. I placed my off-duty weapon in a holster at the small of my back and wore a scruffy brown corduroy sport coat to cover it up.

EJ was sitting on the curb in front of the station house when I arrived. I loaded him into my red-and-white '57 Ford pickup. He told me what he knew about the whorehouse on the 20-minute ride to Watie Junction. According to him, there were five girls—now presumably four—who lived and worked there. He said the only one he knew other than Sheryl was named Annette or something like that. I knew where the brothel was but pretended I didn't. I let EJ show me the way.

Officially, it is none of my business if the law in Watie Junction and Tilghman County turn a blind eye to the existence of a local bordello. The way it's arranged, there's not much they could do, even if they wanted to. The brothel is a shabby house trailer sitting at the edge of a large parking area next to Jerry's Cafe. The state line runs across the parking lot. Jerry's is on the Oklahoma side. The whorehouse lies in Texas. It's a convenient set-up for degenerates who like to eat in one state and screw in another.

The County Mounties on the Texas side are spread as thin as mustard on a peanut butter sandwich. They are inclined to look at it as a Tilghman County problem. Sheriff Burton and the Watie Junction police, on the other hand, profess it to be a Texas concern. The upshot is, nothing gets done. Some folks whisper that certain elected officials have a financial stake in the enterprise. I've been assured by those same elected officials such a scurrilous rumor has no basis in fact.

The sun had set by the time we arrived but it was still light out. I felt like grabbing a bite, so we went into the diner and had ourselves a hamburger and fries. I read a copy of *The Watie Junction News*, while EJ flirted with our pretty redheaded waitress. She was at least five years older than him and indifferent to his charms.

The hiring of a new high school football coach had supplanted our murder in the headlines, although the paper did run a short piece about it. It quoted Agent Jones as saying law enforcement was hot on the killer's trail, which was news to me. Last I heard, they were stuck on the hobo's girlfriend angle, which I saw as more of a half-assed guess than an actual theory.

We'd just about finished eating when the streetlights in the parking light came on. I took this as our cue to approach the ladies. The trailer they used for their dirty sinful activities was painted an ugly swimming-pool green, with dark-blue trim. It was about 40 feet long and ten feet wide—bigger than a camper, but not big enough for five adult females to live and work in, I wouldn't think. There wasn't any skirting around the bottom, in case the need for a quick getaway presented itself.

I paid our bill and we went out to the truck. I moved it close enough to the trailer to get a clear view but not so close that we'd draw attention to ourselves. No sooner had we got situated, a tractor trailer pulled up and blew its horn. A girl wearing a pink mini skirt and purple polka-dotted halter top came out and flirted with the driver. Another truck followed. Another girl came out of the trailer. I couldn't hear what they were saying, but it seemed apparent they were negotiating terms, after which the girl would climb into the cab. According to EJ, neither of the hookers was who we were looking for. I got tired of waiting and was just about to go knocking on the trailer door, when our girl saved me the trouble and came out on her own.

"That's her," he said. She looked like Elly May Clampett, if Uncle Jed's favorite niece had ended up turning tricks on the Sunset Strip instead of sunbathing next to the cee-ment pond, which I guess that was the point. She wore a red-and-white checked shirt unbuttoned and tied tightly under her conspicuously large breasts, which were as nicely suntanned as the rest of her and mostly exposed to the elements. Her shorts might've began life as a pair of blue jeans, although there wasn't enough fabric left to say for certain. Like Elly May, she cinched them with a piece of rope. Her hair was the texture of cotton candy and bleached as white as her fancy high-heeled cowgirl boots with red stitching and valentine hearts running up the sides.

"Her name's Annette?" I asked EJ again.

"Something like that," EJ said. "I'm not real sure."

She strutted right up to my window, wearing a big phony smile and several layers of make-up. Up close she looked older, but was still attractive in that trashy way most respectable men won't admit they like.

I make no pretense of being respectable.

"You boys lookin' for some fun?" she asked.

"Why don't you hop in and find out?"

"I don't do two at a time, sweetheart, I should tell you right off," she said. "Y'all gotta take turns."

I nodded and smiled. "Your name's Annette, right?"

She shook her head and continued smiling her counterfeit smile. "No, shug, it's Yvette, with a Y." She winked and did something obscene with her tongue. "It's French."

"Ah, that's right," I said. "Well, Yvette, I don't want to upset you or anything, I got to tell you I'm a police officer and I'd like to ask you a few questions about your friend Sheryl."

Yvette's smile disappeared faster than a jar of moonshine at a barn dance. "You trying to find who killed Sheryl?"

"I am. I got no reason to bother you other than to ask for your help."

She tensed-up like a stray cat ready to turn tail if I looked at her cross-eyed. "Listen, I gotta make some money tonight. I have to make a car payment tomorrow."

"I'd be happy to pay you for your time."

I wondered what Karen would think when she did our books. I

never submitted a voucher for a prostitute before.

We negotiated a price and she walked over the passenger side. I tossed EJ a quarter and told him to go get himself a coke. "I need to talk to Yvette in private," I said.

She recognized him. "Oh, hi!" she said. "How you holding up, sweetie?"

EJ didn't say anything, just double-timed it over to the diner.

"Sit by the window where I can see you," I called after him. "And I want change for that quarter."

I watched as EJ sat in a booth by the window as instructed. I'd expected him to bitch. It made me suspicious that he didn't.

Yvette got in. "Mind if I smoke?" she asked and lit up before I could answer.

I started to unfold one of the flyers with the artist's sketch on it. Yvette reached over and placed her hand over it. "That's ok, sweetheart," she said. "I saw it. It's her."

I looked toward the diner at EJ. All I saw through the glass was the back of his head. I reckoned he was eyeballing that redheaded waitress.

I turned my attention back to Yvette. It required every bit of gentlemanliness I had not to let my eyes wander too far south. That cab had gotten a helluva lot smaller since she got in.

I asked if she and Sheryl had been close friends.

"I wouldn't exactly say we were friends at all, really, not outside work," she said. "I kind of looked out for her, or at least tried to. She was so young, and being colored and all, she had a hard time. I felt sorry for her."

"When you say, 'she had a hard time,' what do you mean exactly?"

"Oh, you know how people are. Them other girls are mostly white trash themselves, but no matter how low someone is, they always need someone else to look down on."

"So, you looked after her?"

"I tried, anyway. She was so young. Lost, it seemed like. A little angry, a little sad."

"What do you know about her background, where's she from, that sort of thing?"

She gestured in EJ's direction. "I reckon the boyfriend can tell you more than I can."

I looked over and caught him staring at us. He turned away.

"EJ was her boyfriend?"

"I didn't know that was his name. I know Sheryl called him 'my boyfriend.'" Yvette brushed a few brittle strands of hair out of her face and stifled a sneeze. "Sorry, I think I'm catching a cold," she said with sniffle. "Anyway, Sheryl sure thought he was her boyfriend. They acted like boyfriend and girlfriend when I saw them together. Sheryl thought of him kind of like her knight in shining armor. Like he was going to take her away from this."

I pondered that for a bit. The idea of EJ being anyone's knight in shining armor seemed to me every bit as plausible as Truman Capote playing fullback for the Green Bay Packers.

"How'd they get along?" I asked. "Did he ever hit her that you know of?"

"Oh no, nothing like that," she said. "They were always sweet with each other. From what she said, he treated her nice."

"You don't think he'd have hurt her?"

"I been doing this long enough to know any man is capable doing anything to any woman, but in this case, I highly doubt it."

I asked her to tell me what she knew about Sheryl. Like her last name. "You know, she never told me and I never asked," she said. "For all I know, Sheryl might not have been her real first name. She said she was from Oklahoma City. I remember her talking bad about her daddy. Said he'd drink too much and force himself on her, so one day she got sick of it and moved out." She shook her head. "I don't know how much of it was true. Girls in this business tend to make up stories."

A panel truck pulled up and parked next to us just a few feet way. The driver gawked at Yvette through the window, craning his neck like he was trying to get a look at her cleavage. Yvette turned away from me and waved at the fella, wearing that same syrupy smile she'd given me. He grinned back, revealing something less than a full allowance of teeth. I thought he looked like a sweating, slobbering sack of shit. Yvette likely did, too, but her job was to let sacks of shit sweat and slobber on top of her, so she had to be nice. That can't be much of a life, I thought. She turned back to me. The smile vanished and she rolled her eyes a little bit.

"Sheryl said she was 18 when moved in here and started work about a year ago," she said. "I'd bet she wasn't older than 16, though."

I asked about the trailer situation and she explained how they all kicked-in on the rent and coordinated bedroom usage. Sheryl had been the last to move in, so she mostly slept on the couch. She told Yvette she had family in Oklahoma City, who she visited from time to time.

"You have any idea of her family's address?"

"No idea," Yvette said and took a last puff of her cigarette. I was impressed at how fast she'd sucked it down. She cracked the window and tossed it out, careful not to make eye contact with the sack of shit. "Ask the boyfriend. Or that friend he used to bring around sometimes."

"He brought a friend?"

She arched her painted-on eyebrows and pointed an index finger with an extremely long, curved red fingernail in my direction.

"Now, *that* boy's a different story."

From somewhere on her scantily-clad person she produced a pack of Pall Malls and fired up another one. I rolled down my window and leaned out for some air.

"You reckon the friend might've hurt her?" I asked.

She giggled like I'd said the funniest thing. "Lord, no. He was too bashful to say boo. No, I meant the boyfriend treated him awful."

At EJ's mention, I looked over and caught him picking his nose. That boy surely does turn my stomach, I thought.

"You remember what this friend looked like?"

She nodded. "I do. Short, pimply faced teenage boy with greasy brown hair."

"Ever catch his name?"

"I know what the boyfriend called him," she said dubiously, "but I'm pretty sure it wasn't his name."

"What was that?"

She hesitated. "Cunt," she blurted, "if you'll please excuse my French, because I do not like to use such words. Sometimes Cunty, or Cunter, or Cuntface. But always having to do with cunt."

I knew immediately who it had to be and described him to Yvette.

"Sounds like him," Yvette said. "Anyway, that poor thing just took a beating and he never got mad. The boyfriend seemed to get a kick out of treating him so mean. It was so different from the way he treated Sheryl."

I asked how often the friend came and if he'd been there recently. "Not recently, that I know of. He came a few times, but never paid for a party or anything like that. Just sat up there in the diner, while Sheryl and the other one did the deed. After a while he stopped coming. The boyfriend would come alone in that Corvette of his, drive off with Sheryl and bring her back a few hours later with enough money in her purse to cover a night's worth of tricks."

"Did Sheryl ever say anything to you about his friend?"

"Oh sure, she told me he had an awful crush on her. She said he tried to pay once but the boyfriend wouldn't let him, wanted Sheryl all to himself. I know she felt sorry for the little guy."

"Why'd she feel sorry for him?"

"I reckon because he was so pitiful. Sheryl said she got sad just being around him."

How pathetic did you have to be to arouse pity in a teenage prostitute? I wondered.

"Did the friend ever come back without the boyfriend?"

"Not that I know of. If he did, Sheryl never said nothing about it."

"When'd you last see Sheryl?"

"The night she died. I was taking a client inside the trailer and I remember seeing Sheryl out front. I didn't pay much attention. She was gone when I came out. I don't know for sure what time. If I had to guess I'd say between eight and nine."

"Did she come back, do you know"

"If she did, I didn't see her."

"Did she go off on her own like that a lot?"

"We come and go as we please, but we always let each other know. Friday after work's the time Sheryl would usually take off. We like to coordinate our schedules so there'll always be at least two of us here, so we tell each other in advance. Sheryl was always good about letting us know."

"Did she tell you this time?"

"No, she didn't, which I thought was strange. I was more mad than scared, because I had plans, but when she still hadn't come back the next day, I started worrying a little bit. That night, a customer came in and told us about a colored girl's body they found, and I thought it might be her. When I saw that drawing in the newspaper, I knew it was. I figured it wouldn't be long before someone like you would come by."

The sack of shit in the panel truck honked. Yvette glanced over with that smile and mouthed that she'd be right with him. "Listen, I need to get to work," she said.

"Just a couple more things," I said. "How did Sheryl get along with the other girls?"

"Not so great, but it wasn't her fault. They acted like they were afraid they'd turn black by being around her. They wouldn't have done anything to hurt her, though. They got too many problems of their own to go around hurting someone like Sheryl."

Maybe, maybe not.

"Did she have any regular customers?"

"Besides the boyfriend, you mean? There was an older fella she used to complain about."

"What was the problem? Did he hurt her?"

"I don't think so. He was just mean and bossy, I think. Acted like he owned her. A lot of clients are like that. I got the impression this guy was worse than most."

"Did you ever see him?"

"Oh yeh, I saw him a few times. And heard him," She laughed. "Lord, he was loud."

I thought that if I were patronizing a whorehouse I'd be too embarrassed to be loud. "He was older? How old?"

"Well, I reckon he wasn't too old. I guess he was more like your age."

Thanks a lot, Yvette. "So, he was middle-aged, then?"

"Yeh, you could say that." She gave me doe eyes and a flirty pout. "Sorry about that, hon."

I chuckled. "That's ok. I know I'm no spring chicken. Would you recognize him if you saw him again?"

She started to answer then sneezed into her hand. "Bless you," I said.

She smiled her thanks and wiped her nose. "I probably would recognize him," she said, then paused. "I know I would."

I thanked her and let her tend to business. I recommended she drink lots of orange juice, as I'm told it helps ward off colds. She graciously offered me a discount on her usual services, which I politely declined.

I spent the next few minutes trying to talk to the other hookers, but they were busy and I felt guilty about getting in their way. I thought it'd be better if I or someone else came back when things weren't so hectic. I understood that this was a dusk-to-dawn operation, but I was too tired to wait. I'd send Bernard or Kenny later. I fetched EJ from the diner and we headed back to Burr.

We rode in silence for a while. "Who's Cunter?" I asked.

By the light of the dashboard I could see him flinch. He took a few seconds to answer. Presumably, he was weighing the pros and cons of handing me a line of crap. In the end, he reckoned it wasn't worth the trouble.

"He's just a guy at school. Kevin Gunter."

Exactly who I suspected. Kevin's the son of Nate Gunter—Edgar, Sr.'s doormat, back in the day.

"Kevin a friend of yours?"

He laughed.

"He thinks so."

"He's not?"

He leaned back in his seat and acted bored.

"I used to let him hang around. I got tired of him."

"Why do you call him Cunter?"

"Because his last name is Gunter and he's a little cunt."

I had to stop talking right then or I was afraid I might hit him. Later, I'd ask whatever questions needed to be asked.

It was almost midnight before we got back to Burr. I saw EJ's mama peeking out from behind the curtain when I dropped him off. Edgar was nowhere to be seen.

CHAPTER NINETEEN

In some ways Nate Gunter was like the other kids I went to school with. He wasn't too smart, but he didn't stand out in that respect. Burr hasn't produced many Rhodes Scholars.

Getting disowned by his daddy was a major cause of Nate's problems. The Gunters split up before Nate was old enough to walk. Normally, it's hard for a couple to get a divorce in Oklahoma. That is, except when one of the parties—especially the woman—gets caught screwing around. Nate's mama made a science of screwing around.

Noreen Martin got pregnant with Nate while she was in high school. The pool of potential daddies comprised half the male student body. She kept them in suspense up to the moment they wheeled her into the delivery room, when a nurse asked who the father was and Noreen screamed, "Randy Gunter!" I'm told the collective sigh of relief could be heard as far away as Tulsa.

Randy did the right thing by Noreen, not that he loved or even liked her very much. The unhappy couple dropped out of school and moved into the bunkhouse on Randy's folks' place. They hadn't been married a year when Randy came home one night and found his blushing bride in bed with the captain of the Burr High School basketball team, whose season was subsequently cut short, thanks to a load of birdshot deposited into his skinny backside by the wronged husband.

Having salvaged his dignity with only the slightest legal

repercussions—this is rural Oklahoma, after all, where honor shootings are respected, if not explicitly encouraged—the Gunters expelled both Noreen and the two-year-old boy they were never convinced was Randy's anyway. Noreen was paid alimony and childcare as part of the divorce agreement. She was also deeded a tiny, unpainted cinderblock house on the edge of the Gunter property, where she and Nate lived. Before long, the humiliation of being cuckolded by a girl like Noreen became too much for Randy and his folks, and they moved away. Noreen, on the other hand, was never unduly prone to embarrassment. She stayed in Burr and raised Nate. Last time I checked, she was still living in that cinderblock house. She never did get around to having it painted.

People used to say the doors of Noreen's house were always open to teenage boys looking to sample the sweet mysteries of life, but I have my doubts. Certainly, by the time Nate was in high school, Noreen had stopped being so easy. You could always find somebody who knew someone else who'd bedded Noreen, but I never actually met anyone who confessed to having done it himself. Lord knows, she was no sex goddess. My memory is her lying on the couch in a dirty pink satin robe and fuzzy blue slippers, her hair in curlers, reading movie magazines and chain-smoking Old Golds. Drinking Boone's Farm Strawberry Hill through a straw.

Except for the money he sent Noreen every month like clockwork, Randy had no contact with his son, and Nate grew up without a father. Over the years, that role was filled in some twisted capacity by Edgar Bixby, so it was a cruel blow when Edgar went off to college and left Nate behind, just like his daddy did. I remember it about killed Nate. He stayed around Burr, working odd jobs and haunting the fringes of the high school crowd. He'd sit in the back of the bleachers at home football games and hang out at the soda fountain at Miller's—looking sad and lonely, and smelling like an outhouse.

Meanwhile, Karen Dean moved to Burr. She was a couple years behind me in school, but we became fast friends, anyway. Karen barely knew Nate, but she had the world's biggest heart. She saw him moping around in a dismal state and cajoled me into being his friend.

I pitied Nate, I really did, but being around him was about as much fun as a visit to the butt doctor. I said as much to Karen, but she's always had a way of getting a person to do things he doesn't want to do. Before I knew it, Nate was following me around, everywhere I went.

I let him. For a while. Then something happened.

•   •   •   •   •

A defining ritual for teenage boys in my day was to spend Saturday nights driving around trying to pick-up girls. Few were successful—or at least not nearly as successful as they would later make it sound—but the very attempt was a time-honored rite. No boy worth his weight in gas-station-restroom condoms would deny himself the adventure of trying and failing to get laid.

Nate Gunter had been denied that thrill, for reasons mostly having to do with his general unattractiveness. A lack of familiarity with such basic tools of hygiene as a toothbrush and bar of soap did not endear him to anyone. Also, cruising was invariably a two-man operation. Failure was frequent and expected. No one wanted to spend Saturday night alone in a car. Edgar was the closest thing he had to a friend, and Edgar wouldn't be seen dead with Nate on a Saturday night. Nate never had anyone to partner with. That is, until I entered the picture.

One Saturday night a few months into our engineered friendship, Nate got it into his head we were going to try something he'd once thought impossible: drive to Alva, cruise the main drag and try to pick-up girls. Based mostly on wishful thinking, boys from Burr universally believed that girls from Alva were not only more attractive, but more promiscuous than the hometown kind. Personally, I had never pursued that line of inquiry, being more than happy to date girls from Burr … that is, when my obsession with Denise Kinney was not too debilitating.

I was indifferent to the idea, but Nate had this heart set on it. He'd taken a bath and brushed his teeth and put on clean clothes for the occasion. I didn't want to burst his bubble, so I consented to go along. I had little faith in the myth about the girls from Alva, but I figured it might be like having faith in God. The worst thing that could happen is that you wasted whatever time you spent praying.

I figured Nate could use my help if he was to have any chance at all. I generally did ok with girls, owing at least somewhat to my prowess on the football field. Nate, on the other hand, couldn't get kissed if he walked into a whorehouse with a suitcase full of 100-dollar bills. Without me, he had no chance. With me, maybe a little bit.

Before we could worry about getting Nate a girlfriend, we had to find a viable means of transportation. Between the two of us, our only vehicle was Nate's old Ford flareside pickup, which hadn't run for weeks. He figured the battery was shot, but had procured an allegedly functional replacement from a source I considered unreliable. I expressed my skepticism but Nate waved off my concerns. "Don't worry," he said. "Everything's under control."

Nate used to say that a lot, which is funny, because in all the years I've known him, I don't think he's ever had a single goddam thing under control.

The plan was to swap-out the good battery for the bad, drive the thirty miles or so to Alva and cruise Main Street. After that, I guess the hope was that a girl or two would jump in the truck or otherwise magically appear.

Over the years, my daddy tried to teach me what he knew about cars, which was a fair amount, but I never cared to learn and didn't pay attention. Nate claimed to know a little bit, so I decided to trust him. The sun had already gone down when I got dropped off at Nate's, so we had to hurry. We didn't have a flashlight and it was getting darker by the minute. Before long, we were working by porch light.

It doesn't take any special aptitude to install a car battery, but even so, we had a terrible time. One look at the corroded cables and I reckoned we were in for it. Nate assured me otherwise, but he would've said anything to make me stay. At one point, he lost his grip on the old battery and almost dropped it on my foot. I banged my head on the hood latch trying to get out of the way, and suffered a bloody gash. I was *this* close to going home, but Nate apologized so hard I had to give in.

Of course, it started to rain, because this is Nate Gunter we're talking about. The new battery was too big to fit, and the porch light was too dim for us to see worth a damn. The worse things got, the more manic Nate got. "Tonight's the night, buddy!" he yelped with the misplaced optimism of a Chihuahua trying to mount a Great Dane. I reckon there's a first time for everything, but I wouldn't have bet a penny Nate would come within a hundred yards of a female that night, even if we did get the car running.

We finally got it in crosswise and tied it down as best we could, by which time it was coming down in buckets, drenching us from head to toe. I took a celebratory piss behind the house and we got in the car, glad to be out of the rain.

"Cross your fingers," said Nate, and turned the key. Nothing. He got out, messed with the connections, and tried again. Nothing. Either the new battery was no better than the old one, or the problem lay somewhere else. In any case, we were going nowhere.

Nate about lost his mind. Earlier, he'd been happy and optimistic and his hair was washed and his breath wasn't too foul and he'd seemed almost normal. Now, he screamed and cussed and pounded the roof of the pickup and howled like a maimed coyote. My tries at consoling him only made things worse, so I sat quietly in the dark, watched the rain splatter on the windshield and wished I was somewhere else.

After a while, his rage reduced itself to spastic whimpers. I asked him if he wanted to go in the house and listen to the radio. "Maybe we can catch the end of *Gangbusters*."

"Nah, mama's on the couch," he hiccupped, his chin quivering. "Probably listening to *Your Hit Parade*." Nate hated that program, I suspect because his mother liked it so much. Noreen spent a lot of time by that radio, probably dreaming Bing Crosby would show up and take her away from all this.

"Can I stay at your house tonight?" Nate asked suddenly. He

sounded so pitiful, I couldn't say no. I said we should tell his mama he was coming over, but he didn't want to. "Let's just go," he said. Noreen didn't have a telephone, so I couldn't call my folks to come pick us up. We walked the two miles to my house in the rain. Once there, my mama gave us towels and made us dry off before we came in the house. She made us sandwiches and we listened to the radio for a while, then went to bed. Nate was gone when I got up in the morning.

He avoided me after that night, which, I'm ashamed to say, was fine with me. Not long after that came the night at the lake with Denny, which resulted in me joining the Marines and Nate Gunter exiting from my life. After my return as police chief our paths occasionally crossed, but for the most part in the years since I came back I've had very little to do with Nate.

I couldn't avoid him now if I wanted to question his son. I could ask one of my officers to do it, but then I'd have to explain all about Nate, and I didn't have the energy for that. The best thing is to do the job myself. I'm not real good at delegating.

·　　·　　·　　·　　·

I hardly slept after my night at the whorehouse. I was out of bourbon, so I drank a six-pack of Brown Derby. The beer made me a little drowsy, but that was offset by having to crawl out of bed to pee every 15 minutes. After my fourth trip, I decided to stay up. I read 100-or-so pages of a novel about a US president running for reelection who was as crazy as a box of frogs. It kept me entertained until the sun came up, when I fried up a half-pound of bacon and drank three cups of instant coffee. I dragged my least-dirty uniform out of the hamper, got dressed, and headed out, hoping to catch the Gunters before they left for the day.

Nate and Kevin live in a little house located on Cedar Street, just off US 14 on the north side of the road, 50 yards or so from our red, white, and blue water tower with the name of the town in six-foot-high letters and the words "Home of the Patriots" painted underneath. Across the street are a pair of grain elevators—one almost brand-new and white as snow; the other at least 50 years old, the wooden outsides gray and rotten and twisting like a Slinky. Locals call it the Leaning Tower of Burr. Cedar Street is unpaved except for a layer of chat the town puts down once a year. At one end of the street is a small chicken farm tended by the man who lays the chat; on the other end, a few rusty steel storage sheds and a prefabricated aluminum garage where the school parks its buses. The Gunters are the street's only human occupants.

Nate's place has ugly gray Insul-Brick siding with sections torn off where you could see tar paper and rotted wood underneath. Years ago, it was the post office. The post office moved to Main Street in the '30s, and the building was converted into a very small house. It's been vacant more often than not over the years. Its tradition of being poorly maintained was kept alive by its two current occupants. There once was a third, but Mrs. Gunter left some time back to pursue her childhood dream of not being married to Nate.

Parked in the street was the same Ford pickup Nate and I tried to fix that rainy night twenty years earlier. The hard-packed dirt driveway was empty, so I backed the Fury in.

I strolled over and took a look at the truck, for old times' sake,

A bad battery was now the least of its problems. The once dark blue paint had faded to a cloudy grayish-green color, alternating with large patches of brown rust. The seats were worn through to the springs. The step on the driver's side was bent downwards so it almost scraped the ground, and the front end looked like it had lost a game of chicken with a dinosaur.

A mailbox sat in the yard to the side of the truck. Once upon a time, it had been painted in a stars-and-stripes design like the nearby water tower, but now it had faded almost white. Someone or something—a blindfolded epileptic monkey would be my guess—had scrawled "Gunter" across the side in black magic marker. I noticed the flag on the side of the box sagged toward the ground. I absent-mindedly tried to push it into its original position. It came off in my hand. I opened the flap to put the flag inside, but the flap came off in my other hand. I looked around to see if anyone was watching, then stuffed the broken pieces into the box.

The door to the house stood wide open. I knocked and asked in a loud voice if anyone was home. No one responded, so I let myself in.

The front room was about ten-feet across and extended back another fifteen feet or so. The floor—where visible beneath the layers of empty beer cans, dirty clothes, hamburger wrappers and assorted other garbage—was covered in ancient red-and-white-striped linoleum, worn black in spots. It peeled around the edges, and you could see underneath another, older layer of blue-and-green-plaid linoleum.

The walls were a dark-brown wood veneer paneling, with a random assortment of gouges, as if the monkey who lettered the mailbox had also decorated the interior using a claw hammer. On one side of the room was a single electrical outlet with a tangle of adaptors and extension cords plugged into it. Among other things, there was a portable GE television set stacked on top of a huge out-of-date Zenith floor model with a round porthole-type screen; a blender containing some kind of vaguely green, once-liquid-but-now-solid material with what looked like a dead mouse trapped in it; and a glowing Schlitz clock with a "Sooners" bumper sticker stuck over the part that should've said *The Beer that Made Milwaukee Famous*. On the other side of the room, a plywood closet was built-out from the wall, covered by a tattered and mildewed gold-colored plastic shower curtain instead of a door.

A framed high school picture of Noreen was being used to partially obscure one of the larger holes in the wall. The only other decoration was the cover of a program from the 1956 Texas-Oklahoma football game, scotch-taped to a door that I surmised led to another room. A decrepit box fan was jammed in the front window. It ran full blast, but even at this early hour it wasn't doing much to cool things down.

I helloed a couple more times and got no answer. I opened the door with the football program on it and walked into the next room. It was windowless and dark. I was running my hand along the wall looking for a light switch when I heard the screen door slam. I rushed back to the living room to find the shower curtain had been ripped down in haste. Someone had been hiding in the closet and was making tracks trying to get away.

Through the open front door, I saw Kevin Gunter carrying a rifle and running across the street in the direction of the Leaning Tower. I yelled and chased after him, but he had young legs and a head start. He disappeared into the building before I could make it across the street.

The Leaning Tower had a pair of doors that opened outward. They hung loose on their hinges and were held partly shut by a padlocked chain running through a pair of handles. A rattlesnake or an underfed teenage boy might fit through the narrow gap, but I met neither description. A neatly hand-lettered sign said, "NO TRESPASSING: VIOLATORS WILL BE PERSECUTED."

Close enough for me to get the gist.

I stuck my head through the opening. "Kevin, you don't want to be going in there," I yelled.

I heard him climbing steps.

"Birds are scared to land on that thing."

No answer, just more creaking steps. I reckon the damn thing hadn't been used to store wheat since Oklahoma got statehood. Even if I could get in, following him up those rotten stairs was a bad idea. I decided to rely on my powers of persuasion.

"Kevin, come on now, I just want to ask you a few questions," I shouted. "You aren't in any trouble yet, but you will be if you use that gun."

More footsteps. The wood above made small cracking sounds.

"Alright, Kevin. I'll just wait over by my car for you to come out. I'll be there when you're ready to talk."

I walked back to the Fury and leaned up against it, arms and legs crossed, trying to be casual so Kevin's mind would be eased if he was to look. I was irritated, but I didn't want Kevin to know or it might take forever to get him out. I got close enough to the open car window so I could grab my revolver from the glove compartment if I needed to. I made a good target but I didn't think Kevin would shoot at me.

I was mistaken.

I'd been standing there about a minute when I saw something move in a large opening near the top of the building. I grabbed my gun but it was too late.

I heard quick 'pop' and 'pffft' sounds and felt a sharp pain on my thigh like I'd been stung by bee. A second later it happened again, this time on my forearm. That one drew blood.

I suddenly recognized that I was in the midst of a gun battle. Fortunately, my opposite number was armed only with a BB gun. I looked up at the window and saw Kevin take aim again. I yanked open the car door and crouched behind it.

Armed retaliation was out of the question, of course. You can't use a .357 on a kid pelting you with a Daisy air rifle, even if you are an officer of the law.

"Kevin, is this about the mailbox?" I yelled. "I'm very sorry about that. I'll pay to get it fixed."

Thwack. A fourth BB struck the windshield, causing a spiderweb-shaped crack.

"C'mon now, Kevin, you cracked the window of my car. My deputy won't like that. Better you talk to me before he gets his hands on you."

Thwack. A BB hit the door I was hiding behind. The young desperado was beyond reason.

I thought to call Karen for backup, but the shame of being bested by a teenager with a Red Ryder BB gun would be hard to live down. If I timed it right, I could cross over to the other side of the road and take shelter beside the building before Kevin could pelt me with too many more rounds. That would at least draw his shots away from the Fury. God knows, Bernard would be heartbroken at the damage already done.

I took another shot to the door, then ran across the street as fast as my achy knees would carry me. Before I was halfway there, I felt a sting on the back of my neck.

The boy was a good shot.

"Goddammit, Kevin, you're gonna put someone's eye out."

I just had to say that.

Out of nowhere, a brittle, sobbing voice shouted, "I didn't kill her!"

Whatever I expected to hear, it wasn't that. "Kevin, no one is saying you did. We're just looking for folks who knew her. We want to find out who she was."

"You're lying. EJ told me last night. He said you think I did it and that you were coming to arrest me."

"Kevin, I don't know where EJ got that, but it's not true. I just want to ask you some questions. I was hoping you can help us find whoever did it."

After a lengthy pause, he said in a shaky voice, "I'll come down if you promise not to put me in jail."

"Kevin, I'm not going to put you in jail, but I'll have to talk to your daddy about this. You know where I can find him?"

"No, I ain't seen him."

"Alright, don't worry about it, we'll track him down. The hard part's gonna be explaining to Deputy Cousins how his car got its windshield broke."

"I'm sorry," he said so quiet I could barely hear.

"That's ok son, we'll sort things out. Right now, you need to come down and talk to me for a few minutes before you get off to school."

From there, I heard footsteps, then a sudden *crack*—loud, this time, followed by the sound of wood splintering and a solid thump, like someone had fallen out a plane without a parachute.

I ripped the doors off their hinges and went inside. Kevin lay there, bloody and twisted, in a pile of broken, rotten wood.

He wouldn't be going to school today.

CHAPTER TWENTY

I radioed Karen, told her what had happened, and had her call Pate's Funeral Home and Dr. Pepper.

Pate's operated Burr's only ambulance, and Dr. Pepper is our only doctor.

Dr. Donald Pepper, to be precise. His office hours are 10, two, and four. Laugh if you want. He's used to it. We all are.

Pate's jet-black Cadillac combination hearse-and-ambulance arrived the same time as Dr. Pepper's big, jet-black Coupe deVille. Bernard showed up in his truck shortly thereafter, with Karen alongside. Karen rushed over to Kevin and held his hand and told him everything was going to be ok. Bernard stood dumbstruck at the damage visited upon his beloved Fury. It was hardly noticeable to anyone but him, but he took it hard. Karen and I got out of the way as the medics began their ministrations.

After a couple of minutes. Dr. Pepper took me aside. He reckoned they were dealing with a concussion and a broken collarbone. "Perhaps some broken ribs, too," he added. "He's in pain, but he'll be fine. We should get him to Baptist Hospital in Oklahoma City, though, just to be safe. A surgeon may want to perform an exploratory in case there's internal bleeding."

The attendants placed Kevin on a stretcher. I leaned over him and told him they were going to take him to a hospital and they'd fix him right up. "Deputy Cousins is going to ride with you and make sure they treat you right."

His eyes got big. "You said he'd be mad because of what I did to his car." His voice was so hoarse I could barely understand.

"Don't worry, son. Deputy Cousins is the forgiving type."

Bernard looked at Kevin over my shoulder. "Don't worry, Kevin," he said. "There ain't nothing that can't be fixed." I know it pained him to say that.

Bernard crawled in the back of the ambulance with Kevin and the attendants. They pulled out, followed by Dr. Pepper in his Coupe de Ville.

Karen and I cleaned up as best we could. What was left of the wood from the stairs was so rotten, it crumbled in our hands. The town should've demolished that death trap a long time ago. I thought how Nate should sue but hoped he wouldn't, in case the city fathers might decide my salary is a luxury they could no longer afford.

We commiserated about Kevin on the drive back and I filled her in on the latest developments. "Let me try to understand this," she said, once I'd finished the story of my Watie Junction whorehouse adventure. "The murdered girl was a prostitute named Sheryl. We don't know her last name, or even if Sheryl is her real first name. A homely old hooker who used to work with her says Sheryl was EJ's girlfriend. EJ denies it. He says he was just paying her for sex and she wound up falling in love with him. This homely old hooker also says that Kevin—EJ's so-called friend—had a crush on Sheryl, but the feelings were not reciprocated."

I took a corner too sharp going too fast. She gasped and grabbed the dashboard to steady herself. It took her a few seconds to recover. "When you finished asking questions, the hooker offered you a freebie, which you say you declined. Do I have it right so far?"

"More or less, except you added the part about the hooker being old and homely yourself. She wasn't either old or homely. And she offered me a discount, not a freebie. Which I don't just *say* I declined. I *did* decline."

"Mm-hmm," Karen said. "I expect she offers that same deal to all law officers."

I felt guilty without exactly knowing why.

"Anyway," she continued her summary, "this morning on the way to the office, you stopped by the Gunter place, looking for Nate or Kevin. Nate wasn't home but Kevin was. Somehow the two of you got into a BB-gun shootout. Kevin fell through an upper-story floor of the Leaning Tower, but not before telling you EJ had phoned him last night and told him that he was the prime suspect in the murder." She took a deep breath. "That about the size of it? Oh, and I almost forgot. At some point, you pretty much destroyed the Gunters' mailbox."

"It wasn't really a shoot-out, since I didn't return fire, but yeh, that's it in a nutshell."

I parked in my designated spot in front of the station. The sun near blinded me and the heat made my skin tingle as I got out of the car. "By the way," I said as we made our way to the door, "I'd like to think she offered me that discount on account of I'm so handsome."

"You keep telling yourself that," Karen drawled.

The office proved at least a little cooler than the street outside. First thing I did was call the OSBI. I got Heckscher on the line. I told him Sheryl's name and what else I'd learned, thinking it would make a difference. It didn't seem to. He couldn't hardly wait for me to finish so he could tell me some news of his own.

"We've just had a break in the case," he said. "We got a call a half hour ago. A Wichita patrolman arrested a drunken Indian getting off a freight car the morning after your girl was found."

Spoken like a true paleface.

"He was carrying a small suitcase or bag of some kind," he said. "Inside was a woman's purse with a wallet and an Oklahoma driver's license in the name of one Sheryl Foster. There were also some women's clothes with streaks of blood. Hold on a second."

He held his hand over the mouthpiece. I heard muffled speech but couldn't understand what was being said. He came back on the line. "Let me give you to Ovell," he said. I heard the phone change hands.

"Chief, this is Agent Jones. Did you just tell John Joe your hooker's name was Sheryl?"

I replied in the affirmative.

"Well, the birth date on this Sheryl Foster's driver's license is 1947, which makes her about the same age as your gal. Says she's a negro. If it's the same girl, I'd say we got our murderer. We're going up later today to talk to the Indian. With any luck, we'll get extradition and bring him back, toot sweet."

For some reason I felt numb, like I'd been given an all-over shot of Novocain. I guess I didn't realize how much I'd invested in finding the girl's killer myself.

"You find out where she lived?" I asked. Of course they did, if they had her driver's license. But it was all I could think of to say.

"On the east side, here in the city. We called and got hold of a woman who I reckon is her mother. We're sending a couple of officers right now to talk to her. Hopefully she'll be able to identify the body."

Hopefully for her sake she won't, I thought. "Did he have the murder weapon on him?" I asked.

"No, he must've gotten rid of it at some point."

Why would he have kept her clothes but discarded the weapon? Something about this felt wrong, even if I couldn't exactly put my finger on what it was.

I started thinking out loud, trying to sort it out in my mind.

"So, if he killed her on the train and dumped her where we found her, how'd she board the train in the first place? We know it doesn't stop anywhere near Watie Junction, and that's where she was last spotted. We also know she wasn't killed at the scene, since there was hardly any blood."

"Those are some good questions, Chief, but I'm sure if we set our minds to it we'll be able to match the facts to the evidence."

I wasn't sure what he meant by that, but whatever it was, it didn't sound good. "Listen, Agent Jones, I don't want to tell you boys how to do your business, but it might be worth your while to follow up with some of the locals I've talked to."

"Let's see where this Indian takes us," he replied generously. "If it turns out he's not the killer, we'll look somewhere else."

Judging by his tone, I'd say he'd just about shut the door on that possibility.

I wanted to keep on good terms with Jones, so I fought to hide my lack of regard for their investigation while still pressing my point. "I appreciate the work you've put in on this, Ovell, but I'm beginning to think there might be some viable suspects here in Burr." I told him in brief what I'd described to Heckscher, including my just-concluded fracas with Kevin and his unprovoked denial of guilt. "I just think it's a little early to be counting our chickens," I concluded.

"I understand your concerns," he said between lung-racking coughing jags, "but we feel pretty strongly that this is the guy. You can continue to look into things on that end, though, if you want, at least until we charge this fella."

In other words, we hicks could play in the sandbox while the big boys did the real work.

"We're going up to Wichita right now," he said. "We'll give you a call and let you know where we stand once we get back."

I asked for and he gave me the girl's address. We said our goodbyes.

So that's it, I thought. Finished before we even got started.

·   ·   ·   ·   ·

The more I considered it, the less sense it made.

I sat down in my usual spot on the edge of Karen's desk and related my conversation with Agents Jones and Heckscher, careful to include the part about the latter being a self-important jackass.

"That's good, right?" she said. "Not the part about him being a self-important jackass, but the rest of it."

"It's good if they got the right man," I said, "but too much doesn't fit. I mean, where was she killed? We know it wasn't where we found her. How did she get to where she was? I don't see any way she could've gotten on that train, considering when and where she was last seen."

"If this fella didn't do it, how'd he get her stuff?"

"That's a good question and I'll be darned if I know. Maybe he did it and I'm not smart enough to figure out how."

"You will," she said with more confidence than I inspired in myself.

I went back to my office and picked up the piece of paper where I'd written Sheryl's address. I recognized the street. "I have her mama's address," I said. "I could go talk to her, see what she can tell us."

"I guess you don't need me to tell you to be gentle," Karen said.

"Probably not, but I can bear hearing it."

I asked her to check the schedules to establish if it was possible for Sheryl and her killer to have caught a north-bound train south of where we found her, given the time and distances involved. I then asked who we had coming in. She said Kenny would be in shortly and Jeff was scheduled for that afternoon. I should have plenty of time to drive to Oklahoma City and back.

"I'd also appreciate if you do what you can to track down Nate Gunter while I'm gone," I said. "I know he did some work for Bill McKibben at the gravel pit awhile back. You might want to start there." Nate needed to know what had happened to his son.

I also asked her to attempt to contact the former Mrs. Gunter, who—last I heard—had moved to Las Vegas. "I don't remember her first name, unfortunately," I said.

"I do," said Karen. "It's Betty. Her maiden name was Thornhill, but who knows what she's calling herself now. Probably not Mrs. Gunter."

"I trust your investigative skills."

She scribbled something down on a pad of paper. "What about his grandma?" she asked.

I'd forgotten about Noreen. "That's right, she's still living in that old house. Give her a call. It's not even ten o'clock. Maybe she won't have crawled too deep into the bottle. Tell her if she needs a ride into the city she can come with me."

I went back to my office and sat down, only to pop right back up. "You know what? We need to have someone talk to the baseball coach and confirm EJ's alibi."

She scribbled some more on her pad. "I think Jeff can handle that," she said.

The phone rang. Karen picked up. It was Cousins. They'd arrived at Baptist Hospital and Kevin was about to undergo exploratory surgery to see if there were any internal bleeding. The doctor didn't think there was but wanted to make sure. I told Bernard it was likely he'd have to stay with Kevin overnight. I said I'd bring him a change of clothes and see him in a couple of hours.

Yet another thing came to mind. "I know I'm putting a lot on your plate, Red," I said, "but I'd be much obliged if you could have the boys poke around and try to find out who stole Daffodil. I'm reasonably sure that Indian they found up in Wichita isn't responsible for that."

"I'll do it, if the *next* thing you put on my plate is a sirloin steak. You owe me a nice dinner, anyway."

"Sounds like a deal." I winked and gave her my best Clark Gable grin.

She snorted. "Don't try to charm me, drugstore cowboy."

I went back to my office and shut the door. My mind fixated on the fifth of Old Grand-Dad in my desk drawer. I know having a drink so early in the day is a bad idea. That doesn't mean I can't want one.

I distracted myself by attending to some paperwork Karen had left for me. On top was a questionnaire about local police methods sent out by the governor 's office. I fill out the same damn form every year and typically give nonsense answers to see if anybody will notice. They never do. Under "Describe all law enforcement functions under which your office has primary responsibility," I wrote: "Repel attacks by flying monkeys." I felt regretful having written it, as I reckon flying monkeys are more likely to be looking for bananas than people. Maybe I will have that drink, after all, I decided.

CHAPTER TWENTY-ONE

I called the Plymouth dealership in Temple City to check on a replacement windshield for the Fury. They didn't have one in stock and would have to order it. I'd need to drive it as it was for a few days, crack and all.

I was still a little concerned about my father. He'd been his usual contrary self the other day, but digging up his yard like that was strange. The fact he didn't give me a real reason bothered me, even though he never was much for explaining things. I thought he might get some satisfaction from how his brothel suggestion panned out, however, so I drove over to pay a visit.

The hole was wider and deeper than before. The pile of dirt next to it was at least four-feet-high. He'd left his front door wide open, so I announced myself and walked back to the kitchen. Dad stood at the sink, washing the breakfast dishes.

We exchanged our usual semi-civil greetings. I asked what he hoped to find in the front yard. He barked that it was none of my business, which was a good sign.

"I thought you'd like to know, your idea about the whorehouse was a good one," I said. I described Sheryl's connection to EJ Bixby and told how the OSBI had caught an Indian fella in Wichita with her purse. "They think they've cracked the case."

"Cracked their heads is more like it," Dad said. He finished the dishes and turned to me. His jowls quivered almost imperceptibly — a sure sign he was being more than just crotchety. "That don't make a bit of sense. There's no way that girl could've been on that train. The railroad doesn't go through Watie Junction. The closest place she could've gotten on before Burr is in Texas. That don't make no goddam sense at all."

I said I thought it unlikely, as well, and proposed they were more easily sold on their solution than they should be.

He slapped an open palm on the counter with a thwack. "Damn right," he said. "She ain't a person to them. She's just another nigger."

• • • • •

The word exploded like an atom bomb. Dad had never used it in my presence. In fact, I've seen him confront other people who use it. He's no radical, but over the years he's often spoken in defense of colored folks and Indians.

One time when I was little, some men got dressed-up in their KKK outfits and marched in the Armistice Day parade. My dad walked up to the group's leader—the grand dragon or whatever they call the idiot wearing the fanciest robe—in the middle of the street and pulled off his mask. Told him he ought to be ashamed of himself. Afterwards, I asked him why he did it. He said it was because those men were cowards, and he hates cowards. I didn't understand it at the time. I thought maybe they'd just gotten their parades mixed-up, thinking it was Halloween instead of Armistice Day.

That's not to say he always acted in such an upright manner.

Years later, a group of white men—doubtless many of the same yahoos who marched in that parade—set fire to the home of Burr's last remaining negro family. At one time, Burr had a sizable population of negroes, but the peckerwoods did their best to run them off and mostly succeeded. Clarence Younger and his brood were the final holdouts. A few bigots couldn't wait for them to leave on their own and figured to give them a nudge by burning down their house, although, truth be told, it was little more than a tar-paper shack. No one was physically harmed, although I reckon the Younger children had nightmares for quite some time.

Mr. Younger was surely aware my father often took the side of the negroes. He drove up to our home the day after his own burned down, his old Model T bucking and clattering like a barrel of bolts rolling down a hill. His eldest son Gabriel sat in the passenger seat. Gabe and I used to go fishing. I waved from the doorway. Gabe waved back.

Dad told me to go in the other room while he and Clarence talked. I hid around a corner and listened. Clarence explained what had happened, but my father already knew. Mr. Younger asked if his family could stay in an outbuilding on our farm. He said he'd be happy to pay. Dad hemmed and hawed and finally made up some excuse to say no.

After the Youngers left, Dad told me not to tell mama they'd been there. That night at dinner, she talked about the burning of the Younger place and how it was a terrible thing. Dad nodded but didn't say much. I felt like I was lying to her by not telling about Mr. Younger's visit, but I wasn't about to go against my father. I was surprised and disappointed by the whole episode. I had an image of my dad as someone who stood up to bullies. I never understood why he refused to help Mr. Younger. It affected me for a long time afterward. Maybe it still does.

I never saw the Youngers again.

·   ·   ·   ·   ·

This time, dad seemed to take the whole situation personally, like Sheryl Foster was a member of the family and not someone he'd never so much as laid eyes on. He was at least partly right about the OSBI not pursuing the case as hard as they should. I'd thought the same thing from the beginning, Still, I gave in to my natural urge to argue over every little thing.

"Dad, I met those boys from the OSBI who're working this," I said. "One of them's prejudiced, but the one in charge seems to be ok.

Their problem is they don't have the time or help to do a thorough job."

"Bullshit," he said, then withdrew into himself. He doesn't like to show his feelings. Not even to his son. Especially not his son.

I excused myself to use the toilet, thinking it might give us both time to cool down. Generally, I try to keep things close to the vest unless I'm sure the person I'm with shares my opinion. More often than not, Dad and I feel the same way about things, but we're too stubborn to admit it and we end up fighting. God knows why.

He'd left the kitchen by the time I returned. I heard a small engine start up outside. I walked out through the side door and saw him on his lawnmower, a signal our conversation was over. He didn't see me wave goodbye, or at least pretended not to.

CHAPTER TWENTY-TWO

As I've made clear, my experience solving murders is limited, but I have studied the subject pretty extensively, and if I've learned anything, it's when a woman gets murdered, the perpetrator is usually a husband or boyfriend. So, when Jim Bob Hall let slip that EJ Bixby had been seeing a girl who turned out to be our victim, my mind trained itself on young Edgar, Jr. like a laser beam.

But EJ had an alibi, and the Wichita police had apprehended a man carrying a bag full of incriminating evidence. Even a rookie murder investigator like myself could see there wasn't much left to do.

Still, there were too many questions for my mind to rest easy.

For instance, what to make of that World's Fair coin? I know that coin did not throw itself on those train tracks, just as sure as I know Bernard Cousins's middle name is Rubottom. Someone—maybe the person who killed Sheryl Foster—dropped it or otherwise lost or discarded the dang thing.

I couldn't imagine anybody from Burr (or, for that matter, the whole of Tilghman County) visiting New York. They'd be as likely to take a trip to Mars. The fact remained, however: the coin came from somewhere. Finding out where might help me find out who. Finding out who might help me sleep sounder.

About all I know about the fair is that it opened a year ago in a part of the Borough of Queens called Flushing Meadows (which conjures some strange pictures in my mind). I recall seeing a report on a TV news program about the Oklahoma exhibit around the time it started. I don't believe I'd heard or read a single word about it since. I aimed to change that.

The Burr library owes its existence to Annabelle Bixby, Deke Bixby's wife. Annabelle is like Denny, in that she could have done much better job finding a man if she put some effort into it, or at least moved someplace with a wider selection. Unlike her piss-poor excuse for a husband, Annabelle's a genuinely nice person who I believe must lay awake nights thinking of ways to improve our town. Fortunately for bookworms like myself, the Burr Public Library is her pet project. She sponsored and campaigned for the bond issue that built it, and hosts twice-yearly all-you-can-eat pancake breakfasts and spaghetti dinners to raise the money necessary to stock it with books.

The librarian is a young woman by the name of Kate Hennessey. Kate's the picture of what you'd expect a small-town librarian to be: near-sighted, shy, and quiet as a mouse with laryngitis. Get her going on the latest Agatha Christie or Ross MacDonald whodunnit, however, and Kate lights-up from the inside. She'll talk your ear off about books if you let her.

The library is located on Main Street in a red brick building a few doors down and across from the police station. I drove there straight from my father's house.

Kate and I typically swap opinions about what we're reading, but today my mind was otherwise occupied. I barged in and found her sitting behind the check-out desk drinking a cup of something steaming hot and reading a book called *The Killer Inside Me*. I'd been meaning to read it myself and another day I might have said so. Today I got down to brass tacks.

"What can tell me about the New York World's Fair?"

If my abruptness caught her off-guard, she didn't show it.

"1939, or the one going on now?"

"This one. Specifically, I'd like to know about the State of Oklahoma exhibit."

She took a sip of coffee and folded her arms across her chest.

"Hmmm," she said. "I doubt we have much, to be honest. It's kind of old news by now."

"I'll take whatever you got."

She chewed on her thumbnail and thought for a second. She said, "I'll be right back," then got up from her chair and disappeared into her inner sanctum. I heard boxes being moved and paper being rustled. After a couple of minutes, she re-emerged with some reading material. "Would this help?" she asked.

She handed me a copy of a magazine called *Oklahoma Spotlight*. On the cover was a picture of a dignified-to-the-point-of-being-pissed-off looking Indian in full headdress and regalia. The caption read, "World's Fair Special."

"It might," I said. I took it to a table in the back.

Oklahoma Spotlight is a harmless piece of Okie propaganda published a few times a year by the state tourism board. It's the last place I'd go for hard news, but I'll occasionally read it in the beauty salon while I'm waiting to get my hair cut. Sometimes I even learn something.

Calling it a "World's Fair Special" was an egregious act of false advertising. Information about Oklahoma's exhibit comprised a short blurb in the table of contents about the state's official World's Fair emblem, and a few paragraphs that explained how Oklahoma was such a great place, Jesus would've lived here if his daddy had let him. None of this did me a bit of good. However, on the back page was a list of Oklahomans involved with the fair, which I reckoned might bear some looking into.

I asked Kate if I could borrow the magazine and she said that would be fine. I drove back to the station … meaning, I moved the Fury from one side of the street to the other. I could've left it where it was, but I'm kind of partial to my "Reserved for Chief Hardy" parking spot.

·   ·   ·   ·   ·

I found Karen smoking and reading a paperback and listening to

Buck Owens sing about how some folks with more money than sense were going to put him in the movies and make him a big star. I sang along until Karen shut me up.

"I'd have y'all arrested for disturbing the peace if the police around here weren't so unreliable," she said without looking up from her book.

"You're lucky I'm such an understanding boss."

"Like you'd ever fire me. I run this place and you know it."

"I'd agree with you if I wasn't afraid it'd give you a bigger head than you already got."

She stubbed out her cigarette in the green-plaid beanbag ashtray on her desk and laid down her book. "I tried but could not find Nate Gunter," she said. "Bill McKibben says he's been doing some work for him, but he hasn't shown up since Friday. As far as I can tell, nobody in town has seen him since then."

Friday was the night Sheryl Foster was killed.

The only thing connecting Sheryl to Nate was Kevin, but him disappearing around the time she was killed and the boy's BB-gun assault and strange non-confession made my antennas twitch.

"Keep trying," I said. "What about Noreen?"

"Noreen was already three sheets to the wind when I called. She said she can't leave the house because of her 'lady problem,' which could mean a bunch of different things, but I suspect in this case means she's gotten so fat she can't fit through the door of her house." Karen's a sweetheart, but she can be catty at times.

"About what I expected. Any news on Betty Gunter, or Thornhill, or whatever she's calling herself these days?"

"You're gonna want to give me a raise after this," she grinned and wriggled her shoulders. "I tracked Betty Gunter to a place in California called Nightbird Ranch."

"What, pray tell, is Nightbird Ranch?"

"Well sir, I'm glad you asked. Nightbird Ranch is what folks out there call a 'commune.' From what I can tell, it's a group of people who live together but don't believe in personal property. They roam the countryside, camping where they can get permission or squatting if they can't. Sooner or later they get kicked off whatever land they're on and go somewhere else. When last seen, they were hunkered down in Sonoma County, which as I understand it, is north of San Francisco."

"I don't even want to know how you discovered that," I chuckled.

"The heck you don't. It was a lot of work and I'm going to make you listen." She leaned forward with her elbows on the desk and rested her chin in her hands. "Betty had been living in Las Vegas under her maiden name of Thornhill, which was in the phone book, thank you Jesus." She said it conspiratorial-like, which was kind of sexy, to tell the truth.

"I called the number. Betty wasn't there but her ex-roommate was. She was a real jabber jaws. She said Betty used to be a cocktail waitress at a casino until one day she read about this Nightbird Ranch in a magazine. Betty was fed up with serving drinks and thought this 'commune' lifestyle thing sounded good, so she gave away her stuff and moved to California looking to track them down. Apparently, she found 'em, because a couple of weeks later she calls her roommate. Says she's changed her name to Moon Spray and she's 'resigned from civilization.' Those were her exact words." I thought I sensed a tiny bit of envy in Karen's tone. "Of course, this has been a while ago," she added. "The roommate says this Nightbird crew gets kicked out of everywhere they go, so it's anybody's guess if she's still in that Sonoma place. I wouldn't expect to find her any time soon."

I wouldn't necessarily blame Karen for feeling envious. The idea of "resigning from civilization" had some redeeming value. However, my main concern was how I might eventually have to tell Nate his ex-wife's name was now "Moon Spray."

"That's some fine detective work." I said—a little patronizingly, so she wouldn't think I was excessively dazzled. I perused my mental checklist and came upon an item regarding Daffodil Bixby. "Speaking of cockamamie stories, did Jeff talk to the baseball coach about EJ's alibi?"

"He did. He says it checks out."

"I guess that's good," I said, although part of me would've loved to pin Sheryl Foster's murder on EJ.

I walked back into my office, leaving the door slightly ajar in a way we both understand is an invitation for Karen to join me. She did, carrying a pencil and pad of paper, just in case. She placed the pencil behind her right ear and sat in a chair across from my desk.

I pulled out my enamel cup and bottle of bourbon. I noticed Karen hadn't refilled it since the last time.

"What's this?" I said, holding it up for her inspection. For a few seconds, all I heard was the hum of the electric clock on my desk.

"Looks like an almost empty bottle of Old Grand-Dad."

"I can see that. The question is: why's it almost empty?"

"Because you been drinking it, I suppose," she said, looking me square in the eye.

I was being sent a message.

"Alright. I get it," I said at last.

"I just figure you been drinking a little overly much," she said, sounding a little apologetic. "Maybe it's time I quit helping you."

She was right, but it annoyed me all the same. I poured the last of the bourbon into the cup and swallowed half of it in one gulp. I leaned back against the wall, lifting the chair's front legs off the floor. The booze warmed my insides and loosened-up my thoughts, which is the best reason I can think of to not stop drinking.

She gave me a vaguely disapproving look and crossed her legs. I noticed she was wearing a new pair of Levis. My mind wandered to the fact she fills them out better than the average woman her age has any right to expect. I'm not saying 34 is old, but Karen's figure puts most college girls to shame.

Harboring such unprofessional feelings is a sign that the alcohol is starting to do its job.

"Alright," I said. "fair enough."

I couldn't remember why I'd brought her back to my office. I knew it wasn't to admire her looks, though that wasn't the worst reason. Damn, what was it? "Oh, that's right," I said mostly to myself. "Red, I am in need of your woman's intuition."

She snorted. "Don't talk to me about women's intuition."

"What's the matter with women's intuition?"

"Women's intuition is an excuse a man uses when a woman figures out something he can't," she scoffed. "It can't be because she's as smart as he is. Or smarter."

I don't know many men one-tenth as smart as Karen Dean, and I'll testify to that in court.

"Nah," she continued sarcastically, "it has to be because she was some mysterious power emanating from her lady parts."

"I never thought of it that way," I said, eager to avoid her wrath which can be considerable. "Maybe you're right."

"No 'maybe' about it," she grumbled.

"I should have said, 'I am in need of your intelligence and insight.'"

"That's better. What's on your mind?"

I told her about my trip to the library and showed her the *Oklahoma Spotlight* with the Indian chief on the cover. She thumbed through it.

"You're thinking about that coin and where it came from," she said after a spell.

"I am."

"First thing I thought was that it belonged to someone who went to the World's Fair or someone who knows someone who went."

"Or someone who works for or at the World's Fair," I said. "Read the article. It's short."

As she read, I heard the outer door open from the street. Kenny stuck his head in my office, reporting for his shift. I asked him to man the phone for a minute until Karen and I were done.

She set the magazine down on my desk. "Honestly, hon, I don't see anything here that helps us."

I picked it up and turned to the list of names of people involved with the Oklahoma exhibit. "I admit, it's a needle in a haystack, but I expect any of those folks would have access to one of those coins."

"They're likely spread out all over the state."

"Which is why I'd like you to narrow it down to citizens of Tilghman County," I said. "That makes it more like finding a baseball bat in a haystack."

If she was amused by my clever wordplay, she didn't show it. "I guess I can do that soon as you're out of my hair," she said with a distinct lack of enthusiasm. It was hard to blame her. Talking on the phone with a bunch of self-important county politicians is way down at the bottom of any sane person's list of fun things to do. "I don't see how that requires any special intelligence and insight," she said. "Or women's intuition, if there was such a thing."

"You're right, it doesn't," I said. "Really, I just wanted to hear what you think about this whole mess. If you suspect anyone in particular."

She slid the pencil back behind her ear and tossed the pad on my desk. "It might just be the person they caught. He did have her stuff."

"He did. It could be him," I said. "But let's think who it would be if it wasn't him."

She pursed her lips, closed her eyes, then opened them again. "Well, the obvious choice is EJ, but he's got an alibi."

"Which I need to check out myself, since I don't trust Jeff as far as I can throw him. Anyway, go on. If it isn't the Indian fella, and it can't be EJ, then who?"

Her eyes and darted around in exasperation like she was trying to follow the movements of a mosquito. "It could've been anyone, Emmett. It doesn't have to be someone we know. In fact, it's more than likely that it was some person we don't know and never will."

That was probably true, which discouraged me right down to my bones, the more I thought about it.

"When you put it that way, I guess we better hope it was that Indian, then," I said.

I might be beat but I wasn't licked yet. I sure as hell wasn't going to fold my tent, at least not before I spoke with Sheryl's mother. I needed to be on my way to the city if I was going to give myself time to talk to her and check on Kevin. I called in Kenny and gave him a list of things that needed to be done, some related to the murder, some not. I told him to bear down on finding our pig-napper.

Goddammit, we were going to solve at least one of the crimes on our plate or die trying.

CHAPTER TWENTY-THREE

Kevin didn't have any family members there to hold his hand while he was hospitalized. His mother was off gallivanting in California and his father had disappeared into thin air. I thought having Bernard stay with him overnight was the Christian thing to do. I'm not a Christian, but Bernard is.

I stopped by Bernard's house to pick him up a change of clothes to take to the city. I have a key, not that it matters. He always leaves it unlocked. He's unusually trusting for a cop. The only clean clothes I could find was a spare uniform. Other than socks and underwear, there were no civvies in his closet or dresser drawers. Maybe he dropped them off at the laundromat. Maybe he doesn't own any. I can't say I'd be surprised if that were the case, although I wouldn't consider it healthy.

There are limits to how devoted a person should be to his job.

I took the uniform, some socks and boxer shorts, and hit the road. After fifteen minutes of driving, I got a cramp in my neck from having to contort myself to see around crack in the windshield left by the BB gun. It almost would've been better if he'd used a real gun and shot out the whole goddam windshield. At least that way I could see where I was going.

Folks think that since we can drive as fast as we want, run stoplights, eat doughnuts and drink beer behind the wheel, driving a police car must be a dance in the flower patch. They are mistaken. For one thing, people slow down ten miles-per-hour below the speed limit when they see you coming up behind them, meaning you have to pass them if you want to make good time. The longer I follow a fella, the pokier he gets, sometimes to the point that it feels like we're going in reverse. You can hit your lights and get them to pull over, but I don't like doing that. Today I decided it was necessary if I wanted to reach my destination before I reached retirement age. I expect I made a few folks crap their pants thinking I was about to write them a ticket, but I got to the city with time to spare.

My first stop was the East Side address the OSBI got from Sheryl Foster's driver's license.

Thanks to Jim Crow laws dating to Alfalfa Bill Murray's governorship, the East Side has long been Oklahoma City's semi-official colored neighborhood. I've been going there since high school. Marceline Hardy took particular pleasure in flaunting race laws. She called them "ignorant," and I reckon they are. Once I turned 16, she started taking me on rounds of the area's jazz clubs. I looked a lot older than I was, so I had no trouble. Almost always, we were the only white faces in the house. The colored folks tended to be friendly to us, or at least polite.

I remember one time we went to this place—Slaughter's Hall, I believe it was—to hear the great tenor saxophonist, Illinois Jacquet. On this occasion, there was another white person present, a young saxophonist about my age. He asked to sit-in with the band. I envied his courage and thought he did ok, at least until Mr. Jacquet had his turn. By the time Illinois finished, the boy was looking for a hole to crawl in. At the end of the song, Illinois pounded his chest and yelled "Me Tarzan!" The crowd howled. Even the kid had to laugh. Afterwards, mama and I went up to meet Mr. Jacquet. She told him I was a saxophone player, too, and that one of these days I'd be up there, just like that young man. "That boy did all right," he chuckled. "Showed me something." We talked a little bit. He told me to bring my horn next time. I said I would, but never did.

The East Side is different now. Jazz clubs are fewer. Businesses have closed or moved elsewhere. The negro population has spread out to other parts of the city.

The Foster place was one of the more well-kept buildings on its street—a small single-story, asphalt-shingled house a couple blocks away from what had once been the neighborhood's main drag. On the porch next door, three elderly colored gentlemen sat around shooting the breeze. They stopped laughing when I drove up and regarded me with suspicion as I got out of the Fury. I stood out like a sore thumb, with my uniform and general caucasian-ness. I'm dark complexioned enough to be confused for an Indian, but not enough to pass as a negro.

"How are y'all?" I said. "Hot one, ain't it?"

"It sure is," one of them replied. The youngest couldn't have been a day younger than 75 and they dressed their age. Each wore the same basic old-man uniform: a beat-up old fedora of felt or straw; a short-sleeved dress shirt with a white undershirt visible underneath; a pair of shiny, worn-out dress pants that must have been washed a few hundred times, and loafers or house slippers without socks. I judged the one who spoke-up to be the oldest, based mainly on the whiteness of his whiskers.

"You a long ways from home, aren't you, sheriff?" he said. "You lost?"

"No sir, I'm not lost, and I'm not a sheriff. Just regular police. You're right, though. I am a long way from home."

I climbed the steps to the Foster's porch. "Don't let me interrupt y'all," I said to the old men.

"Oh, we won't, we won't," one said, and they all laughed.

I contemplated my plan of action. Heckscher had told me they sent police out to break the news to Sheryl's mother. Still, it was possible they hadn't been there yet. I didn't want to be the one, but I had to be ready just in case. I steeled myself and rang the doorbell. The door opened a crack. A small child peeked out. He didn't say a word.

"Hello, son," I said. "Is your mama home?"

"My mama don't live here," he said.

"Oh. Well, is Mrs. Foster home?"

The child shut the door and a few seconds later, a slim, light-skinned young negro woman appeared. She'd obviously been crying. "I'm Alice Foster," she said. "How can I help you?"

Her voice shook and her eyes were red-rimmed. It was clear I wouldn't be the one to break the news.

She wore white, flat-soled canvas shoes and a light-blue uniform of the type worn by nurses and waitresses. Her first name was sewn over one breast in cursive writing and her hair was pulled back and stuffed into a hair net, so I was betting she was the former. She wore pink lipstick but no other makeup. She couldn't have been older than 25, obviously too young to be Sheryl's mother.

I introduced myself and explained my visit. She nodded sadly and led me into the living room. She offered me a chair and sat on a couch catty-corner from me.

"Two policemen came by this morning," she said. "They told me what happened. They asked me to identify her body. It was her." She dabbed her eyes with a lace handkerchief. "I just got back from the morgue a few minutes ago."

I expressed my condolences. I said I needed to ask her some questions and that I'd try not to take up too much of her time.

"You ask all the questions you want," she said quietly. "I have a little while before I have to go to work. I can talk for a while."

I was at a loss for a graceful opening. "You have a lovely home," was the best I could do.

"Thank you. Sheryl and I grew up in this house." She blew her nose lightly. "You'll have to excuse me," she said. Her voice shook. "I'm not at my best." Fresh tears welled in the corners of her eyes.

I discreetly inspected the living room. It was small and sparsely furnished, but neat as a pin. The couch and easy chair were a bland shade of green. In front of them was a light-brown wooden coffee table, with matching end tables. Framed photographs, presumably of family members, hung on the walls. A sandy-haired, blue-eyed Jesus occupied place of honor over the fireplace. Karen Dean has the same print hanging in her dining room. One time I expressed the opinion he resembled one of those long-haired marijuana-smoking beatniks you see in Life magazine. Karen didn't think that was funny.

The little boy peeked at me from behind the sofa. He made a funny face. I smiled. He giggled and crawled over to where Alice sat.

I told her what I knew about the death of her sister, including the part about me finding her body. I explained I was conducting my own investigation independent of the OSBI.

"I'd been led to believe you were Sheryl's mother," I said. "Obviously, that's incorrect."

"I'm her older sister. Our mother died a couple of years ago. My father's dead, also. He died in Korea during the war, when Sheryl was a baby. He never even met her." Apparently, the story Yvette told about Sheryl's father forcing himself on her was untrue, unless there was a stepfather involved. I asked Alice if there was. She shook her head.

Her silence was drenched with sorrow. Looking for something to say, I gestured toward the boy. "That's a handsome young man. Yours?"

"No, he's the neighbor's child. I watch him until his sister gets out of school." She wiped her nose daintily. "I had to take him with me to see my sister. A police lady watched him while I—" She inhaled deeply and exhaled in hitches and pauses. "She should be here to pick him up soon."

She stood uneasily. "Let's go get you a snack, Raymond. Excuse me for a moment." She led the boy by the shoulders into the kitchen. I heard dishes clatter and recognized the sound of milk being poured into a glass. She told the boy to stay put while she talked to me. From the other room, she asked if I'd care for something to drink. I declined and she returned to the living room.

I realized no matter how I phrased my next bit of news, it would inflict additional pain on a woman who surely couldn't bear much more. But it had to be said. "Miss Foster, I hate to have to tell you this, but it's necessary if we're going to find out who did this. Do you understand?" She nodded. I took a deep breath. "We've determined Sheryl was working as a prostitute out of a house trailer near Watie Junction in Tilghman County. Were you aware of this?"

Surprisingly, she didn't flinch. "Sheryl always had money," Alice said. "I didn't know what she was doing for it, but I suspected it was something like that. She never told me anything." Her eyes were drawn to the sound made by tree branches scratching against a window. As faint as it was, it seemed indecently loud, given the circumstances. "I hardly ever saw her," she continued. "Sheryl hasn't been staying here much, and when she did, she slept all day. I work nights at a pancake house over near the state capitol. We don't spend much time together."

"When was the last time?"

"Friday morning. She'd been gone for several days. She says she rents an apartment in Nichols Hills." Nichols Hills is a rich white community, surrounded by Oklahoma City on three sides, but not officially part of it. All the rich oilmen live there. Alice gave an unamused chuckle. "I know it's a lie, but that's just Sheryl's way. She lies to make her life seem better than it is. Or was." Alice looked down at her lap and smoothed an invisible wrinkle in her dress. "She might've fooled herself, but she didn't fool me."

"What time was it?"

"I heard her come in, so it must've been near dawn. I checked on her when I got up, around 7:00. She was asleep. She stayed in bed all day. Didn't get up until just before I left for work around 3:30."

"Did you talk to her before you left?"

"Not that I recall. We passed each other in the hall as I was going out. I was running late because the boy's sister was late picking him up. Maybe it was closer to three-forty-five."

"Did she act normal?" I asked. "Did you notice anything different about her behavior?"

"I don't think so, but we didn't speak. I barely even saw her, I was in such a hurry."

"Did Sheryl have a boyfriend?"

"She used to say she was seeing a rich white boy and that he was crazy about her and wanted to marry her. I didn't believe it. She lived in a fantasy world. Always has. Our mama spoiled her rotten, her being the youngest. She used to talk about how she was going to—"

Her voice cracked. She covered her face with her hands. "Sheryl would talk about a lot of crazy things that were never going to happen."

After a respectful silence, I asked if Sheryl had ever mentioned the boyfriend's name.

"She called him Eddie. She never said his last name."

"Did she say anything else about him? Where he lived? What he looked like? How old?"

"One thing she was always talking about was his fancy car. Sheryl said it was same as the one on that television show about two boys driving across the country."

"Route 66?" I said.

"Yes, that's the one," she said.

The car on Route 66 is a Corvette. EJ Bixby drives one, too.

"I don't know if this matters to you," I said, "but Sheryl really was seeing a rich young white boy. He drives a car like that." I did not disclose the particulars of their relationship.

Alice's brow furrowed. "He didn't have anything to do with her getting killed, though, did he?" she asked. "The policeman who was here before said they caught an Indian up in Wichita who had her purse and her clothes, and that they were all bloody. They said it looks like he was the one who did it."

"Maybe he is. We don't know yet, for sure. The OSBI have their theories and I have mine."

Alice sat back and almost disappeared into the cushions of the chair, mournful and defeated. "It doesn't matter. Knowing who did it won't bring her back."

There wasn't much I could say to that.

"I know this may sound like a strange question," I said, "but did Sheryl ever go to the World's Fair in New York?"

Alice almost laughed through her tears. "I don't know every place that girl was off to, but I do know she never went to New York. She used to talk about it because it was a dream of hers, but she never did it." She wiped her eyes. "Now she never will."

I pulled out a photo of the coin. "The reason I ask is because we found this near where Sheryl was found."

She looked at it for several seconds. "I never saw anything like that."

The doorbell rang. "That's the boy's sister," she said, smoothing her hair and wiping away tears as she got up from the couch.

"Miss Foster, did Sheryl have her own room?" I asked.

"Yes, she did."

"Would you mind if I take a look?"

"No, you go right ahead," she said. "It's down the hall to your right." She moved to answer the door and I stepped into the hallway.

Sheryl's room was tiny, about the size of a walk-in closet. There was a single twin bed with a flowered spread. A pink bureau and yellow nightstand competed for the remaining space. The sliver of floor was covered in blue-and-white-checked linoleum. The air smelled like candy. Pictures of music stars and movie actors and actresses cut out of magazines were taped to the walls. Some were negroes, some were white. One of the colored girls I'd seen on Ed Sullivan, but I couldn't remember her name.

I went through her drawers, not knowing what I was looking for. There were panties and socks and blouses and skirts. A few dresses hung on a rod. Nothing you'd expect a prostitute to wear. A pair of red high heels on the floor was the only hint the room had been occupied by anyone other than a typical high school girl.

On a wooden bookshelf nailed to the wall above her bed was a row of more than a dozen books with yellow spines. I immediately knew what they were. It seemed Sheryl Foster and I had Nancy Drew in common. I read all the Nancy Drew books when I was a kid. Mama never understood why I didn't prefer the Hardy Boys, especially since we had the same last name. I reckon it was because I had a crush on the idea of someone like Nancy. There aren't many girls like her in Burr, Oklahoma.

I cringed a little when I saw she also had a copy of *The Adventures of Huckleberry Finn*. I loved it, but I reckon I might feel different if I was colored. On the nightstand was an issue of *Ebony* magazine with a photograph of the negro preacher Martin Luther King, walking hand-in-hand and arm-in-arm with a group of people, both white and colored. The caption said, "50,000 March On Montgomery." The bigots around here hate Mr. King, although I know some white folks who sympathize with his cause. Not many, but a few. My dad, for one. And me.

I picked up the magazine and leafed through it, wondering what Dr. King and Sheryl and Alice thought about Huckleberry Finn. I wondered what they thought about Huck's pal, Jim.

When I returned, the boy was gone and Alice stood by herself in the middle of the living room, clutching a small white handbag.

"I'm sorry but I should be going," she said.

"Of course. Thank you for speaking to me. I might have some more questions later."

"That's fine," she said, and we walked over to the door.

"Sheryl must've liked Nancy Drew," I said.

Alice gave me a sorrowful smile. "Oh yes. That's how she learned to read. I read the first one to her over and over until she memorized every word. She read every book in the series several times. Nancy was her hero."

On the wall next to the door was a color photo of a beautiful young girl with a playful smile, a slight space between her teeth, and eyes the color of a 7-Up bottle. She sat looking playfully at the camera, chin resting on cupped palms. She wore a silver charm bracelet. One charm had a girl on a horse; another was a little telephone dial with a red stone set in the center; another had a cheerleader's megaphone with the initials "S.F." engraved on it.

"Is that Sheryl?" I said. She was clearly younger in the photo, but I recognized her immediately.

"Yes, it is," Alice said. "She hated that picture because she was smiling with her mouth open. She was self-conscious about that little gap in her teeth."

"She was a cheerleader?"

"Yes, she was," Alice said. "How did you know?"

"The megaphone on her charm bracelet."

"Ah. Our mother bought her that bracelet for making the honor roll. Yes, she was a cheerleader at Douglass High School for a time. She dropped out after ninth grade, when mama died. The picture was taken in the fall. Mama died in the spring."

"Can I borrow it?" I asked. "It might help in our investigation. I promise to give it back."

"Yes, certainly." She took it down from the wall and handed it to me.

We walked together. The gathering of old men had dispersed. I offered Alice a ride. She said she had her own car and pointed at an aged sky-blue Nash Rambler parked across the street. I got behind the wheel of the Fury and rolled down the windows. I laid the photo on the seat next to me and started the car. Alice stood on the sidewalk in the shade of an elm tree, her hands together at her waist clasping her handbag, waiting for me to leave.

As I put the car in gear, she baby-stepped up to the passenger-side window. I stopped. "I thought of something else," she said. "Sheryl said the boy's daddy didn't approve. She said it was because he was a dirty old man and was jealous." She stepped back and waved primly, as if she'd said all there was to say. I thanked her and drove away. In the mirror, I saw Alice stride in the opposite direction, chin up, head held high. The sky-blue Nash remained parked at the curb.

CHAPTER TWENTY-FOUR

Bernard sat in the hospital waiting room reading Guns & Ammo magazine as I arrived. "They're not letting him have any visitors," he said.

"We'll see about that," I said and went looking for Kevin's nurse. I asked a woman behind the admissions desk. "Mr. Gunter's nurse is right there behind you," she said.

I almost tripped over her. She was four-feet, ten inches of bosom, brazenness, and unquestioned authority. I foolishly tried to sweet talk her, which earned me a pitying smile. I related Kevin's family situation in lamentable detail. My story didn't make her cry, but it got us in to see him. She closed a curtain around his bed to give us some privacy. "Just a few minutes," she said.

It hurt my heart a little bit to see the state Kevin was in. At first, I thought it might make him feel better if I could make him laugh. "Son," I said, "you look like you took a swan dive into a bucket of cow shit." He didn't seem to think it was funny, but just looked at me through glassy eyes. I looked around for a place to park myself and realized the nurse had walked in right behind me. "Pardon my language, ma'am," I said. "Don't worry," she said tartly. "I ain't a Baptist."

Kevin wasn't in any kind of a laughing mood. He lay pale as a sheet except for the blotches of acne covering his face, which stood out more than ever. Snakes of matted brown hair fell across his greasy forehead. A tube went in his nose and some kind of brace looped around his neck and shoulders.

"They just gave him something for the pain," said Bernard.

"Oh yeh, he's high as a kite," the nurse said brightly as she fussed over him.

"I need to ask him some questions, if that's ok," I said.

"You can ask. I wouldn't expect much in the way of answers, though," she said, and sashayed out.

Kevin's eyelids drooped and his bloodshot eyeballs rolled back in his head. His mouth hung open and drool ran down his chin. Even from where I stood, his breath smelled like week-old roadkill. Healthy, Kevin Gunter is no prime specimen. Banged-up like that, he was painful to look at.

"Kevin," I said, "it's Chief Hardy. Can you hear me?"

His head moved vaguely in my direction. "Ah'm sorry ah shaw chew wi' mah beebee gun," he said, trying to focus but still looking all googly-eyed.

"That's ok, son," I said. "We're looking for your daddy. We can't find him and we want him to know you're in here. Do you know where we could find him?"

"I ain't seen 'im since Sat'day morning," he said, slowly. He slurred his words, fighting a losing battle against the effects the drugs they'd given him. "He 'uz out all night. Slam 'a door when he got home. Woke me up. I wen' back to sleep and when I got up he 'uz gone again."

"You remember what time, Kevin?"

"The beer clock said 6:20." I remembered the Schlitz clock with the Sooners bumper sticker hanging in his living room.

"And you haven't seen him since?"

He nodded then shook his head, like he wasn't sure which was the correct response.

"Ah'm so thirsty," he said. His tongue lolled out of his mouth.

"The nurse says he can't have water. Just ice chips, a little at a time," said Bernard. He gestured toward a cup on the bed stand. I fed Kevin some with a plastic spoon. His opened his gullet like a hungry baby bird.

"Did you talk to your daddy when you saw him? Did he say where he'd been?" I asked.

"Misserbissbee," he said drunkenly.

"Say that again, Kevin," I said.

He screwed up his face and tried to sit up straight, but it hurt too much and he slumped back onto his pillow. "Miss-er ... Biss-bee," he said, trying hard to make himself understood. Mister Bixby. "Misser Bissbee ha' a job for 'im, bu' ah don' know what it was."

"Kevin, was that Edgar Bixby or Deke Bixby?"

"Misser Bissbee` ha' a job for 'im ..." he said again. I thought it likely he didn't know which one. It was probably Edgar, but it would be easy enough to find out for sure.

I asked him what kind of job, but he just moaned miserably. "Ok, Kevin, we'll keep trying to find your daddy," I said. He nodded so slightly I could barely see his head move, then shut his eyes. The nurse opened the curtain.

"That's it for now, boys," she said. "This young 'un needs his rest." I asked how long he'd be in intensive care. She said most likely overnight. "He's not as bad as he looks," she said. "If there aren't any complications, we'll move him to a room tomorrow."

I thanked her and we vacated. I asked Bernard to walk with me out to the car. A blast of heat like a flame-thrower greeted us as we exited the hospital. The acrid smell of newly laid asphalt assaulted my nose. Mama used to call the sense of smell our "old factory" sense. I didn't understand where that came from, until years after she died.

"Did he say anything in the ambulance about Sheryl Foster?" I asked him.

"No sir, not a word," he said. "He was just semi-conscious during the trip." He stopped and raised up one of his shoes to look at, like you do when you think you've stepped in dog shit, except it was because the tar in the parking lot was sticky.

I checked my own shoes. They were fine. We resumed walking. "What about later?" I asked.

"No, they took him straight to surgery," he said, "then to recovery and back to intensive care. I didn't hardly get to talk to him at all before you showed up."

"Well, I hope you don't have plans for the evening, because one of us needs to stay here, at least until he gets sent to a room," I said. "No one knows where his daddy is. Karen tracked down his mother, but there's no way of getting in touch with her. By this time of the day I'm sure his grandma's drunk herself unconscious. That leaves us. I don't want the poor kid to be alone, for now, at least."

I filled him in about recent developments as best I could. What Alice told me about Sheryl's boyfriend's daddy being jealous got Bernard's attention. "That sounds just like Edgar," he said.

"It does," I agreed. "It also sounds like he might have had something of his own going on with the girl."

"I can imagine him being jealous," Bernard said. "Even of his son. He doesn't want anyone to have anything he doesn't have."

We still hadn't found the car and I realized we'd been looking in the wrong place. I did a 180-degree turn and spied the Fury parked on the far end. We trudged in that direction. "She was a hooker," I said. "He could've had her anytime he wanted. All it would've taken was money, and he has plenty of that."

"Unless she refused to be with him anyway, money or no. Which she might've done if she found out he was EJ's father."

Our feet made weird slapping and peeling sounds as we walked across the gummy blacktop.

"If Edgar wanted her for himself and couldn't have her, that's motive, right there," said Bernard. "You think it's fishy how Nate was out all night on Friday? Is there some connection between him and Sheryl?"

"Nate? Not that we know of, directly, at least. That prostitute friend of Sheryl's says Kevin had a crush on Sheryl."

"Could Kevin have told Nate about Sheryl, and Nate got mad and went and killed her? Why would he do that?"

"He wouldn't," I said. "I have no idea where Nate is or why he disappeared, but I guarantee it's not because he killed Sheryl Foster. Nate Gunter wouldn't hurt a fly." Unless Edgar Bixby told him to, I thought. But all that ended a long time ago.

We reached the car. Bernard absentmindedly ran his hands over the BB dents. We stood on either side without getting in and stared across the roof at each other, thinking.

I broke the lull. "Almost all we know about EJ and Sheryl is what Yvette told us. Until today, when Alice told me Sheryl had said EJ wanted to marry her. Call me a pessimist, but that sounds an awful lot like a fantasy cooked up by a sad and desperate young girl. I reckon we'll see Dick Nixon French-kiss Bobby Kennedy before Edgar lets his son marry a colored girl, never mind a prostitute." I took off my hat and wiped my forehead with my shirtsleeve. You could almost see the heat rise up off the blacktop. "On the other hand, I believe EJ or even Edgar would've made her think it was possible if it got them what they wanted. We need to talk to Edgar."

Bernard nodded. "I'd better get back inside. Don't want to leave the boy alone for too long."

"You go ahead and git," I said and handed him the clean clothes. "Tomorrow you and Kenny are going out to that brothel and talk to those girls. See who they're working for. Whoever it is would be a suspect, too."

"Sounds like a plan. Kenny and I'll go out there as soon as I get home." I'm sure he couldn't wait. Babysitting wasn't part of his job description, although to tell the truth, I'm not sure I ever gave him one.

·   ·   ·   ·   ·

Next stop was the OSBI offices. I thought it prudent to check with Agents Jones and Heckscher, in case they'd returned from Wichita. I didn't expect they had, but maybe I'd get lucky.

Closing time was nigh. I arrived to find the stenographer, Miss White, the last person left. Today she was decked-out all in blue instead of brown. We chatted a little and she informed me Jones and Heckscher had not gotten back. I thought she was actually kind of pretty behind those cat-eye glasses. I considered asking her to dinner until I noticed an autographed photo of Billy Graham on her desk and decided not to.

I drove back to the East side, looking to postpone my upcoming sleepless night as long as possible. I stopped at a newsstand and bought a copy of *The Black Dispatch*, the negro newspaper. I check it when I'm in town, to see what musicians are playing the local jazz establishments. Used to be the white papers wouldn't carry ads for black businesses. I'm not sure if that still holds. I prefer the *Dispatch* anyway.

I stopped at a diner and ordered chicken-fried steak with mashed potatoes. My waitress was a sour-dispositioned white woman of indeterminate age, with varicose veins that looked like a map of the state highway system. I thought I detected her giving me a dirty look when she saw I was reading the *Dispatch*. I smiled sweetly and asked for a cup of coffee. She asked me how I liked it and I said black. She walked away mumbling something.

I read that Roy Eldridge was playing Ruth's Bar-B-Q. Roy was one of Marceline Hardy's favorite trumpet players. I liked him plenty, myself. I was tempted to go see him, but waltzing into a club on the East Side wearing a badge would be asking for trouble. Parking the Fury after dark didn't sound like an especially good idea, either. Instead of going out to hear music, I stopped into a 7-Eleven next door to the diner and bought a six-pack of Schlitz. I set it down beside me on the front seat, popped one open, and headed back to Burr.

I pulled up to my house a few minutes after midnight. Dizzy waited at the front door. I hoped she'd hadn't gotten into Ethel's trash while I was gone. She trotted in behind me, laid down in her usual spot beside the La-Z-Boy and fell asleep.

I opened the last Schlitz, sat down and went over the autopsy report again. I focused on the part that said the scrapes and gouges and broken bones she suffered had been incurred post-mortem. She died of a slashed throat, but those other injuries happened afterwards. That would be consistent with her being killed on a train and then thrown off. It could also simply mean that whoever dumped her body wasn't very careful. My mood dropped a few notches below miserable. I considered getting out my saxophone and blowing a few notes, but it was late, and anyway I was too tired.

I watched TV until it went off the air, then took out the picture of Sheryl her sister had given me. I looked at it for a long time. I never did fall asleep.

CHAPTER TWENTY-FIVE

To me, the crack of dawn is typically just another signal I've laid awake all night worrying about things I can't change. I must admit, however, there's something especially beautiful about mornings—the way the early sunlight makes everything seem realer, somehow: lit by fire and more distinct, like a Charles Russell painting come to life, without the cowboys and Indians cluttering up the landscape.

I thought of that while driving in to work.

I beat Karen to the station for one of the rare times in recent memory. I put on the coffee myself, and sat at my desk. I'd brought the photo of Sheryl. The frame had a cardboard flap on the back so it could be stood up. I placed it on my desk facing me so I could see it and be reminded.

Karen came in ten minutes later, followed within the hour by the others. I'd called the meeting to update everyone—except Bernard, of course, who was still in the city—not just about what we'd found, but also about what I saw as our enhanced role in finding the killer.

"The OSBI has apprehended a suspect in our murder," I began. Facing me across my desk were Jeff, Kenny, and Karen, drinking coffee and squinting. They drank coffee and squinted into the sun shining through the window to my back. Jeff lit a cigarette. The smoke danced through the sunbeams like a spoonful of milk in a pitcher of water.

I explained about the man who'd been arrested in the Wichita train yard in possession of a bag containing the victim's personal effects, including her driver's license and blood-streaked clothing. I told them about my visit to Alice Foster's house.

I turned the photo around so they could see. "Her name is Sheryl Foster, age 17, of Oklahoma City," I said. "Apparently she's been working as a prostitute out of house trailer parked just barely over the Texas line near Watie Junction." I sipped my coffee. "EJ Bixby admits to being a customer, although we have reason to believe there might be more to it than that. I spoke to two acquaintances of Miss Foster who characterized EJ or someone matching his description as Sheryl's boyfriend. In most cases, this would make him the prime suspect. His alibi has him returning from a baseball game in Anadarko at the time of the girl's death. Jeff says it checks out."

"Yes sir, it does," said Jeff. He glanced at the picture. "I spoke to several of the boys on the team, and they all told me the bus didn't get back until after ten."

"Did you speak to the coach?" I asked.

He moved his mouth but nothing came out except cigarette smoke. "No, I didn't," he managed. "He teaches at the elementary school during the day and I ain't seen him."

As a boss, I know it's important to maintain my composure, even when my laziest, most feeble-brained underling surpasses his previous capacity for being an idiot. And the truth is, I may have been irritated at Jeff, but I was just as irritated at myself for giving him a task I should've known he'd screw up. I decided not to throw good money after bad and turned to Kenny, who I trusted to do the job right.

"Kenny, you track down Coach—what's his name?"

"Shannon," Karen said. "Dale Shannon."

"—Coach Shannon," I continued, "and ask him everything you can think to ask about the baseball team's trip to Anadarko on the day of the murder. We especially need to know when the game ended and what time the bus got back to Burr."

"—and if EJ was on the bus," said Karen.

"That's right," I said.

I tilted my chair against the wall and frowned at Jeff. He looked like Dizzy does when I catch her doing her business on the living room floor. It would've been easy to say something to make him feel better. But I didn't think he deserved to feel better.

I let my chair legs fall back to the floor and continued. I told them everything I'd discovered about Sheryl Foster—how both her folks were dead; how she'd been a good student and a cheerleader, but after her mother died something had gone wrong. I told them she had dreams of going to New York but had never been. I told how Alice had never seen the World's Fair pendant. I described the posters on Sheryl's wall and the magazine with Reverend King on the cover. The only thing I left out was her love of Nancy Drew, which seemed too sad and hit too close to home.

The last thing I talked about was the manner of her death. "She died from a loss of blood, which had obviously occurred elsewhere. She had sexual intercourse earlier in the day, but there were no signs it had been forced, so rape does not seem to have been involved." I paused. "Of course, her being a prostitute complicates matters in that regard."

"C'mon," Jeff blurted. "You can't rape a whore."

I could feel Karen tense. I glared at Jeff. "Son, you're having a real bad day already. I advise you to cut your losses and keep your mouth shut."

His gaped at me like he couldn't believe I'd taken offense. He started to defend himself but I cut him off. "That's enough," I said. "You need to think before you speak from now on." I almost added, what he really needed to do was consider whether he wanted to continue being a police officer.

Karen's color was still up, but she kept quiet. I admired her restraint.

I returned to the subject at hand. "The OSBI thinks they about have this thing solved," I concluded, "but they gave us a green light to continue looking at things on our end until they're 100% sure. So that's what we'll do."

Karen and Kenny nodded. Jeff stood with his arms crossed and head down.

"Now for our second order of business: Daffodil Bixby. Where do we stand?"

"I haven't found anyone willing to talk at school," said Jeff quietly, sounding humble for a change. "I'm sure someone will, eventually."

Karen scoffed. "It shouldn't be too dang hard to find out from a group of teenagers in a town of less than 2,000 people which one of them stole a two-thousand-pound pig. Whoever did it is probably so proud he's told every person in town under the age of 17."

"Go after the weakest kid in school," said Kenny. "Lean on him a little bit."

"That'd be Kevin Gunter," said Jeff.

Even a blind pig finds an acorn now and then. "Good thinking, Jeff," I said. "Karen, when we're done, give Bernard a call at the hospital and have him ask Kevin if he knows who took Daffodil. Jeff, how about you lean on the second-weakest kid and get me some names."

I asked Kenny if he'd made any progress locating Nate Gunter.

"I asked darn near everyone in town," he said, "A few folks saw him last Friday night at Edna's, but nobody seems to have seen him since. Bill McKibben said he didn't come to work Saturday or Monday and that if he doesn't show up today he's out of a job."

"What time was he at Edna's?"

"I couldn't get an exact time. There was a shift change at 9:00. The first crew didn't remember seeing Nate, but the second one did."

"You've checked his house."

"Several times, at least once-an-hour all day yesterday beginning around 3:30 until 11 or so. I left him a note to call us. He never showed up and we never heard from him. Checked again this morning on my way here. Still nobody home."

"Who's friends with Nate these days?" I said. "If he has any."

"I've seen him at Edna's a few times with Wesley Harmon," said Jeff. Wesley runs the Sinclair station outside of town, not far from where we found Sheryl's body.

I asked Kenny if he'd talked to Wesley. "No, I didn't think to go out there," he said. "I could this afternoon, if you want."

"No, I'll do it myself," I said. "I'll go when we're done here."

"Hope you're ready to talk some football," Karen said in a wry voice. Wesley is the most rabid University of Oklahoma football fan in town, which is saying a lot, since just about everyone aside from Everett Hardy and his damn-fool son Emmett is a Sooner fan. Wes is worse than most, in that he won't hardly talk about anything else. I'm the opposite. Since high school, I've become indifferent to the sport, although I keep up with it some, out of self-defense.

"Can anybody tell me who's playing quarterback for them next fall?" I said.

"Nobody worth a damn," said Jeff. Jeff's almost as bad as Wes, except Wes is generally optimistic; Jeff can't say anything positive. He thinks they've gone downhill every year since he left school.

It was barely eight o'clock and already I was tempted to call it a day. My eyes felt like they'd been soaked in lye. My breath could've killed a buffalo at 20 paces.

I had one more issue to address.

"Jeff, go out to Edgar's and ask him if he knew Sheryl." Edgar likes Jeff because of the OU connection, and, I suspect, because they have similar bigoted attitudes on a multitude of subjects. "Take one of the flyers. I'm sure he's already seen it, but show it to him anyway. Don't mention anything about her relationship with EJ unless he brings it up. Can you handle that?"

"Yes, Chief."

I looked at Karen. "Am I forgetting anything, Red?"

"More than likely, but I don't know what it would be," she said. "I imagine one of us'll think of it soon enough."

CHAPTER TWENTY-SIX

Wes Harmon and I have been pretty good friends since we were teenagers, though to be honest, I tend to steer clear of him these days, to avoid the inevitable football discussions.

I do make an exception when it comes to patronizing his business. Folks tell the story how Wes took apart and put back together his first engine when he was eight. I don't doubt it. He's the best in town at what he does. He gets my trade, football talk or no.

I pulled up to the pumps and watched him roll out from underneath a Ford Falcon parked in the service bay. He waved and walked toward me while I mentally reviewed what little I knew about the Sooners' upcoming prospects.

Wes was well on his way to being dirty as a coal miner, as usual. That boy gets filthier faster than any mechanic I've ever seen. He starts every morning with a spotless green jumpsuit. By lunch, it and every other part of him is black with grease. All Wes has to do is unlock the garage in the morning and the grime jumps all over him.

He greeted me with a smile. "Emmett, how ya doing?" he said as he wiped his hands on a red oil rag. He didn't bother offering his hand. He knows he's dirty.

"Hey there, Wes," I said. "I'm doin' fine and dandy." For some reason I tend to exaggerate my drawl when talking to people I went to school with. My ex-wife was from up north; she used to say talking like that's going to get me beaten-up one day. She didn't understand redneck is my native tongue.

"How about you?" I asked. "Everything alright?"

"Fair-to-middlin'," he said. "Lookin' forward to football season. Damn, it's got to be better than last year, don't ya think?" I nodded like I cared. "They need to bring Coach Wilkinson outta retirement if things don't get better," he said. You don't have to be Sooner fan to know who Bud Wilkinson is. If college football is a religion, Bud is its Pope.

I interjected a few unspecific comments and Wes held forth on how worthless the present coach is, and how he's going to end up coaching Pop Warner if he's not careful. It took a few minutes before I could steer the conversation around to the purpose of my visit.

"Wes, you seen Nate Gunter the last few days?" I asked. "His boy's up at Baptist Hospital in Oklahoma City and we haven't been able to get in touch with Nate. No one's seen hide-nor-hair of him since last week."

"Kevin's in the hospital?" he asked. "What in hell happened?"

I told him in broad terms, leaving out the BB gun shoot-out. I have my pride.

"I'm sorry to hear that," he said. He spat tobacco juice into a paper cup. "Kevin drove in here the other night. Matter of fact, it was the night that girl got killed up the road."

The hair on my neck stood up. "You were here that night?" I said. "I figured you'd have been closed up."

"Normally I would've, but nah, I stayed late," he said. "I turned off the pumps at the regular time and stayed to finish up that Falcon over there. I was planning to close early on Saturday, so I wanted to get it done." He looked disgustedly back at the Falcon. "Unfortunately, I didn't."

"The place was dark when I passed by about eleven," I said.

"You must've just missed me," he said. "I left about ten-forty-five."

I felt disgusted with myself for not checking with him earlier. I kind of took my pissed-offedness out on him. "You should've come to me before this," I said.

"I'm sorry, Emmett," he said, "but I didn't see how it was important. Saturday morning I was in a hurry to get out of here so I could make it to Norman in time for the Varsity-Alumni game." He spit and wiped a piece of tobacco off his lip. "I stayed overnight at my sister's in Noble and got home late Sunday. I meant to call you Monday, but I got so busy, I didn't have time. I was gonna do it today, though." He shrugged. "It's not like I saw a lot. Could be nothing."

"What'd you see?" I asked.

"Like I said before," he said. "I saw Kevin. I was working in the service bay. My lift's broke, so I was underneath that Ford most of the evening. About the only time I came out was when Kevin drove up in his daddy's pickup. I rolled out from under the car, yelled I was closed, and they drove off."

"What time?" I asked.

"I can't rightly say. It was dark, I know that. It would've been after nine. How much after, I don't know."

"Anyone with him?" I asked.

"Edgar Bixby's boy was in the passenger seat," he said. "I don't know why they bothered coming in. My canopy lights were off. Might be they saw the garage lights were on and thought they'd take a chance. Anyway, I recognized that old truck, and the moon was bright enough, so I could see Edgar, Jr. with him."

"You told them you were closed and they drove off?" I said.

"Yup."

He excused himself to attend to a customer, leaving me to digest this new piece of information.

Wes pumped some gas and exchanged some football talk with a fella in a blue Valiant. He finished and we got back to talking.

"About Nate. You seen him recently?" I asked.

"I saw him the next morning, in fact, first thing. He was here when I opened. Driving a new car," he said, then quickly corrected himself. "New for him, I should say. A red 1960 Impala sedan. Nice car."

Nate never has two nickels to rub together, never mind the money for a new car or even a decent used one. "He say where he got it?" I asked.

"He told me Ernie Bosworth's." Ernie runs a used car dealership on the North end of town on the way to Butcherville.

"He say when?"

"No, but it must've been the last day or so, because I saw him last Wednesday or Thursday driving that old pickup."

"Where'd he get the money?"

"You tell me."

"You two talk?"

"I tried, but he didn't have much to say."

"Did you talk about the killing?" I asked.

"I didn't know about it yet," he said. "Nate was my first customer of the day. If he knew about it, he didn't mention it. I heard about that from someone else later on, after Nate had left."

"What did you talk about?" I asked.

"Oh, we yakked a little about how hot it's been," he said. "or at least I did. I mentioned I saw his boy the night before, but he didn't say nothing to that." He looked thoughtful. "I talked some football, not that Nate's too interested. Not everybody's as big a Sooner fan as you and me." He stroked his chin, leaving a streak of grease. "Oh, I remember," he said, snapping his fingers. "I asked him if he wanted to go to Norman with me."

"What'd he say?"

"He said no, he had some place he needed to be."

"He say where?"

"No, just said there was somewhere he had to be and that was it." Another car pulled up. Wesley started to go over but the driver got out and helped himself. They exchanged brief pleasantries and Wes resumed our conversation. "We didn't talk about nothing else," he said. "Someone came in with a flat I had to take care of. By the time I finished, Nate was gone."

I asked if Nate had behaved unusual in any way. Wesley put on his thinking cap. "You wanna hear something unusual?" he asked with a smile. "I'll tell you what was unusual: he left me a ten-dollar bill but just bought three dollars-worth of gas. That was unusual."

He walked over to the other pump and picked up a clipboard sitting on top. "I always leave this here for people to sign their credit card receipts. Nate fitted a ten under the clip and drove off. Didn't wait for his change. That never happens. Nate don't have that kind of money to throw around." He spit again. "I guess I'll give it to him next time I see him," he said almost under his breath.

I asked if there'd been anything else different about the way Nate had acted that night.

Wes considered it. "He was a little jumpy, is all," he said. "But you know Nate. He's always a little jumpy."

He couldn't tell me much else. He'd been in the service bay the entire time and all he could see of the road was a sliver out the garage door. He'd been focused on that Ford's U-joints.

I excused myself and Wes went back to working on the Ford. I radioed Karen from the Fury. "Red, did Kenny get hold of Coach Shannon?" We're not so formal that we use all those "10-4s" and "10-20s" big police forces use.

"Hon, I just got off the phone with him," she said. "You're never gonna guess what he told me."

"Wait a minute," I said. "I thought I told Kenny to do that."

"Kenny went to Coach Shannon's house," she said. "He wasn't home so Kenny told his wife to have him call when he got back. He did. I answered the phone. I know what you want to know, so I asked." She bit off the words. "Now, do you want to hear what he said or not?"

She waited for me to answer. "Yes," I said.

"He says the Dairy Queen they stopped at wasn't in Anadarko. It was in Watie Junction."

I had to think for a second why that was important. EJ said the bus stopped at a Dairy Queen on the way back from the game. He thought it was Anadarko but wasn't sure.

"That's the kind of mix up a kid would make," I said. "It could be an honest mistake."

"Wait, though, that's not all," she said. "Coach said when the team got back to Burr, EJ wasn't on the bus. Apparently, he snuck out the back as they were leaving Dairy Queen."

"EJ got off the bus in Watie Junction?"

"He did," she said. "Some boys told Coach what happened when they got back. EJ told the other kids he had permission." I felt my face getting red, thinking about how Jeff had screwed-up every aspect of what I'd asked him to do.

"He called Edgar and offered to go back and look for him," she said, "but Edgar told him he thought he knew where he was, and he'd take care of it. Coach said Edgar was mad as hell. Threatened to have him fired and everything."

"That means EJ's alibi is shot."

"It doesn't look good. He gets off to see Sheryl and she turns up dead a few hours later."

"Did Coach Shannon say anything else?"

"Oh, you're gonna love this," she said, "or maybe you'll hate it, I don't know. Anyway, Coach said Edgar called the next morning and told him he'd decided not to make an issue of it. Said it would be better for everyone if they let it drop."

"I don't love it or hate it," I said, "but it gives me one more thing to excogitate."

"'Excogitate,'" she exclaimed. "What in God's name does that mean?"

"It means 'consider,' or 'mull over,'" I said. "Got it out of the dictionary the other day. You like it?"

She giggled. "You're a piece of work, you know that?"

I told her I'd spoken to Wesley and would fill her in when I got back. Presently, I needed her to call the highway patrol and put out an all points bulletin on Nate Gunter. "No one's seen him since last Saturday morning," I said. "He needs to be told about his son."

"Should I say he's wanted for questioning regarding Sheryl Foster?" she asked.

"Let's not put that out there just yet," I said. "Make it about Kevin. I don't know how Agents Jones and Heckscher are going to like it when they find out how aggressive we're being with this." Especially since they seemed convinced they'd already gotten their man.

I asked her if Jeff had shown Edgar the picture of Sheryl. "He did," she said. "Edgar says he's never met her and doesn't know who she is."

We over-and-outed. I walked over to the service bay to thank Wes. "I gotta git," I said. "If you see or hear from Nate, give us a call."

"Should I tell him about his boy?" he asked.

"Tell you what, ask him to call us, ok? Tell him it's an urgent matter involving Kevin," I said. "We'll take it from there." I began walking away when another question popped into my mind. "Wes, you're sure there was only two people in that truck?" I asked. "Could there have been someone else. Maybe sitting in the middle?"

He thought on it. "I don't think so," he said. "Not unless they was lyin' down in back."

CHAPTER TWENTY-SEVEN

I got back to find Karen hunched over the phone, hands wrapped around the handset like she was afraid it would scoot off on its own if she loosened her grip.

"Uh-huh, uh-huh," she said. "Ok—but—ok, I understand, but you need to come home. Your boy needs you, hon." I caught her eye. She mouthed one word: "Nate."

"That's Nate on the phone?" I asked. I have this bad habit of repeating what I've just been told. "Let me talk to him."

"Ok, now Nate, I got Chief Hardy here," she said. "he wants to talk to you. No, no, don't—." She put down the phone and her body sagged. "He hung up," she said.

"What's that all about?" I asked.

"Oh, Lord," she said. "He's been calling home trying to get through to Kevin. He finally got so worried he called us. I told him what happened."

"Where is he?"

"He wouldn't say. I know he called from a pay phone and it was long-distance, because the operator broke-in a couple of times to ask him to put in more money."

"Think the operator could tell you where the call came from?" I asked.

"Can't hurt to ask," she said.

I went back into my office and opened some mail while Karen

talked to the operator. She ended the call. "She says she'll call back in a few minutes," she said.

"Can it be done?" I asked.

"Maybe," Karen said. "She's not supposed to. I told her the caller's little boy is in the hospital and made it sound even sadder than it is, but that wasn't enough. I had to get creative."

"What do you mean, 'creative?'"

"I had to pull rank," she added sheepishly.

"You don't have any rank," I said.

"She doesn't know that," she said. "If anyone asks, I'm Deputy Karen Dean of the Burr Police Department."

Girl's got cojones, I'll give her that. "Impersonating an officer of the law is a serious offense," I joked.

She winked. "I wouldn't worry about it," she said. "I have low friends in high places."

The phone rang. Karen answered, said thank you once or twice and said "yes" and "no" a few times. She wrote something down, said another thank you, and hung up.

"She could only narrow it down to an area code," she said. "702. Nevada."

"Las Vegas," I said. "Where he thinks his ex is."

I asked her to contact the highway patrol and cancel the APB on Nate, then call the Las Vegas police department and Nevada State police and ask for their help in tracking him down. "Give them Betty's last known address and phone number," I said. "Tell them he's driving a red 1960 Chevy Impala."

"You got a plate number?" she said.

"No, but Nate told Wesley he got it off Ernie Bosworth's lot. Give Ernie a call and get the plate and registration from him."

"I'll do it right now."

Karen dialed-up Ernie. I could tell from her end of the conversation that Nate didn't get the car from him. She thanked him and hung up.

"Never had one to sell," she said.

"Why would Nate lie about that?" I asked.

"Maybe he stole it," she said.

"I doubt it," I said, "but we should probably check with the state boys about any stolen red Impalas."

She asked what else I got out of Wesley. I outlined the relevant points.

"That puts EJ Bixby and Kevin Gunter right near where you found the body, right before you found it," she said.

"Shortly after Sheryl Foster was last seen alive."

A car honked several times on the street. I got out of my chair and stuck my head out the front door to see if there was a problem. Nothing, as far as I could tell. I walked back to my desk and sat.

"Gonna bring him in?" Karen asked.

"Who?" I said, knowing full well.

"Edgar Bixby, Jr."

"Is Daffodil Bixby the world's fattest pig?" I said.

"Depends on who you ask," she said. "Not according to the Red Chinese."

"Well, there you go," I said.

$\bullet \quad \bullet \quad \bullet \quad \bullet \quad \bullet$

Getting EJ out of school in the middle of the day turned out to be more of a challenge than I thought. Rather than make a fuss, I decided to wait until school was out.

I used the time to search for Nate. I asked Bill Haygood and his crew of regulars at the barber shop if they's seen him. None had. I went to Miller's, had a chocolate soda and argued politics with Pat Sherry, the local locksmith and a card-carrying member of the John Birch Society. Neither Pat nor anyone else at Miller's had seen Nate.

I dropped by Jesus Is Lord Hair Salon and let Cathy Stallcup give me a trim. I like Bill Haygood, but I'd rather let a mental patient cut my hair with a lawnmower. As it is, Cathy spent the entire time complaining about her boss. By the time she finished, I was ready to find me that mental patient or else give Bill another chance. On my way out the door I asked her about Nate. She hadn't seen him.

I made a final stop at the library and asked Kate if she subscribed to any car magazines. She did. I rummaged through the stacks until I found what I was looking for—a 1959 issue of *Motor World* with a red 1960 Impala on the cover. Kate was happy to let me borrow it. I told her I hadn't forgotten about the issue of *Oklahoma Spotlight* and she said I could take my time with it.

I got back to the station in time to catch a phone call from Agent Ovell Jones of the OSBI.

"Agent Jones," I said. "You back from corn country?"

"Heckscher and I just got back with our suspect. Took most of yesterday afternoon to get extradition, so we didn't head out until this morning."

"What'd you find out?"

"I believe we got our killer. Name's Eugene Henry Yellowhorse, age 42, recently escaped from Beckham County jail in Sayre, where he was being held for sexual assault of a minor. He was found carrying a blue and white Pan American Airlines overnight bag we believe belonged to Sheryl Foster. Her purse and clothes were inside. The purse had her personal effects: wallet and keys and so on—a change of underwear, some makeup. The clothes were streaked with blood: Type A-positive, same as the victim."

Things looked bad for this Eugene Yellowhorse. Still, all I could think of was why he'd be carrying around the bloody clothes. I asked Jones.

"It's not what I would do but I'm not a murdering psychopath." He coughed and I thought how I could almost smell the smoke over the phone. "If these assholes were smart, we wouldn't catch them as often as we do," he said.

"No murder weapon?"

"No, he wasn't so dumb that he held on to that."

I expressed my reservations, saying there was no way he could've picked-up Sheryl at Watie Junction, jumped a freight, killed her on the train, then dumped the body where we found it.

"Part of a murder inquiry is finding answers to questions like that," he said. "It's early in this one, but we will, don't worry."

I recounted what I discovered since we'd last spoken, with special emphasis on the part about EJ Bixby being nearby around the time she was last seen alive. Agent Jones commended my diligence, but remained unmoved.

"That's interesting, Chief," he said. "But let me ask you this. Do you have any physical evidence? Because we do. And we have motive, which is basically that Gene Yellowhorse is a violent woman-hating piece of shit who chooses his victims at random. He has a record going back to when he was a teenager. Three convictions for felony assault since the age of 16. As a juvenile, he didn't do hard time for the first two, But he went away for five years for rape and aggravated assault as an adult back in '57. His most recent arrest was a month ago. This is a bad man we're talking about." I didn't doubt that.

I asked what he'd gotten out of him in the interrogation.

"Not a confession, that's for sure. He said a buddy had given him a ride as far as Alva where he hopped a freight. He said the girl's bag was already in the box car when he got on, which is what you'd expect him to say. He was so scared when I told him he was looking at the electric chair, I'd have felt sorry for him if he wasn't such a lowlife."

I asked how he explained being in possession of the bloody clothes.

"He says he didn't know what was in the bag, it was too dark in the box car, so he waited until he got off to go through it." I heard him take another pull off his cigarette. "To be fair, that squares with the arresting officer's account," he said. "Yellowhorse was rummaging around in the bag when they caught him."

"If that's true, he didn't know what was in the bag, which means he's not our man."

"*If* it's true. But it's not. We caught him with the dead girl's effects a long ways from where she was found, which puts Gene's butt cheeks in the electric chair. Frankly, if they need a volunteer to pull the switch, I'll be first in line."

I'm not the kind to argue for the sake of arguing, but I was concerned Agent Jones had taken a wrong turn and was almost too far from the main road to go back. I told him that in so many words.

"If I never heard of Eugene Yellowhorse, I might agree," he said, "but even with what you've told me, we got too much on this fella to ignore."

I couldn't argue with that.

He finished by once again telling me to feel free to continue my own investigation. I rang off thinking he was a decent fella, however misled. I almost felt bad about those mean thoughts I'd had about him.

· · · · ·

Kenny got off work at the hardware store at 3:00. By 3:05, he was standing in front of my desk.

"What took you so long?"

"Sorry, Chief. I had to change into my uniform."

"I'm kidding, son."

I told him about the events of the day and said there'd been a change in plans, that he was to pick-up EJ at school and bring him in, as inconspicuously as possible. I didn't want folks talking about it until there was something for them to talk about.

Jeff came in and I sent him on patrol. Kenny had the Fury, so Jeff had to use his own car with a magnetic flasher on the roof. None of the boys like to do that, feeling it makes them look less official. Jeff knew he was in my doghouse, however, so he had the good sense not to fuss.

I couldn't find the notes from the first time I'd talked to EJ, then remembered I'd thrown them in the trash. I dug them out and tried to read them. They were no more legible than they'd been before, but I tried hard and was able to decipher enough to remind me what ground needed to be covered.

I opened my bottom desk drawer to check on my supply of liquid courage. Instead of the depleted bottle of Old Grand-Dad I'd expected to find, there was an unopened bottle of Smirnoff vodka—with a note: "At least they can't smell this on your breath—Karen."

That girl thinks of everything.

CHAPTER TWENTY-EIGHT

I called Jimmy Jack and told him we intended to question EJ. Five minutes later, he and Edgar drove up in Edgar's bronze Lincoln. They parked in one of our "Reserved for Official Vehicles" spots. The temptation to have them move the car was profound, but I resisted. No need to fan the flames. Things were bound to get heated enough as it was.

Edgar barged in with Jimmy Jack on his heels. Jimmy Jack tried to slow down Edgar by grabbing at his arm, but Edgar jerked it away. I stepped aside without a word and olé-d them into my office.

Edgar ignored my offer to sit. His contorted face resembled the business end of that prize-winning pig he was so proud of.

"You must not like your job very much, you wife-stealing bastard," he said.

It warms my heart to see Edgar act like a spoiled five-year-old, like he always does when things don't go his way.

"Why, hello to you, too, Edgar," I said with my best used-car-salesman smile.

I gestured toward the outer office. "Could I remind you to watch your language," I said in a confidential tone. "There's a lady present." I raised my voice. "I'm sorry you had to hear that, Miss Dean," I said. "Thank you kindly, Chief Hardy," she replied primly.

I thought Edgar might try something physical, which at that moment I would've welcomed as an excuse to beat him senseless.

Jimmy Jack ruined my fun by grabbing him by the pants pocket and tugging him down into a chair. "I want to know why you're not out trying to find who stole my livestock," he spat, "instead of accusing my son of some stupid bullshit."

"Now hold on, Edgar," I said. "I'm not accusing anyone of anything, but that girl being dead on the train tracks isn't some stupid bullshit. It's murder, and whoever did it needs to be caught and punished. Your son might've been the last one to see her alive."

He didn't react, which I took as a sign I wasn't telling him anything he hadn't figured out on his own. "We need some answers out of EJ," I said. "And I mean real answers, not the trash he was peddling in here the other day."

"C'mon now, boys," said Jimmy Jack, with his greasy politician's manner. "We're all friends here, ain't we?"

"We sure as hell ain't," Edgar said. "Never was."

Even a busted clock is right twice a day.

"Edgar, dammit, sit down and be quiet." Jimmy Jack said. "Let me handle this."

Look at Jimmy Jack, talking back to Edgar. I didn't think he had it in him.

Karen peeked in the door. "Could I get anyone in here a cup of coffee?" she said.

Jimmy Jack raised a weary hand. "Cream and two sugars," he said. Judging by the croak in his voice, standing up to his biggest client just now had taken a couple of years off his life.

"Edgar?" she said. Edgar didn't answer. If I were to try my hand at reading his mind, I'd say he was considering whether to burn me alive or bury me up to my neck next to a fire ant hill and pour honey over my head. "Ok, nothing for you," she said a tiny bit sarcastically. "Chief?"

"I'll take some orange juice," I said with a wink, hoping my meaning was clear.

It was clear enough, but did not solicit the desired response. "We don't have any orange juice," she said pointedly. Damn.

The trouble with vodka is it doesn't mix with coffee. I couldn't pull the bottle out of my desk with Edgar and Jimmy Jack sitting there, anyway. Poor planning on my part.

Jimmy Jack asked if he might have a moment with his client. I made them promise not to touch anything and joined Karen in the outer office. I shut the door to give them some privacy.

"Orange juice," she said with disdain.

"Yeh, I know," I said. "It was worth a try."

While we waited for Abbott and Costello to concoct their legal strategy, I considered whether to call Rex McKinnis, the Tilghman County prosecutor, and let him in on what I was up to. Unlike his predecessor—a career politician who looked out for the interests of the oil and cattle millionaires but God help you if you worked for a living—I knew Rex to be fair and honest.

Karen must've been reading my mind. "You gonna call Rex?" she asked.

"I'm not sure," I said. "Depends on what happens with those two. And the boy." We sat in silence, me cleaning my fingernails with a toothpick and Karen going over the instructions on how to put together a toy oven she bought as a birthday present for her niece. Looked to me like all you had to do was screw in a lightbulb. I never read instructions.

"You'd best keep his phone number handy, just in case," I said. She nodded and kept reading.

Kenny should've been here with EJ by now, I thought. I got him on the radio. He said there had been some unforeseen difficulties, but the situation was now under control. He walked in two minutes later, holding EJ by the elbow, as if the boy had tried to make a break for it.

"What took you so long?" I asked.

"EJ must not have a rear-view mirror," Kenny replied. "Wouldn't pull over when I hit my lights. As a matter of fact, I believe he sped up. I hope I'm wrong about that."

"I didn't see you, OK?" EJ said in that whiny, defensive way teenagers talk when they've been caught red-handed.

Kenny rolled his eyes, shook his head and tossed EJ's keys on Karen's desk. He informed us they'd left EJ's hot rod parked on the shoulder of the highway. I said I'd send Jeff or Bernard out to get it.

"Speaking of Deputy Cousins," I said to Karen, "have you heard from him today?"

"Oh, I clean forgot to tell you," she said. "He called when you were out this morning and said he was on his way home. The hospital arranged for some church ladies in the city to come and sit with Kevin until his kin can visit."

"Any idea when he'll be back?

"Bernard or Kevin?"

"Both, I guess."

"Apparently Kevin's going to be there another few days," she said. "Bernard should be here any minute."

I asked Kenny to answer the phone so Karen could take notes. I caught the scent of her perfume as she passed by. I always liked it and wish she'd wear it more often. It bucked me up a little bit. I took EJ by the shoulder and guided him into my office, shutting the door behind us.

CHAPTER TWENTY-NINE

Edgar and Jimmy Jack cleared a space between them. EJ pulled up a chair and sat down.

I'm often inclined to begin an interrogation by sticking the needle in, especially if I consider the subject especially stupid and unpleasant. As in this case.

"First of all, EJ," I said, "I want to tell you how sorry I am."

"About what?"

"About what happened to your good friend Kevin Gunter."

He shrugged and wiped his nose with the back of his hand.

"You must feel terrible. Been up to visit him yet?"

"I told you before, he ain't really my friend. He just follows me around like a damn puppy."

I dropped my jaw and pretended to be surprised. "Really? That's not what I heard."

I picked up a pencil and tapped out a swing rhythm on the side of my enamel cup. "Anyway, I'd like to thank you boys for coming in on such short notice. I don't want to scare y'all, but for the record, this is an official interview. We call Miss Dean 'The Human Tape Recorder' because she's so good at shorthand. She'll be writing everything down, in case I can't remember at a later date what we all said."

Karen doesn't really know shorthand; she just writes real fast. I looked over at her and saw the shadow of a smile.

"Chief," said Jimmy Jack, "I want it noted we came here voluntarily."

"I'm not sure EJ trying to outrun my deputy counts as voluntary, but I'll make sure my stenographer puts that on the record. Did you get that, Miss Dean?"

"Mm-hmm," she said. "'Mr. Preston says his client's here voluntarily even though he tried to escape."

Edgar's eyes looked about to bulge out of their sockets and he started to sputter when Jimmy Jack cut him off. "Hold on, Edgar," he said and patted his client on the knee. "They're just kiddin' around. Aren't you, Emmett?"

"Y'all know Miss Dean's sense of humor," I said, "She used to write jokes for Bob Hope before she came to work for us."

Jimmy Jack grinned his fake good ol' boy grin. Edgar steamed. EJ sulked.

"Let's get down to business." I felt a tiny twinge of mercy and issued a warning. "Y'all should know, we're going to talk about some things EJ might not want his daddy to hear."

"Edgar's aware of the boy's relationship with the colored girl," Jimmy Jack said.

"Is that so? Her name is Sheryl Foster, by the way. How long have you known, Edgar?"

Evidently Edgar's strategy was to ignore my questions and try to scowl me to death.

"We're not going to address that," Jimmy Jack answered. "What matters is that he knows."

Nothing suspicious about that. "Alright, we'll let it go for now."

I realized I was still wearing my hat. I took it off and placed it over a small statue of Elvis that Kenny gave me as a joke for Christmas last year. The way the hat hung, all you could see was Elvis's feet, which I reckon is the least interesting part of his body. "Let's get the most important question out of the way first," I said. "Where were you, EJ, on the night Sheryl was killed?"

"I already told you." He spoke slowly, like a redneck might try to explain the intricacies of *The Beverly Hillbillies* to Shakespeare. "I went with the baseball team to Anadarko for a game then came back on the bus."

"You said the bus stopped at a Dairy Queen in Anadarko on the way home, is that right?"

"Yeh."

I got tired of playing with the pencil and flipped it on the desk. It almost rolled off but I caught it in time. "See, now, that just ain't so, EJ. Your coach says the Dairy Queen wasn't in Anadarko. He said it was in Watie Junction."

Jimmy Jack chortled. "C'mon, now Emmett. Give the boy a break. EJ said he *thought* it was in Anadarko. He couldn't remember for sure."

"Either way, he's lying," I said. "Coach Shannon says he snuck off the bus before it left the Dairy Queen."

The realization I'd seen through his ingenious plan shocked EJ into silence. I could almost see the hamster wheel in his head spin as he tried to contrive a substitute lie. "I had to take a piss, is why," he blurted. "I got off the bus to take a piss, and it was gone when I got back."

I know I shouldn't have, but somehow, I expected more of the boy. "Son, that's an insult to my intelligence. I'm not even going to waste time on it." I got up and eased out of my chair and sat on the front edge of my desk, right in front of him. I leaned in six inches from his face like I was daring him to look at me. He didn't. "What's relevant here is the fact you got off the bus in Watie Junction around the time Sheryl was last seen. Within two hours, a witness saw you riding around with Kevin Gunter, less than a quarter-mile from where we found her body. I don't know about you, but that sounds fishy to me. Can you help me with that?"

EJ scratched his face and looked over at Jimmy Jack, who gawked like he was as interested to hear the boy's explanation as I was. I swear, I'd sooner have Gomer Pyle defend me in court.

I kept pushing. "I reckon Kevin Gunter will be able to shed some light on things. Once he's back on his feet."

He raised his eyes at me for the first time. "I called Gunter and he drove to Watie Junction and got me. I didn't say nothin' about it because I didn't want my dad to know."

I strolled back to my chair and sat down. "What didn't you want your dad to know? That you were in Watie Junction? That you were stupid enough to miss the bus? Or was it because you didn't want him to know *why* you missed the bus?" His expression was becoming almost as hateful as his father's. "If that was why, you shouldn't have bothered. According to Jimmy Jack, your daddy already knew about you and Sheryl."

"I didn't know he knew."

I was inclined to believe that.

Edgar sat mute, straight as a stick. He didn't need to speak. I could tell what he was thinking just by looking at him. I thought I'd try poking the snake to see if it would strike. "Edgar, you told the coach you knew where EJ was, and that you'd handle it yourself. You knew he got off the bus in Watie Junction to see Sheryl. Didn't you?" He still glowered. If I didn't know better, I'd have thought he had a stroke.

Jimmy Jack decided it was time to impersonate a competent attorney. "We're not going to go into what Edgar did or did not know, and when he did or did not know it, Emmett."

Very nice, Jimmy Jack! I thought.

"Edgar knew why EJ got off the bus," I said. "If he wants to pretend he didn't, that's his prerogative. But what matters are facts, and the facts are: EJ was near that brothel when she was last seen alive, and in the vicinity of where her body was dumped, just a few minutes before it was discovered. Those are two mighty big coincidences." I paused. "I'm not sure I believe in coincidences that big."

Jimmy Jack stood up. "That's about enough of this," he said. "You're letting your dislike of Edgar influence the way you're doing your job, and we're not going to sit still for that."

"You sure, Jimmy Jack? I think Edgar must like sitting still. I don't think he's moved a muscle since EJ got here." I regarded Edgar with mock concern. "Can you talk, buddy? You want me to call Dr. Pepper?" I snapped my fingers in front of his face. "Blink twice for yes." I thought that might earn me a punch in the face, but all that happened was his expression just got darker.

Jimmy Jack either didn't get or didn't like my little joke. "We're leaving," he said.

They filed out. "You're in over your head, Emmett," Jimmy Jack said. "If I were you, I'd let the professionals deal with this. I heard the OSBI made an arrest. You'd best leave it to them and stop harassing my clients, if you know what's good for you."

Jimmy Jack Preston talking about someone being in over his head is like Dean Martin expounding the virtues of tee-totaling. "Ok, Jimmy Jack, you can stop with the bullshit. I understand you're only doing your job. Just make sure those boys can be contacted in case I need to talk to them again."

"My clients are free go wherever they want whenever they please, and there's nothing you can do about it. Let's go, gentlemen." When the going gets tough, Jimmy Jack tends to lose his drawl and fall back on that New England accent he picked up at Yale.

The three of them filed out. Edgar lurched like an irate cigar store Indian. EJ smirked like the whole thing was a joke.

Bernard was in Karen's chair talking to Kenny when the rest of us emerged from my office. She gave him a stern look and he popped up so quick, you'd think he'd been sitting on a lit cigarette. All of us watched through the front window as the Bixbys and Jimmy Jack walked to their car. I noticed a piece of paper stuck under one of his wiper blades. Edgar pulled it out, looked at it, then started to yell and dance crazily, arms jerking and jowls jiggling, with spittle running down his chin like a rabid Saint Bernard. Finally, he tore it up, threw the pieces to the wind, and drove away, tires squealing.

"What in hell was that all about?" I said.

"I wrote him a ticket," said Bernard as innocent as a newborn babe. "He was parked illegally."

"Good job, Deputy," I laughed. "Chase him down and give him another one for littering."

CHAPTER THIRTY

When I finally recovered from busting a gut from laughing at Edgar, I decided I'd call the county prosecutor.

Tilghman County District Attorney Rex McKinnis grew up in Red Plains, Oklahoma at the same time I went to school in Burr. Red Plains is another itty-bitty bump-in-the-blacktop—like Burr, except smaller. Our football team beat theirs like a borrowed mule. Rex played in the line. He claims to have knocked me on my ass a few times. Maybe it happened, although I have my doubts.

Up to now, Rex had only dealt with the OSBI on this case. I thought I'd better let him know what we were up to.

Talking on the phone makes me nervous and I hate it, but sometimes it cannot be avoided. I considered taking a gulp of vodka straight out of the bottle, then I noticed it was after five. I figured if I dawdled any longer I might miss Rex, so I skipped the booze and dialed. Lucky for me, Rex doesn't keep bankers' hours and I got him right away.

After a short exchange of small-town yakking and law-enforcement gossip, I told him about our investigation and what we'd discovered. I sold it like a box of laundry soap, since I figured maybe that's what it would take to persuade him to take it seriously.

He didn't say anything for a few seconds. "You still there?" I asked.

"I'm still here. Just thinking."

Still more seconds passed. "You could be onto something," he said.

I exhaled heavily. I hadn't even noticed I'd been holding my breath.

"Listen Rex, I'm no Sam Spade, but this whole thing with the Bixbys smells bad," I said. "Consider what Alice Foster said Sheryl said about EJ's daddy being jealous. That sounds like Edgar knew about Sheryl, and might've had something going with her, too. If that's true, it puts him in the picture, don't you think?"

"It might. You make some good points, but I'm not convinced. Compelling physical evidence links Gene Yellowhorse to the victim. What you're telling me doesn't change or nullify that." My hopes sank. "We're seriously considering offering him a deal," he said. "Second-degree murder. Life without parole."

Not a terrible bargain if he actually killed her. A grave injustice if he didn't, I don't care how bad a guy he is. "It wouldn't be the first time an innocent man pleaded out to avoid the death penalty," I said.

"No, it wouldn't, but his claim to have found that bag on the train would be a hard sell to a jury, and he knows it. Hold on," he rasped, "I got to drink something. I feel like I swallowed a mouthful of dirt." I reckoned his choice of on-the-job liquid refreshment was less potent than yours truly's.

He drank something and came back on the line. "I'll tell you what, you follow your inquiry and see where it leads. Sometimes an investigation uncovers more than one plausible scenario."

That wasn't 100% what I wanted to hear, but it was better than nothing. He asked if I needed some help in the way of sheriff's deputies. I said thanks but no thanks. There did not figure to be any car chases or shootouts in my immediate future. I chose not to mention details of the BB gun fiasco.

"Ok, keep after it," he said. "I should warn you, though, unless you give us something more within the next couple of days, we're going to charge Yellowhorse. I'm fairly certain he'll plead to second degree."

I got him to promise to contact me before that happened. He said he would, and we hung up. I looked up from my desk and saw Karen standing there.

"He give you the go-ahead?" she asked.

"In a way," I said. I stood and stretched before I remembered that I'd unbuckled my belt and undone my trousers, which I occasionally do if I'm at my desk and figure to be sitting for a long time. I managed to grab my pants before they fell below my knees, though Karen might've gotten a glimpse of my jockey shorts. "Sorry about that," I said.

She appeared greatly amused. "Not at all."

I buttoned-up and otherwise situated myself. "I'm hungry," I said. "Wanna go get some dinner?"

"Well, I was gonna go home and wash my hair, but a girl's got to eat."

"A girl does," I agreed.

· · · · ·

When I say the Piazza is Burr's only real restaurant, I mean it's the one place in town that has tables and chairs and waitresses, and a menu you can hold in your hands and not have to read off a board. We've also got the Burger Mart, but it's just a hamburger stand, with drive-up service and picnic tables that don't get much use except in the summer. If it's a good home-style meal you're after, the Piazza's all she wrote, unless you want to drive a half-hour or so to one of our neighboring metropolises, like Temple City or Alva.

Some of the Piazza's food is very good, and it's not too pricey. You can get their specialty—chicken-fried steak platter, which includes your choice of mashed or baked potato, vegetable of the day (grown locally in-season, so it's fresh in the summertime), Texas toast, and the main course smothered in cream gravy—for $1.85.

For some reason, the owners decided to give their restaurant an Italian name and decorate it in a Venetian style, which is odd because it's not actually an Italian restaurant. In fact, the one Italian dish they have—spaghetti—might be the worst thing on the menu. On the walls are scenes of gondolas piloted by fellas with dark, curly mustaches, and red-and-white-striped shirts. The booths and chairs are red, the tablecloths white. The lighting's turned down low, but every table has a candle in a wine bottle that makes it possible to see what you're eating. I guess the owner figures an Italian theme lends the place class and makes it romantic. Maybe it does, at that. It's a nice place to take a girl on a date.

Not that this was a date. This was Karen and me.

We took a booth in the back. "Don't tell me I don't know how to treat a lady," I said.

"Why Mr. Hardy, I declare, I am unaccustomed to dining in such luxury." she said. "If I'm not mistaken, the last meal you bought me was a hot dog at a football game last fall."

"Uh, I believe you're forgetting the hamburger from Burger Mart I bought you for lunch a couple of weeks ago."

"Of course. How silly of me."

Our waitress was Jeannie Klinglesmith, a graduate of Burr High School *circa* 1960. Jeannie's a former homecoming queen who married her childhood sweetheart right out of school, after which things went downhill precipitously. If she'd chosen better, she might've ended up like Denny Bixby—not especially happy, but with nice clothes and a big house and a new car in the garage whenever her husband screwed up. Unfortunately, Jeannie's husband never got a chance to atone for his screw-ups. Not long after they married, he got a job at the gas plant, then blew himself up lighting a cigarette while cleaning the inside of a storage tank. Fortunately, the couple did not procreate.

Jeannie's been single since then. I would recommend she stay that way, as long as she lives here, at least. Burr is not overpopulated with desirable eligible bachelors.

I can always tell when someone doesn't like me and I am confident in my surmise that Jeannie Klinglesmith would rather gargle with battery acid than give me the time of day. That's inconvenient, since I eat there at least once a week and she's usually my waitress. But I reckon there's not much I can do. I've tried being extra nice and tipping big, but it doesn't make any difference. Could be it's not me, but the world that's the matter. I'd understand if she felt that way.

She brought over our menus and glasses of water with a minimum of politeness and walked away.

"Is it my imagination or is that girl rude?" I asked Karen.

"She did seem a little snippy just now."

"Maybe it's me."

"Maybe it *is* you, hon. Just because you look like Philip Marlowe doesn't mean all the girls have to like you." Karen thinks I favor Dick Powell, the actor who played Marlowe in *Murder, My Sweet*, which happens to be her favorite movie. Better Powell than Humphrey Bogart, who played Marlowe in *The Big Sleep*. I've always thought Bogie looked like he'd gotten his face caught in a taffy-pulling machine.

I already knew I was going to order the chicken-fried steak. Karen smoked two cigarettes down to the filter while trying to decide.

"What I really want is chicken-fried steak," she said.

"I believe when you suggested this outing you mentioned something about having a sirloin."

"Haven't you ever heard the saying, 'It's a girl's prerogative to change her mind?' I changed my mind. I want chicken-fried steak."

"Then order it."

"But that's what you're getting."

"Why do you care? If you want chicken-fried steak, get chicken-fried steak."

"We should get something different so we can share."

For reasons I am unable to fathom, Karen always wants to share when we eat out. I never do.

"I'm sorry ma'am, but I'd really prefer not to share," I said in the same exaggeratedly respectful tone I use when I write someone a speeding ticket. "I plan to eat my chicken-fried steak all by myself. If you want to share, you can share my green beans and Texas toast." I dislike green beans, and toast just takes up valuable stomach room that's better used to stow meat and potato.

If she was bothered by my sarcasm, she didn't show it. "Why

don't you like to share?" As if we'd never had this conversation.

"Because I want chicken-fried steak. I don't want what you're having, unless you're having chicken-fried steak. In that case, I'll share."

"Well, I'm going to have spaghetti."

As mentioned, the Piazza's spaghetti is awful—just limp noodles and ketchup, is all it is. I considered pointing that out, but decided otherwise. "You can have all the spaghetti you want," I said, "but don't plan on picking chicken-fried steak off my plate, because it ain't gonna happen."

She made a face. "You're a strange one, Emmett Hardy."

"That may very well be true, but I don't see what's so strange about wanting to eat what *I* want to eat and not what *you* want to eat."

"Men," she said.

"Women," I said.

"Can I have your order?" Jeannie said.

.   .   .   .   .

My meal was delicious. Judging by how much of it she left on the plate, Karen's was not. You can go into just about any restaurant or diner in this state and get a good chicken-fried steak, but I would recommend that you not order spaghetti unless it's the specialty of the house. Even then, I'd make sure the cook speaks Italian.

Of course, Karen tried to poach off my plate when she thought I wasn't looking. I let her. I love my chicken-fried steak, but I'm not a monster.

Between bites we talked about this and that, little of it having to do with work. Karen described in great detail a new TV show about a rich New York lawyer who decides he wants to be a farmer and moves to the sticks with his high-society wife. One of the neighbors has a super-smart pig and I was reminded of Daffodil. Karen said the show was hilarious.

We talked about a couple of local boys in the Army who'd gotten drafted and sent to Viet Nam. Karen said she saw the wife of a local businessman steal a ladies' panty girdle off a neighbor's clothesline. I was skeptical, but Karen doesn't lie, so I reckon it must be true. We avoided talking about ourselves, since we spend so much time together and know pretty much all there is to know—and what we don't know, we know better than to ask.

When it was time to go, Jeannie was nowhere to be found. Another waitress brought us our check. She said Jeannie's shift had ended. We'd been sitting there longer than I thought.

We exited into the parking lot. The sun had set, but the sky was still more light than dark. The moon was orange in the sky and I could already see the Big Dipper. I raised my arms to stretch and noticed the lower half of my belly hung over my belt a little more than it should, and I knew I couldn't blame it all on the chicken-fried steak I'd just consumed. As we got in my truck, I noticed Jeannie, over in the shadows at the far corner of the restaurant, watching the road like she was expecting a ride. I'd just started my engine and was about to pull out when a bronze Lincoln Continental turned in the next to where Jeannie was. She got in, scooted over, and gave Edgar Bixby a big ol' open-mouthed kiss.

CHAPTER THIRTY-ONE

One of these days I'm going to learn sleeping on a La-Z-Boy is not conducive to getting a good night's rest, and that downing a half-bottle of bourbon after dinner just makes it worse.

One of these days, but not today.

Last time we talked, Denny had let slip her suspicion Edgar was having an affair. She didn't seem to know who the girl was, and I didn't give it any thought ... although if I had, Jeannie Klinglesmith would've been on the short list. Jeannie's exactly the kind of girl I'd expect Edgar to screw-around with: young, pretty, desperate, and not very smart. Who knew what effect their coupling would have on our investigation? Maybe none. At the moment, it was simply another item stuffed into a brain already overflowing with things I'd rather not think about.

As usual, after dinner Karen and I went our separate ways. We've always been close friends. On a few occasions, we've been on the verge of becoming more than that, but obstacles always present themselves. She won't say it, but I suspect one is my tendency to try and drink away my problems. The overriding reason might just be that neither one of us knows how to take the first step.

I drank my Old Grand-Dad and sank into a sleep about as restful as a rollercoaster ride. I dreamed I was in high school, but at my present age. I wandered the halls of Burr High, hunting for Sheryl Foster. Everyone I asked smiled and acted like they knew where she was, but they wouldn't tell me. After a while, I heard familiar voices coming from a janitor's closet. I opened the door and looked in. There was Sheryl and Denny, sitting on a couple of upturned mop buckets, chatting-away like long-lost sisters. I tried to ask them how they knew each other, but they just talked and laughed like I wasn't there. I finally realized they were laughing at me. That woke me with a start. In my dreams, Denny's humiliated me a million times in a million different ways over the years. This was Sheryl's first appearance.

I couldn't go back to sleep, so I finished my book about the crazy president. The vice president saved the world at the last minute.

· · · · ·

I take weekends off when I can—which is, to be honest, most of the time—but it'd been over a week since we'd discovered Sheryl Foster's body and I felt like I needed to keep the pedal down. I changed out of yesterday's dirty uniform into a clean one that I'd forgotten was in the back of my closet. I needed to go into work and hear what Kenny and Bernard had discovered on their visit to the brothel.

Bernard's dearly beloved—the Fury—was parked in front of the station when I arrived, meaning he'd beaten me to work. I'd been hogging his sweetheart for the last few days, so I let him drive it to Watie Junction. He and Kenny had planned their visit for three or four in the morning, when they figured the girls would be least busy. Knowing Bernard, he'd driven straight here after they'd finished.

There was a pot of fresh-brewed coffee ready when I walked in the door, but no country music on the radio. Both Karen and Bernard had gotten a head start on the coffee.

"You look like you can use a cup or three or four," she said.

"At least," I said. She poured the coffee into the same enamel cup I drink my Old Grand-Dad out of. I gave it a sniff to make sure it was plain Folger's. It was, but I wouldn't have turned it down if it wasn't.

I don't normally get hangover headaches, but today was the exception that proves the rule. It felt like someone had cracked open my skull, stuffed it full of rotten meat, and sewed it back up with a railroad spike and some broken shoelaces. I was inclined to blame my impairment on not being able to sleep, and not an overabundance of liquor, although truth be told, it was a what-came-first-the-chicken-or-the-egg-type of situation. In any case, just standing up was a chore, so I invited the pair back to my office where I could talk and sit at the same time. Karen grabbed a chair and Bernard leaned up against the door frame. Both enjoyed their morning cigarettes. I didn't complain, even though the smoke made me even more light-headed than I already was. "Heard from Kenny?" I asked.

"He went home to get some sleep," said Karen.

"Fair enough. Bernard, how was your night at the house of ill repute?"

He smiled shyly and squinted through those thick glasses of his. "You mean the whorehouse?" he asked.

I allowed that I did.

"Alright, first of all, there ain't no man running the place. No pimp or nothing. The whores run the whole thing all by themselves. They kick in for rent on the trailer and other expenses. If they're bribing someone to stay open, they won't admit it, but I think maybe they aren't, believe it or not. They call themselves *independent contractors.*"

"Good for them, I guess. Tell me about 'em."

"Four ladies work there. Krystal, spelled with a 'K,' Yvette, Ginger, and Mary Ann."

Karen spit out a mouthful of coffee. "Are you serious?" she said. "Ginger and Mary Ann?"

"I reckon Gilligan and the Skipper must be regular customers," I said.

Bernard clearly didn't understand what we were talking about. I don't think he watches much television.

"Go on, little buddy," I said.

He squinted some more and blew smoke through his nostrils. Like Puff the Magic Dragon if Puff wore a pair of thick Harold Lloyd glasses. "There used to be five," he said. "They haven't replaced Sheryl. There isn't enough room for five, anyway, or so they said. They just did it to save money."

"I like a thrifty hooker, myself," I said. Karen gave me a dirty look and I resolved to limit further attempts at humor.

Bernard gave an explanation of their operation, most of which I knew already from my conversation with Yvette. I listened with half an ear until he got to the part about them seeing Sheryl the night of her death.

"Krystal's the only one who thought she saw Sheryl go anywhere," he said. "She was busy with a customer, but she thinks she may have seen her get into a car."

"Could she describe the car?" I asked.

He shook his head and pooched out his lips in an exaggerated frown. "Not really," he said. "She said she thought it was kind of big, and it might've been red, but she couldn't be sure. She didn't get a good look. She wasn't sure about anything, not even if it was Sheryl she saw. None of the other girls saw it, either, so it might be that Krystal ain't the most dependable witness."

"But it was definitely a car and not a pickup or a truck?" Karen said.

"No, she was sure about that. It was a car."

"What else?" I asked.

"Yvette, the one you talked to before, she told me a couple of things. She recognized a picture of the World's Fair pendant. She said Sheryl already had it when they started working together. That was over a year ago. Sheryl told Yvette she'd gotten it from a regular client when she worked in Oklahoma City. A state senator. He knew she was crazy about going to New York, so he gave it to her as a souvenir."

If that were true, and it probably was, our most important item of physical evidence was worthless. The coin must've come off or was ripped from her body when she was dumped. Oh well, at least I'd learned something about the World's Fair.

"Yvette also said she's been thinking since y'all talked. She might've seen some middle-aged fella who used to come to see Sheryl." He looked puzzled. "She said I should make sure I say he was 'middle-aged' and not 'old.' Said you'd know why."

I assured him I did and told him to go on.

"Anyway, she says her memory's been playing tricks on her these days, but she thinks she saw him that Friday night."

"Was he with Sheryl?"

"No, she said he was alone, up near the diner. She said he stood around, looking at what was going on by the trailer. Like he was trying to decide to come over or not."

"Did she see what he was driving?"

"No, he was on foot when she saw him. She thinks it was the man y'all had talked about, though. He was a long way away, so she couldn't be 100% sure."

I wondered if the fella in question was who I suspected it was.

"One more thing," Bernard said. "Ginger says she saw EJ get rough with Sheryl one time. Grabbed her hard, pushed and slapped her, that kind of stuff."

Karen leaned forward in her chair. She pursed her lips started shook her head in small, quick motions, like she does when she's starting to get riled. "He did it once, he could do it again," she said. I nodded in agreement.

I noticed I was starting to sweat and wondered if it was the heat or my debilitated condition. I chose to believe it was the heat. We generally try to save money on our electric bill by leaving our little air-conditioner off until later in the day. Our penny-pinching usually becomes a casualty of the weather by June at the latest. It might happen in April this year.

"I know it's not part of the case or anything," Bernard said, "but I wonder what makes a girl turn out like that? I mean, once they realized we weren't there to give 'em a hard time, they seemed just regular, you know? Ginger is kind of stuck-up, but the others are nice. They didn't even mind that we parked the Fury out front. They said they were tired and ready to call it a night. Said parking a police car there was like putting out a 'Closed' sign."

"Karen," I said, "you're the lady of the house, what do you think?"

She looked annoyed. "What do I think about prostitution? I'm against it."

"Well, obviously you're against it," I said. "I'm asking why do you think girls fall into that life."

She leaned back in her chair and sighed. For a second seemed too tired to answer. "Emmett, don't make me explain it," she said. "You're smart enough to figure it out for yourself."

"I'm not sure I am."

Judging by her tone and facial expression, her estimation of my cognitive abilities at that moment was not especially high. "Let me tell you something," she said, "I've known a lot of women who weren't prostitutes, who felt like what they had to do to survive wasn't much better." She started pursing her lips and shaking her head again and using her hands to help her talk. "Men run the world and we girls basically do as we're told. We aren't police chiefs, we're dispatchers. We aren't bosses, we're secretaries. We do what y'all let us do. In the case of Sheryl, she was colored and I imagine that makes everything about ten times worse, plus she lost both her folks so young—"

I braced myself for more but nothing came. I thought about suggesting it was God's will that things turn out the way they do, but I'm not much of a believer, and anyway I'd expect my mama would rise up from her grave and tan my hide if I said something so stupid. That is, if Karen didn't beat her to it.

"Pour me some of that vodka you got hid in your drawer," she snapped.

The two things Karen Dean does when she's angry are cuss and drink. She starts doing either one, you'd best get out her way or do what she says. Especially at nine o'clock in the morning.

I poured double shots of Smirnoff into two paper cups. Karen downed hers in one gulp. I had to space out my sips. Straight vodka is nasty enough any time, never mind first thing in the morning.

Bernard clearly held our indulgence in low regard. "I guess I'll take the Fury out for a while," he grumped. Bernard's a bit of a horse-faced schoolmarm, if you want to know the truth.

Karen tossed her cup into the trash, folded her arms and put her feet up on my desk. I'll be honest, I don't mind a bit when she drinks, because that's when she lets down her defenses and becomes most like herself—defiant and tomboy-like and ready to kick some tail. "Sheryl Foster said or did something a man didn't like and got killed for it," she said.

I reckoned she was right on the money, but I didn't say so. At the moment, I don't think Karen was in a frame of mind to hear me say anything more on the subject.

CHAPTER THIRTY-TWO

The phone rang off the hook all morning. Somehow, every pissed-off citizen in town seemed to know I'd be in the office. It was like they'd saved-up all their bitching and moaning for the weekend.

John Curtis is a life insurance salesman with a Kansas accent who did not realize when he moved here that a majority of Burr-ites consider his product to be a form of gambling and therefore an affront to Jesus. John called this morning to say he'd had enough and was getting the hell out of town. Unfortunately, his next-door neighbor's raggedy lawn made it hard for him to sell his house. He pestered me to cite the neighbor for being a public nuisance or unlicensed weed-growing or something. I told John it'd be better if he handled the problem himself, and to call back if there was no way to resolve the situation without resorting to gun play.

Doris Schrader called with the sad tale of the death of her Siamese cat, Miss Pussykins. A power line had sagged from its pole and dropped a power line into her back yard. The cat got too close and electrocuted herself. It can hardly be said that Miss Pussykins' was a premature death; She'd just celebrated her 19th birthday a couple of weeks earlier (there'd been a front-page article about the milestone in *The Burr Gazette*, with pictures and everything). I expressed my sympathies and advised Doris to contact Oklahoma Gas & Electric.

LaVerne Salisbury called to say she'd be in Tulsa for a week and asked if we could suspend her mail delivery. I told her to call the post office and said we'd miss her while she was gone.

Then Rex McKinnis called to say he'd decided to charge Gene Yellowhorse for the murder of Sheryl Foster, which I took as worse news than John Curtis's departure, Miss Pussykins' demise, and LaVerne's mail problem all put together.

. . . . .

Rex informed me there'd been a breakthrough. Yellowhorse's cellmate had agreed to testify that the Indian told him he'd raped and killed Sheryl. The fact that the cellmate was a three-time loser did not dissuade Rex.

"Sounds to me like someone's looking for a 'Get Out of Jail Free' card," I said.

"I imagine he is, but credibility won't be an issue if the case never goes to court," he said. "I can use his statement to convince Yellowhorse his only reasonable course is to plead to second-degree murder. With his record, he'll more than likely spend the rest of his life in prison, but that's better than the electric chair, which he'll almost certainly get, otherwise."

"I'd say congratulations, Rex, except I believe you got the wrong man."

"I don't think so, Emmett. How far have you gotten with that investigation of yours?" He didn't need to tell me it no longer mattered.

Nevertheless, I sold my new information as best I could. I told him what the hookers said and whatever else I could think of that might change his mind. Rex was sympathetic but wouldn't budge.

"The only way to turn me around at this point is with a confession. Do it before this Yellowhorse deal gets set in stone, I'll reconsider. But I'm not unhappy with what we have."

"Being 'not unhappy' is not the same as being happy."

"In this business, it can be close enough."

"Like horseshoes."

"And hand grenades."

. . . . .

Bernard was out writing tickets at the speed trap. Kenny was due to come in later. God knows where Jeff was. I left Karen to hold down the fort and took off in my pickup. I had a lot to do in a short time, and I didn't know where to start. That's what I told myself, anyway.

· · · · ·

The Thunderbird was the lone car in the driveway when I arrived at the Bixby place.

I climbed the steps to the porch, making sure my boots fell heavy and loud so Denny'd hear me coming. She pulled the drapes aside a couple of inches and peeked out, then opened the door. A blast of central air-conditioning hit my face like a bucket of ice water.

She wore a peach-colored sleeveless blouse and a pair of denim shorts, although you could say the shorts were wearing her, they were so tight. Her blond hair was pulled back into a pony tail tied by a navy-blue ribbon. She didn't wear a spot of makeup. Didn't need it. I've known that woman thirty years and she still makes my heart thump like a nine-pound hammer.

The last time I'd been inside her house was a party for brother-in-law Deke promoting one of his runs for town council. That was a good ten years ago. It was even fancier now than it was then.

In the entrance there was a huge oil painting of US cavalry soldiers in blue uniforms and gray Stetsons kicking the shit out of some Indians. Opposite that was a small bronze sculpture of a Pony Express rider on a marble pedestal. I guessed the painting was by Charles Russell and the sculpture by Frederic Remington, but it could've been the other way around. Both men's work tends to be highly prized by Oklahoma cattle and oil millionaires with social pretensions.

From there we stepped into a living room that was bigger than my whole house.

Against one wall was an enormous fireplace with andirons shaped like bucking broncos and a mantelpiece carved with likenesses of

John Wayne, Gene Autry, and, I believe, Gary Cooper—although the one of Coop looked more like Danny Kaye, if you ask me. The walls were covered in walnut paneling, the floor in dense, olive-colored shag carpet. The furniture was constructed of heavy cuts of dark, varnished wood, and hand-tooled leather. The side table lamps were made of horseshoes welded together in a fancy design that I'm sure wasn't meant to look like a pair of female breasts, but did. Large photographs of oil wells and livestock covered one wall. Edgar's hunting trophies hung on another: stuffed elk and buffalo heads, and a number of smaller animals, as well. On the opposite wall was a painting of Bud Wilkinson. Next to Bud was a portrait of Daffodil Bixby, in all her prize-winning glory.

Whoever decorated the place, it sure as hell wasn't Denny, who I'm reasonably certain has no fondness for football or disembodied animal heads or giant pigs. For a girl who always wanted to be rich, Denny is surprisingly un-fancy. I reckon she was glad to let Edgar and whoever he hired handle the interior design.

She motioned me to sit, so I plunked down on the larger of two overstuffed leather couches sitting across from one another. "Would you care for a drink?" she asked. "Or don't you indulge while in uniform?" Before I could answer she made for the bar, stumbling slightly over a seam on the carpet. It looked she'd gotten a head start with the booze.

"I'll have some bourbon if you got any."

"You name it, we got it." She wobbled back to the second couch carrying a bottle of Jim Beam and a couple of glasses, which she filled nearly to the brim. She slid one across the coffee table to me. A few drops of amber liquid spilled over the side. Denny didn't seem to care.

"According to your husband, I tried to force myself on you last time I was here," I said. "I'm surprised you let me in the front door."

She waved her hand limply and lifted her glass for a toast. "Here's to Chief Emmett Hardy. The one who got away."

My ears burned. "Pushed away, is more like it." I regretted the words as soon as they left my mouth.

"Ha!" she said and tossed back her drink. "If you're here to play the rejected schoolboy, you can just turn around and leave, right this minute."

I'd made a mistake, but what's done is done. "I'm sorry, but goddammit Denny, you can't go and tease me like that."

"Tease you?" she laughed incredulously. "What in hell is our relationship but a big tease, anyway? That's what friends do. They tease and poke fun."

"Well, it gets to the point where it's just mean, is all."

"Oh, is little ol' Denny being mean to poor Emmett again? Is that what this is about?" She poured herself another two-fingers and drank most of it. "Are you going to give me the 'you just married Edgar for his money and now you're paying the price, blah, blah, blah?'"

"I never said that to you, Denny."

"No, but you thought it, just like everyone else in town. Why can't y'all just give it a rest? Let me live my life." She made a short, harsh sound that could've been a laugh or a cry.

I didn't know what to say so I didn't say anything.

She leaned forward with the drink held close enough to her mouth that she could sip in-between sentences. "Don't get me wrong," she almost slurred. "I understand perfectly. You've been in love with me since we were little. For all I know, you still are. And you blame me for not being in love with you. But I can't, Emmett Hardy, I can't. Never could, never will. I'm sorry, but it just isn't going to happen. I cared about you too much to pretend otherwise."

It seemed like there was something underneath the words she was trying to say, but I couldn't put my finger on what it was. Might be something I knew but couldn't admit to myself.

She gazed at me with red eyes, blinking slowly, her head wobbling slightly from side to side. It could be that she couldn't hold her booze like she used to, or had finally discovered a level of consumption that would get her stinking drunk. "Do you understand?" she said, gently now. "I'm sorry, but that's the way it is. I love you to death, but I don't feel romantic about you."

Whatever I'd expected when I showed up at her door, this wasn't it. I couldn't even be sure why I'd come, to be honest. I'd only known I had to go somewhere. I sure hadn't gone there to be shamed and/or squashed like a bug, but that's what happened. I downed the drink she'd given me and poured another big one. I drank it a single gulp, hoping the effect might help me regain some self-respect. It didn't.

"Jesus, Emmett. Think of all the time you wasted moping over me. Most of the girls in school were in love with you. Karen Dean was. Probably still is." She reached toward an engraved gold case on the coffee table and fumbled trying to extricate a cigarette. She finally got one lit and took a drag. "I never asked you about that woman you married back east when you got out of the Army. What happened with her?"

I didn't see any point in lying. "She wasn't you."

She sighed and seemed to shrink a little, like all the air had been let out of her. "I'm sorry Emmett, I should keep my big fat mouth shut." She got up, a drink in one hand and a smoke in the other. She walked over to a set of sliding glass doors that looked out onto her backyard. They'd put in a swimming pool since the last time I'd visited. A dirty inflatable green dinosaur, like a child would use, floated on the water. It appeared to have been there awhile.

She turned around too fast and had to brace herself against the doorframe to keep from falling over. "I'm in a terrible mood and you caught me at a bad time." She leaned back against the glass door. "Believe it or not, it hurts me that I hurt you. Always has." Her voice broke. "You're a good man and deserve to be happy. But it's not my fault you're not. It's cruel of you to blame me. I've got enough on my shoulders."

I nodded like one of those plastic puppies people put on their dashboards. I downed the last of my bourbon and promised myself not to drink any more until I was safe at home in my La-Z-Boy.

Denny wagged a finger in my direction and smiled ironically. "You couldn't have saved me, ok? The fact I'm miserable has nothing to do with you, just like the fact you're miserable has nothing to do with me." God, she was drunk. Denny never used to get drunk. We're getting old, I thought.

My voice was shaky but I discovered it still worked. "Ok," I said. "I'm just—I'm sorry." I wasn't sure why, specifically, but I knew over the years I'd done something to hurt her, even if I wasn't completely sure what it was. I sank deep into the couch, drained. By everything.

Every goddam thing.

Denny sat next to me and put her head on my shoulder. The bourbon on her breath depressed me, but also reminded me of better times. We sat there for a while without saying anything.

Out of nowhere, she burst out laughing. "Do you remember that time we took your daddy's car to play miniature golf?" I started laughing despite myself.

My dad bought a brand-new 1947 Hudson with some of his natural gas windfall. Against his better judgment, he loaned it to me one night to take Denny miniature golfing. He made me promise upon pain of death that no harm would come to it. Golf Pair O' Dice was like a Warner Brothers cartoon come to life. Every hole had a giant-sized version of Bugs Bunny or Daffy Duck or Porky Pig. I remember one in particular involving the Roadrunner and a guillotine. The trick was to knock the ball through a space between Roadrunner's legs before the blade came down and cut Wile E. Coyote's head off. It took me at least half-a-dozen times to make it through. Denny got a hole-in-one. In fact, she kicked the hell out of me overall. We had a great time.

After we finished, Denny asked me to buy her a Coke. I gave her the keys so she could get into the car while I went to the concession stand. When I returned, the car's rear end was hanging over the edge of a drainage ditch. Denny had decided she was going to back-out the car for me, even though she'd never driven in her life. She backed up well-enough, but couldn't figure out how to stop in time. The car got caught on the curb and seesawed, the front wheels sitting lightly on the ground and the rear wheels suspended in mid-air. Denny was bawling and I felt like crying myself, thinking what my father would do if the car was damaged. She started to get out but the car began falling into the ditch, so I pushed her back in. I made her sit tight until we could get rescued.

"I guess I tried to forget," I said. Of course, I wouldn't, if I lived to be one hundred.

Denny couldn't stop laughing. "I remember the look on your face. You were so sure your daddy was going to kill you."

"He might've if he ever found out."

"But he didn't. And now we can laugh."

"It sure as hell didn't seem very funny at the time."

"No, I guess it didn't."

We got quiet again.

"I missed being your friend," she said softly.

"I missed being yours, too."

I thought I should exit before I embarrassed myself beyond the point of no return. I got up to leave.

"You're going already? Why'd you come, anyway? Not because you wanted to be abused by me, surely."

I didn't want to say it was because I was considering putting most of her family in jail— which come to think of it was the main reason— so I blurted the first thing that came to mind. "I wanted to ask Edgar about Daffodil."

"Oh, that damn pig. Well, I'm pretty sure Edgar's not gonna want to talk to you, after everything that's been going on." I cringed inwardly. I didn't know whether she knew about my talk with her menfolk the day before. If she did, she made no indication. "If you want to try and hunt him down, he's in Temple City," she said with what seemed like a tinge of melancholy. "That's what he told me, anyway. He's staying overnight at the Casa Grande Hotel."

I thought of Jeannie Klinglesmith. Maybe Denny was thinking about her, too. Or someone like her.

"I'll track him down there," I said, intending to do no such thing.

"He should be back tomorrow in time for church."

That Edgar Bixby is allowed within a mile of a church of any kind is all the evidence I need that there is no God.

Denny craned her neck and gave me a sloppy kiss on the cheek. "I do love you in my own way, you know," she said with a sad smile.

"I know," I said.

I did. Not that it helped much.

CHAPTER THIRTY-THREE

I raised Karen on the two-way as I drove back to town and asked if she had a phone book handy.

"Got it right here, hon," she said.

"I need Jeannie Klinglesmith's address."

"Uh-oh," she said. "I can see where this is headed." She gave me the address. "Watch your step."

"I'll try."

Jeannie lived in a trim little ranch-style house in Redbud Acres, Burr's one genuine housing development. A builder named Harry "Red" Budbill constructed 12 nearly identical houses on spec right after World War II. Harry read about what was going on in Levittown, NY, and thought it'd go over big here. Unfortunately for him, supply exceeded demand and he fell behind on his loan payments. The bank—in the person of local Scrooge-in-Training Deke Bixby—took over. Deke sold the houses cheaper than Harry could. Twelve families ended-up getting a bargain, the first and only time anyone in Burr got a good deal from a Bixby. It didn't turn out so well for poor Harry. In his despair, he tried drinking himself to death, but it took too long, so he hanged himself from a windmill north of town, instead.

Redbud Acres has one street and Jeannie lived at the far end. No vehicles were parked in front of her house, so I could be pretty sure Edgar wasn't there. I was jumping without a parachute, but I figured even free-falling was preferable to standing still. I rang the doorbell.

No one answered, thanks to the loud American Bandstand-style music coming from somewhere inside. I knocked hard a dozen times. Finally, a female voice yelled, "Hold on, I'm coming!"

I'd guess the pretty young brunette who answered the door was in her mid-20s, although guessing women's ages is not one of my strengths. She wore a low-cut dress of alternating yellow and blue stripes with large white buttons up the front. It was short enough to have gotten her sent home from school if she'd been a few years younger. Her light brown hair had been hair-sprayed into the shape of a motorcycle helmet, with a flip at the bottom. Tight white boots came almost up to her knees. She'd turned down the music but it was still audible—some overaged teenager singing "baby, baby," over and over.

Her smile reached from here to Tuesday. "Hey!" she chirped. "What can I do for you?"

Right off, I was leery. Nobody's that happy when visited by the police. I sniffed the air, thinking she might be smoking some illegal substance, but all I could detect was some kind of perfume that smelled like the inside of a box of Luden's Cough Drops.

"Hi, yourself," I said. "Is Jeannie home?"

"Sure! I mean, no!" She laughed. "I'm sorry, I'm a little distracted. Would you like to come in?"

I demurred, thinking she might try to tickle me to death or feed me to some giant man-eating houseplant. "I'm just looking to talk to Jeannie. Nothing serious, I'm hoping she can help me find a friend of mine."

"I'm her roommate. Maybe I can help." She whacked her forehead with the palm of her hand and pretended she'd knocked herself silly. "Whoops, I forgot to introduce myself. I'm Peggy Miller."

With some effort, I managed *not* to sneak a peak at Peggy Miller's shapely legs, which were a great deal more exposed than I am accustomed to seeing.

"Glad to know you, Miss Miller.

I had to look somewhere, it would've been impolite not to, so I looked in her eyes. They were heavily mascaraed and shadowed, but I could tell they were brown with flecks of green.

"Glad to know you—" she squinted at my nameplate, "Chief Hardy. Oh! I've heard of you. You rescued a skunk out from under Ethel Blankenship's house a couple of weeks ago."

"It was Ella Burton's house and it was a stray cat got stuck in a bucket of black paint, but yeh, that was me."

"It's an honor to meet you, sir! I'll tell Jeannie you came by."

"You wouldn't happen to know where I can find her, do you? Or when she'll be home?"

"She's out of town for the weekend. She should be back for church tomorrow, though. Who's your friend? I might know him."

"His name's Edgar Bixby," I said, still trying not to let my eyes wander. I'm a gentleman always, but I'm also a male of the species and being in close proximity to an attractive young woman dressed like a New York fashion model made me unusually self-conscious. I'm old enough to be her father, I thought. Or her much older brother.

At the mention of Edgar, her 1000-watt smile died down to about a 5-watt. "I don't know anybody by that name."

Peggy Miller is a bad liar, I thought.

"Are you sure?" I said. "I think I remember Edgar saying Jeannie's roommate was pretty as a picture."

Big mistake. Her smile disappeared and she smoothed the front of her dress, like she was trying to make the fabric cover more than it was designed to. I admit, it's possible my attempt to avoid looking at her legs had failed.

"Well, Chief Hardy, I know I shouldn't fib to a police officer, so I suppose I deserve it if you fib to me. But I don't like it." She moved behind the door, closing it most of the way, so all I could see was half of her face. "I'll tell you the truth. Edgar Bixby has been in this house many times, and I've heard him mention your name in a way that makes me think you two aren't friends."

If there are classes in talking to women, I should sign up right away. "You're right, Miss Miller," I said. "I apologize. Edgar Bixby and I are not friends. Far from it, if you want to know the truth."

She opened the door a little wider. "I'm not supposed to tell anyone Jeannie and him are carrying on, but you're the police, so I guess it's ok." She laid an index finger aside her cheek and looked off to the side. "It's kind of my duty as a citizen, right?" The idea seemed to cheer her up. I nodded and smiled. She grinned back and opened the door the rest of the way. Peggy Miller is not one to hold a grudge.

"If he doesn't like you, that must mean you're ok. Any enemy of Edgar is a friend of mine!" She stopped trying to adjust her dress. "What do you want to know?"

I explained briefly how I knew Jeannie had been seeing Edgar, and I needed to find him as soon as possible in connection with a matter I was investigating. Peggy asked if it was about the girl who was killed. I said I couldn't discuss it.

"Oh, never mind," she said, "I'll tell you anyway." She leaned forward and stage-whispered like she was revealing a state secret. "Edgar took Jeannie to Temple City last night after she got off work. She said they were going to stay overnight at the Casa Grande Hotel. I expect they'll be there tonight, too."

I thought of Denny and felt sad for her, despite myself.

"Does Edgar come around much?"

"Too much, if you ask me. Sometimes they go back in Jeannie's room, but mostly he takes her somewhere."

I thanked her for her help. "If what you're doing means Edgar won't be coming around anymore, I thank *you*," she said. "I don't understand why Jeannie puts up with him. No amount of fancy dinners or presents are worth it."

We said our goodbyes and I turned to leave. I hadn't stepped down off the porch before I thought of something else. "Sorry, Peggy, but there's one more thing. What kind of car does Edgar drive?"

"It's big and red and kind of futuristic looking. I can't remember what it's called."

Edgar's Lincoln is big, but it's not red, nor is it futuristic. Denny's Thunderbird is red but it's not especially big.

I knew a car that fit the description. I had a picture, but I'd left it in the Fury.

"Would you remember the name if you heard it?"

"I think so."

"Impala?"

"That's it!" she said, slapping her forehead again. "An Impala. Cherry-red."

"One last thing, I promise. Do you remember if Edgar was here a week ago last Friday night?"

"That's funny, because ordinarily I wouldn't. But actually, I do, because that night there was this crazy thing on Johnny Carson. That Indian fella from Daniel Boone threw an axe at this picture of a cowboy and hit him right in the you-know-whats." She giggled. "Jeannie watched it with me. She didn't laugh. I think she was still mad at Edgar."

"Why was she mad at Edgar?"

"Oh, the usual reason. He was mean to her. He was supposed to take her to some fancy restaurant, but called and cancelled at the last minute. Oh boy, was Jeannie mad. I never saw her so mad, and she's mad a lot."

"You remember what time it was?"

"I'd say about eight-thirty. Jeannie gets off work at eight. She came home and changed clothes real fast. She was waiting for him to pick her up when he called."

I thanked her again. "You've been a great help. It's nice to have met you."

She grinned hugely. I noticed she had a slight overbite which I thought was just as cute as the dickens. "You're welcome! Should I tell Jeannie you were here?"

I hated to ask Peggy Miller to lie, if for no other reason than I reckoned she was too honest to be a good liar. On the other hand, there were certain advantages to keeping Jeannie in the dark.

"Would you mind not mentioning it to her for the time being?" I asked. "No need to worry. She's not in any trouble, but it might be better if she didn't discuss this with Edgar."

Peggy stood to attention and saluted. "Roger wilco, Chief. Glad to be of service! Come around any time. We never close!"

I heard her laugh and turn up the music as I walked back to my car.

Damn, I thought. If I was that happy all the time, I think I'd kill myself.

CHAPTER THIRTY-FOUR

Karen's voice crackled over the radio when I got back to the pickup

"What's up?" I said.

"I've been trying to get hold of you for the last half-hour."

"I've been busy."

"Well, you need to listen to this," she said. "I got a call from one of the church ladies looking after Kevin Gunter. The hospital released him this morning."

"Released him?" I said. "To who?"

"His daddy."

I guess Nate's back from Las Vegas.

"I don't suppose they know where they were headed?"

"Not really. The nurse I talked to said Nate gave his home address on the discharge papers, but who knows if that's where they're going."

"What time was he discharged?"

"About two hours ago."

"Have Kenny or Bernard drive over to Nate's and wait."

"I'll send Kenny. He just came in. Bernard needed to go home and get some sleep. Jeff's out on patrol."

"If Nate's heading back to Burr, he should be here soon."

For all I knew, he could've been bound for France, although I can't picture Nate wearing a beret and eating snails. Burr was a better bet.

I remembered Karen had been working on her day off, so I told her to have our calls forwarded to the sheriff's department and take the rest of the day off.

"I won't argue with you, boss. Where are you now?"

"Outside Jeannie Klinglesmith's house. I talked to her roommate. I'll tell you about it later."

I started the truck, holding the microphone in one hand and wrestling with the clutch in the other. "I'm heading over to the high school," I said. "It looked like they were getting ready for a ball game when I drove by earlier."

I got the truck in gear and pulled onto the highway without looking both ways. A passing semi missed taking off my front bumper by about an inch. He gave his horn an angry blast. I pointed to the magnetic emergency light on my roof. I don't think it carried much weight with him. At such times, I miss the Fury.

Karen was unaware of my brush with catastrophe. "What are you fixing to do?" she asked.

"Let's say I intend to have a private chat with EJ Bixby. Without his lawyer present."

"Be careful. Don't break any laws."

"Girl, I am the law, or haven't you heard?" I could almost hear her roll her eyes.

"Yeh, you're a regular Judge Roy Bean," she said.

"Don't worry. I'm not necessarily looking for something to use in court. I just want some answers."

"Speaking of answers, Jeff discovered who stole Daffodil. A high school kid named Chuck Hyatt. He had some help, but he planned the deal."

Hearing we'd found our pig-napper made me feel happier than I expected it would. Maybe it was a good omen. "That's Darren Hyatt's boy," I said. "Call Darren. Set up a time for them to come in before church tomorrow. I should at least put a scare into Chuck."

·   ·   ·   ·   ·

The high school baseball team plays its games at the same field where, once upon a time, Edgar Bixby stole my Pepper Martin glove. Unlike the football stadium, which is the nicest structure in town, the baseball field is only a step above a cow pasture. Other than a set of puny bleachers they added when I wasn't paying attention, it hasn't changed much since the old days.

A game was still going on. EJ's Corvette was parked in foul territory. I pulled up next to it.

The visitors had the bases loaded when I arrived. I asked a bored-looking fella in a blue and yellow CAT Diesel Power cap if he knew the score. He spit a wad of chewing tobacco through the backstop in the direction of the umpire and said we were losing nine-zip. Just then, a big burly farm boy on the other team hit the ball out of sight, way out into the same weeds where Edgar used to hit them against us kids. He preened like a peacock running the bases. 13-zip.

The next batter poked a weak grounder toward first base. EJ fielded it easily and stepped on the bag for the third out. On the way back to the bench, he said something to the pitcher. The pitcher took offense and shoved EJ. EJ shoved back, and before you knew it, the whole team was on the field pulling them apart. Adversity doesn't bring out the best in everyone.

The Patriots went down one-two-three in the bottom of the ninth. Coach Shannon gathered them in the dugout on the first base side and yelled about how they were a team and had to stick together and they should direct their fight toward their opponent. He looked straight at EJ the whole time. EJ made a big show out of not paying attention. No one else seemed very interested, either. The coach got tired of listening to himself after a couple of minutes and sent them home.

I know EJ saw me but he wouldn't look over. Instead, he jogged toward his car, hoping for a quick getaway. No dice. I headed him off.

"EJ, why don't you come and sit in my truck a minute. We need to talk."

"I ain't supposed to talk to you without my lawyer," he said walking backwards toward his car.

"C'mon, now. That's only if we're conducting a formal interview." That wasn't entirely true, but he didn't have to know that. "I'm just trying to get a clear picture of what happened the night Sheryl Foster was killed."

"I told you, I don't know nothing about it."

"I know you did, but maybe you do and you just forgot. I'll bet if you think real hard you can remember something that'll help."

That gave him pause. He stood there craning his neck this way and that like he expected someone to come to his rescue. No one did. He lowered his head and kicked up a clump of dirt. "Alright," he said resignedly, and got in the truck.

I got in beside him and started the engine. "You didn't say we was going anywhere," he said.

"We're just going to drive around a little bit. I think better when I'm driving."

I avoided Main Street and turned onto 14 near the edge of town. There weren't many folks out-and-about this late in the day, but I didn't want to take a chance on anyone seeing me with EJ. I noticed him scratching a red spot on his arm.

"Mosquito bite?" I asked.

"Yeh, I guess," he said.

I sensed him getting nervous when he realized where we were headed, but he didn't say anything. Just kept scratching the mosquito bite.

It was seven o'clock but it was still hotter than the devil's waiting room. The sun lay low in the Western sky, blinding me as I drove. I pulled down my visor and hoped for the best.

A blue sawhorse was tipped over on its side a few yards from where we'd found Sheryl's body. I couldn't be sure if it was supposed to be there or the highway patrol forgot about it.

"Let's walk," I said.

EJ was still scratching his arm. "I don't feel like it," he said. "I just got done playing. I'm tired."

"Come on," I cajoled. "You got plenty of energy." He still balked. "Let's go," I said in a voice I reserve for those times I'm about to kick someone's rear end. He sighed and got out of the truck.

I started toward rise on the tracks. EJ lagged behind. "Come on, while we're young," I said. He followed, seeing he had no choice in the matter. We hadn't had rain in over a month, so the white painted outline of the body on the incline was still vivid.

"This was where we found her," I said.

He stood blank-faced, looking down at the spot, still scratching his arm. The area around the mosquito bite had turned the color of an overripe strawberry.

"She was naked and bloody when we found her," I said. "See these?" I crouched and picked up a few of the crushed rocks. "See how jagged they are? The railroad fellas call it 'ballast.' It's what holds the tracks in place. They cut Sheryl bad. I guess it didn't matter, since she was dead by the time she was dumped. Whoever killed her threw her body down like she was a sack of trash. I reckon they thought she didn't deserve any better since she was colored."

He remained impassive, looking down at the spot and scratching his arm. He was starting to draw blood.

I was going to get some kind of response out of him if it took all night. "You don't care if that's where we found your girlfriend, naked with her throat cut?" I rose from my crouch. My knees popped, just like they did that night. "Maybe I was wrong about you. Maybe you did kill her."

That got his attention. "You always thought I did," he said. "Ain't that what this is about?"

"I never said I thought you killed her, EJ. I can't imagine why you would. But based on the way you've lied, I'm starting to think you did."

An urge to drink intruded upon my thoughts. I felt like a shot or two of bourbon might file-down my irritation and dull the sadness of being in that place and reliving that night. I did what I could to push the idea out of my mind. Focus was required.

"The biggest lie you tell is about not caring for Sheryl," I said. "I think you did care, and even though you've been a pain in this town's ass over the years, I don't think you're a killer. I think you're mostly lying to stay out of trouble with your daddy." I paused to let it sink in. "Let me tell you, there are worse things than being in trouble with Edgar. I've been in trouble with him all my life, and I've done alright."

At that, his eyes welled-up. I tried feeling sorry for him but I might as well have been watching a rock cry. Still, I had to pretend. "Help me, EJ," I said. "Help me find out who did this."

He shook his head a few times. I'd poked a hole in his defense, but the wall still stood. I handed him a handkerchief. He dried his eyes and wiped his arm where it had started to bleed from the scratching. I motioned for him to keep it. "Let's go back to the car," I said. "Might as well sit."

EJ sat in the truck, red-faced with snot running out his nose, staring blankly out the windshield at the train tracks. In the distance was his home. The porch light was on and I wondered if Denny was watching us. Maybe EJ was wondering the same thing.

Out of nowhere, he said, "What do you want to know?"

"I want to know who did it."

"I don't know," he said too quick.

"If you know, EJ, you'd best tell. Withholding evidence makes you an accessory. You're 19. You can be tried as an adult and sent to McAlester." I did not describe how pretty young boys like him are treated in prison. I'd play that card later, if I needed it. "Trust me, you don't want that," was all I said.

"I don't know, okay?" he said in a panicky voice.

"Sure, sure, alright, EJ, calm down." I didn't want to antagonize the boy any more than necessary. What I was doing—talking to him without his folks or a lawyer present—was at the very least unethical, if not illegal. I didn't want it to come back and bite me later.

A change of tack was in order. "Tell me what you did after you ditched the bus," I said.

I knew what he did, and he knew I knew. But I wanted to hear him say it.

"I went to see Sheryl. I didn't plan on it, but when the bus stopped I just did it." He shrugged. "I figured I could get someone to pick me up later or I could hitchhike home."

"So, you went to the whorehouse?"

"Yeh. I walked there from the Dairy Queen."

"What'd you do when you got there?"

He looked at me like it was a stupid question. Which I suppose, it was. "I tried to find Sheryl. I saw her outside the trailer. She was about to start working and said she didn't have time to talk to me, so I left."

"So that's it? You just left? You stranded yourself 20 miles from home to spend time with her, she turns you down, and you give up so easy?" I shook my head. "Boy, if it was me, I'd have tried to make her at least take a break." I swatted at a June bug that had flown in through the window. "Hell," I said, "I might even insist."

"I didn't give up easy. I tried hard, but she wouldn't do it."

I waited for more, but all he did was scratch his arm.

"So, what did you do next?"

"I didn't have any money because I was still in my baseball uniform, so I borrowed some change from her to make a phone call to get someone to pick me up."

"EJ, I'm sorry, but this doesn't smell right." I reckoned harping on his natural feeling of male superiority might get the job done. "I can't believe you'd let a girl toy with you like that."

He stuck his chest out and squared his jaw. "I didn't, okay? I told her I'd let her off the hook this time, but it better not happen again." He sat back and banged his head against the truck's rear window. "Jesus Christ, she didn't have time, is all. I wasn't going to kidnap her."

"So, you weren't mad at her, then."

"No." He paused and looked thoughtful. "You didn't get mad at Sheryl. She was too good a person." It must be true if someone as spoiled as EJ could see it. That she could be so decent in the face of what she was up against made the whole thing even more depressing.

I asked him who he called. Kevin Gunter.

"I thought you hated Kevin Gunter."

"I don't hate him. I just think he's a pussy."

"A pussy who'll help you when you're in a tough spot."

"He can be all right sometimes." In other words, he has his uses. The right tool for the right job.

"Where'd he pick you up?"

"Dairy Queen."

"Why not the whorehouse? Why'd you go back?"

"I don't know," he said. "I just did. I don't like being around that place. Bunch of creeps and losers."

"Where'd you first meet Sheryl?"

"A bunch of us guys went up there last fall after a football game."

"So, you met her there. At the whorehouse."

"Well, yeh."

I did not ask which he was, a creep or a loser.

He claimed not to know what time Kevin picked him up, just that it was still light out. He said they went straight back to Burr and drove around some when they got to town. I asked if they stopped anywhere.

"No ... oh, wait. We did. Kind of. We needed some gas, so Kevin pulled into the Sinclair station out near my house. The lights were still on so we thought it might be open, but it wasn't."

"What time was it?"

He threw his head back and bumped his head again. "You keep asking me what time it was," he said, rubbing the back of his head. "I don't know. I don't wear a watch. It was dark. That's all I know."

"Did anybody see you pull into the Sinclair?"

"Yeh. That numb-nuts mechanic of theirs was working in the garage. He hollered they was closed when we pulled up to the pumps, so we just drove on through."

"What'd you do for gas?"

"Kevin said he had enough to get home and that he'd get some the next day. My car was parked at the school so I just had him drive me there and I went home."

I listened to the crickets. A gust of wind brought the smell of cow manure through my open window. I reckoned some of what EJ said could've been true. It was mostly what he didn't say that bothered me.

I backtracked. "Tell me again what happened when you got to the whorehouse."

"Don't you listen?" Clearly, he considered me one of the ten dumbest sumbitches on the planet. "I saw Sheryl and I left. That's all."

"No, I want to hear what you did exactly. From when you snuck off the bus to when Kevin picked you up at the Dairy Queen."

"I walked from the Dairy Queen to the whorehouse." He spoke slow and with exaggerated precision, like I was a small child. "When I got there she was outside the trailer, so I went up to her."

"Was she glad to see you?"

"I guess she was. She was always glad to see me."

"What else?"

"I don't know. I reckon I said, 'surprise' and she smiled, and I asked her if we could go out back where we sometimes go, but she said she had to work, so I left."

At this point I was convinced he was making it up on the spot.

"You didn't argue? You didn't get mad?"

"I told you, I said she better not do it again, and I left." He sniffed and said quietly, "I keep telling you."

"Did you see her with anyone else? When you were walking away?"

"No, I walked to the diner to use the phone. When I turned around she was gone."

"You didn't see where she went."

"No."

"Did you see anyone you knew? A customer who seemed familiar? Someone from Burr?"

"No, uh-uh." He said it too quick. The question made him uncomfortable. I pressed him.

"How 'bout a red Chevy Impala?"

He hesitated. "No, nothing like that," he said.

"Do you know anyone who drives a red Impala?"

"No, I don't. I can't think of any."

Maybe not everything he was saying was a lie, but if you wrote the true parts down, there wouldn't be enough to wallpaper an outhouse. I glared at him and gave him the silent treatment, but it didn't take. He just looked down at the mosquito bite. His arm was smeared with blood. He'd said all he was going to say. For now.

"Alright, EJ. We'd best get you back to your car. I'll bet your mama's waiting dinner on you."

"Huh," he said. "if you think that, you don't know my mama."

I had to laugh. "I guess I don't," I said.

CHAPTER THIRTY-FIVE

By the time I dropped off EJ at his car it was almost dark. I followed him most of the way home partly because he drives like a maniac and partly because I wanted him to know I was watching him. After that, I drove by the station. The lights were off. Karen had gone home earlier, Kenny's shift was over, and Jeff was on-call. During off-hours, our phone calls are forwarded to the sheriff's department. They contact me at home if my services are required.

Bernard was at the Gunter house waiting for Nate and Kevin to show up. I was supposed to relieve him, but my stomach demanded immediate attention. I drove home, put a Swanson's Fried Chicken TV dinner in the oven, and had a jelly glass of Old Grand-Dad. I wolfed down my food and drained the bourbon, then picked a paperback off the stack of books next to the La-Z-Boy. I thought I'd read while I waited for Nate. Could be a long night.

·　　·　　·　　·　　·

Bernard had parked the Fury across from the Gunters', to one side of the Leaning Tower so it could not be easily detected. I maneuvered my truck alongside.

I rolled down my window. "Time to trade vehicles," I said. Bernard groaned and banged his fist lightly on the steering wheel. "I'm just kidding, son. You can keep the car." We got out and met in front of the Fury.

"Any luck?" I asked, careful not to get within sniffing distance. Bernard knows I drink but I don't like to flaunt it in front of him. For some reason, I want him to think the best of me.

"Nope," he said. "I haven't taken my eye off that house since I got here. No Nate, no Kevin, no nothing."

I recounted the latest developments, leaving out the visit to Denny, which hadn't accomplished much, other than to make me feel like an ass.

The subject of the red car came up.

"I've got to believe Edgar's Impala and Nate's Impala are one and the same," I said.

"I ain't never seen one around town, never mind two," he said.

"I bet he parks it somewhere out of sight so he can use it when he goes tomcatting with Jeannie Klinglesmith, or whoever else."

Bernard nodded. "Everyone in the county knows that Lincoln of his. He's not likely to use it to cheat on his wife or park it in front of a whorehouse."

"No, not likely," I agreed. "The question is, why'd Nate have it?"

Bernard extracted a crooked cigarette from a rumpled pack in his shirt pocket. "I guess Edgar could've sold it to him."

"I reckon we'll have to ask one or the other," I said.

Bernard worked to straighten out the cigarette enough to be smoked. "Any reason to think the Impala's the same car Krystal with a K saw Sheryl get into?" he asked.

"There's a good reason, if Edgar had something going on with Sheryl."

He searched his pockets for a Zippo. He couldn't find it and gave me a questioning look. I don't carry matches. He leaned through the car window and groped around in the front seat until he found his lighter. He fired up the cigarette and relaxed.

I had to admit, it was a lovely evening to try to solve a murder. The weather was perfect—one of those late-April nights where you don't feel heat or chill and the air is dewy and even the odors of livestock shit and freshly laid asphalt don't seem so objectionable. The sky was high and wide, and the stars shone like diamonds scattered across a blanket of black velvet. If I didn't know better, I might've forgotten I was at work.

But I did know better. "We know Coach Shannon called Edgar and told him that EJ got left behind in Watie Junction," I said. "If Edgar knew about EJ and Sheryl, he must have suspected the boy ditched the bus to meet-up with her."

"Edgar probably just took off and went after him."

I lightly slapped the hood. "I'd bet this girl's pink slip that's what he did." Bernard nodded and brushed away an invisible spot of dirt where I'd touched the car.

"Peggy Miller says Edgar called and cancelled his date with Jeannie about the same time coach called Edgar about EJ," I said.

"So, Edgar drives to the whorehouse looking for EJ," said Bernard. "Sheryl tells him EJ was there earlier but Kevin picked him up."

"Maybe Edgar figures to get a little nookie while he's there. He takes Sheryl off somewhere. Something goes wrong. Maybe she starts feeling bad about cheating on her boyfriend with his father—"

"Gee, I don't know why she'd feel bad about that," said Bernard.

I chuckled and slapped him lightly on the back. Bernard's appreciation of irony is uneven and I like to encourage it when I can.

"Anyway," I said, "for whatever reason, let's say Sheryl threatens Edgar—says she's going to tell everybody about her relationships with the Bixbys. Edgar can't have that, so he kills her. He takes her back to Burr in the trunk of the Impala and dumps her on the train tracks."

Bernard made a face and shrugged. "I don't know," he said, "it could've happened that way. But would Edgar kill her just for that? Why would he care what she said? He thinks he can get away with anything."

That was a good point, but I wasn't about to let my theory go down without a fight. "If we could get Krystal with a K to identify one of Edgar's cars as the one she saw Sheryl get into—"

"*Thinks* she saw."

"*Thinks* she saw," I agreed, "and if Yvette can finger him as the fella who used to bother Sheryl, and if he was the one outside the diner on the night Sheryl was killed ...." I took a deep breath. "I'd say we'd have grounds for bringing him in for questioning, at the very least."

I was starting to feel proud of myself.

Bernard licked his finger and used it to extinguish his cigarette. He stuck the half-smoked butt back in the pack. "If we can put him and the car and Sheryl in the same place at the same time, we've got him as the last person to see her alive." He slid the pack into his shirt pocket. "But what about Nate?"

Good point. What about Nate? He was involved on some level, but I wasn't sure how. Nate's role might shoot my theory all to hell.

"We need to talk to him," I said. Brevity is the soul of face-saving.

I hated like hell to ask Bernard to do anything else, but I had another task that needed to be completed before the sun rose on a new day. I retrieved the magazine with the Impala on the cover from the glove box.

"Take this over to the whorehouse and ask Krystal if this is the car she saw Sheryl get into," I said. "Ask all of them if they've seen it before. While you're at it, ask Yvette if she remembers what kind of car Sheryl's middle-aged guy drove. I didn't think to ask when I questioned her before."

I should've known it was impossible to overwork Bernard. He perked up like Dizzy does when I ask her if she wants to go for a ride. I told him not to bother coming back, but to radio me after he talked to the girls. He drove off in a cloud of red dust.

I liberated the flask of bourbon I keep under the seat if my truck. I slid behind the wheel and stretched my legs out as far as they'd go. Once somewhat comfortable, I took a healthy swig of brain medicine, switched on my flashlight, and opened my book to page one.

I'd gotten all the way to page 50 by the time Bernard reported in. It was one of those "good news/bad news" deals. The bad news was that Krystal decided she hadn't seen Sheryl getting into a car that night, after all. The good news was, all the girls recognized the

Impala. What's more, Yvette said that Sheryl's regular drove a car just like it, and she was pretty sure she saw it parked by the diner on the night in question. That gave us something to work on and I felt good about it. I thanked Bernard, promised him a raise and told him to go home and get some rest. I reckoned those women might be in line for that $1000 reward, even though I still had no idea how where I was going to get it, never mind a boost in pay for Bernard.

From that point, things started going sideways. My mind entertained uncharitable visions having to do with Edgar Bixby rotting in jail and me putting him there, animated in no small part by the celebratory intake of the contents of my flask. I remember getting out of the vehicle and counting stars as I relieved myself in the area between the truck and the Leaning Tower, banging my head on the door frame as I got back in, and trying to decode the words in my book as they swirled around on the page like those little noodle-y letters in a bowl of alphabet soup. I remember thinking: Uh-oh, I hope Nate doesn't show up because I'm in no shape to deal with him tonight. I reckon that was my last thought, or close to it, before I either passed out or fell asleep.

I dreamed Bernard and I were playing miniature golf at Golf Pair O'Dice, only we used live mice instead of golf balls. I remember trying to hit them real soft so I wouldn't hurt them. They kept squeaking and scurrying away and we'd have to take a new one out of a bag that looked just like the white purse Alice Foster carried the day I went to talk to her about her sister. I reckon it was inspired by a Bugs Bunny or Tom and Jerry cartoon I saw a long time ago. After a while, the mouse squeaks modulated into the throaty rumble of a Chevy V-8. Even in my half-conscious state, I was aware of the crunch of gravel and the glare of high-beams flashing across my face. I ignored it and kept playing with my little rodent buddies until I realized what was happening.

I opened my eyes just in time to see a red Impala pull into Nate Gunter's driveway.

CHAPTER THIRTY-SIX

My subsequent actions, however well-meaning, were sabotaged by unforgivable stupidity and an overabundance of bourbon. If I were to be more honest with myself than I usually am, I'd have to say both factors were inextricably entwined.

I almost fell trying to get out of the truck too fast. I got my arm caught in the steering wheel and almost wrenched my right shoulder out of socket. Somehow, I managed not to land on my ass or my face. At that moment, I couldn't have told one from the other. I commenced my drunkard's walk across the street in the direction of the Gunters'.

Nate had switched off the Impala's headlights. He got out of the car and crossed over to help Kevin, whose right arm was in a sling.

I should've approached Nate like I would a skittish mare. Instead, I came at him like he was a stray dog crapping in my front yard. "Hold on there, Nate," I yelled. "You're under arrest."

My enjoinder did not have the desired effect.

Nate's face twisted with surprise and fear and I wouldn't be surprised if he'd peed his pants. He yelled something at Kevin, who went in the house. Nate got back in the car. He cranked it and for a second I thought he'd flooded it, but he got it going and drove away before I could get close enough to intervene. I'd never seen him move so fast, not that he needed to. In my condition, I couldn't have outmaneuvered a three-legged mule.

I hadn't taken two steps before I tripped and dropped my keys. As

Nate made his getaway, I crawled on my hands and knees in the dark like a blind rooster pecking at the last kernel of corn. By the time I recovered the keys, Nate had a sizable lead.

Of course, Nate being Nate, he didn't do much with it.

He drove to the end of Cedar Street and turned onto Highway 14 heading west. I followed a half-minute later, by which time Nate's taillights were a pair of blurry red dots in the distance. I had no business driving, never mind chasing someone. I'd managed to sleep-off some of the booze's effects. However, I was still not in full possession of my faculties. But Nate had to be caught, and I was the officer at the scene.

Somehow, I managed to keep my truck on the road and Nate in sight. Given my abject state and his considerable head start, I had little hope of catching him. If things had gone his way, he would've driven through town and crossed into Texas, and I would've driven into a ditch.

But things rarely go Nate's way and they weren't about to start now. As so often happens, fate—combined with his own ineptitude—dealt him another pernicious blow.

In his rush, Nate had decided to try to outrace a tractor-trailer approaching the intersection of US 14 and State Highway 43. The truck was heading north. Nate was heading west. The truck driver slowed down at the blinking yellow light. Nate sped up. The truck got there first. Nate realized too late he'd lost the race and hit the brakes doing about 50 mph. He flew into a long uncontrolled skid. He swerved and missed the truck but couldn't avoid the only other car on the street, a black Rambler parked in front of Edna's. He crashed headlong into the Rambler's quarter panel on the driver's side, burrowed underneath it and lifted its rear end two or three feet in the air, before coming to a full stop. He slammed the Impala into reverse, but only managed to jerk the conjoined cars backwards a few feet before giving up and shutting off his engine.

I viewed the show from a rapidly diminishing distance. Undistracted and unimpaired, I reckon I could've slowed-down in time, but I might've forgot I was driving and anyway my reaction time was for shit. Once I realized I needed to stop, it was almost too late.

My brakes locked and I skidded. I steered to avoid the rear end of the tractor-trailer and tipped up on two wheels. I almost went into a roll, but gravity did its duty and the car slammed down on all four tires. Unfortunately, I'd also jumped the curb and landed on the sidewalk, ultimately coming to a stop a squirrel's eyelash shy of the plate glass window in the empty storefront next to Edna's. By some miracle I had avoided actually crashing into anything, although I had bumped my forehead hard against the steering wheel.

I extricated myself and rushed over to attend to Nate. "Don't worry," I could hear him mumble to himself. "Everything's under control."

But of course, nothing was.

. . . . .

The demolished Rambler belonged to Ray Nugent, the weekend bartender at Edna's. It's such an ugly damn car, you might think Nate had done Ray a favor.

Ray didn't see it that way. He'd been cleaning up when he heard the crash. He rushed out holding a wet mop. He shouted a few choice curses and blasphemes of the sort you might hear from a man who had not recently found himself in the Lord's good graces.

His attention then fell on the driver. Or who he thought was the driver. "Goddammit, Edgar, what in Christ's name is going on?" he said, before realizing it was someone else at the wheel. "What in hell, Nate? Did you steal Edgar's car?"

At least one other person knew Edgar had been driving that Impala.

Nate was busy trying to disentangle himself from the wreckage. He repeatedly banged his shoulder against the car door, trying to get it to open. The collision had knocked everything out of whack. The trucker and I pulled on the door while Nate pushed, until we finally got the damn thing open.

"You ok?" I asked him.

"Yeh," he said. He stood and stretched, trying out his limbs and hands and fingers, making sure everything still worked the way it was supposed to. He lifted the gray and white Farmer's Co-op cap he was wearing and ran his hand over his head, looking for bumps or gashes. There were none. All in all, he appeared fine, although *fine* for Nate isn't always the same as *fine* for a regular person.

The trucker asked if he could go. I took down his information and sent him on his way. He hadn't broken any laws.

I turned to Nate. "You, on the other hand, need to come with me."

I walked him over to my pickup, which was still up on the sidewalk. Nate got in without a fuss. "Are you going to behave, or do I need to cuff you?"

He shrugged. "I ain't going nowhere."

I raised Bernard on the radio. He said he'd be there in five minutes. I told Nate to stay put and walked to where Ray was mourning the loss of his car.

"What in hell, Emmett?" he said. "What in goddam hell?"

I considered cracking a joke then decided it would probably make matters worse, so I just tried to console him as best I could. I said it was Nate's fault and that I'd put it in writing, if it would help with his insurance. He walked out in the middle of the road, hands on his hips, looking up at the stars for heavenly help that I was sure would not come. Meanwhile, I picked up pieces of shattered glass out from under my back wheels and tossed them onto the Rambler's floorboards. Last thing I needed was a flat tire.

Bernard arrived five minutes later with his red emergency lights on. He walked over to where I stood and marveled at the unholy union of Impala and Rambler. "What in the world happened here?" he asked.

"Nate showed up," I said. "Chaos ensued."

"I guess it did," he said and gave me a suspicious look. I reckon he'd gotten a whiff of my breath.

I filled him in on the details, taking care not to slur my words. I'd swear on a stack of bibles I wasn't drunk, but things were complicated enough and I didn't want to make them worse. I explained what I wanted him to do and asked if he needed my help.

"Nah, I called Jeff. His babies were keeping him up, anyway. He sounded glad to get out of there. You do what you need to do. We'll be fine."

I felt queasy, and the gas fumes were making it worse. The quicker I removed myself, the better. "Ok," I said, "I'm going to drive Nate back to the station and get to the bottom of a few things."

Bernard hesitated like he wanted to say something but wasn't sure he should. "You good to drive, Chief?" he asked softly and kindly.

I was embarrassed he felt like he had to ask, so I snapped back, "I reckon I can drive a hundred yards down the street." I stomped over to my pickup with my nose out-of-joint. I got the truck righted and onto the street without too much trouble and drove Nate to the station. We got out of the truck, and as I led him through the front door, I grabbed his arm more roughly than I needed to. I was in that kind of mood.

I pointed at the holding cell. "You want to talk?" I said, red-eyed and about as mad as I ever get. "Or should I put you in there and let the Sheriff come get you?"

He stared back, looking hurt.

"You know me, Emmett," he said. "I'll talk."

CHAPTER THIRTY-SEVEN

I pulled up the wooden school chair and motioned for Nate to sit. We stared across my desk at each other for a long spell. He had the look of a man who'd lost his last dollar betting the sun would rise in the west. Let's go, baby. Just this once.

"Nate, what in hell's going on?"

"Emmett, swear to God, I don't know. I figured if you was after me, I must be in trouble."

"C'mon, now Nate, that's not it and you know it. You ran for a reason."

"I swear, Emmet, you said I was under arrest and I just got scared, that's all."

I had to admit, it made sense. I silently cussed myself for drinking too much and falling asleep and generally making a mess of the situation.

"Well, I apologize for that, Nate. I wasn't thinking straight. I should've just said I needed to talk to you."

His head drooped and he slumped in the chair. "That's ok," he muttered. I could see he felt ashamed. Nate feels ashamed even when he hasn't done anything wrong. This time it looked as though he had a reason.

He looked up at me out from under the bill of his cap. "Is it because Edgar told you I stole his car?"

That was a new twist. "Edgar didn't tell me anything of the kind,

Nate," I said. "Did you steal his car?"

"No, I didn't. He gave it to me. But I knew there was something wrong the way he done it."

"Did he sign over the pink slip?"

"He did. You can check for yourself."

"Well, then, it's yours," I said. "That don't sound much like Edgar, though."

"I had to do something for it," Nate said. "He wanted me to drive it out of state. He said he'd give me a thousand dollars if I did."

It would normally take Nate two or three months hauling gravel to make that much money. "Where'd he ask you to take it?" I asked

"He didn't care, so long it was far away. It couldn't just be to Texas, though. He said I could keep the car." He shook his head. "I should've known it was too good to be true."

I already knew where he went, but he told me anyway. "I drove to Las Vegas, where my ex-wife lives. At least, that's where she used to live. I was going to try to get back with her now that I had some cash."

He asked for some water. I gave him a cup and he drank it down. I told him to start at the beginning.

.   .   .   .   .

A thin stream of water dripped out the side of his mouth and down his chin. "Last Friday night I went to Edna's and I saw Edgar. He said he had a job for me."

"You sure it was Friday?" I asked. "I talked to everybody at Edna's who was working Friday. Nobody saw Edgar."

"Probably I was the only one who saw him. I don't think he even came in. I ran into him on my way to the men's room."

"How'd you do that, if he never came in?

"You know how the back door at Edna's is right next to the restroom, and how it's always open? Edgar was standing outside there in the dark. It was almost like he was waiting for me. Now that I think about it, he did kind of act like he didn't want no one to see him.

He said he had a job for me. I told him to wait 'til after I took a whiz."

I thought about the bad old days when how Edgar used to take advantage of Nate. I thought that had ended a long time ago. Maybe I was wrong.

"You do a lot of work for Edgar?"

"Not a lot. Sometimes I help him haul stuff and fix things. He pays me pretty good."

"Not a thousand bucks, I reckon." Edgar throws pennies around like tractor tires.

"Oh, hell no," he said, chuckling softly despite himself. "Most he ever give me was a hundred dollars one time to paint his outbuildings. Made me do it twice before he'd pay me." He made a wry face. "Uh-uh, he never gave me nothing like a thousand dollars before." He crumpled up the paper cup and tossed it in the direction of the trash can. He missed by a couple of feet.

"We went out back of Edna's," Nate said. "The Impala was there. Edgar said he needed it to disappear and that if I drove it somewhere a long way away he'd give a thousand dollars and let me keep the car."

"He didn't tell you where?"

"No, he just said it had to go away. Those were his exact words. 'It has to go away.' He said I couldn't even wait until morning. I had to do it that very minute."

"Did he say why?"

"He said he'd been using it to take around another woman and he didn't want his wife to find out. He said someone told her and she was looking for the car, so he had to get rid of it."

The only person in the world who trusts Edgar Bixby enough to believe such a cockamamie story is Nate Gunter. He's always had an unlimited capacity to accept Edgar's bullshit as gospel.

He must've guessed what I was thinking. "I know it sounds fishy," he said. "But I did it anyway. I never owned a car that slick, and a thousand dollars is a lot of money."

"You remember what time it was?"

"I don't know. Tell the truth, I was so drunk I hardly knew which way was up. It was late, I know that."

"So, what happened next?" I asked. "He just give you the money and say, 'see ya later'?"

Nate shook his head. "No, we drove the car over to the bank so he could get the money."

"Where's your pickup in all this?"

"I was on foot. I don't mind walking. Kevin needed the truck anyway."

So I'd heard. "The bank's closed that time of night," I said.

Nate shrugged. "Edgar had a key," he said.

Of course he did. A key he got from his brother the bank president.

I nodded for Nate to continue.

"He opened a safe in Deke's office and took out a bunch of cash and put it in one of those money bags. He said it was a thousand dollars and it was mine as long as I did what we'd talked about. He said I couldn't tell anyone what I was doing or where I was going, not even Kevin. He didn't even want to know where. All I had to do was stay away until he said it was safe to come back. I asked him how long and he said a couple of weeks, maybe more. Then he gave me the keys to the Impala and left."

"How'd he get home?"

"That Lincoln of his was parked at the bank."

I pondered whether that meant he had help from someone besides Nate. "Did you see anyone else?" I asked.

"No, it was just me and Edgar."

"Ok, so what next? I know you didn't do what he said. You didn't leave that night, because you filled up at Wes Harmon's Sinclair the next morning."

"Nah, I just made it as far as the lake. I hid-out there and slept until morning, then I snuck back into town."

"You went home and saw Kevin."

"Yeh, and I picked up some clothes and things. Kevin was still in bed. I looked in on him and told him I was going to do some work for Mr. Bixby." He made a face and swallowed hard a couple of times.

"I'm sorry, Emmett, but my throat's dry as hell. Could I have some more water?" I got him another cup. He drank it down and asked for another. He downed that one just as quick.

"I decided to drive to Las Vegas and find Kevin's mother," he said, a little less hoarse than before. "I thought if she saw I had a good car and all that money, maybe she'd get back with me. That maybe I'd send for Kevin later and we could be together again as a family."

I thought that was pitiful, but I couldn't let myself get distracted by another account of Nate Gunter's misbegotten life. "You stopped at Wes's on the way out of town," I said.

"Yeh, I stopped for gas. He wanted to talk football. I 'bout never got out of there."

I almost mentioned he had a load of change coming to him, but decided I'd leave that to Wes.

"I just prayed I wouldn't run into Edgar," he said.

"After you filled up, you took off for Las Vegas."

"More or less. I stopped a few places for gas and to eat. I slept in the car."

"What did you do when you got there?"

"I hunted for Betty—that's my ex-wife's name. Turns out she'd been living in a trailer on the outskirts of town. A lady who shared it with her said she'd gone to join some religious group in California. That messed-up my plans. I stayed at a cheap motel for a couple of days. I thought about driving to California, but I decided not to. I wasn't going to get Betty back, no matter what I did. I stayed in Vegas, drank a lot, and lost a little bit of money playing slot machines."

"How much of the thousand is left?"

"Most of it. I was careful not to spend too much."

"Where is it now?"

"I gave it to Kevin before you started chasing me. There's a space behind a wall where we hide important stuff."

He was going to need that money, one way or the other.

"I guess you found out about Kevin getting hurt when you called us."

"Yeh, he wasn't answering the phone so I got worried and called you guys. Karen told me what happened."

"And you hung up."

"I know, I'm sorry about that," he said. "I panicked when Karen said she was gonna make me talk to you. Ever since Edgar gave me the car and the money I've felt like I did something wrong. I thought maybe it was a trick—that Edgar was gonna tell you I stole the car and have me arrested."

"Well, that's not what happened. If the car was signed over to you, it's yours and there's nothing Edgar can do about it. Not that it matters much now."

Kevin sighed through chapped lips. "Dang it, I'll never have a car that nice again." He looked like he was going to cry.

I was angry at him and sorry for him at the same time, which is how I always felt about him when we were kids. Part of me wanted to kick him the butt and tell him to grow a pair of balls, but that wouldn't accomplish anything. Instead, I asked him his plan for coming home from Las Vegas.

"I thought I'd drive straight through to Oklahoma City and see Kevin at the hospital," he said. "I figured if I stayed away from Burr, I'd be ok."

But you're never ok, are you, Nate? I asked him if there was anything in the car when he got it.

He looked puzzled. "Like what?"

"Oh, I don't know. Personal stuff Edgar might've forgotten to take out before he gave it to you." A bloody knife, for instance.

"No. There wasn't nothing."

"Did you look in the trunk?"

"Just to throw my suitcase in."

"Anything there?"

"Just the spare tire, as far as I know."

"You didn't look close?"

"No, I don't think so. I reckon I'd have noticed if there was something."

Maybe you would. Maybe you wouldn't.

"Tell you what, Nate," I said. "Why don't we go look in that trunk right now?"

•   •   •   •   •

The Impala and Rambler—or what was left of them—were still mashed together like a pair of Siamese twins. Ray had presumably gone home to lament his car's demise. Jeff had arrived. He and Bernard sat and smoked at the curb, waiting for the tow trucks. It occurred to me that we'd been giving them a lot of business lately.

My officers started to get up. I motioned for them to stay seated. "Nate and I are going to check some things." I asked Bernard if I could borrow the flashlight he keeps on his belt.

I wriggled into the disfigured Impala and shined the light in the glove compartment. I found the title. It was still in Edgar's name, but he'd signed it over to Nate, dated the day after Sheryl Foster's murder.

"Nate, did you remove anything from the car after you got it from Edgar?"

"I never took nothing out if it. Look inside. It's a mess. I ain't thrown nothing away."

He wasn't lying. The floor was covered with hamburger wrappers and paper cups and empty Brown Derby cans. It stank of cigarettes and beer and dirty socks, like Nate had been living in it.

I rummaged around without finding evidence of anything except that Nate was a slob. If that was a crime, he'd have belonged in jail. Jesus Christ, I thought, Nate's about wrecked this car already, then I remembered: he literally had, less than an hour ago. Some people can't have nice things.

"Nate, I read about how some fella invented this thing called a trash can."

He didn't respond except to shuffle his feet.

In the distance, I heard the sound of an engine approaching from the south. The tow trucks coming from Temple City. Took them long enough.

I removed the keys from the Impala's ignition. "Except for the garbage, is there anything here that wasn't here before Edgar gave you the car?"

That got Bernard and Jeff's attention. "Edgar Bixby gave you this car?" they asked at the same time. Nate nodded sheepishly.

"Nate, answer my question. Was there anything in it when you got it that belonged to Edgar?"

He shook his head.

I walked around to the rear of the car. The trunk was about the only thing not banged up after the wreck. It popped open without a hitch. The inside was lined with a gray vinyl mat. It was mostly empty except for the spare tire, which was held in place by a large wing-nut and bolt mechanism. I ran the flashlight over every inch but didn't find anything. I was close to giving up when I came upon a dark spot at the edge of the mat where it met the wall of the trunk underneath the latch. It was two or three inches in diameter and reddish-brown with irregular edges. I felt that sick feeling you get when you're right about something you'd rather be wrong about.

I called Jeff and Bernard over and pointed to the spot. "What's that look like to you?" I asked.

"That's a blood stain," said Bernard.

"Uh-huh, that's what it looks like," said Jeff.

"Nate come over here and look at this." He slunk over. "You know where that came from?"

"No, Emmett, I don't. It must've been there from before."

I decided I needed to take the mat all the way out so I could see better, but to do that I had to remove the spare tire. Bernard held the flashlight for me and I unscrewed the wing nut holding the wheel in place. I got it all the way off and lifted up the tire. I saw a glint of something silver that had been underneath it. I grabbed the flashlight away from Bernard and shined it on the object. I knew I'd seen it before, but it took me a second to remember where.

"Bernard, I want you to see this," I said. "That look familiar to you?"

Bernard stood with his arms crossed and thought about it for a few seconds. A lightbulb went off over his head. "Is that what I think it is?" he asked.

"If it's not, we're having the same hallucination."

I walked back to the Fury and pulled an evidence envelope out of a pocket behind the front seat. I lifted the object from the trunk using the tip of a Bic pen. I placed it in the envelope, folded it shut, and put it in my shirt pocket.

I slammed the trunk. "Nate," I said, "you're under arrest."

The pair of tow trucks swung into view. The high beams passed across Nate's face. In that second, I thought he looked like a rodeo clown about to have his chest ventilated by a bull. Afraid, but resigned to a fate he's seen coming for a long time. I wouldn't say he seemed guilty, but he didn't seem surprised, either. If you put a gun to my head, I'd say he was just sad.

Like he always done since we were kids.

CHAPTER THIRTY-EIGHT

I left Bernard in charge of getting the wreckage squared away. Jeff rode back to the station with Nate and me.

Nate whimpered that he'd done nothing wrong—he didn't steal the car and didn't know where that thing I'd found had come from and I shouldn't listen to Edgar or whoever else was badmouthing him.

"I know you didn't steal it," I said. "That's not the issue. This is about that girl who was murdered. Or didn't you hear about that in your travels?"

"You think I killed that colored girl?" he said, more amazed than upset. "Emmett, you know me. I can't even shoot a rabbit."

I knew he was squeamish, but everyone has a breaking point. Maybe Nate had finally reached his that night. In my heart I didn't believe it, but it was possible.

"I'm not saying you killed her," I said. "On the other hand, I don't know you didn't. You were driving a car with a bloodstain in the trunk, and something tells me that blood belonged to the murdered girl."

I took off my hat and dropped it on Karen's desk. My brain was mush. "I need to slow things down before my head explodes," I told Nate. "I'm going to lock you up for as long as it takes me to figure out what to do next."

I pushed him into the cage, slammed the cell door behind him, and returned to the reception area, thinking that whoever thought locating the holding cell in the chief's office instead of out front where it belonged ought to have his police-station-designing license revoked. I left the door to my office cracked so I could hear what Nate was up to.

My watch read twenty-five or six minutes to four in the morning. I had cotton mouth and my head felt like someone had hammered a half-dozen ten-penny nails into it. I wished I hadn't drunk so much, Then I remembered I'd almost wrecked my truck, and I wished it even more.

I got to make some changes.

Jeff sat on the bench against the wall. "You don't really think he killed that girl, do you?" he stage-whispered so Nate couldn't hear.

"Nah. Nate cries when he runs over a skunk. Anyway, I got plenty of witnesses who saw him at Edna's at the time the girl was murdered. I think it's more likely Edgar had something to do with it."

"Why?"

"Well, he's an asshole, for one thing," I said. "Besides, I got at least one witness who says Edgar's been screwing Sheryl. Those prostitutes think they saw him and his Impala at the whorehouse the night our girl disappeared. We know Edgar used that car to carry-on with women who aren't his wife. I know for a fact that one of them is Jeannie Klinglesmith. I strongly suspect another was Sheryl Foster."

The front door opened and Bernard came in off the street. "If Edgar or Nate want what's left of that car," he said, "it'll be at the Sheriff's impound lot in Temple City."

I called the sheriff's office and told them to expect the remains of a wrecked Impala, and that it was material to a criminal investigation and should be treated accordingly.

A noise like a chainsaw having intimate relations with a jackhammer came from my office. It was Nate, snoring away, dead to the world.

I closed the door to give us some peace.

"I'm going to need you boys back here by eight. Kenny and Karen, too."

Jeff groaned and Bernard nodded.

"That's the good news. The bad news is one of y'all is going to have to stay here with Nate."

I told them to work it out for themselves. Whoever drew the short straw needed to call Kenny and Karen, as well.

I was just pulling away from the curb when Jeff walked out the door. Bernard had either lost the coin flip or volunteered. Knowing him, it was the latter. If there's a God, I hope he takes notice of how hard that boy works. He deserves some kind of reward. More than I can give him.

·   ·   ·   ·   ·

A grumpy assembly of Burr's Finest greeted me first thing. Karen had brought a box of miniature doughnuts and brewed a pot of coffee. The refreshments helped, but the mood remained dour.

Think you got it bad? I felt like saying. Try looking at it from where I sit.

I purposely didn't look in the mirror when I got up after only a couple hours of sleep. I already know what death warmed over looks like. Kenny was the only one of my three officers who didn't appear to have slept on a bed of nails. In fact, he was bouncing around like rubber ball in a clothes dryer. "Jeff and Bernard say today's D-Day," he chirped. Jeff and Bernard shot death rays at him with their eyes.

My stomach growled and I helped myself to a mini doughnut. "We're not invading France," I said. "We're hauling in Edgar Bixby to ask him some more questions." I poured myself a cup of coffee. "Might not turn out to be anything."

Karen was as perturbed as the rest, but for a different reason. "Jeff says you think Edgar killed that girl. If that's true, why's poor Nate Gunter locked-up in your office?"

"Emmett!" Nate called from the next room. "Is that you? When are you going to let me out?"

Debating Nate was not on the morning's agenda. "Be quiet, Nate," I half-shouted through the door. "I'm keeping you in protective custody."

"From who?"

"C'mon, Nate," I said. "You know who."

He was silent for a second. "Yeh, I guess I do." I heard a clatter as he dropped onto his bunk. "I'm sorry about the car, Emmett." He sounded as pitiful as a box of sick puppies.

"I know you are, bud."

He meant the Impala, of course, but I flashed back to that night he and I tried to replace the battery in an old Ford pickup.

I brought my crew up to speed and concluded with an assurance we were going to everything within our power to apprehend Sheryl Foster's killer. "We're going to re-question everyone in this town who knew her," I said in a lowered my voice so Nate wouldn't hear. "That means Edgar and EJ Bixby, and Kevin Gunter."

I took another donut and downed it with more coffee.

"Nate, I've been meaning to ask," I said, loud enough for him to hear. "Did you ever meet that girl who was killed?"

"No, I don't even know who she was."

Karen gestured toward my office. "What're you going to do with him?" she said, obviously vexed. "You know he didn't have anything to do with this."

"He did, whether he realizes it or not. But mainly this is about keeping Edgar away from him until we get things figured out."

"Aren't we required to let him talk to a lawyer?" asked Kenny.

"Nate, you want to call a lawyer?" I shouted.

"You think I should?"

"Not right now. Maybe later."

"Alright, then."

"You want to call anyone else?"

"Ain't no one to call."

I reckoned that takes care of that.

"Bernard and Kenny," I said, "you ride out to Edgar's with me. Karen, if you will, try to keep Nate happy while we're gone. Jeff, get him something to eat. You can let him out of the cage, but stay close-by in case he gets ornery. I don't expect he will. Lock him up if you have to leave Karen alone with him."

"Like Nate's going to do anything to hurt me," she scoffed.

"Better to be safe than sorry."

The growl in my stomach had become a cantankerous roar. Those itty-bitty doughnuts hadn't done diddly squat. I considered getting some breakfast, myself, but figured I had too much to do.

I consoled myself by thinking I wouldn't be hungry for long. Dealing with the Bixbys would surely put me off my feed.

·　·　·　·　·

The Bixby cars—minus the red Impala—were nose-to-tail on the circular driveway in front of that big ugly brown house. Everything appeared normal. Edgar strutted toward us from the outbuilding or barn or whatever he calls that miniature pig palace about a hundred or so yards away, where I imagine Daffodil enjoys a lifestyle like the Queen of Sheba. If Edgar had any thought of being in trouble, you couldn't tell by looking at him.

I forced myself to keep a straight face, not wanting to appear too excited at the prospect of putting his sorry ass in jail for the rest of his life.

"Hello, Edgar," I said, to which he replied, "What do you want?" about as neighborly as a rattlesnake.

"I need you to come with me."

"Where?"

"Back to the station. I need to ask you some questions." With Bernard and Kenny standing close on either side, Edgar looked like the meat in a go-directly-to-jail sandwich.

"Ask 'em here," he said.

"They're the kind that need to be asked at the station. You go tell Denny where you're going, and come with us."

I reckon if he'd been armed, he might've taken a shot at me. But like I say, he hadn't expected trouble, so after some slightly hostile verbal resistance, he deigned to cooperate. I sent Bernard inside with him to make sure he didn't grab a shotgun. They came back out a minute later, accompanied by Denny, who wasn't happy.

"Emmett, what's going on here?" she said.

"We've got some questions we need to ask Edgar."

"This better not be about what I think it's about," she said, her voice shaking in anger.

I'd expected her to be mad, but I guess I was surprised she was mad at me.

"I don't know what you think this is about, Denny. Edgar has some things to answer for, and we're going to attend to it."

"Call Jimmy Jack," Edgar said. "Tell him to meet us at the station. Make sure he knows we're at the police station in town and not at the sheriff's."

"All right, sweetheart."

If my last conversation with Denny had not flushed twenty-years of wishful thinking down the toilet, hearing her call that bald-headed one-eyebrowed piece of garbage "sweetheart" surely did the trick. For a second, I thought I might puke up those mini donuts.

"Cuff him," I said.

Edgar made a move to get at me, but before he could, Bernard grabbed him by the back of his collar, lifted him a foot off the ground, and threw him into the back seat. Bernard and Kenny got in and sat on either side of him. Seeing Edgar sitting there foaming at the mouth gave me some satisfaction, but not as much as it should have.

I radioed the station and told Karen to have Jeff escort Nate home and babysit him until further notice. I didn't need Edgar and Nate crossing paths. Karen said "10-4" but forgot to take her finger off the button, so I could hear Jeff bitch over the open mic.

"Tell Jeff I heard that," I said.

After a burst of static, she answered. "He says he's sorry."

"Tell him this is a fluid situation that calls for tactical flexibility."

I could almost hear Karen's eyes roll. "Oh, I'm sure that'll help," she said.

·   ·   ·   ·   ·

We arrived back at the station before Jimmy Jack, which I counted as a positive. I didn't expect Edgar to talk without him, but you never know. Maybe I could get under his skin enough to make him say something he'd later regret. One thing I'm good at is getting under Edgar's skin.

Karen sat at her desk reading Look magazine and humming along to the radio, which at that moment was playing a putrid pile of musical night soil called "I Feel Fine" by the Beatles. That spring, it seemed like every song on the radio was by either them or Buck Owens. I'll take Charlie Parker, thanks.

"Please turn that off, Miss Dean," I said. Ordinarily she might have jabbed back, but she knew better than to do that under the circumstances. She grabbed her steno pad and we led Edgar into my office.

Bernard removed the handcuffs. He placed an insistent hand on Edgar's shoulder and sat him down in our most uncomfortable folding chair, then backed off and slouched against the door frame with his arms crossed and a cigarette hanging out of one side of his mouth. Kenny stood in the corner with his hands in his pockets, his head tilted quizzically, chewing on a toothpick. Karen sat in a chair at the end of my desk, legs crossed, prim and proper in her Sunday best: a yellow-and-blue-flowered dress and white patent-leather heels. Evidently, she'd hoped we'd finish in time for her to attend church. I didn't like her chances.

Edgar rubbed his wrists and glowered. The hem of his jeans rode halfway up his shins, his fat thighs open for business.

"Edgar, last night Nate Gunter wrecked a red Chevy Impala that has your name on the title," I began. "I know he didn't steal it, because the title had your signature on it where you signed it over to him. Nate tells me you gave it to him, along with one thousand dollars, on the condition he drive it as far away from Burr as possible."

His jaw jutted and slid side-to-side and his eyes had a dull, dangerous look. Resorting to violence wasn't an option, so I reckoned he was trying to decide whether to just flat-out lie or try to skate around the truth. He settled on a combination. "None of that's true," he said, "but even it was, I don't see how that's any of your goddam business."

"Well, number one, *all* of it is true. Number two, it *is* my business, because we found something in that car that belonged to Sheryl Foster."

His eyes narrowed. "Like hell you did," he said.

"Like hell I didn't."

I turned around the portrait of Sheryl on my desk, so Edgar could see it. "Take a look, Edgar."

He glanced at it for half-a-second.

"Yeh, so what? A picture of some nigger girl I never laid eyes on."

"Well, that's a dozen different kinds of bullshit, Edgar. I got more witnesses than I need who'll testify you were paying that girl for sex. But forget that for the time being. I want you to look at what she's wearing on her wrist. What do you think that is?"

He grudgingly took a closer look.

"What do you see?" I asked.

"I don't know. You talking about that goddam bracelet?"

"Yes, indeed," I said, and pulled an evidence envelope out of my top desk drawer. I turned it over shook it a couple of times. Onto my desk fell a small silver charm in the shape of a cheerleader's megaphone. The initials "S.F." were engraved on one side.

I saw a hint of panic in his eyes. "What in hell does that have to do with anything?" he said.

"I'm going to tell you," I said. I moved the charm toward him with the tip of a pencil. "Look at this, then look at the bracelet in the photograph. My eyesight's not the best, but I'd say they're the same." His eyes were now glued to the charm like he was willing it to disappear. He reached to pick it up. I grabbed his wrist. "No touching," I said. "Evidence."

I had Kenny, Bernard, and Karen gather around. "Y'all take a look at this. Don't this charm and the one as in the picture look to be the same?"

"I believe it does," said Karen.

"Yessir, it's the same one," said Bernard.

"Sure is," said Kenny.

"What do you think, Edgar?" I asked. "Does that look the same to you?"

"I don't think a goddam thing, is what I think. It don't have nothing to do with me."

"I think you're missing something, Edgar." I pointed out the initials. "You see those letters? 'S' and 'F?' They stand for 'Sheryl Foster.' Sheryl's mama had it specially engraved." I pointed to it in the photo. "See, right there? There isn't another one like it in the whole world."

I lifted it with the pencil and put it back in the envelope.

"Guess where we found it?"

"I don't give a shit where you found it."

"Well, you should, Edgar. You really should. Because we found it in the trunk of that Impala you gave Nate."

Edgar was sweating by now and a shade or two paler than he'd been when he walked in the door. Bernard took advantage of his discomposure to remind me of something. "Don't forget to tell him about the bloodstain," he said.

I studied Edgar, trying not to smile, because I was enjoying his pain. You might say he was reluctant to return my gaze.

"That's right, Officer Cousins," I said, "I almost forgot. We also found a spot of blood in the trunk, Edgar, and we're laying money it came from Sheryl Foster. We're going to have the forensic folks test it, but we're pretty sure it'll turn out to be hers. You want a piece of that action?"

If he'd looked dangerous before, now he looked anything but. Now he just looked trapped and confused. I could tell his mind was hard at work, trying to think up some whopper to explain everything away. But so far he was unable.

"It'd be good for everybody including yourself if you could clear it up," I continued. "Tell me there's a reasonable interpretation of the facts I haven't thought of. Because the way it looks now is you killed that girl, drove her out to the railroad tracks near your place and dumped her. I reckon you hoped whoever found her would think she got thrown off a freight train. Pretty half-assed plan, if you ask me." I didn't want to tell him it was almost enough to fool Agents Jones and Heckscher.

He sat there thinking, then opened his mouth like he was about to say something. I would've liked to have heard what it was, but Jimmy Jack burst in before he could say anything.

"Emmett, what the hell's going on here?" Jimmy Jack bellowed. Denny must've gotten him out of bed. He looked like he'd gotten dressed in the dark. He wore a plaid, short-sleeved shirt over golf slacks that were a different kind of plaid, and a pair of brown loafers with no socks. He didn't wear a hat, revealing a flaky red scalp with a few scattered hairs that looked like they'd been combed with a garden rake. I'd never seen him looking so un-fancy. He knew he looked foolish and it showed in his demeanor. He grabbed a chair, looking sheepish.

I did not comment on his dishevelment but instead focused on the matter at hand. "We're holding Edgar for questioning in the murder of Sheryl Foster."

"Based on what evidence?" he asked, sounding more like James Johnson Preston the Third from Connecticut than Jimmy Jack, the Shady Oilman's Best Friend.

I explained it all to him, especially the part about the car, the bloodstain, and the little megaphone charm.

"That's a load of horseshit," he huffed. "Have you charged him?"

"No, I haven't, but I'm in no hurry. I can hold him 72 hours before that's necessary." I sat back and crossed my legs and tried not to look overly impressed with myself. "Yeh, Jimmy Jack, I expect your client will be here for a while."

He demanded to speak to Edgar in private, so the rest of us repaired to the front. After a few minutes, he called us back in.

First thing Jimmy Jack did was ask if it was alright if his client had a chew. I said ok to that. Edgar pulled a pouch of Red Man from his shirt pocket and bit off a plug. Jimmy Jack manifested a spit cup out of thin air and handed it to his client.

"Alright, Edgar," I said, "at this point I'm going to say you're under no obligation to answer any questions that might force you to incriminate yourself, but anything you say could be used against you in court. Do you understand?"

Edgar looked at Jimmy Jack, who nodded at Edgar, who nodded at us.

"Ok," I said. "Let's start again. Edgar, did you know Sheryl Foster?"

"I did."

Apparently, there had been a change in defense tactics.

"How?"

"Deke told me Jim Bob Hall had seen EJ in a car out at the lake with a colored girl," he said. His pronunciation was fuzzy on account of the tobacco.

"That doesn't explain how you knew her. Where'd you enter the picture?"

He spat in the cup. "First, I knew *about* her, then I knew her."

"So, when Jim Bob told you he'd seen EJ with a colored girl, that was the first you heard about it."

"That's what I said."

"And you didn't know her at that point."

"No, I didn't."

"Did you talk to EJ after Deke told you about what Jim Bob said?"

"No."

"Why not?"

He spat again. "I just didn't."

"Edgar, I know if I looked in your closet I'd probably find a white hood or two, so don't tell me you didn't blow your top when you found your boy was dating a colored girl."

"I didn't say I didn't care. I just said I didn't say nothing to him about it."

"You let it go on."

Spit. "Yup."

"Without doing anything about it."

"Yup." *Spit.* "Well, no." He wiped some tobacco off his lower lip.

"Which is it? Yes or no?"

"I did something about it without EJ knowing. Or at least I tried to."

"What?"

Spit. "I spied on him."

"You spied on him. How?"

"I told Jim Bob to call me next time he saw EJ at the lake with that girl. He called one night and I went out there. I followed EJ when he took her back to Watie Junction."

Looked like Jim Bob had known more than he let on. "Where'd they go?" I asked.

"To that trailer house on the Texas line. The one with the whores."

He made some wet hacking noises and spit the whole slimy brown wad into the cup.

I tried to ignore how disgusting it had been. "Did you talk to her?" I asked.

"Not that night. I turned around and drove home."

I waited for him to continue but he just sat, slumped to one side, leftover tobacco juice trickling down his chin. "Wipe your damn face," I said and handed him a tissue. He cleaned himself then let the tissue drop to the floor. He didn't offer any more information.

I was starting to think I was going to have to pull this story out of him with a block and tackle. "I suppose you must've been mad at EJ," I said.

He didn't answer. I started to repeat the question, when he spoke up.

"I wanted to kill him."

Now we're getting somewhere.

"But you killed the girl, instead."

Jimmy Jack jumped up so that the chair legs skidded and shrieked on the linoleum. "Whoa, Emmett, he didn't say any such thing." He sat back down like he was afraid of making that sound again. "Don't go putting words in his mouth."

"No, I wouldn't want to do that. That wouldn't be as much fun."

"Very funny," Edgar said. "You're a regular Ed Sullivan."

I just grinned.

"Ok, Edgar," I said, "let's try this: You followed EJ and found out he was seeing a negro and that she was a prostitute. You were afraid he might be serious about her and the idea didn't sit too well with you."

"I was never going to let it get that far."

He said it quietly, almost without moving his lips.

His menacing tone moved his counsel to intervene. Jimmy Jack placed a hand on Edgar's shoulder and said, "What Edgar means is, he'd never have given EJ permission to marry that girl." He paused and added, "Not that it would've come to that. Puppy love's all it was."

Knowing EJ, I doubted it was love of any kind. "When did you meet Sheryl?" I asked.

"The night after I followed them out there."

"What car did you take?"

"I took the Impala."

"Why?"

"I didn't want people seeing my Lincoln parked in front of a damned whorehouse, is why."

"Where'd you get the Impala, anyway?"

"Bought it used at a dealership in Arlington about a year ago. Deke and I flew down there in his Cessna for an oil industry convention. I drove it back. I kept it in the barn out in back of the bank and only drove it on special occasions."

"Like when you feel like tomcatting around with Jeannie Klinglesmith?"

That didn't faze him. "Maybe like that," he said.

I motioned for him to go on.

"So, I waited outside until the girl was free. She came over to my car. I asked her how much. She said ten dollars. I said that was a lot of money and I hoped it'd be worth it. She said it would be if I took her to a motel. I told her I knew a place. It wasn't a motel but it was nice."

"Where?"

"Out at the lake."

"Burr Lake? Same as where EJ took her?"

"Yup."

It's scary how that bastard's mind works, I thought. "So, what happened? Did you just talk, or did you decide to get your money's worth?"

"If you're asking if I screwed her, hell yes I did." Edgar doesn't like to get cheated. "I was going to just tell her to stay away from EJ, but she was a damn sexy thing up close. I figured if I was going to pay, I might as well get something for my money." He grinned. "She was right, too. It was worth it." He glanced sideways at Karen like he was trying to get a rise out of her. She kept her head down but I could almost see the steam coming out her ears.

"Is that when you told her who you were and why you'd come to see her in the first place?"

"Nah, I didn't say nothing about EJ. I figured if she'd screw me for ten dollars then it could be she was probably just screwing EJ for the money, too. If that's how he wants to spend his allowance, I wasn't going to stop him. Hell, I won't lie. I wanted to go back for more, myself."

"You didn't mind she was a negro?"

"Being colored don't plug no holes," he said and I thought if there was any way I could pull the switch on Edgar in the electric chair, I'd do it.

"Where were you Friday night, April 23rd?"

"I guess you think you already know, so why don't you tell me?"

I wondered if Peggy Miller had spilled the beans about my visit. That girl was too happy to keep secrets. Not that it much mattered at this point.

"That's not how it works," I said. "You talk, I listen." I pointed at Karen. "She writes it down."

Jimmy Jack leaned over and whispered in his client's ear for several seconds. Whatever he said made Edgar sneer. Finally, Jimmy Jack finished and Edgar began to tell his tale.

The story's beginning aligned with what Denny had told me, as far as it went. They'd gone out to eat in Woodward in the early evening, which took a couple of hours. They split-up around seven. Edgar said he went home to take a bath for his date with Jeannie. He was about to leave when Coach Shannon called to tell him about how EJ had gotten off the bus in Watie Junction. Edgar called Jeannie and cancelled their date, drove to the bank and switched cars, retrieving the Impala from the rusting prefab sheet-metal building belonging to his brother. He then drove to Watie Junction.

"What time was it when you hit the road?" I asked.

"I'd say it was between eight and eight-thirty."

"So, what did you do next?"

"I went to the whorehouse, but EJ wasn't there. I drove to the Dairy Queen. He wasn't there either, so I drove some around Watie Junction looking for him. That took some time."

"Couldn't have taken very long. Watie Junction's not that big."

"I don't know how long it took," he said, irritated. "I looked there, then I drove back to Burr and looked here. I couldn't find him, so I went home."

"Where'd you look?"

"Everywhere."

"The lake?"

"The lake is part of everywhere, so yeh, I looked at the goddam lake."

"Where else?"

"What part of 'everywhere' do you not understand?" he said. "Goddammit, Burr ain't Dallas. It takes five minutes to drive up and down the whole town twice. Fifteen, if you go to Butcherville and out to the lake. Which I did."

"That's my point," I said. "You couldn't have spent a helluva lot of time looking. Sheryl Foster was last seen between eight and eight-thirty. You say you were on your way to the whorehouse at that time. We found her body a little before eleven. I need to know where you were and what you were doing up until then."

"It took him some time to search Watie Junction and to drive back here, don't forget," Jimmy Jack said.

"I'd rather Edgar answer the questions, Jimmy Jack."

"Just trying to help, Emmett, just trying to help."

I turned my attention back to Edgar. "Well?" I said.

He tried to act angry and misunderstood, but I was pretty sure it was just that: an act. "It took as long as it took," he said. "I don't know how long. I got tired of looking for him and I drove the Impala back to the bank and picked up the Lincoln. I was home by ten-thirty, which is when I discovered my pig was missing and called y'all."

"If someone says they saw Sheryl Foster get in that Impala of yours at eight-thirty or nine," I said, "that person would be mistaken." I did not have a witness who said that—Krystal with a 'K' had changed her story, which was always shaky, anyway—but I hoped I might trick him.

He called my bluff. "That person would be lying his ass off," he laughed.

The thing is, Sheryl *had* been in that car. She'd been in the *trunk*. Edgar was starting to get cocky again, and that was getting on my last nerve. "How do you explain that piece of charm bracelet we found?" I asked. "How do you explain the blood?"

"How the hell would I know? It's Nate's car. Ask him."

Nate had no reason to even know Sheryl existed at that point unless Kevin had told him, which I strongly doubted. No one had connected him with her in any way.

"You sold Nate the car?"

"Hell, yes. You don't think I'd give it to him?"

"That's what Nate says happened. He says you gave him the car and a thousand dollars if he'd drive it out of the state and stay away for a while."

"That's horseshit. Nate's been after me to sell him that car since I got it. I got tired of him asking and sold it to him." By now his self-confidence had returned. "I got eight-hundred dollars, which was a hundred more than I paid for it." It's just like Edgar to brag about making a profit at the same time he's being investigated for nearly cutting some poor girl's head off.

"This was that same night?"

"That's right" he said. "I got the call saying y'all weren't coming and I was pissed off. I drove to Edna's to drink and ran into Nate. He started going on about how he had to have that car and so-on and so-forth, and I just decided to sell it to him."

"Did you have it when you went to Edna's?"

"I'd picked it back up on my way there."

"Why would you do that?"

"I didn't want anyone seeing my Lincoln parked outside Edna's," he said huffily. "I got a reputation to maintain."

If he had a car that matched his reputation, he'd be driving a garbage truck.

"Did anyone see you talking to Nate?"

"I doubt it. I parked behind Edna's and bumped into him as I was going in the back door. He cornered me. I never even went in. He wore me down quick, trying to get me to sell him that car. I said I'd take nine-hundred, and then I let him jew me down to eight hundred. He said he didn't have it but he could get it. I told him we were buddies and I knew he was good for it. I signed over the pink slip and that's all she wrote."

"Nate says you gave it to him for nothing."

"Well, technically I did, since no money changed hands. But I expected payment. Still do. Eight-hundred dollars. Says so on the bill of sale." Knowing Nate, he hadn't even looked at the bill of sale. I hadn't seen it, but I hadn't been looking for one. I asked Karen to call over to the sheriff when we were done and ask them to check the glove compartment.

"If Nate says I gave him that car, he's lying or else was too drunk to remember," Edgar said. "Wouldn't surprise me either way."

Somewhere I'd gotten off-track in my questioning, but I wasn't sure where. For one thing, Edgar's explanation as to why he'd picked up the Impala on the way to Edna's didn't make sense. Ray Nugent had recognized the Impala as Edgar's after it crashed into his Rambler, which likely meant Edgar had parked it in front of Edna's before. If Ray knew about it, then others undoubtedly did, too. All I needed to do was ask around. But there was more to it than that.

I blundered along and hoped I'd recover. "Nate says you two went to the bank. You opened a safe in Deke's office and gave him a thousand dollars. He says you told him he could have the money and the car if he'd drive it out of state and stay away for a while."

"Oh, that's ridiculous, Emmett," he said. "The only reason we drove over to the bank was so he could drop me off at my car. When have you ever known me to give away a nickel, never mind a car, never mind a thousand bucks cash? I gave him a bargain because he's a buddy, but that's as far as it goes. I sure as hell didn't give him no thousand dollars."

It made sense, but I knew it was a crock. "Thing is, Edgar," I said in a voice I reserve for my most slow-witted suspects, "Nate still has most of the money. I don't know where he'd have gotten it, if not from you."

"Don't ask me. If he's mean enough to kill some poor nigger girl, he's mean enough to hold-up a few liquor stores."

That made me so mad I had to stop for a minute to cool off. I imagined cutting off his privates with a rusty hacksaw and that made me feel a little better. Suddenly, it hit me. I realized where I'd gone wrong. Whether he'd sold the car or given it to Nate made no difference.

I couldn't believe I hadn't caught it right off.

Edgar had screwed up the timeline. If he'd gotten home around ten thirty then gone out again, he would've had possession of the Impala *after* Sheryl's body had been dumped. He admitted as much. If the blood in the trunk was hers, it had to have gotten there before he gave the car to Nate. His little scheme to frame Nate had a hole in it big enough to drive a Sherman tank through.

I almost couldn't decide who I wanted to throttle more: Edgar, for contriving such a thick-headed alibi, or myself, for not seeing it immediately. On the other hand, I did feel like I'd shrugged a 50-pound bag of fertilizer off my shoulders.

"You know what, Edgar?" I said. "It doesn't matter a good goddam whether you sold that car to Nate, or gave it to him, or carved it out of a giant bar of soap."

I took off my boots and set my stockinged feet on my desk, not caring when I almost upset Edgar's tobacco juice. I tossed my hat in the general direction of a hook on the wall, something I do every day and always miss. Today I didn't. I took it as a good omen. "Hell, I'd almost feel sorry for you if I wasn't sure you killed Sheryl Foster," I said. "All that crap about Edna's and running into Nate and selling him the car. None of that matters."

As far as the Bobbsey Twins were concerned, I might as well have been speaking Swahili. Karen, on the other hand, wrote down everything with a grim smile on her face, while Kenny and Bernard moved nearer the door in case Edgar tried to make a break for it. My people understood what was happening even if Edgar did not.

"Let me explain it, since by God you're so stupid you can't figure it out for yourselves," I said. "By the time you say you'd sold or gave Nate the car—it doesn't matter which—we'd already found the body. Understand?"

Kenny let out a huge guffaw. Edgar and Jimmy Jack sat stunned and flustered, like I'd caught them diddling one another.

"You didn't give Nate the car until after you'd killed the girl, you goddam idiot," I said. "That means you had to have been the one who stuffed her in the trunk. You basically admitted it with that pitiful story." I turned to Jimmy Jack. "And you let him tell it. That might be even worse."

Jimmy Jack made like I'd insulted him, but he knew he'd screwed up. Edgar got silent as a monk. That conceited expression he always wears like a sign telling the world how much money he has was gone.

"You're going to need more evidence than you got," Jimmy Jack sputtered.

He was right, of course, but I knew Edgar killed Sheryl Foster and I wouldn't sleep until I had enough evidence to fry him. "I got plenty for now. I suspect we'll lift up a few rocks and find all we'll need to convict."

I stood. "Edgar Bixby, you're under arrest for the murder of Sheryl Foster. I'll be calling the DA about pressing charges. He'll likely want you transferred to the county jail."

He'd also procure a search warrant for the Bixby place, but I didn't mention that. No need to give anybody a head start on destroying evidence.

Edgar wore the expression of a man learning for the first time how it feels to be called to account for all the hurt he'd caused. I relished that look, I'll be real honest.

Bernard took Edgar by the arm, led him to the cell, and locked him up. I was satisfied I had the right man. But I didn't throw away the key. Not yet.

CHAPTER THIRTY-NINE

Nailing Edgar to the cross put me in a better mood, so I gave my people time off to attend church. I didn't go, nor would anyone expect me to. Everyone around here figures I'm hell-bound, as well they should, I suppose. God and I stopped being on speaking terms my first week in Korea when I witnessed a buddy getting vaporized by an artillery shell. Since that day, jazz and bourbon have been my only religion.

I was nevertheless happy to hold down the fort while others tend to their immortal souls. I might be a hopeless case, but those who can still be saved should be afforded every opportunity.

While Edgar stewed in his cell, I borrowed Karen's desk and called District Attorney McKinnis at home. Mrs. McKinnis answered. She was sick in bed and Rex had taken their kids to church. I said I hoped she'd feel better soon and asked her to have him return my call as soon as possible.

I considered calling the sheriff then decided to hold off. I'm not sure why.

I called over to Nate's and talked to Jeff. He said everything was fine, except Kevin had asked Nate some questions that Nate didn't care to answer. I asked him the nature of the questions, but Jeff didn't want to say, since both father and son were sitting right there. I didn't tell him what had happened with Edgar because he'd tell Nate and I wanted to tell Nate myself.

The thought of a drink crossed my mind until I remembered all I had was vodka and nothing to mix it with. I seemed to be finding excuses not to drink that Smirnoff. If Karen substituted it for Old Grand-Dad as a way of getting me to cut down on my daytime drinking, her plan was working.

If I couldn't indulge, I'd sleep. I turned on the radio. It played a song called "What's New, Pussycat?" I braved Edgar's insults long enough to retrieve the fedora from my office, slammed the door on him mid-tirade, and sat back down at Karen's desk. I pulled the hat over my eyes and put my feet up. Within a minute, I was out like a light.

I slept for a half-hour before being woken up by Darren Hyatt. He and his son Chuck had arrived for their Daffodil appointment, which I'd forgotten about. I greeted them as politely as I could, considering my groggy state. I took the radio back to my office and turned the music up loud enough so Edgar wouldn't be able to hear us talk.

The Hyatts grabbed a couple of chairs and made themselves at home. Darren and I made small talk while Chuck sat quiet and nervous. After saying all there was to say about the weather, we got down to brass tacks. "Chuck," I said, "I understand you got something to tell me."

Chuck looked sorrowfully at his dad, who nodded his encouragement. "Yes sir," Chuck said in a shaky voice. "I wanted to tell you that it was me who stole Daffodil and that I'm sorry. I didn't mean no harm."

"He feels real bad about it, Emmett," said Darren. "I just found out yesterday. He says he's wanted to apologize for a few days, but he was scared to. There's more to it than just stealing that pig." He placed his hand on his son's shoulder. "Go on. Tell him."

There was an ominous tone to what Darren had said that I chose not to notice. Right then, the prospect of solving the Daffodil caper seemed like a welcome distraction.

I leaned back and readied myself for a good yarn. "Let's hear it," I said. Little did I know Chuck Hyatt's pig story would wind up kicking the ever-loving crap out of this town.

· · · · ·

"EJ was kind of in on it," Chuck began shamefaced. "I mean, it's not like he actually helped. He had a baseball game or something. But we told him what we were thinking about doing and he thought it was funny. I don't think he likes that pig very much."

I reckon to EJ, Daffodil must seem like a goody-two-shoes older sister who gets straight A's and wins prizes for penmanship, only instead of penmanship, Daffodil wins prizes for being the world's fattest pig.

"What did he do to help?" I asked.

"He gave us a key to the barn and told us when would be the best time to do it."

"That'd be Friday night, huh?"

"Yeh. He said his folks always went out to eat on Fridays, and usually didn't come home until late, so that'd give us plenty of time."

"I assume you didn't move that gigantic son of a gun all by yourself. You going to tell me who helped?"

He didn't want to but he understood he had to. He named Freddie Wright and Derek Drummond. I knew both to be good kids. "Derek's girlfriend, too. Lisa Pickles." I didn't know her. "She's the only one of us who's worked with pigs," he added.

"You need a good pig rustler if you're going to rustle pigs," I said.

He half-smiled, like he wasn't sure if I was joking or not.

"What'd you four desperadoes use to haul that animal, anyway?"

"We hitched Derek's dad's livestock trailer to the back of my truck."

"Mm-hmm," I said, and listened to the details of their caper. Chuck described how surprised he was to discover an 1800-pound pig has a mind of its own, and mentioned how Daffodil's accommodations were fancier than his family's, which visibly irritated his daddy. "Don't worry, Darren," I said. "I've been in your house and it's a lot nicer than mine."

Ordinarily you'd feel sorry for a boy who preferred a pig pen to his own house, but of course Daffodil was royalty.

I'd already determined I was going to give Chuck a slap on the wrist, so I let him ramble. My mind had wandered when said something that got my undivided attention. "We were having a heck of a time trying to get her out of that barn and onto the trailer," he said. "We hadn't been at it long when we heard Mr. Bixby's car driving up."

The possibility that the pig-nappers might have witnessed Edgar's actions had not occurred to me. Goddammit, it's like I always say: Sam Spade, I ain't.

"He couldn't see us as long as he stayed up by the house," Chuck said. "We hid and kept quiet. After a while, we heard the doors slam. I peeked again and saw him walking toward us. Luckily, the phone rang and he turned around and went back inside. He came out again a few minutes later and drove away."

That actually confirmed some of Edgar's story, but it didn't change anything

Chuck described how they ultimately got Daffodil loaded into the trailer, thanks mostly to the heroic efforts of Lisa Pickles, who knows how to speak Latin or whatever language pigs speak. He added a few unnecessary details, after which he stopped and I reckoned he was done.

"Well, you shouldn't have done what you did," I said, "but it's not a capital offense. Edgar's got enough on his plate these days. I'm confident I can talk him out of pressing charges."

Chuck seemed less than relieved, which I thought strange, considering I'd just let him off the hook.

"You know, Darren," I said, "in colonial times they'd have lashed Chuck in the town square, or cut off his ears for doing what he did."

"I'm sure he's grateful, Chief Hardy," Darren said. "It's just that he hasn't told you the whole story." He put an arm on his boy. "Go ahead, son, tell him the rest."

Chuck said he was thirsty and I told him to help himself to a drink of water. He did, then sat back down. He didn't say anything for a minute. I considered giving him a nudge, but he eventually picked up where he'd left off.

"It was almost dark when we finally got her loaded," he said. "We were about to make our getaway when we saw headlights. A couple cars pulled off the highway and drove toward the house. We were scared, so we hid and waited."

The front door opened. Karen strolled in singing "Amazing Grace" under her breath. She must've sensed something big was going on. She stopped in the middle of a verse and sat down.

"Who was it?"

"It was a car and a pickup. I couldn't tell who, at first, because like I said, it was getting dark and I was peeking around the corner of the barn. But when they parked I could see Mr. Bixby was in the car by himself. It wasn't the Lincoln he'd been driving before, though. It was a red Chevy I'd never seen before."

"Who was in the truck?"

"I knew that right off. It was that old Ford pickup Kevin Gunter drives."

I felt a pain in my chest. Part of me wanted to stop right there and walk away.

"Kevin was driving?" Chuck nodded. "Was anyone with him?"

"Yeh, EJ was with him."

The front door opened again. Kenny and Bernard came in, laughing about something. They saw all the serious faces and got serious themselves. They moved to opposite corners of the room. Watched and listened.

"Chuck, do you know what time it was when they drove up?"

He rubbed his eyes with the palms of his hands and yawned, as if all this talking had worn him out. He held out his wrist and showed us a silver Timex. The band was loose and had crept up his arm. "I looked at my watch when we finished to see long it had taken us. It was a few minutes before ten o'clock." He shook his arm and the watch slid back down to where it was supposed to be. He gave me a questioning look, like he was asking permission to continue. I nodded.

"So, EJ and Mr. Bixby talked a little bit. Then they started yelling and pushing each other. Kevin started screaming at them to stop and they calmed down."

"What it was all about?"

"I couldn't tell. Mainly they were just cussing each other."

"Alright," I said. "Go on"

He blinked hard a couple of times. "This is the part where I'm afraid you're going to get mad, because it's something I should've told you back when it happened."

"Don't worry about that right now. Just tell me what you saw."

He took a deep breath. "Ok," he said. "After they stopped yelling, I could tell Kevin was upset about something. I think he might even have been crying. Anyway, they all went to the back of the pickup and opened the tailgate. They lifted up a tarp and looked underneath at something. I couldn't see what."

He leaned forward and rested his elbows on his knees. His hands were clasped together so tight, the tips of his fingers looked like tiny crimson balloons. "They talked some more, then they closed the tailgate and put the tarp back over whatever it was. They got in the pickup, but I guess the battery was dead and it wouldn't start, so they took out whatever was under the tarp and put it in the trunk of the car. It was pretty dark by that time and I couldn't tell what it was. Later on, after I heard about that colored girl who got killed, I thought it could've been about the size of a person's body."

For some reason, instead of focusing on the depressing implications of what he'd said, I thought how it was good to hear a boy Chuck's age use "colored" instead of that other uglier word, and that maybe today's kids are growing up less prejudiced than their folks. There's always hope.

"Go on," I said.

"That was all," he said like he couldn't wait to finish and be done with it. "They got in the Chevy and drove off. We waited until they were down the road and out of sight, and hauled ass out of there."

"They went toward town?"

"Yep. Toward Burr."

"Where'd you go after you left the Bixby's?"

He relaxed some, now that the worst was over. "We took Daffodil to Principal Midkiff's house. We knew he was out of town, so we put Daffodil in his car port as a joke. Senior pranks are kind of a tradition, in case you don't know."

"I know. I ain't that old." I remember how during my own senior year I ran a pair of red long-handle underwear up the flagpole before school one day. Got away with it, too.

"Alright, Chuck. Like I say, you shouldn't have done it, but I don't think you got anything to worry about. What you saw might be more important than the fact you temporarily absconded with a pig."

I told him he might have to testify in court, which I'm sure he didn't like hearing. He didn't complain, though. I reckon he counted himself lucky, all things considered. I also said it might be a good idea to stay clear of EJ until this got cleared up. Both Chuck and Darren agreed that was an excellent suggestion.

I asked Chuck why he didn't come to me earlier. "I was going to, Chief Hardy, I promise, even if y'all didn't catch me. It took me some time to get up the courage."

I wasn't mad at him. He's a kid, and kids do stupid things. Neither he nor his dad had asked about the thousand-dollar reward, to their everlasting credit. In fact, no one had expressed an interest in the money so far, which was a good thing, since I didn't have it, nor did I have a plan to get it. I hoped whoever helped find the killer might forgo the cash out of a sense of civic responsibility. Or shame. Shame would work fine.

In the end, the boy did the right thing, and that's what's important. "Aw, Chuck, there's no need to be afraid of me. Everyone knows I'm a pussycat."

CHAPTER FORTY

I asked Karen to try getting hold of District Attorney McKinnis again. Chuck's story had gotten my heart racing, and when my heart races, the rest of me does, too.

Karen finally got through to Rex.

"Hey Rex," I said, "have you charged Yellowhorse yet?"

"We worked out a deal with his lawyer late Friday. I'm going to run it by the judge tomorrow morning."

"Buddy, I hate to throw sand in the wheels of justice, but you might want to consider canceling that meeting."

· · · · ·

Besides Edgar, Chuck's story had also implicated Kevin and EJ. To what extent, I didn't know and was not especially excited to investigate, even though I knew it was necessary. Between the two, I figured Kevin would be the easier nut to crack. I dislike taking advantage of the weak, but that's often the nature of my business. I left Bernard and Karen to watch over Edgar. I took Jeff and Kenny with me.

If I had my druthers, I'd have never set foot in Nate Gunter's place again, but you can't always get what you want. Pulling up to the house, I could see the only thing that had changed since my last visit was someone had used duct tape in a failed attempt to fix the broken mailbox that I'd made worse.

The screen door was shut but the front door was open. Nate welcomed us.

Inside, things were the same as they'd been the day of the BB-gun fight, right down to the broken curtain rod and the holes in the walls. The window fan was running full speed.

Nate didn't look any better than he had earlier in the day. His thin, prematurely gray hair stuck out all over in greasy, confused wisps. His scalp was bright and shiny red, like he'd fallen asleep with his head in the oven.

"Hey Nate, how you holding up?" I asked.

"Not bad," he said, sounding very bad indeed. "What's going on?"

"We need to talk to Kevin. Is he around?"

"Yeh, he's—"

The back door slammed shut. Holy shit, I thought; I've been through this before.

The four of us rushed through the cramped house and out the back door, to find Kevin attempting to escape.

"What the hell—? Kevin, where you goin', son?" Nate yelled.

Kevin crossed the train tracks and highway without a glance in either direction. He squeezed through a wire fence and ran through a field, green-to-the-horizon with young wheat. He wasn't running for his health but to get away, and that made him faster than he might ordinarily have been. I didn't blame him for trying, but I couldn't let it happen.

Jeff, Kenny, and I took off after him. I'd only gone about five steps before my knees gave out and I had to pull up. The others kept up the chase, with Nate clumping along behind like an old jalopy with a couple of flat tires. Kenny got an angle and closed. Kevin's no more an athlete than his daddy. The added juice lent by panic wouldn't be enough to outrun Kenny, who won track medals in high school. Kenny tackled him with Jeff close behind.

Kevin cried out as they lifted him off the ground. I remembered his broken collarbone and hollered for them to be careful. I broke my own collarbone as a kid and know how much it hurts. Kevin wore the same kind of brace and sling contraption the doctor had given me. Tears ran down his face. I felt damned sorry for him.

"What in hell's going on?" Nate said. "Emmett, are they arresting Kevin?"

"C'mon, bud, let's go back to the house and talk about it."

· · · · ·

Jeff and Kenny deposited Kevin on Nate's living room couch. Gently, as per my orders. The couch had originally been upholstered in some kind of brown Naugahyde, but most of it had worn away to reveal pitted foam rubber, exposed black springs, and a splintered wooden frame. The chrome-and-red-vinyl kitchen chair where I sat was in a similar state of decomposition.

Kenny removed Kevin's cuffs. He and Jeff arranged themselves near the two exits, front and back, in case Kevin got any ideas.

Kevin slumped forward, mouth lolling open, oily brown hair thicker than his dad's but just as messy. His right arm hung uselessly from a white cotton sling. The malignant acne on his face and neck showed in angry contrast to his pale, sweaty skin. The tears had given way to a vacant, pained stare.

Nate sat next to him. Side-by-side, they looked like a picture of the beginning and end of a single sad, misspent life.

Kevin looked lost. Nate looked old. The whole scene was as depressing as hell, but I had a job to do.

I told them I was going to ask Kevin some questions. "He doesn't have to answer them if he doesn't want to," I said, "but his cooperation could benefit him later if he's charged with a crime. Do you understand?"

Nate summoned what was left of his self-respect in support of the boy. "Ask him whatever you want, Emmett. He ain't got nothing to hide." I admired his expression of aggrieved bravado, even if it was as counterfeit as a bottle of snake oil, since it was entirely for his son's benefit.

He slapped Kevin on the thigh and said, "Tell Chief Hardy what he wants to know." Kevin's head moved in something like a nod. I reminded myself not to be too harsh in my questioning. I needed to break him. I did not desire to shatter him into a million pieces.

"Kevin, someone told me a story this morning that involved you. It disturbed me to hear it. Do you know what I'm talking about?"

He stared at a spot on the far wall so intently, I almost looked to see what was there. He shrugged after a few seconds and began picking at a patch on the couch. He tore small pieces of foam rubber from the cushion and tossed them onto a dirty linoleum floor that was already covered in unwashed clothes and assorted food wrappers.

"It involved you and EJ Bixby and his father." Kevin's eyes were pink around the edges. His face was tear-stained, his expression blank. "This person saw the three of y'all take something out the back of your truck and put it in the trunk of a red Impala."

Kevin picked some more at the cushion. I pressed on.

"Kevin, this witness thought it could've been a dead body." Nate flinched. "Can you tell me anything about that?" Kevin gave an almost-invisible shrug and flicked another piece of foam onto the floor.

Nate broke in. "Emmett, you're not saying—" I held up my hand to cut him off.

I could either keep being nice or I could bear down. It occurred to me that alternating the two strategies might be the best way to go. I gritted my teeth and screwed up my face as if struggling to control my temper.

"Alright, Kevin," I said loud enough to be heard a block away. Both the boy and his father jumped, startled. "You're too big to be sitting there crying like a baby. You're a grown man. It's time to start acting like one."

Kevin sat up a little straighter and wiped his runny nose on the sleeve of his dirty white t-shirt.

"My witness says he saw you, EJ and Edgar Bixby move something that looked like dead body from the bed of your truck into the trunk of a red Impala the night of Sheryl Foster's death. You remember anything about that?"

"I don't know," he whispered. "Maybe."

"Speak up, son. I can't hear you."

"I don't know," he blurted. "Maybe."

I got the feeling it wouldn't take much more pushing. "Do you know, or don't you?" He shrugged again, although this time it was more like a cringe. "You know what I'm asking, don't you?" He nodded but didn't say anything. "Were you at the Bixbys' that night? Was there a bundle hidden under a tarp in the back of your truck?" His eyes were lifeless. "Was it Sheryl Foster?"

Nate went fish-belly pale, but he kept quiet. Kevin's chin dropped to his chest and he sat as still as a statue except for his right hand, which pried more and bigger chunks of foam from the couch.

"My witness tells me you boys loaded this bundle into the trunk of that Impala and drove to where we found Sheryl Foster's body." I wasn't 100% certain they'd driven straight to where they dumped the body, but he didn't have to know that. It was a safe assumption, at any rate.

Kevin abruptly stopped pulling out pieces of foam and began sinking his fingers deep into the cushion, like an Old West doctor trying to gouge a bullet from the chest of a wounded gunfighter.

"This would've been about an hour before we discovered Sheryl Foster. Last night I found a piece of a bracelet that belonged to Sheryl." I leaned forward until my face was inches from his. "Look at me," I said and lightly slapped his face. He winced and glanced up just for a second. "I found it in a car your daddy was driving. A red Impala. You understand what that means?"

I'm not sure he did, but he nodded anyway. Nate knew. I could tell by his terrified expression.

"I've got a picture of Sheryl wearing that bracelet. Her mama gave it to her. She wore it every day. She had it on when you and EJ and Mr. Bixby loaded her body into Mr. Bixby's car. Either a piece of that bracelet came off in the car, or someone put it there to make it look like your daddy killed her. Either way, it adds up to you and the Bixby's and maybe your daddy being charged with murder."

Desperation cracked the mask of pride Nate had tried-on and found unsuitable. "That's crazy, Emmett," he said, terror-stricken, his voice rising to a falsetto. "We talked about this last night. Kevin didn't have nothing to do with that girl." He reached over and turned Kevin's head to face him. "Tell him, son. Tell him you didn't have nothing to do with that girl, dead or alive."

Kevin jerked his head away and wouldn't look at his father. His chin quivered and his chest began to heave. He stopped digging into the cushion and began slapping the couch with the hand attached to his good arm. "No, no, no," he said rhythmically, gradually rising in intensity.

"No, no, no, no, no, no," he shook his head and chanted. His movements got more frantic and his voice rose steadily. He slapped the backrest, with both hands now, ignoring the agony I knew that broken collar bone was causing him, hitting patches of vinyl so each smack sounded like a firecracker going off. He thrashed back and forth and cried and he ground his teeth and moaned and said things I couldn't understand—like he was speaking in tongues and calling for God to help: he didn't mean for it to happen, he loved her and he was sorry for wanting to be with her and for killing her, and he asked her and his daddy and his mama and Jesus to forgive him, and then he slammed his fists against the sides of his head and screamed and scratched his face until he drew blood but he didn't feel it, because the pain inside was so much worse, and he wanted to rid himself of it like a wild animal gnawing its leg off trying to escape a steel trap.

Nate tried to put his arms around him but the boy would not be consoled, and still he writhed and sobbed. Through his own tears Nate asked how he could help, and said he loved his son and everything would be all right, even though he and I and especially Kevin knew it wouldn't, not for a long time. Maybe never.

CHAPTER FORTY-ONE

Kevin's breakdown had sucked the air out of the room. I'd figured he'd get upset, but I'd expected he'd give me something I could use against Edgar and EJ, not confess to the crime himself. His admission was about the most depressing thing I'd ever heard, made worse by the way he said it. Still, I needed more. The general thrust was clear, but as you'd expect from a statement produced as a result of an nervous breakdown, details were lacking. He'd given vent to a lot of emotion, as had his father. Both were seriously debilitated. I wasn't feeling so wonderful, myself. We all needed a break.

I called Karen and asked her to bring us something to eat. It was afternoon and most of us hadn't had anything but those little doughnuts for breakfast.

Nate turned on the TV, trying to be a good host, I guess. One of the channels was showing *White Heat*, the Jimmy Cagney film. Karen arrived with hamburgers and fries from the Burger Mart and joined us for lunch. We ate and watched as Cody Jarrett climbed a flaming gas tank and got blown all to hell.

Made it, Ma. Top of the world.

No one talked except to say pass the salt.

The movie ended and the food disappeared and it was time to get back to work. I asked Kevin if he was ready to talk some more, and he said he was. I told Nate, both he and Kevin had a right to remain silent and could have a lawyer present if they wanted. Nate said never mind about that, I trust you to be fair, Emmett, let's just get started.

I asked Karen to take it all down.

"I was sitting here watching TV when the phone rang," Kevin said. The prior misuse of his vocal cords had him sounding like he'd swallowed gravel. "EJ said he was in Watie Junction with Sheryl and needed a ride back to Burr."

The fan was making too much noise and I told Jeff to turn it off. He couldn't figure out which button to push, so he just jerked the plug out of the wall.

"What did you say?" I asked Kevin.

"When? You mean just now?"

My patience had about worn to a nub, but I tried to keep it hid as best I could. "No, I mean what did you say to EJ when he asked you to pick up him and Sheryl?"

"Oh, ok. I didn't want to go, is what I said."

"Why not?"

"Because I was trying not to be friends with him anymore."

If you'd done that earlier you would've saved yourself some grief, I thought.

"Why was that?" I said.

"Because he treats me so bad. I'm just tired of it, so I said no."

"What did EJ say when you told him no?"

"He argued with me and tried to get me to come. He said he'd let me drive his car, which I didn't care about."

It must've surprised EJ to find not everyone thinks his expensive car is a big deal.

"So, what happened?" I asked.

"He kept asking and arguing and I kept saying no, until he told me that if I came, he'd let me do it with Sheryl."

"He said he'd let you have sex with her?"

Add pimping to EJ's other sterling qualities.

"Yeh," Kevin said. "I partly didn't believe him, because before he wouldn't let me even if I paid. And anyway, I didn't think it was for him to say."

"Did you ever pay Sheryl for sex?"

"Well, I liked her a lot—a real lot—but I didn't want to pay to be with her," he said. "That was her job, and I don't think she liked it very much. I mostly just liked being around her, when I'd take EJ out there sometimes. She's lots nicer to me than the girls at school."

"How often did you take EJ out there?"

"A bunch of times at first. He didn't want to park his car in front because he thought one of his daddy's friends would see it."

There are too many father/son parallels to keep up with on this case, I thought.

"But after a while he didn't care. He started driving himself, so I stopped going."

"Ok, so he said you could have relations with Sheryl if you'd go pick them up. I'm guessing you said yes."

He nodded. "Pretty much. I told him I didn't want to do it with her unless she wanted to do it with me."

It must've been his last few grains of pride that caused him to say that.

"What did he say?" I asked.

"He said she did want to." Kevin said it like he was still amazed at the memory. "I didn't believe him, because when he said it, I could hear Sheryl talking in the background. She sounded mad. EJ held his hand over the phone, so I couldn't hear very well, but I could tell they were arguing. Hold on, wait a second—"

Something caught in his throat and he coughed. All the dust in the air. He took a long swallow of his Coke and was able to go on.

"Anyway, EJ came back on the line and said Sheryl wanted to talk to me and he gave her the phone. She said if I came and picked them up, we'd go out to the lake and have some fun. I asked her if that was what she wanted and she said yes. So, I said ok, I'd come and get them. I picked them up at the Dairy Queen in Watie Junction."

I took a swallow of my own Coke and wished it had some bourbon in it.

"EJ said he knew someone in Watie Junction who'd buy us beer. I thought EJ was calling him Jaybird, but it might've been Jailbird. Anyway, EJ gave him 10 dollars and told him that if he bought us a couple six packs of Lone Star he could keep the change. So that's what he did."

For some reason Kevin seemed to want a reaction, so I nodded, which seemed to satisfy him.

"We took Jaybird home, then EJ asked if I had my pup tent with me. He said he wanted to camp out. Sometimes I sleep out at the lake because it gets so hot in the house. I usually carry the tent with me in the back of the truck." His voice was still hoarse but he seemed a little less morose.

"When we got there, EJ wanted us to go someplace you couldn't see from the bait shop. He said Jim Bob Hall—you know Jim Bob, who owns the shop? EJ says he's a dirty old man who likes to spy on people who go out there to make out." That sounds about right, I thought. "I usually camp behind a little stand of cottonwoods on the far side of the lake," Kevin said. "That's where we went."

He took another sip of his Coke and flicked a chunk of foam off the couch. It landed in someone's else's cup of orange Fanta sitting on the coffee table. That's what you get for taking off the lid. Kevin clenched his jaw and squeezed his eyes open-and-shut a couple of times. He moved his lips, but nothing came out.

Nate broke the silence. "Go on, son. The truth shall set you free."

I didn't know whether to laugh or cry when he said that.

I don't think Kevin did, either. He seemed to be groping for a way to start. Out of nowhere he looked at Karen like he wanted something from her but didn't know what it was or how to ask. Karen gave him that sweet smile of hers. Well, I guess that's what he needed. He smiled back faintly and finished his story.

CHAPTER FORTY-TWO

"I mostly remember her eyes." Kevin spoke so softly I could barely hear. "I never seen anyone with eyes like hers." His looked like someone who'd spent a night in paradise and aimed to spend the rest of his life trying to get back.

I had to turn away. I remembered her eyes, too. I'd carried the vision with me since that night. I didn't want him to know we had that in common.

I didn't want to share.

"I set up the tent and spread out a blanket inside. EJ thanked me for the ride and said I should come back and pick them up in the morning. I said, hold on, now, what about our deal? He laughed at me and said there'd been a change of plans. I started to get mad but Sheryl told him to stop teasing me. She said she'd go into the tent with me, like they said. EJ said 'Ok, it's your funeral.' He'd been drinking already, so maybe he was a little drunk, I don't know. I wasn't.

"Sheryl and I went into the tent. She took off her clothes and showed me what to do, because I didn't really know." He ran his hands through his greasy hair and wiped them on his jeans. "It was wonderful. She was real nice and told me that she loved EJ but she liked me, too." His voice broke. "I was pretty happy there for a minute."

He sat rocking back and forth with his hands wedged between his knees, blinking hard, trying to keep from crying again. "Ok, so I got dressed. Sheryl wrapped the blanket around herself and we crawled out of the tent. EJ sat leaning back up against a tree, holding that Buck knife he always carries. He was flipping it into the ground next to him, over and over, like he was playing mumbly-peg. I could tell he was mad before he even said anything. He had a funny expression on his face. A smile, but a mean smile, not happy. He asked Sheryl if she had fun, and if my thing was longer than his. He asked her if she wanted to marry me instead of him. He tried to pretend he was kidding, but I could tell he wasn't. He kept getting madder and madder and started calling her a whore and a slut and a bunch of other names. Sheryl got upset and cried and said she did it with me so she could spend time with him—that he was the one she loved. It was like EJ couldn't hear what she as saying. She tried to get him to hold her, but he pushed her away. He wouldn't stop cussing at her. I told him that I knew Sheryl was his girl, but he said I was a pussy and to go to hell. Then he hit me in the stomach as hard as he could. It knocked the wind out of me. I fell down. Sheryl came over to see if I was ok. That made EJ even madder. He pulled her away from me, grabbed her from behind and reached around—"

He'd been faltering, but now he came to a stop.

The room was quiet except for the sound of wind blowing in through the open door and windows, and clouds of dust hitting up against the side of the house. Outside, a crow cawed. I peeked out the screen door and saw it perched on a power line across the street. "Nevermore," I whispered to myself. The Edgar who wrote that was from Baltimore, I remembered. He was writing about a raven, not a crow. This was a crow.

"EJ reached around with the knife and cut her throat."

He began to cry. "She bled all over the place," he said. "She moved her mouth like she was trying to talk, but nothing came out, just gurgling sounds and blood bubbles." His voice took on an air of horrified wonder, like he didn't want to believe what had happened. "I couldn't do anything. One minute she was trying to help me, the next she was dead."

I felt some relief on at least one count. "You didn't kill her, then," I said.

"No, but it's my fault she's dead," he shouted through the tears.

I don't think I've never wanted to be someplace else more than I did at that moment.

No one else made a sound. Kenny stood leaning against the doorframe, looking outside at whatever there was to see—Nate's truck and the grain elevators and the broken mailbox, and maybe that crow, if it hadn't flown away. Jeff sat in a mangy antique armchair, legs stretched out and arms crossed, staring at the floor. Nate gave his son what comfort he could. Karen moved to the couch and sat on the other side of the boy. Almost instinctively, he moved to embrace her and cry on her shoulder. She hugged and cried right back.

All I could think was: The story's not over yet.

After a couple of minutes, Kevin wiped his eyes with a paper napkin and sat up straight, trying to rescue a shred of dignity, I suspect.

"EJ didn't say anything the whole time he was killing her," he said in an even voice. "He just let her drop to the ground. He threw-up in some weeds then laid down with his eyes closed. After a while he got up and started bossing me around. Said we were in this together and I was a guilty as he was and we had to stick together or we'd both go to the electric chair."

The only way that's going to happen is with EJ sitting in it, I thought. With Kevin watching from the other side of the glass. If there's any justice in the world.

"How did he act?" I asked. "Sad? Angry?"

"He was more worried than anything." Kevin was hiccupping from all the crying. "He started talking fast, telling me to put her in the bed of the truck. He said we were going to find his daddy and ask for help. I reckoned Mr. Bixby would know what to do, so I did what he said."

"You covered her with the tent?"

"EJ wanted to wrap her up in it, but my daddy gave it to me for my birthday and I didn't want to ruin it, so we just covered her up with it."

"Was she carrying a purse, or a bag of some kind?"

"She had a blue and white bag. It was more like a little suitcase. It had her purse in it, I remember. I started to put her dress back on but EJ said to forget it, leave her the way she was, so I just used it to wipe some of the blood off her, then stuffed it into the bag and took it with us."

"What did you do with the blanket?" I asked.

"I burned it in the trash barrel out back after we were done."

I made a mental note to check that barrel. "Then you went looking for Mr. Bixby?""Yeh, we went by Edna's and the Piazza and everywhere else around town but we couldn't find him. EJ thought he might've gone home, so we headed that way. EJ wanted to get rid of the knife. He'd thrown it in the back of the truck and it was rattling around making a racket. He said he didn't think Wes Harmon kept his gas tanks locked and we could drop it into one of them and no one would ever find it. We thought the Sinclair was closed but we saw Wes working on a car when we pulled in, so we drove away."

I asked if they found Mr. Bixby.

"Yeh, we did, right after that. We ran into him on the highway coming from the other direction."

"What car was he driving?"

"That car he gave my daddy. The Impala. We stopped next to him on the road and EJ said he had something important he needed to talk to him about. He told us to follow him and we went to their house."

"What did y'all do when you got there?"

"We parked and got out. EJ told his daddy he accidentally killed a whore and we had her in the back of my pick up. Mr. Bixby got real mad and asked if it was Sheryl."

"He called her Sheryl? Like he knew who she was?"

"Yes sir, he asked if it was Sheryl who EJ killed. EJ asked him how he knew about her, and Mr. Bixby said because he'd been screwing her himself. EJ exploded when he heard that, and pushed Mr. Bixby. They got in a fight. I yelled a bunch and they stopped."

He took a drink of his Coke and continued. "Mr. Bixby wanted to see her, so we lifted up the tent and showed him. He told us to get in the truck but the battery was dead. He made us put her in the trunk of the Impala. He was in a hurry because he didn't want his wife to see him driving it, and we needed to leave before she got home. First, he started to go out to the lake, then he said he had a better idea and turned around. He went a little past the Sinclair and pulled over next to the train tracks. We sat there in the dark for a few minutes until we heard a whistle. Mr. Bixby took the bag with Sheryl's things and laid down in the weeds next to the tracks waiting for the train to come. Mr. Bixby ran up to the tracks and tried to chuck the bag into a boxcar with its doors open, but he missed and the bag bounced off, so he had to wait for another one that had an open door. It was a real long train. He made it the second time, then ran back and hid in the tall grass until it was gone, I guess so no one in the caboose would see him."

So, it turns out Eugene Yellowhorse was telling the truth, maybe for the first time in his life. Sorry for the inconvenience, Gene. We'd let you go but we can't on account of all those other crimes you did.

Kevin finished his Coke. He was still thirsty and asked for a drink of water. Nate got it for him. Kevin drank most of it in one gulp. He wiped his mouth with the back of his hand. Small drops lingered in the dark peach fuzz over his top lip.

"Mr. Bixby told us to get Sheryl's body out of the trunk," he said. A light went on behind his eyes. "You know what? She was wearing that bracelet when we took her out of the trunk. EJ saw it. He took it off her wrist, real careful. Mr. Bixby kept telling him to hurry, but EJ did it slow, like he didn't want to hurt her. I'll bet he's still got it."

I hope he does, I thought.

"Mr. Bixby told us to take her arms and legs and throw her as hard as we could against—" He paused. "You know how the ground rises up to the tracks? I forget what they call it."

"An embankment," Kenny said, the first words he'd spoken since he'd run down Kevin. I noticed for the first time how Kenny's eyes were wide and his mouth curled in an expression of disgust and amazement. I glanced at the others in the room and they looked much the same. I think it felt to all of us like the boy were revealing secrets of some hideous universe festering just beneath the surface of our own.

"Yeh, that's it," Kevin said. "He told EJ and me to throw her against the embankment, so we did. She didn't weigh much, so it wasn't hard. The first time we did it, he said she wasn't busted-up enough to look like she'd fallen off a train, so he made us do it again and again. After we done it three or four times, he said it was ok."

I gave Kevin time to say more but he didn't. I asked him what happened next.

"Nothing. We just left her there and went back to the Bixby place. Mr. Bixby gave my truck a jump and I came home."

I reckon that would've been at about the same time I was sitting down to watch Ed Ames teach Johnny Carson how to throw a tomahawk.

One major question remained unanswered.

"What did you do with the knife?"

Kevin chewed his bottom lip for a few seconds, then nodded like he'd won an argument with himself. He got up from the couch. Kenny and Jeff moved towards him. "I ain't going anywhere, I promise," he said. "I just need to fetch something. I ain't even going to leave this room."

"Let him do what he needs to do," I said.

Kevin walked over to the wall where the picture of his grandma Noreen hung. He took it down, revealing a gash in the paneling. Tacked to the wall were two short lengths of string leading down into the hole. Kevin tugged on one and pulled out a transparent Piggly Wiggly bread bag. He placed it on the table.

I didn't have to open it to see what was inside. It was a Buck folding knife, the blood still tacky from being wrapped in plastic since the night of the murder.

"I ain't never touched it with my hands," he said. "EJ forgot about it and left it in the back of my truck. He called me later that night and told me to get rid of it. I told him I threw it in the lake."

He hung his head.

"I guess I lied."

CHAPTER FORTY-THREE

The afternoon ran its course. The hot, dry wind blew through the window, spinning the fan Jeff had earlier disarmed. The blades cast a moving shadow on Karen, Kevin and Nate on the battered couch. I was reminded of something I'd seen when I was little, a memory of the Great Depression: two men my dad's age, stick-thin and pasty as cadavers, dressed in filthy overalls and sweat-stained undershirts, begging the man behind the counter at Miller's for something to eat. I don't recall if he gave them anything, but I do remember the overhead fan cast a similar shadow across their ruined faces.

I absent-mindedly ran my tongue over my teeth and tasted the grit I'd breathed in over the course of the day. I spit some into the handkerchief I carry for that express purpose. The Dust Bowl's been over for a long time, but Oklahoma can still be a dirty place.

We sat hot and uncomfortable, not saying much. The question of what to do hung in the air.

If the folks in that room thought I had a master plan, they were very much mistaken. If asked, I would've said I was more than ready to turn over this mess to Sheriff Murray or Agents Jones and Heckscher or whoever else might be kind enough to take it off my hands. I was done being a detective.

But I had a pretty good idea how things would play out.

Kevin would testify and be believed, although I expected Jimmy Jack, or whoever EJ's lawyer is, to try to put the blame on him. It wouldn't work. Chuck's story supported Kevin's, and there was the bloody knife with EJ's fingerprints all over it. Edgar was in deep shit, as well. The tire marks at the scene would match the Impala, and the bloodstain and megaphone charm we found in the trunk implicated him as an accessory. Still, he has money and powerful friends. It was possible he'd finagle out of it some way.

Kevin's role in bringing EJ to justice—and the fact he was only 17 and therefore still a minor—should keep him out of the most serious trouble. He'd spend some time in reform school, but would have the chance to live out his adult life a free man. Or as free as a man in his circumstances can ever be.

I doubted even a jury of 12 prejudiced white people—which he was likely to get—would exonerate EJ, although you can never tell. The fact Sheryl Foster was colored and a prostitute certainly made his conviction less of a sure thing. In a perfect world, both Bixbys would receive the punishment they deserved, but this world ain't perfect. Not by a long shot.

In any case, it wasn't my problem and I was glad about that. I'm not paid enough to decide who gets punished and what that punishment will be.

I tried calling the sheriff from Nate's house but couldn't get the phone to work, so I had to wait until we got back to the station. I radioed ahead to Bernard and had him drive Edgar to the county jail so he wouldn't have to share our little holding cell with the Gunters. Kenny transported Nate and Kevin. I rode with Karen. We hardly spoke. Even back at the station, no one said much. When we did talk, it was in quiet, almost whispered tones. I think we all were a little ashamed, although I'm not sure any of us knew exactly why.

I called Rex McKinnis and Sheriff Murray and told them what had happened. "Gene Yellowhorse sure will be disappointed," said Rex drily. "I think he was counting on spending more time in our lockup before going back to McAlester." I asked him to pass along my regrets.

Burt Murray said he'd have his deputies meet my people at the Bixby place to arrest EJ. He asked if I wanted to be in on it. I said no.

Jeff and Kenny were straining at their leashes. I let them go.

Karen finished transcribing Kevin's statement. He signed it. Neither he or his father read it. I locked them both in the holding cell. I didn't know what to charge Nate with, but I felt sure the DA would think of something. Bernard returned with a couple sheriff's deputies, who took the Gunters into custody. Bernard was happy to ride along with them to Temple City.

The next hours passed in a fog. A rotating cast of sheriff's deputies and curious townsfolk came in and out. Neither Karen nor I turned on the lights, even as the shadows got long. I suppose we implicitly decided semi-darkness fit the occasion. The phone rang and the police radio buzzed non-stop. Word came that EJ had been apprehended without incident, although his mother had apparently thrown a conniption. A search of EJ's underwear drawer turned-up an empty Skoal can with Sheryl's bracelet inside. Sheriff Murray came by to congratulate me in person. I shook his hand and must've said something funny because I remember he laughed. One of DA McKinnis' assistants called and asked for the transcripts of the statements we'd taken. I said I'd get right on it, but by then I was running on fumes and I couldn't recall how many there'd been or who they were. Karen pried the phone out of my hand and took over.

I remember at some point I started to dial Alice Foster's number, but realized I didn't know what to say. Even if I did, I didn't have the energy to say it, so I put if off until later. I thought my dad would want to know, too, but I couldn't call him, either. Like it or not, my words about this were liable to affect people deeply, and that was more responsibility than I cared to assume at the moment.

Denny called, crying hysterically and yelling into the phone. I couldn't understand a word, not that it mattered. Her meaning was clear enough. I felt bad for her, but no more than I did for everyone else involved. I had to hang up before she could bring me lower, because if I sunk any deeper I thought I might just disappear. I told Karen I didn't want to talk to anyone and closed the door to my office. I leaned back in my chair and tried to pretend it was my La-Z-Boy. I pulled my fedora over my eyes and fell asleep.

It was dark outside by the time Karen opened my door and woke me up.

"Just wanted to see how you were doing," she said.

"Whoa," I said, squinting at the bright light coming through the doorway. "How long have I been out?"

"A couple of hours."

"Did I miss anything?"

"Agents Jones and Heckscher came in, wanting to talk to you. I told 'em nothing short of the Second Coming would get me to wake you up."

"I bet they loved that."

She shrugged and smiled.

"Anything else?"

"Nothing we couldn't handle. Nothing that can't wait until morning."

I noticed she'd changed out of her church clothes into blue jeans, a red-checked blouse, and a pair of fancy-stitched boots.

"I guess you went home at some point," I said.

"Yeh, I did. Cathy Stallcup came by with some cupcakes she baked for you. I asked her to stay while I went home and took a shower. Told her not to bother you."

"Figured I needed a babysitter, huh?"

"Can't be too careful."

We smiled at one another.

"It's been a heck of a day," she said.

"I might put in stronger terms, but yeh, it was."

She closed the door and sat down in the chair across from my desk. The only light came in from under the door and the half-moon shining through the window.

"How are you doing?" she asked. I noticed she was wearing that perfume I like.

"I'm fine." My voice shook the slightest bit, which surprised me, although maybe it shouldn't have, given the events of the last few days. "About as good as can be expected. You?"

"I'm ok." She arched an eyebrow in that way that makes her look like Vivien Leigh, who I had a crush on as a boy. I suddenly realized it wasn't just nervous exhaustion that made my voice shake. Maybe she wore that perfume because she knows I like it.

We talked but didn't tease the way we usually do. I suppose we've always used jokes as a way to avoid trying and failing at something neither of us had ever been very good at. The stakes had always seemed too high. We both had too much to lose. Our friendship was that important.

"You going home?" she asked.

"I suppose I should."

There was a pause you could ride an elephant through sideways. "Feel like company?" she finally asked, with the tiniest catch in her voice.

I could've said yes and who knows what might've happened. But the timing couldn't have been worse.

It pained me to say it, but it had to be said. "As much as I value your companionship, ma'am, I think I'd best spend this evening alone with my thoughts."

Her smile might've betrayed a hint of regret. Or relief. Maybe both. "I understand," she said. She reached across the desk and took my hand. I let her. She got up after a few seconds and opened the door. She stood half in shadow, half in light. I couldn't make out the expression on her face, but I knew it would be one of kindness, because that's just the way she is. Not for the first time, I pondered what it would be like to be with her—really *with* her—and understood if I were to do that, I'd have to cut loose a truckload of thoughts and feelings that had weighed me down for too long. For the first time, it seemed like that was something I could do. If that happened, it would be the only good thing to come out of all this this.

I followed her into the front office and watched as she gathered a few items off her desk and swept them into her purse.

"Another big day tomorrow," she said.

"I reckon you're right about that. Like you are about most things."

"You sure you're ok?"

"Yeh, I'll be fine. You go on, now."

"Alright, then. I got some laundry that needs doing."

I thought she might come over and kiss me on the cheek, but she didn't. On her way out, she turned to say goodbye. Our eyes met.

I'd forgotten hers were green.

"Good night, Chief Hardy."

"Good night, Red."

. . . . .

I puttered around the office for a while. It was after midnight before I got out of there. I thought it unwise to drive, since my immediate plans involved drinking to excess. A vehicle parked in my driveway could be a dangerous temptation. Given the mood I was in, there's no telling where I would've gone or what I might've done.

Edna's was closed, but Ray Nugent was back in the office doing the books. I persuaded him to sell me a bottle of Old Grand-Dad, albeit at a greatly inflated price. I'd mostly resisted the Song of the Volga Boatmen issuing forth from my desk drawer, and I'd had second thoughts about my drinking habits after my car chase with Nate. Hell, maybe I'll quit at some point, but not tonight. Tonight, I'd strip down to my t-shirt and BVDs, retire to my La-Z-Boy and drown my not inconsiderable sorrows. It was Sunday night—Monday morning, actually. Johnny Carson wouldn't be on, but there'd be a late movie. Or maybe I'd get roaring drunk, pull out my saxophone and wake the neighbors. I hadn't done that in a while.

It was as hot as it'd been all day. It felt like the sun hadn't set, but changed out of its work clothes into something dark and less conspicuous. I didn't mind. Sometimes a hot night can soothe like a mother's embrace.

The air was sweet—that is, if you don't mind sniffing a little alfalfa and cow manure. Burr's official smell.

Walking home, I ran into Dizzy. On her way back from Ethel Blankenship's, no doubt. Ethel cooks for her extended family on Sundays and dumps the scraps in her trash can, much to Dizzy's delight. Gorging on Ethel's leftovers is a weekly tradition for Diz. I generally don't even feed her on Sundays, knowing she's getting gourmet fare from Ethel. Silly dog needs to lose weight.

She was still licking her chops, having obviously gotten her fill. She trotted beside me, panting, as happy as a clam.

"Nothing like feeding on other folks' garbage, is there, Diz?" I said.

Dizzy looked up at me, wagged her tail and smiled. Dogs are so damn easy to please.

Thank you so much for reading one of our **Crime Fiction** novels.
If you enjoyed our book, please check out our recommended title for your
next great read!

Caught in a Web by Joseph Lewis

"This important, nail-biting crime thriller about MS-13 sets the bar very
high. One of the year's best thrillers." *–BEST THRILLERS*

View other Black Rose Writing titles at www.blackrosewriting.com/books

and use promo code **PRINT** to receive a **20% discount** when purchasing

Made in the USA
Coppell, TX
20 March 2024

30304388R00184